THE
VIPER

BY J. R. WARD

THE BLACK DAGGER BROTHERHOOD SERIES

Dark Lover

Lover Eternal

Lover Awakened

Lover Revealed

Lover Unbound

Lover Enshrined

The Black Dagger

Brotherhood:

An Insider's Guide

Lover Avenged

Lover Mine

Lover Unleashed

Lover Reborn

Lover at Last

The King

The Shadows

The Beast

The Chosen

The Thief

The Savior

The Sinner

Lover Unveiled

Lover Arisen

THE BLACK DAGGER LEGACY SERIES

Blood Kiss

Blood Vow

Blood Fury

Blood Truth

THE BLACK DAGGER BROTHERHOOD WORLD

Dearest Ivie

Prisoner of Night

Where Winter Finds You

A Warm Heart in Winter

THE LAIR OF THE WOLVEN SERIES

Claimed

THE BLACK DAGGER BROTHERHOOD: PRISON CAMP

The Jackal

The Wolf

The Viper

NOVELS OF THE FALLEN ANGELS

Covet

Crave

Envy

Rapture

Possession

Immortal

THE BOURBON KINGS SERIES

The Bourbon Kings

The Angels' Share

Devil's Cut

J.R. WARD

THE VIPER

◆ THE BLACK DAGGER BROTHERHOOD ◆
PRISON CAMP

GALLERY BOOKS

New York · London · Toronto · Sydney · New Delhi

Gallery Books
An Imprint of Simon & Schuster, Inc.
1230 Avenue of the Americas
New York, NY 10020

First Gallery Books hardcover edition September 2022

GALLERY BOOKS and colophon are registered trademarks of Simon & Schuster, Inc.

For information about special discounts for bulk purchases, please contact Simon & Schuster Special Sales at 1-866-506-1949 or business@simonandschuster.com.

The Simon & Schuster Speakers Bureau can bring authors to your live event. For more information or to book an event, contact the Simon & Schuster Speakers Bureau at 1-866-248-3049 or visit our website at www.simonspeakers.com.

Interior design by Davina Mock-Maniscalco

Manufactured in the United States of America

10 9 8 7 6 5 4 3 2 1

Library of Congress Control Number: 2022942435

ISBN 978-1-9821-7990-8
ISBN 978-1-9821-7992-2 (ebook)

To a male of worth,
who always saw the beauty underneath,
and the female who let him into her heart.

GLOSSARY OF TERMS AND PROPER NOUNS

ahstrux nohtrum (n.) Private guard with license to kill who is granted his or her position by the King.

ahvenge (v.) Act of mortal retribution, carried out typically by a male loved one.

Black Dagger Brotherhood (pr. n.) Highly trained vampire warriors who protect their species against the Lessening Society. As a result of selective breeding within the race, Brothers possess immense physical and mental strength, as well as rapid healing capabilities. They are not siblings for the most part, and are inducted into the Brotherhood upon nomination by the Brothers. Aggressive, self-reliant, and secretive by nature, they are the subjects of legend and objects of reverence within the vampire world. They may be killed only by the most serious of wounds, e.g., a gunshot or stab to the heart, etc.

blood slave (n.) Male or female vampire who has been subjugated to serve the blood needs of another. The practice of keeping blood slaves has been outlawed.

the Chosen (pr. n.) Female vampires who had been bred to serve the Scribe Virgin. In the past, they were spiritually rather than temporally focused, but that changed with the ascendance of the final Primale, who freed them from the Sanctuary. With the Scribe Virgin removing herself from her role, they are completely autonomous and learning to live on earth. They do continue to meet the blood needs of unmated members of the Brotherhood, as well as Brothers who cannot feed from their *shellans* or injured fighters.

chrih (n.) Symbol of honorable death in the Old Language.

cohntehst (n.) Conflict between two males competing for the right to be a female's mate.

Dhunhd (pr. n.) Hell.

doggen (n.) Member of the servant class within the vampire world. *Doggen* have old, conservative traditions about service to their superiors, following a formal code of dress and behavior. They are able to go out during the day, but they age relatively quickly. Life expectancy is approximately five hundred years.

ehros (n.) A Chosen trained in the matter of sexual arts.

exhile dhoble (n.) The evil or cursed twin, the one born second.

the Fade (pr. n.) Non-temporal realm where the dead reunite with their loved ones and pass eternity.

First Family (pr. n.) The King and Queen of the vampires, and any children they may have.

ghardian (n.) Custodian of an individual. There are varying degrees of *ghardians*, with the most powerful being that of a *sehcluded* female.

glymera (n.) The social core of the aristocracy, roughly equivalent to Regency England's *ton*.

hellren (n.) Male vampire who has been mated to a female. Males may take more than one female as mate.

hyslop (n. or v.) Term referring to a lapse in judgment, typically resulting in the compromise of the mechanical operations of a vehicle or otherwise motorized conveyance of some kind. For example, leaving one's keys in one's car as it is parked outside the family home overnight, whereupon said vehicle is stolen.

leahdyre (n.) A person of power and influence.

leelan (adj. or n.) A term of endearment loosely translated as "dearest one."

Lessening Society (pr. n.) Order of slayers convened by the Omega for the purpose of eradicating the vampire species.

lesser (n.) De-souled human who targets vampires for extermination as a member of the Lessening Society. *Lessers* must be stabbed through the chest in order to be killed; otherwise they are ageless. They do not eat or drink and are impotent. Over time, their hair, skin, and irises lose pigmentation until they are blond, blushless, and pale-eyed. They smell like baby powder. Inducted into the society by the Omega, they retain a ceramic jar thereafter into which their heart was placed after it was removed.

lewlhen (n.) Gift.

lheage (n.) A term of respect used by a sexual submissive to refer to their dominant.

Lhenihan (pr. n.) A mythic beast renowned for its sexual prowess. In modern slang, refers to a male of preternatural size and sexual stamina.

lys (n.) Torture tool used to remove the eyes.

mahmen (n.) Mother. Used both as an identifier and a term of affection.

mhis (n.) The masking of a given physical environment; the creation of a field of illusion.

nalla (n., f.) or *nallum* (n., m.) Beloved.

needing period (n.) Female vampire's time of fertility, generally lasting for two days and accompanied by intense sexual cravings. Occurs approximately five years after a female's transition and then once a decade thereafter. All males respond to some degree if they are around a female in her need. It can be a dangerous time, with conflicts and fights breaking out between competing males, particularly if the female is not mated.

newling (n.) A virgin.

the Omega (pr. n.) Malevolent, mystical figure who has targeted the vampires for extinction out of resentment directed toward the Scribe Virgin. Exists in a non-temporal realm and has extensive powers, though not the power of creation.

phearsom (adj.) Term referring to the potency of a male's sexual organs. Literal translation something close to "worthy of entering a female."

Princeps (pr. n.) Highest level of the vampire aristocracy, second only to members of the First Family or the Scribe Virgin's Chosen. Must be born to the title; it may not be conferred.

pyrocant (n.) Refers to a critical weakness in an individual. The weakness can be internal, such as an addiction, or external, such as a lover.

rahlman (n.) Savior.

rythe (n.) Ritual manner of asserting honor granted by one who has offended another. If accepted, the offended chooses a weapon and strikes the offender, who presents him- or herself without defenses.

the Scribe Virgin (pr. n.) Mystical force who previously was counselor to the King as well as the keeper of vampire archives and the dispenser of privileges. Existed in a non-temporal realm and had extensive powers, but has recently stepped down and given her station to another. Capable of a single act of creation, which she expended to bring the vampires into existence.

sehclusion (n.) Status conferred by the King upon a female of the aristocracy as a result of a petition by the female's family. Places the female under the sole direction of her *ghardian*, typically the eldest male in her household. Her *ghardian* then has the legal right to determine all manner of her life, restricting at will any and all interactions she has with the world.

shellan (n.) Female vampire who has been mated to a male. Females generally do not take more than one mate due to the highly territorial nature of bonded males.

symphath (n.) Subspecies within the vampire race characterized by the ability and desire to manipulate emotions in others (for the purposes of an energy exchange), among other traits. Historically, they have been discriminated against and, during certain eras, hunted by vampires. They are near extinction.

talhman (n.) The evil side of an individual. A dark stain on the soul that requires expression if it is not properly expunged.

the Tomb (pr. n.) Sacred vault of the Black Dagger Brotherhood. Used as a ceremonial site as well as a storage facility for the jars of *lessers*. Ceremonies performed there include inductions, funerals, and disciplinary actions against Brothers. No one may enter except for members of the Brotherhood, the Scribe Virgin or her successor, or candidates for induction.

trahyner (n.) Word used between males of mutual respect and affection. Translated loosely as "beloved friend."

transition (n.) Critical moment in a vampire's life when he or she transforms into an adult. Thereafter, he or she must drink the blood of the opposite sex to survive and is unable to withstand sunlight. Occurs generally in the mid-twenties. Some vampires do not survive their transitions, males in particular. Prior to their transitions, vampires are physically weak, sexually unaware and unresponsive, and unable to dematerialize.

vampire (n.) Member of a species separate from that of *Homo sapiens*. Vampires must drink the blood of the opposite sex to survive. Human blood will keep them alive, though the strength does not last long. Following their transitions, which occur in their mid-twenties, they are unable to go out into sunlight and must feed from the vein regularly. Vampires cannot "convert" humans through a bite or transfer of blood, though they are in rare cases able to breed with the other species. Vampires can dematerialize at will, though they must be able to calm themselves and concentrate to do so and may not carry anything heavy with them. They are able to strip the memories of humans, provided such memories are short-term. Some vampires are able to read minds. Life expectancy is upward of a thousand years, or in some cases, even longer.

wahlker (n.) An individual who has died and returned to the living from the Fade. They are accorded great respect and are revered for their travails.

whard (n.) Equivalent of a godfather or godmother to an individual.

PROLOGUE

1824 (Human Years)
Caldwell, New York

Kanemille, son of Ulyss the Elder, rode upon a fine steed through the moonlit forest, the shod hooves of his favorite stallion muffled by the layers of pine needles and fallen leaves. The chill of November had come unto the land, a promise of winter's frosted embrace, and in truth, though the lower temperature complicated some manners of life and livelihood, he relished the change of season.

There was nothing he liked better than a warm hearth upon a cold night.

As he broke free of the tree line, his horse followed without direction the beaten path that skirted the meadow and approached the rear gardens of Kane's manor house. Indeed, when he had crossed the ocean to settle here in the New World a mere year prior, he had not expected so much of the Old World to be found in his relocation. Yet from the Georgian-style home he inhabited, to its grounds and stables, to the very landscape of his property, he felt wonderfully at ease.

Then again, perhaps it was more being newly mated that gave him a glow of soul-deep comfort and an optimistic and kindly disposition to various and sundry.

Lo, his beloved leelan, Cordelhia, was a female of worth, and how lucky was he. And to think the mating had almost not occurred.

As was the proper fashion among families of the glymera, their union had been arranged, the pairing set up between her family here and what was left of his own back in the motherland. His aged aunt had functioned as his representative, and the bargain had been a right and proper one, struck with Cordelhia's mahmen as her sire had gone unto the Fade the previous year. In exchange for Kane's pledge to come across the ocean and proffer himself at the mating ceremony, he had been granted this grand estate, fully staffed and furnished, along with six fine carriage horses, four trotters, and a herd of dairy cows. There had also been a very sizable payment rendered in his name, one that provided an ample allowance for his new shellan and household.

When his aunt had presented the fruits of her negotiation unto him, his initial refusal had sent the elderly female into a flailing paroxysm. Part of his hard stance had been the fact that he had known aught of her plans for him. The other part had been a reticence to shackle himself into a loveless mating. Yet his aunt's pleas from what had turned out to be her deathbed had been heart-wrenching. The last of the elder generation of the bloodline, she had feared she would not serve the vow she had made unto her sister to see Kanemille into a settled adulthood. This was the only way, she had maintained, and she was running out of time, given her declining health and very advanced age.

As if he could say no to that.

And then she had passed, going unto the Fade.

Her death had racked him with guilt, for surely the upset he had caused had hastened her departure, and after the mourning period, he had found her staff other positions, sold her assets which were now his, and come to the New World to fulfill her final wishes.

Whereupon so many blessings had found him, and all were unexpected.

From the moment the veil had been lifted from his beloved's visage, he had fallen in love. Cordelhia was lovely as a Shakespeare rose upon the eyes, but it was her demure grace and modesty that truly struck him.

He had expected to have to endure his aunt's last wish. Instead, he often found himself praying that she was watching down from the Fade, satisfied with her efforts and touched by his sincere gratitude for what he should have recognized all along as the right and proper course for his life.

Closing in on the stables, his horse let out a whinny, and as its mates answered from the paddock, Kane's eyes went unto the glow of his manse. The welcoming yellow light of countless oil lamps streamed from out of the windowpanes on all floors, sunshine upon the frosted grounds.

His blood quickened upon the approach. His heart jumped. His soul smiled.

His dominant hand left the reins and double-checked that his saddlebag had held with constancy its contents.

His errand had been in service to a special request from his shellan. Of late, she had had trouble sleeping, and the sachet of lavender and herbs had been ordered by the village healer to help her rest more easily.

What a pleasure to do something for his female.

Traversing the rear stone wall of the gardens, he proceeded unto the stable. The horses were kept downwind of the manor, the architect of the estate having considered the prevailing wind direction as well as the natural buffers of a rise and fall of the terrain with regard to the placement. More whinnies percolated into the night, and beneath him, his steed began to prance.

Someone else was glad to return home.

The stable facility was open at both ends, and the oil lamps suspended down the center aisle of the stalls cast another lot of warm, inviting illumination. Pulling up on the reins, he dismounted as his stallion jogged in place and threw its head. With Kane's boots on the ground, he drew the horse into the—

No stable hand came forth.

"Tomy?" he called out.

Though there was much noise about, the chuffing and stamping in the stalls a chorus with which he was well familiar, the lack of a response turned to silence the sounds.

"Tomy." Wrapping the reins through an eyelet, Kane raised his voice. "Where are you . . . ?"

He stopped. Looked over his shoulder. Sniffed the air.

A terrible feeling gathered within his ribs and he strode down the aisle.

The tack room was at the fore of the stable, and in addition to housing the saddles and bridles and other provisions of an equestrian nature, Tomy's private subterranean quarters were entered through its narrow confines.

The door to the steps that descended into the earth was closed. Was the keeper of horses ill or injured?

Knocking upon the panels, Kane then wrenched them open. "Tomy?"

From the darkness below, there came no reply. There was no scent of occupation, either.

Forcing himself to remain calm, Kane strode away, passing by the saddles upon their posts, and the tendrils of leathers with their bits, and the wooden buckets. All was familiar, and yet he was abruptly lost.

At the head of the stables, he looked out to the manor house and took solace in how undisturbed it all appeared. Further, he reminded himself that there were countless reasons why a busy stable hand would be away from his position. A fence repair. A hay bale delivery. A coyote upon the fringes of the paddocks, requiring dispatch.

Whye'er would one be concerned?

Alas, he knew the answer to that. He had had so much good fortune e'er since he arrived in Caldwell. Too much. Surely the scale must be righted.

When the rest of the household was abed and asleep, that worry kept him awake—and now this. No Tomy. Which was unheard of.

Bracing his body, Kane forced himself not to run unto the manor, but rather course up the walking path as if his mind had not gone immediately, and perhaps with paranoia, to matters of calamity and death. On his approach, his eyes penetrated each window of his grand home and traversed its exterior expanse from footing to roofline, from cornerstone to opposite terminal. The formal structure was a sprawl of rooms, two wings flanking a generous central feature of three stories, and as the silk drapes had all been parted to let in the beauty of the moonlit night, he searched the interior for signs of proper disruption.

When there were no figures moving about at all, he reached to the small of his back. For personal protection, he carried always an ornate, bejeweled dagger, although as an aristocrat, he was not well trained with it.

Yet Cordelhia was within.

He needed to protect her.

Walking around to the front door, he found that the sturdy panels were open, and he knew that some of the doors were also wide on the rear of the house as there was the draw of a breeze coming at his back and no scents greeting his nose.

Dearest Virgin Scribe, they had been robbed.

Tightening his grip on the dagger's hilt, his hand trembled, and he hated his fine breeding and all his years of education and social leisure. He should have found a training camp and hardened himself—

He placed his free palm upon the honed wood of the door, and pushed the weight further forth.

"Cordelhia?" he called out. "Balen?"

The butler's lack of response was more alarming than his shellan *not replying. Balen was always upon any entrance.*

"Balen!"

As Kane's voice echoed, he looked into the dining hall, and regarded the perfectly set table for two. But that had been laid out hours ago, as Last Meal always was.

Underfoot, a Persian carpet he was particularly fond of cushioned his progress to the base of the stairs, and whilst he placed his free hand upon the balustrade, he feared what he would find. As that breeze coming through the house whistled past his back, the hairs on his nape stood up—

"Surprise!"

"Best of birth days, master!"

"Birth day wishes unto you!"

As Kane shouted and jumped back, figures well-known and well-loved presented themselves in a stream that emerged from the library in the rear of the house.

It was the full staff of the manor and the estate, all of whom he valued and appreciated for their individual merits . . . and at the back of the rush, his leelan, his Cordelhia, her blush-colored gown bringing out the spun gold in her hair and the strawberries upon her cheeks and the sapphire of her eyes.

As always, her gaze was downcast, her modesty a cardinal virtue among the glymera, and yet he knew she was delighted at the surprise she no doubt had engineered.

She knew him so well. He was not one for grand parties as was the aristocracy's way, so this was the perfect fashion in which to celebrate the anniversary of his birthing. And though her station was august, not just within this household but in the glymera as a whole, she waited until all the staff had paid their respects unto their master before she came forward.

"Blessings upon this night of your birth, dear Kanemille."

His female was far too chaste to offer her hand or her mouth. But he could not resist presenting himself before her and kissing her throat on her veins, first the left, then the right, directly above the high lace collar of her gown. Her discomfort at his display was in the way her shoulders tightened, but the contact was permissible as they were amongst their servants who were sworn to secrecy and discretion.

It was hardly a liberty given they were properly mated.

As he eased back, he gazed upon the loveliness that was his mate and knew that he was the luckiest male in the New World, and truly, the whole of the Earth.

Within a fortnight, that view of his destiny would be altered.

And the long period of his suffering would commence.

Had he known what awaited him, he would have placed his feelings of dread in a more proper context. They were not, as it turned out, paranoia.

They were prescience.

CHAPTER ONE

Present Day
Willow Hills Sanatorium (deserted)
Connelly, New York

Get the fucking car. Right now—wait! Did you disarm the collars?"

"We'll find out. If our heads blow off, that would be a no."

After this back-and-forth of disembodied male voices, there was a scramble of footfalls that retreated—and an electronic beeping that was short in duration, quiet in volume. And then, silence.

No . . . breathing.

From behind Kane's slammed-shut eyelids, he couldn't tell whether the ragged respiration was his own or another's, and there was little he could do to settle the debate. He lacked the strength to lift the dead weight that was cutting off his vision, but there were other issues outside of that. His wounded body, covered in third-degree burns, was an anchor that kept his cognitive abilities far, far under the hot water of his pain. Processing anything past a simple state of consciousness required concentration he did not have.

Although, if he was having even these thoughts, surely at least some of the inhaling/exhaling was his own—

Well . . . dammit. He was going to throw up.

About ten minutes ago, or it might have been ten hours ago—maybe ten days ago?—they'd given him something to ease his agony, the drug administered into a vein at the crook of his elbow. Almost immediately, there had been a floating sensation that had dimmed everything and created the heavy lids he was trying to raise, and now his stomach was rolling, the nausea nearly as bad as the—

The sound of metal on metal registered.

A gun being checked for ammunition.

The shifting and clicking were enough to cut through what few thoughts he had, taking him back to places in his old life he never liked to visit. However, the tide of recollections about his past refused to heed the barriers he attempted to erect. Images, like grenades, assaulted his mental landscape, their detonations creating craters—

"Kane."

Relieved by the distraction, he turned his head blindly to the male he knew so very well. Dragging open his eyes, he saw nothing. At least . . . he thought his lids were open? He had been recently beaten by some of the prison camp's guards, and the swelling made him feel like his face was a sack of potatoes.

"Apex," he said hoarsely.

"I'm going to pick you up."

Shaking his head, Kane tried to speak further. Movement would be very bad in this instance. Very bad indeed—

"This is our one shot. We have to take it now."

The arms that shoved their way under his body were like rods inserted through his flesh, and he moaned. Then panicked.

"Wait, stop," he choked out.

On his command, Apex froze, and Kane had a thought that no one else could do that to the other prisoner. Apex was a force of nature, an immoral scourge within the camp's confines, whether here at the new location, or in the previous subterranean one. And yet he came to heel for Kane, for reasons that had never been clear.

"We cannot leave." Kane coughed weakly, which made him feel sicker. "What . . . of Lucan. The Jackal—"

"They're gone."

Kane struggled to keep focus. "Where did they go—"

"We can't do this right now. The head of the guards is in the workroom and the shift change is happening. We need to get you out of her private quarters while we can—"

"What about the Executioner—"

"I already told you. He's been taken care of."

"What about Lucan, what about the Jackal—"

"I just answered that. We're going now—"

"What about Nadya?"

He didn't get a reply. And as he was forcibly picked up and carried off, he lost his ability to speak. Sure as if someone had set a charge under his skin and blown him up, his body seemed to lose all structural integrity, becoming nothing but nerve impulses that overwhelmed his brain, even with the drugs. It was all he could do to stay alive—and then he did throw up, bile stinging its way up his throat and souring his mouth. As he began to choke, he was roughly turned in Apex's arms so his mouth cleared.

Another round of beeping.

Stairs, but in his delirium he couldn't tell whether they were ascending or descending. The next thing he was aware of was fresh air. Cold, fresh air. As his lungs inflated, his stomach settled a little, and he became preoccupied with the layers of scent. Pine. Wet dirt. A faint vehicle exhaust—

Gunshots. From behind them.

"Fuck," Apex muttered.

Now, gunshots close by. And a shout as if someone was hit. Followed by another holler.

"Over here!" Mayhem called out.

Fast movement now, and bullets whizzing by, the high-pitched missiles streaking past them.

A stop-short, something opening, and then Apex said, "No, I'm getting in the back seat with him—go! Go!"

With no preamble, he was thrown free of Apex's arms and landed in a tight space that brutally compressed his arms and his torso. The smell of leather flooded his nose, which was pushed into something with a little give to it.

Apex's voice, loud: "Go! Fucking drive!"

A slamming thump was followed by many gunshots now with pings of what he assumed were bullets hitting the panels of the car. Roaring, an engine. Screeching, tires on pavement. Rough rocking, his face smacking into something else, and then his body banging back.

The next thing he knew, the car seemed to be gathering speed—

A burst of sound, shrapnel falling upon him, a sharp rain. Wind now, blaring wind, a rush in his ears and across his raw skin.

"Are you hit!" came Mayhem's voice over the din.

Apex: "Just keep driving, I don't give a fuck!"

"They're coming up on us!"

There was more shooting, and then Kane smelled fresh blood along with gunpowder. And after that, an explosion—

"We're going off-road!"

He wasn't sure who said that because a sudden lurch was followed by a brief period of total smoothness, as if they were airborne, and too bad they couldn't keep flying. There was a bumping return to ground and turbulance that rolled him around—

"Tree!"

The pounding impact as they crashed was so loud, his ears stung, so violent, that pain consumed him even through the haze of the drug, everything taking him back to the moment when he had made the decision to give someone else's true love a chance.

And purposely detonated his own restraint collar.

Finally, he thought as his energy ebbed. He could be reunited with Cordelhia in the Fade.

When he felt no relief at the prospect, no happiness, either, he told himself it was because of his suffering.

It had nothing to do with the nurse that had been left behind, the one who had cared for him with such tenderness and concern, the one who, when Apex had not been by his side, had sat with him as if where his destiny went so did hers . . .

The one whose eyes he had never looked into, and face he had never seen, whose halting movements told a story she had never put into words—and didn't need to for him to understand.

No, his numbness had nothing to do with Nadya.

At all.

◆   ◆   ◆

One grenade.

It turned out Apex found one grenade in the SUV they stole.

What fucking luck.

As they sped away from the prison camp's new location, and bullets shattered both the rear and side windows, he dove for cover into the back seat's wheel well, the fragments of safety glass speckling him like sleet. As a second barrage of bullets pinged off the exterior of the vehicle, he thought of all the fuel in the gas tank, and though his eyes had closed instinctively, he popped them open again pretty damn fast—

The small, fist-sized metal object rolled right into his face, and the palm-contoured, square-ridged little fucker fit just perfectly into his left eye socket. Ever the aggressor, he was ready to punch back when he realized—

Jerking his head toward it, he snatched the thing quick as his next breath. Which was what you did when you won a munitions lottery you weren't aware of having entered.

Perfect timing. Whoever was trying to pump the SUV full of bullets was reloading so there was a pause in the barrage.

Apex pulled the pin while he surged up from the floor. The roaring sound from the open hole where the passenger-side window had been led him better than sight would have, and he moved instinctively. Shoving his torso out of the bullet-created aperture, a blast of wind hit his back as he trained his focus on the tall, boxy vehicle about thirty feet in their wake.

Thanks to its interior lighting, he identified two guards, one behind the wheel looking out over the hood like his eyes were the laser sights of a bazooka, and the other in the passenger seat with his attention trained on his lap.

No time to get in his head about aim. Besides, he had the grenade in the wrong hand, so this was going to be a shit throw.

Shifting his weight, he got even farther out of the window, his dagger hand gripping a handle mounted on the ceiling to hold his body at a bad angle. Good news: The grenade didn't weigh much, and he had the wind working for him. The metal knot of *kaboom!* flew through the air, but the arc was off. Instead of going through the front windshield, it hit the grille—

Nope, bounce was okay. As opposed to going under the vehicle, velocity took the explosive up onto the hood, then up onto that windshield.

Now, goddamn it, *now*—

Nope, bounce was bad. The grenade rode up the slope of that windshield and disappeared as it hit the roof. Where it was going to blow up thin air in their pursuers' wake.

"Fuck!" Apex sucked back into the car. "Faster, we need to go fa—"

The explosion was loud enough so that the sound cut through the blaring wind and the engine roar, and the burst of light was like the sun that Apex remembered from before his transition. Wrenching around in his seat, he saw the brilliant yellow light contained inside the guards' vehicle, the glare beaming out of the glass on all sides and silhouetting the driver and the passenger for a moment.

Before they became just another part of a fruit salad of shrapnel—

"We're going off-road!" Mayhem hollered.

Their vehicle veered over the shoulder and caught something, their velocity undiminished as they enjoyed a brief moment of flight. Then the landing punched Apex up into the roof of the SUV, his head taking the brunt of the impact—meanwhile, Kane was like loose luggage, banging around the place as they landed on three tires, nearly fell off-balance, but somehow kept going.

With a sudden surge, Apex pushed himself over to the male, yanked the seat belt across him, and roughly shoved the clip into its home.

"Tree!" Mayhem shouted.

Apex wrenched his head around. Right in front of the SUV, spotlit by the headlights, was the single largest maple he'd ever seen.

As their driver hit the brakes, the SUV fought the deceleration, fishtailing, weaving again like it was going to tip over. Then there was a bump . . .

. . . a moment of spinning . . .

. . . followed by an impact so great that Apex was thrown into the front of the vehicle. As he banged back into place, he was momentarily stunned, his sight flickering, his hearing going out, his heart rate all that he was aware of.

As their lack of motion persisted, with nothing but the hiss of a ruined engine cutting into the silence, he heard something off in the distance.

Another vehicle, traveling fast toward them.

More guards, he thought as he tasted his own blood.

Fuck . . . but at least they had died trying to get out.

With his eyesight failing, he turned his head and tried to focus on Kane. The male was in a contorted tangle as he lay half on, half off, the bench seat, his bloodstained tunic and bandages making a mummy out of him. He did not appear to be conscious and also wasn't breathing.

"I am sorry," Apex croaked as he started to lose consciousness.

His last thought as he died was that he'd never told the male he loved him.

Probably for the best.

CHAPTER TWO

The King's Audience House
Caldwell, New York

N o, *Annabelle* comes first—"
        "Absolutely not—"
        "Does too."
    "Does not."

As the highly intellectual argument went from a simmer to a par-boil, Vishous, son of the Bloodletter, glanced across what had been a dining room and was now the King's receiving hall—just in time to see his roommate, Butch, look at Rhage like the brother had called some-one's momma a five-finger felon.

"*Annabelle: Creation*," the former homicide cop pronounced. "You watch that first. Everyone knows it."

Hollywood pointed to the guy with his sterling silver, Mint Choco-late Chunk delivery device. A.k.a. soup spoon, because the tea ones were too small. "The origin story has better resonance if you go back to it. More context."

"Why would you start in the middle?"

"Because it's the way the filmmakers made the films. It's in their title. Making, films."

"Thank you, Einstein. You want to draw me a—"

"—portrait? Sure. Do you want it with or without common sense? I mean, if it's the former, you're not subject."

"I was thinking more along the lines of a picture of what goes through your mind when you're losing an argument this badly. Is it a hopeless void?"

"That's my stomach actually."

"Okay, I'll agree with you there."

As the tennis match of insults and cinematic continuity issues continued to roll out, V decided to do some rolling of his own. Unhooking his lean from a sideboard, he walked across a Persian rug that had been hand-loomed and purchased new a good century and a half ago. He could remember when the bowling-alley-long stretch of jewel colors had anchored a dining room table that could seat twenty-four. Now it was Holi lawn for the polished hardwood flooring, no furniture marring its vast, vibrant pattern of swirls except for a pair of armchairs set in front of the hearth down at the far end.

There was only one other seating area. On the opposite side of the elegant, rectangular space, off in the corner like he'd been a bad, bad lawyer and put in a shark tank time-out, the King's solicitor, Saxton, was sitting at his desk. As usual, the male was nattily dressed, his handmade suit and waistcoat as tweed as an Englishman's knickers, as Rhage liked to say, his thick, Dread Pirate Roberts blond hair swept off his handsome face just like Cary Elwes in his prime.

As usual, the male had his aquiline nose buried in a book of the Old Laws, his brows drawn tight, his buffed nails tapping at the corners of the parchment.

Like he didn't like what he was reading.

"You mind if I pull over a chair so I can play with my tobacco?"

The attorney looked up with confusion as if his brain struggled to parallel-process both the spoken and the written word.

"Oh, yes," Saxton said. "Of course. Come, come."

One of those perfectly manicured hands motioned at a spare arm-chair.

V picked up the mahogany ass palace and put it at the edge of the desk. "Thanks."

"You are so welcome. I enjoy the smell of it."

As V parked himself, he took out his pouch of Turkish perfect and a pack of Rizla+ Black King Size Slim papers. "So what's the verdict on outlawing the prison camp."

"I'm still researching the issue."

"I'll say it again—why bother." Rolling up a perfect pinch of leaves, V ran the tip of his tongue down the gum arabic strip. "Wrath's gotten rid of blood slaves and *sehclusion* for females. He can do whatever the hell he wants."

"Yes." Saxton tapped the book of the Old Laws. "But the camp was not established by him. It was a construct of the Council. The *Princeps* were the ones who chartered, endowed, and serviced the facility."

"*Facility?* Is that what that shithole is supposed to be called? Because when we got into the place, it was a fucking nightmare."

"I gather its previous location was very grim."

"We were so close to finding it in time. We missed it by like a night or two at most. Frustrating as hell."

On that note, V glanced across the room. Rhage and Butch were still slapping each other's dicks about Ed and Lorraine Warren movies as well as all manner of personal failings and inadequacies.

"But come on, the Council's been disbanded." V shrugged. "Most of the aristocracy is dead. Who the hell's going to complain? And P.S., fuck the *glymera*."

Saxton smiled as he stretched his arms overhead and moved his neck from side to side. The fact that his hair didn't shift at all was not a fact of Aqua Net. It was because every inch of him was just that refined and well-behaved.

Likely down to his proverbial knickers, which were unlikely to be tweed.

"While I appreciate that sentiment," the solicitor hedged, "nonetheless, we need to be of care. The King is of course free to do what he wishes, but it's my job to ensure that any implications of his actions are presented to him for review."

Even though Saxton was a born and bred aristocrat, he had no love for his class. Then again, he'd been kicked out of his bloodline because he preferred the company of his own sex. The good news was he had found a new family of choice with the Brotherhood and mated a helluva guy. Ruhn was good stuff.

So, yeah, fuck the *glymera*.

"What're they going to do to us?" V started a second roll. "They have no power, and Wrath is democratically elected now. They can't touch him."

The attorney looked back down at the inked symbols on the open folio of parchment. "Yet if we proceed with precision, then there can be no rightful complaints."

"We're just going to raid the place and burn it down. Who's going to rebuild it out of the dozen of the aristocrats that are left."

Assuming they could find the new site. After years of losing track of the *glymera*'s private repository for vampires who pissed them off, the Jackal had gotten free of the place and come to the Brotherhood. By the time they'd all gone back to the underground location, however, the "facility" had been deserted: Whoever was running the camp now had somehow managed to disappear five or six hundred prisoners, an entire drug operation, and all staff and guards, right into thin air. *Poof!*

But to where? They couldn't have gone far, considering.

"I say we cold-lab it." V licked another strip. "Shut it all down with an edict and clean up the paperwork afterward."

"Have you found the location—"

"No, but we're going to. Even if it kills us." He took out another rolling paper, and then barked across the dining room, "Jesus, will you two just look it up on the Internet!"

Butch and Rhage turned and looked at him as if he had suggested putting a "For Sale" sign in front of the mansion. And was prepared to deed Fritz, butler extraordinaire, along with the property.

V jabbed a hand into his ass pocket and took out his Samsung, waving it around. "Not sure if either of you are aware, but you have the world at your fingertips here. Typey-typey."

Butch tugged at the sleeve of his Tom Ford jacket, prim as the good little Catholic boy he had been, and still was. "That's not the point."

"And you shouldn't believe everything you read on the Internet." Hollywood motioned with that bathtub-sized spoon. "Also, we don't really care about what other people think."

"So this is a private jerk-off," V muttered.

"Exactly."

"About a very important horror franchise," Butch footnoted.

For some reason, the sight of the two of them standing there by one of the long windows, Rhage all big, blond, and beautiful, eating out of a Ben & Jerry's container, Butch looking like he was waiting for someone from *GQ* to hand him his Best-Dressed Vampire of the Year award, made V remember the early days of the troika, the three of them single and hanging out in the Pit.

He wouldn't return to that time, even if someone paid him with a lifetime supply of hand-rolleds that he didn't have to twist and lick himself. But they were good memories. Just like the pair of airheads were very good males, very good brothers.

Very good fighters.

V checked the time on his phone. The three of them had been early for tonight's audiences, some kind of buzzy animation making it impossible for them to hang out all the way through First Meal back at the mansion. Wrath would be arriving soon, and not long thereafter, the citizens for their appointments with their King.

V hated this part of his job, cooling his jets while he listened in on private conversations about matings, births, deaths, and property disputes. However, the Black Dagger Brotherhood had always functioned as both the defenders of the species and the King's private guard.

So Wrath never did this on his own.

And who knew, maybe some night, the brothers might be needed.

In the meantime, he was staring down the barrel at six hours of twitching in his shitkickers. When he could be out looking for that fucking prison camp.

The more they couldn't find that place, the more he was determined to hunt down the location. It wasn't that he knew anybody who was currently incarcerated, and he was not a bleeding heart with a rescue complex. He really fucking hated the *glymera*, though, and even if the camp had been co-opted by some faction and wasn't being run by that bunch of self-righteous snots anymore, there was satisfaction in taking a toy with their name on it away.

And okay, yeah . . . maybe he didn't like the idea that there were people in there who'd done nothing wrong. According to the Jackal, there had been a number of murderers thrown behind bars, but there were others who'd been tossed in there who'd done nothing but break social rules that were total bullshit. Like females who had busted out of *sehclusion* or left abusive mates. Males who were competition, politically, socially, romantically.

People who were into their own kind.

FFS, his sex life had never been conventional, so it could have been him. Saxton. Ruhn. Blay and Qhuinn.

So fuck the *glymera*, he thought as he took another pinch out of the pouch.

"We'll find it," he vowed to the King's solicitor. "And I'm going to enjoy blowing it the fuck up."

CHAPTER THREE

In the prison camp's new location, three stories below the abandoned tuberculosis hospital's decaying floors of patient rooms, treatment areas, and administrative offices, two levels beneath where the drug processing was performed by the imprisoned and the private quarters for the Command had been built, and four flights of cracked concrete steps underneath the terrible sleeping conditions of the prisoners . . . a lone nurse draped from head to toe in dingy brown robing was changing the bedsheets on a thin, stained mattress with the kind of care usually reserved for the master suite in one of the aristocracy's finest houses.

As Nadya moved about the rusted metal frame, tucking the rough sheets in between the creaking springs and the forty-year-old padded pallet, the falls of fabric she hid under swung loosely about her scarred face and crippled body. It was a strange contrast, her stiffness, jerks, and hobbles, compared with the flow of the cloth, and she reflected, not for the first time, that she wore what she did partially because it granted her something of what she had lost.

Ease of movement. Grace. Fluidity.

But there were other reasons she covered herself thus.

Flipping a clean blanket out of folds she had rendered it into, she let the woolen weight settle and then smoothed out any wrinkles. Then she bent down with a grimace and picked up the thin, hard pillow from the concrete floor. As she placed the headrest where it belonged, she stared down at the vacant bed.

Until she had to look away.

What she saw around her elevated none of her unsettled mood. Her makeshift facility for the sick, injured, or infirmed among the prisoners was in an abandoned storage room, tucked behind a forest of shelves that still bore the weight of supplies that had been outdated or antiquated twenty years ago. When the camp had been moved here to this old human hospital, it had taken her nights and days to clear the space to set up the row of treatment beds, and as much as she scrubbed the floors and laundered the linens and washed down the walls that she could reach, she did not bother with the dust on the shelves.

There were limits to her energy and she disregarded them at her peril.

She had had two patients thus far. No longer than a night ago, she had washed and remade the bed on the far end, where that human woman had been, where Lucan had watched over her.

Where the wolven had fallen in love with his fated mate.

From Nadya's post in the shadows, she had witnessed the favor growing between them, and she'd recognized it for what it was: a blessing granted by destiny. A relief of suffering, a source of hope in turmoil, a direction when all seemed lost.

A destination when one had no home.

After the woman had left, Nadya had taken similar care with the washing of the sheets and blankets. She had known that Rio would not be back, assuming she survived the return to her people—and therefore she had known that Lucan would not return, for wherever that woman would be, he would go. Thus to honor them, she had stripped and reconstructed the bedding with precision, as if her efforts could somehow impact their future.

As if she held magic in her hands and could aid them along their journey.

Looking back down, she stared at the bed before her. Then she splayed her hands wide once more and ran them over the blankets. As the texture of the coarse wool registered, she pictured the patient who had lain there returning to her clinic, as if she could summon him by will alone. She visualized him coming back to her in the same manner he had first arrived, with Apex and Mayhem holding his weight up by the armpits, his feet not touching the concrete, his head loose, his body injured in shocking ways . . .

But his eyes seeking her out even though her face was hidden beneath her hood.

She imagined Kane with utter specificity, his raw burn wounds, his patchy hair, his mouth drawn tight from the suffering. His withered limbs. His clawed hands that were missing fingers.

She had done what she could for him, but her efforts had made little difference. He had remained on the verge of death until the night before, when the guards had taken him away roughly, with no regard for his compromised condition.

She'd tried to stop them. But the male who had manhandled him had put a gun to her head. She would never forget the look in those cold, pale eyes.

After Kane had been forcefully removed, she'd left the bed as it was, as if it were a beacon Kane's destiny could locate only if she didn't change the sheeting. Which was so stupid.

He was not coming back. And his end had been a terrible one.

She told herself he was finally at peace now. Up in the Fade. With his beloved mate, about whom he had spoken in his delirium.

Sitting down, the rusty springs creaked under her weight, and she had never heard a more lonely sound. Putting her hand on the freshly laundered case, she pictured what hair Kane had had left and tried to feel its texture, its softness, as if she could bring him back if her memories were clear enough.

But that was not how resuscitation worked. Or resurrection—

"Missing someone?"

Nadya jumped up and steadied herself as best she could. The female who loomed in the open doorway was framed by the aisle created by the two blocks of shelving rows. Standing over six feet tall and dressed for war, her powerful body was belted with weapons, her lean, intelligent face drawn in cunning lines. In a prison camp full of depravity and survival instinct run rampant, she was in charge of the guards, running the male squadrons with an iron fist.

Nadya's heart skipped beats and she pulled her hooding down farther, even though it was already in place.

The head of the guards came forward. That she was alone was unusual. That she was utterly unconcerned with a lack of defense behind her was not.

She had taken over after the Executioner was killed, and there would be no one who would get uphill of her.

"You wait until spoken to," she commented in her deep voice.

Nadya bowed slightly, and kept the truth to herself. It was not respect that made her silent, and also not fear. All she could think of was the way that guard had pulled Kane up off the bed by the arm, and even though Kane had cried out in pain, there had been no deference shown for his condition. For the fact that he was already suffering.

Instead, there had been cruel delight. And that horrible male had been sent down here by one and only one person.

Hatred was the reason for the silence.

"I have injured guards," their leader announced. "I'm bringing them here to you. Tell me the supplies you don't have and I'll get them for you."

Nadya cleared her throat. "What kind of injuries?"

"Does it matter? You're going to have to save them one way or another."

"If you want me to tell you what I need, you're going to have to tell me what I'm treating."

As a dark brow arched, Nadya realized that no one had ever called the female by a name. She was just referred to as the head of the guards, or "*muhm*" in the Old Language, in deference to her higher rank.

It was odd to hear the aristocratic term used to refer to someone like her.

"Gunshots. Contusions. Concussions."

"How many patients."

"A dozen."

"I need antibiotics, bandages, and pain relief," Nadya shot back. "Cephalosporin, all the pills you can get. Sulfa pills, too. I want hydrogen peroxide, as much as you can find, and Polysporin or Neosporin in tubes. I'll take any pain relievers, pill form or liquid, even if they're just over-the-counter. Also suturing kits and sterile bandages with tape. But I don't know where you're going to find it all—"

"That's not going to be a problem."

The arrogance wasn't a surprise.

"Let me write it down."

Moving as fast as she could, she went over to a battered desk in the corner and pulled out old stationery that had browned with age, but still bore the header of the hospital's name and address. Her writing was messy, but her mind was clear.

Her mentor's teachings remained with her, that bridge between the vampire and the human worlds still sound, still saving lives—even though she would see each of those guards bleed out if she had the choice.

Nadya returned to the other female and held out the piece of stationery. "Just so we're clear, I can't operate. I don't have the skills beyond simple suturing. I'll do what I can, but I—"

"No," the female snapped as she took the list. "You'll make sure they're fully healed and back in commission. And before you ask, if they need to feed, I will have females brought here."

"There are limits to what I can—"

The head of the guards took out a blade, the steel flashing with the same cold light that was in her eyes. "You better hope they all live. Every one of them. Their lives are yours. Their graves are your own. I'll put a piece of you in each hole I have to dig for any of my males."

Nadya stared through the mesh of her hood—and decided she was just about done with weapons being pointed at her.

"Where did my burn patient go?" she demanded as she pointed at the bed. "What happened to him?"

Weaknesses had to be hidden in the prison camp, and though her physical faults were obvious, she did what she could to camouflage her mental ones: Revealing to this killer that she had developed a tie with Kane was not smart.

But she had to know for sure what she feared in theory.

"He's dead." The head of the guards pivoted and walked out into the forest of shelves. "Your patients are arriving shortly. I'll get you your supplies."

Nadya listened to the retreating footfalls. And knew if she had been in another body, she would have gone after the female. In her mind, she had a fantasy of hand-to-hand combat, but that was never going to happen for so many reasons.

Kane had been a stranger. Yet in his suffering, he had become a part of her.

It was as if she had died, too.

And the prospect of going on without him cast her already gray world into a mourning that reached her soul.

CHAPTER FOUR

The sound of tires crackling over loose gravel entered Apex's ears like shards of glass, the soft volume at odds with the pain the noise caused inside his skull. Meanwhile, in his nose, the smell of blood, gas, burned rubber, and fresh grass was likewise too much to handle. Groaning, he pushed at what was against his face—

He was back in the wheel well of the SUV. Except this time, it was vertical, not horizontal.

Shit, they'd rolled over. And those were more guards pulling up on the shoulder of the road.

As brakes squeaked, he forced himself into motion and patted around for a weapon he didn't have, while off to the left, a car door opened—no, two. And that spelled certain death if he couldn't find something to shoot or stab with—

Footsteps on the ground cover, rustling on the approach. At least two sets, closing in.

No scent that he could catch over all the stench, but like it mattered? He knew what was coming.

Determined to at least go out punching, he flipped around in the tight squeeze, and as his head lifted, he felt a foot on the side of his face. Kane's.

In a sudden surge, he pushed himself up, only to get caught in a tangle of legs and the folds of that cover he'd wrapped Kane in when he'd carried the male out. The seat belt he'd fastened around the other prisoner at the last second was holding what was clearly dead weight in place above him, all those loose, unresponsive limbs making Apex's gut twist.

Batting the blanket aside, he was able to see better, thanks to the glow of the dashboard. Breathing. Okay, at least Kane was breathing. For how long, who the fuck knew.

"Mayhem?" he hissed.

No reply. No movement, either, from the guy behind the wheel who was hanging in his seat from his belt just like Kane was.

With the grim triaging done, Apex assessed whether he could squeeze into the front to look for another grenade or maybe a gun. The impact should have thrown anything loose forward, the kinetic energy of the objects unchanged even as the SUV hit a hard stop—

"Apex," came a voice from what seemed like far, far away. "Don't start shooting, for fuck's sake. It's me."

"*Lucan?*"

"I'm going to get you out of this wreck."

Apex put his hand to his head and winced. Maybe this was because of a concussion? Then again, he'd had a few in his lifetime, and they'd never come with auditory hallucinations before.

"What the hell are you doing here, wolven," he mumbled.

There was a pause. "Are you complaining? Because I'll leave you in this wreck if you'd rather wait for Santa-fucking-Claus."

"Hollow threat, wolf."

But come on, of course the guy would return. That half-breed had too much lupine DNA in him to desert anyone from what he perceived as his clan, and too much vampire in him not to protect those who he thought were his. Even though he'd escaped the prison camp with the human woman he'd claimed as his mate, and in spite of the fact that he shouldn't get anywhere near the place, at least not without a pistol to his pea head, here he was.

"Take Kane first."

Lucan's voice was muffled. "Cover your head."

"What?"

"Cover your damn head, just in case."

An absolutely insane part of Apex wanted to stick his fucking neck out because he was just that kind of a defiant SOB. But he ducked down and took shelter behind the seat.

"Be careful of Kane!" he barked. "And Mayhem!"

Up at the front windshield, there was a dull thud. And then a second that was louder, and a last—

"I'm in." The wolven's voice was clear as a bell now. "Oh, hell, Mayhem . . ."

"Is he dead?" Apex said as he pushed himself up.

"I don't know."

Apex tried to look around, but the blanket's dark folds turned everything into a stage set that had yet to be revealed.

A familiar female voice now: "Unlock the doors."

"Why is Rio here?" Apex demanded. "Are you fucking nuts? The guards are coming. We were followed—"

"Of course you were," Lucan's *shellan* muttered. "That's why we've gotta stop talking and move fast."

It had been a long time since anyone had essentially told him to shut up. Like maybe, ever.

"Take Kane out from up above," he said. "He's not going to make it if you try to get him out of the front."

Conversation now on the periphery, quick and intense, between the wolven and his female. And then there was a rocking—Lucan climbing up onto the side panels as Rio started to rip out what was left of the safety glass from the windshield frame. After that, another round of f-bombs, which Apex didn't need translated to guess the problem: The rear door was jammed.

"Toss me the tire iron," the wolven said to his female.

Another smash, and this time there was a raining of small fragments.

Now Lucan's voice right above: "Okay, Kane. This is going to get rough. I'm sorry—Apex, I've got him. Can you release the seat belt?"

"Yeah." Fighting through the loose limbs and folds of wool, Apex found the belt's anchor. "You ready?"

"Yup."

The resulting groan of pain was hard to hear, and then the load on top of Apex eased in increments while the other prisoner started to be pulled off of him. As the blanket went along for the ride, Apex could finally get a good look at—

"Oh . . . shit," he breathed. "Mayhem."

As Rio squeezed herself into the cockpit, the prisoner didn't acknowledge her—given all the blood running down his face, he had to be either dead or unconscious.

"Apex, release this belt for me, too?"

Shoving his hand forward, he did the duty, and then refocused and tried to help with the Kane evac. The moaning was goddamn awful to hear, but at least it meant there was still life. Although at this rate, the extraction was going to finish the fucking job—

Everything stopped as Kane screamed.

"The blanket's caught," Lucan said. "*Shit.*"

Apex's one and only impulse was to shove as hard as he could, but where was that going to get them other than skinning Kane alive. Either he lost what was left on his bones when the wool wrap came off, or the window with its busted rim of glass did the duty.

See, this was why it was better not to get involved with other people.

Their suffering became your own.

◆　◆　◆

Up on top of the tipped-over SUV, Lucan tried to be gentle with Kane, he really did. But there were limits when you were attempting to drag the dead weight of a male through an opening barely big enough for the size of the guy's shoulders. Plus even emaciated, Kane was over a hundred pounds, and with his body so weak, he was slippery as hell to grip.

And then there was that fucking blanket.

"We're out of time," Apex said from down below. "We've gotta get him out."

This was correct, of course.

As one of Lucan's boots slipped out from under him, he slammed down on the side panel, and lost the ground he'd gained.

"Hang on, buddy," Lucan gritted as he reestablished his foot position. "Just a little farther—on three."

"Got it," Apex called up.

"One . . . two . . . *three*—"

All at once, the prisoner broke free, and with the abrupt release, it was all Lucan could do to keep from losing his balance and taking them both down to the ground. As he steadied himself, he laid the guy out along the flank of the car, and the way that head fell back was truly alarming. Alarming, too, was the blood on the mouth, the bruises on the face. And all those raw wounds that glistened and wept.

Lucan pulled open what was left of one of the eyelids. The whites were showing and nothing else. "Shit—"

Apex leaped out of the broken window like his boots were spring-loaded, the momentum so great that he not only cleared the vehicle, but pulled off a somersault in the air. Landing hard, it was no surprise that he went immediately to Kane, even though he himself had a head wound that was bleeding.

"Is he breathing?"

The question was spoken roughly, and the answer was what it was: Anyone could see that the bare chest was going up and down. But Apex clearly cared so much that he didn't trust his own eyes.

"For the moment," Lucan hedged as he leaned out to the side.

At the front of the SUV, Rio had pulled Mayhem out of the driver's seat and laid him flat on the scruffy weeds. Face up to the sky, the male was moving in an uncoordinated way, arms circling weakly, legs up-and-down'ing, like he was drunk and trying to run.

There was a lot of blood on his face, like a glossy, red mask.

And then things got worse.

Off in the distance, through the tree line, the unmistakable flicker of headlights coming fast was the tick-tock of a doomsday clock.

"We've got company," Rio said.

After which things got worse-er.

Flaring his nostrils, Lucan scented the air and bared his fangs. "Rio, get your gun out."

Cranking his head around, he re-tested the scents coming over on the breeze and got a confirmation that made his pecs tighten. Great. The one thing that he really didn't need added to this shit show.

"Mayhem says it was a wolf," Rio called out. "In the road. He swerved to avoid a wolf."

"Yeah, I can scent it from here."

Lucan measured the approaching vehicles. They were closing in, an inexorable gunfight rolling toward them like a storm surge.

Glancing at Apex, he tossed the male the one gun he had. "Defend them while I go deal with a relative of mine."

Apex caught the weapon and nodded without a word.

Leaping from the side panel of the SUV, Lucan hit the ground and ran down the undercarriage to his mate. "I'll be right back."

"Be careful."

He kissed her quickly and then tore off, jumping up the shallow embankment. The road was unlit, but he didn't need streetlamps to see. The wolf's body was about forty feet away, in the center of the pitted asphalt strip, blood staining the white-and-gray fur of the chest, a gray tongue lolling out of open jaws. Surprisingly, the rib cage was still going up and down. That wasn't going to last.

Even though it had been decades, Lucan recognized the male. It was another of his cousins.

The first had been brought in by the Executioner mere nights ago. For whatever reason, the wolven had come off the mountain and were circling the prison camp—

The growl came directly across from Lucan.

As he lifted his stare to a stand of bushes, a set of glowing blue eyes was locked on him.

"Rio," he said loudly, without looking away from the wolven. "Get back in our car—"

"What?"

"*Get in our car, right now.*"

"But what about—"

"Now!" he barked as he sank down into his thighs and prepared for a fight.

Whether it was going to be on four paws or two feet, that was the only question.

Talk about spoiled for choice.

CHAPTER FIVE

It was with no small measure of confusion that Kane opened his eyes and regarded the night sky above him. Given the pain he had just endured, he had assumed . . . that the next thing he saw would be the foggy landscape of the Fade and the white door he had been told of by *wahlkers*.

But he had no mist, no door. He had only the dreary heavens above the earth, the twinkling stars offering little in the way of beauty and absolutely no mysticism to him.

Although if he was alive, he had a chance to—

"I've got to move you to some better cover. I'm sorry."

Turning his head, he found it difficult to focus on the near-to, but after a moment, the face on a level with his own registered.

"Apex." Dearest Virgin Scribe, his voice was so hoarse. "Wherever are we . . ."

"Brace yourself."

His fellow prisoner left him no time to follow that order, but perhaps it was for the best. As Kane's pain receptors once again became all he knew, the electric shocks boring through him like swords, the contortion of his limbs and spine nothing he could control, he retreated into his skin, the world lost unto him. Those icy cold heavens, too.

It felt like an eternity until he was laid out flat on the ground, and certainly the agony departed on its own schedule, what had arrived with a slamming alacrity retreating upon a leisurely stroll.

He opened his eyes again as a way of enduring the torture. In all his nights of suffering, he'd found that if he could focus on something, anything, outside of himself, he could beat back some of the onslaught—

Mechanicals. As his sight sharpened, he was looking at an interwoven thicket of pipes, shafts, wires, pans: It was a vehicle on its side.

In a flash, he remembered a gunfight, Apex leaning out of a window, throwing something—and then . . .

"You need to leave me," he said to the other male.

When there was no response, he gritted his molars and turned his head up and around. Apex was kneeling beside him, his hands planted on the scourged earth, his body poised as if he were going to attack what was left of the SUV.

"You are going to leave me here," Kane repeated, "and save yourself."

As the other male opened his mouth, he found an octave lower in his tone. "Let me go. I heard what Lucan said. A wolven in the road. And there have to be more in the woods if we hit one, and there will be another flank of guards on top of all that. You're free. You're out of the prison. Go."

The male lowered his eyes, and in the tense silence, Kane studied those harsh, lean features. He had seen much of them since he had detonated his collar and the circlet had exploded. Apex had stayed for hours at his bedside, for reasons he still could not understand.

"You need to save yourself."

Apex didn't reply. Didn't nod or shake his head. He was like a statue, though under his surface, there was heat and life. And aggression.

"Can you move him?"

The female voice was a surprise, and yet expected, given who had pulled Kane out of the back of the toppled vehicle. Lucan's *shellan* was dressed in darkness, and she had a gun in her hand. Though there was blood on her cheek and smudging across her jacket, she was as unflappable as a person in their place of usual habitation.

"Yes," Apex said. "I'll pick him up."

"No," Kane cut in.

"We need to get him and Mayhem in our car with the doors locked."

Apex moved fast. So did the female. And Kane must have passed out as he was picked up because the next thing he knew he was sitting upright, a belt over his shoulder and across his chest, his feet arranged in an alignment so precise, his proper *mahmen* would have approved.

"Kane, lock the door. Do you understand?"

Unable to move his head, his eyes sought the deep voice. Apex, again. Apex, always. Leaning down into the vehicle.

"Dematerialize out of here," Kane commanded.

"Lock it."

A hearty steel panel was slammed, and then Apex jammed his forefinger to the glass, to a little shaft that protruded from the door.

Apex's eyes burned. "I'm not leaving you until you do it."

Kane complied with a fumble of the hand that still had fingers; then he collapsed back into the seat. As his head lolled, he discovered he had a partner in injury. Next to him, Mayhem seemed to be in the same shape, his face covered with blood, his eyes blinking in an uneven rhythm.

"You all right?" the other prisoner mumbled to him.

Kane didn't bother answering as it seemed like a reflexive inquiry, the kind of thing that came from politeness or practicality, even though Mayhem was not known for either—and in any event, the male did not seem to have enough energy to track whatever reply would be proffered.

And oh, interesting. The prisoner had his collar still on, the steel band with its explosive charge and tracking device, intact. Somehow, it must have been disabled or it would have detonated as soon as they were off the grounds.

Forcing his head to other side, Kane stared out of a stretch of milky glass. Up on the road, he saw Lucan straighten from a crouch and focus on something just outside of view. And beyond the male, in the darkness, snaking through a landscape of trees . . . a line of headlights.

Cars. Many. On the approach.

Guards.

Although Kane was not of this modern era, having been locked in time since he had been incarcerated centuries before, he recognized what he was in and what was coming at them. He had seen all kinds of motorized conveyances, the trucks, SUVs, and cars used to transport the drugs that were packaged at the camp and sold for a profit. And he knew how many guards could fit in a lineup like that.

This was going to go very badly. For all of them.

As if a horse spooked, his mind abruptly retreated from the present. But rather than go to a safe void, it went to the worst possible place, sucking him down into memories that he always fought: He went to another night when death had come, although not on tires, but upon footfalls . . .

✦ ✦ ✦

On the evening of his shellan's *last breath, Kane was sitting at his desk in his study, the accounting of his estate before him, the columns of figures and tallies like sand sifting through his palms, nothing sticking except the odd numeral or line title. No matter how oft he reengaged with the material, he tracked none of it, his lack of comprehension forcing him to start and restart.*

And start once more—

Fidgeting in his chair, he relit his pipe because the ember had gone out in its rosewood bowl, and as he puffed out clouds of smoke, they floated up and lingered high in the elegant, masculine room, making him think of steam engines—

When a rhythmic tapping sounded, he was confused as to its origin. Then he tilted to the side and looked under the desk. His heel was bouncing on the rug, animated by the surges of energy that had made it difficult for him to settle in any fashion, in any activity, in any position, for the previous eight nights and days.

He was not the only one within the household who was not feeling himself. As well, his Cordelhia was off, although her symptoms were the opposite to his own. In contrast to his hyperactivity, she had been sluggish and without impulse, neither eating nor sleeping overmuch of late.

And what joy for them both.

Like a present for the anniversary of his birth, her needing was on the arrival. The change of her hormones, the fertile charge, was thick in the air, teasing his nose, causing his fangs to descend and stay in that position, making him restless nearly to the point of insanity. And the servants in the house felt it as well, although given that they were doggen, they were not affected on a visceral level. They did endeavor to provide extra privacy, however, dispatching themselves unto errands that kept them away during both the day and the night in a rotating schedule.

As soon as the full blooming came, supplies would be left and the property monitored from the perimeter until the fertile hours had passed. Indeed, the only way to ease a female's intense cravings was to mount her and service her as only a male could, and though he and his shellan were both aristocrats, biology was a force of nature that could not be negotiated with—and she was reaching her apex soon. He could sense it—and so could she, though he had, of the last two nights, felt as though she were fighting the tide. He could not blame her. The risks of the birthing bed were real, and yet his beloved wanted a young. It was all she spoke of, especially since her brother's shellan had presented a fine son unto the family bloodline this summertime.

Thus Cordelhia was not the only one who was impatient. Her mahmen was a constant source of pressure.

As was custom in both the Old Country and the New World, when a young was born unto an aristocratic family, the mahmen of the new mahmen was invited into the house of the mated pair, for to oversee the initial rearing

by the staff whilst the recovery from the birthing occurred. Following a successful rebound, the mahmen herself would then take over the proper monitoring
of the doggen. In the case of Cordelhia's brother, their mahmen had of course
been denied the opportunity, and Kane gathered that she did not feel things
had been attended to in an appropriate manner with her son's progeny. She
was determined to set the right example in her daughter's household, and intended, as soon as the pregnancy was confirmed, to move in to hire new staff
and train them in a fashion she considered correct.

Kane was surprised she did not anticipate redecorating the entire manor
as well. Although mayhap that was on the docket and had as yet to be com-
municated unto him.

It was . . . such a joy . . . to have the involvement of family. Wasn't it.
Especially one's shellan's.

Although a birth would be a blessing from the Scribe Virgin, assuming
the young was healthy and Cordelhia returned unto full health, an intermi-
nable cohabitation with Milesandhe was nothing to anticipate with glee—
and mayhap his restlessness was both the fertile time and the impending
descent of such an honored, nosy guest—

Unable to remain sitting, Kane's body bolted up on its own, the accounting pages slipping off the blotter as his sleeve caught some of the parchment.
Tugging at the knot of his cravat, he rebuttoned his jacket as he stepped over
the ledger bits and out around his desk.

Crossing the Persian rug, he went to a brass cart laden with cut crystal
decanters, all manner of liquors glowing citrine and ruby and amber in bel-
lies that caught and refracted the light of the oil lamps. Placing his pipe between his teeth, he regarded the selection, even though there was but one
liquor that he e'er imbibed.

To battle his sexual cravings, he had availed himself of very much of the
sherry. Verily, as he lifted the topper of the decanter, it was impossible not to
notice that it had had to be refilled once again. He did not approve of the
vice, yet for the previous few nights, he had been drinking steadily from the
moment he awoke until he passed out at dawn's arrival. It was the only manner in which he could remain partially sane.

His struggle to stay within the boundaries of customary decorum was a shock for him, a reminder that beneath his fine clothes, behind his proper education, lurked an animal, with an animal's base urges to mate, impregnate, and carry forth the species.

So, yes, either he partook or he could not stand himself.

Pouring an ale-sized portion of sherry into a crystal tumbler, he took a bit of misplaced pride that he had made it until—whate'er was the time? He glanced over to the grandfather clock in the corner. Nine forty-nine. So he had made it an hour and twenty minutes, nearly to ten o'clock this evening, before having to lean on the liquid crutch.

As he brought the glass to his mouth, he tilted his head back and his eyes went to the ceiling.

His shellan was right above, he reflected as he swallowed and swallowed.

His beloved was directly above him, a loose silken gown covering her body as she reclined against the softest pillows and her cloud-like bedding platform.

Anxiety curdled in his gut, souring the sherry's warm glow.

They had lain together but three times in the last year, the first being on the night of their mating ceremony. That initial interlude had been an awkward, fumbling affair, him taking her virginity as he had lost his own, her bearing him atop her as a duty she would not shirk. Afterward, as she had sat down gingerly at First Meal hours later, he had worried he had hurt her, but hadn't known how to ask a relative stranger about something so personal.

After that, he had vowed to woo her properly. Though it was his right as her hellren to demand of her his pleasure whenever he was so inclined, he wanted her a willing participant, and so he had set about getting to know her and showing her how cherished she was. With jewels and flowers, moonlit walks about the grounds, and all manner of judicious touches of the hand or shoulder, he had nurtured a connection.

And then he had tried once more. The second time he had attempted to lie with her, she had disrobed as if she were shedding her own skin, and she had laid herself out on her bed with the kind of forbearance one would expect for a healer's examination of a boil. No matter how tempting her bare breasts had been, he hadn't been able to sustain his hardness.

Some months thereafter, upon a final venture, he had tried to coax an arousal from her, seeking her out in the dead of daylight, taking his time, being gentle with her body. She had stopped him and insisted on intercourse. His sex had somehow retained its state, even as she had pulled him on top of her and roughly guided him in; yet he had felt a hollow sadness whilst she had born his release with a stoic resignation.

Subsequently, when she had taken great pains to assure him that she would e'er do her mated duty whenever he wished, he had felt a shame that had soured his blood. That she had carved him to his soul with her soft and sincere words was something he had kept hidden from her.

But she loved him. He never doubted that. She was incredibly atten-tive, and endearing, and the very best mate a hellren *could ask for. Over time, the sexual relationship would grow. In this, he was certain. She had been a* sehcluded *female until her* mahmen *had given her over to Kane, a precious commodity presented in full purity to a loving steward who vowed to continue to protect and cloister her. He must make allowances for her inhibitions.*

He'd just assumed they would have more time before they had to ease her otherwise intolerable cravings with the sexual act. But she knew that when her needing arrived, there would be . . . intimacy . . . to both keep her com-fortable and conceive that which they both wanted—

A sound outside drew his eyes to one of the windows.

With the lanterns glowing in the study, there was naught to be seen out in the walled garden, and yet he stared into the nocturnal void.

When there was no repeat of the noise, he shook his head and poured himself a second serving of sherry. Then he turned about and walked toward his desk, though he did not know what he hoped to accomplish there.

Halfway across the study, his body wobbled, his balance listing as if he were in a wind. Immediately, his eyes shot to the ceiling. With a buffering going through his veins, and a strange pall coming over him, surely this meant the time had arrived—

His legs went loose, the fine carpet with its jewel-like colors rushing up to greet him. The impact was hard, yet curiously, he felt naught whilst the glass spilled its contents and his pipe bounced away from his grip.

Opening his mouth, he drew in a deep breath that felt all wrong. Something was impeding his respiration—

A scent registered.

And then he saw the boots . . . black boots entered his vision.

With his consciousness ebbing, the last thing he noticed was the fresh mud curling around the soles and the heels, as if whoever was wearing them had trampled through the flower beds . . .

◆   ◆   ◆

Kane came back into his awareness on a full-body jerk, as if every vital part of himself awakened and gasped at the same moment. Disoriented, with his temples pounding, and his thoughts sluggish and confused, he tried to piece together what had—

Blood.

The smell of blood was overwhelming.

As panic enlivened him, he lifted his heavy head. Though his blurred eyes provided him with little detail, he knew where he was. He was in the flower-draped enclave of his shellan's private quarters. And the blood was hers.

"Cordelhia . . . ?"

Fear gave him strength to push past the logy fog and focus his eyes . . .

"Cordelhia!"

His shellan was lying across her bed, her bare arm hanging loosely off the soft mattress and monogrammed sheets, a river of blood running down the inside of her elbow and her wrist . . . before pooling in her upturned palm and dripping off the tips of her fingers.

On a wave of horror, Kane attempted desperately to propel himself up from the floor, to go unto her, to try to revive her with his voice, his touch, his vein. His body refused all call to movement, however, only his head bobbing up and down—

A scream shattered the silence.

In the doorway, his shellan's mahmen *stood in all her finery, her formal dress still complemented by her matching silk-and-fur overcoat because there had been no staff to remove it from her shoulders.*

"*You have killed my daughter!*" *she said in horror.* "*My daughter is dead!*"

CHAPTER SIX

Standing over the body of his cousin, Lucan palmed a knife and pointed it toward the other wolven who was hiding in the bushes off the shoulder of the road. In his peripheral vision, he measured the progress of the approaching cars that were no doubt full of guards—but mostly, he noted the shadowy movement around the Monte Carlo. Someone was getting stuffed in the back—Kane. And then Apex slammed the door shut and barked at the window.

Rio better be getting behind that wheel. Belting herself in. Cranking the engine on and hitting the fucking gas.

No engine. Not yet. *Fuck.*

"You don't want to do this," he told the wolven who remained hidden. Then he nodded off into the distance. "There's company coming. And a fight between you and me is going to guarantee that you meet my friends in uniforms. You're not going to like them."

There was a rustling, and then the other male revealed himself in his bare naked, two-legged form.

Oh, great. But he wasn't surprised: "Callum."

"Lucan, cousin mine." The male's eyes went up and down, not that he hadn't already done a full inventory of his opponent. With a fighter like him, those kinds of assessments were instantaneous. "You're just as I remember."

"Likewise." Lucan sank down into his thighs and brought the knife to chest level. "You don't want to do this."

There was zero chance that fine piece of advice was going to be taken. Callum was the oldest of the three who had framed Lucan, and the male was still powerfully built and, as always, uncompromising, his flexibility that of an anvil. An I-beam. The front grille of a tank. With white hair and glowing ice-blue eyes, he was moonlight made corporeal—and imbued with the aggression of a charging bull.

The good news? He hadn't brought up a weapon. And given that he was naked, Mother Nature provided only one concealed-carry holster, and there was no reason to think that—

Abruptly, the wolven turned his back on Lucan and focused on the approaching vehicles. Then, without another word, he leaped back into the cover of the bushes, making no sound.

As the shadows consumed the male, Lucan looked down at the dying wolven before him. In his fantasies, he had seen his cousins kicking the bucket in horrible ways—so this should have been a good thing, an outcome that was easy to move on from.

"Fuck."

He had a mate to protect, friends to save, and a fight that was rolling up on him. He needed to take cover, get a gun back, and pray that somehow they could hold out long enough to do mortal damage to this particular squad of guards.

Before the next group showed up.

Why the fuck wasn't he moving. "*Fuck.*"

Against everything that made any sense, he shoved his knife into his waistband, bent over, and picked up the wolven who had betrayed him and framed him for murder. As he marched down the embankment with the body, he cursed his DNA. Pack animals found it nearly impossible to leave someone from their clan behind. Even when there were reasons why they should never, ever give a goddamn about that relative.

He didn't make it to goal.

Before he reached the Monte Carlo, the lineup of blacked-out SUVs arrived and the shooting started, the guards firing off rounds even before the vehicles braked. As bullets whizzed by Lucan's head, he ducked and weaved as best he could, while his cousin's loose limbs flopped around and made balance the kind of challenge he didn't need.

Plus Jesus, the sonofabitch had been a member of the clean plate club. His cousin weighed as much as a piano.

Rio's voice was loud and welcome: "I'm covering you!"

It was the sweetest thing his mate had ever said to him, and man, she had good aim. The instant she started firing, the high-pitched pings of bullets hitting steel panels were a symphony to his ears, and they were also a game changer: Incoming fire stopped altogether.

Not that that was going to last.

His boots grabbed for traction as he rounded the trunk of the car that he'd stolen a lifetime ago, and as soon as he had cover, he all but tossed his cousin's body to the ground like it was a log.

A sharp whistle brought his head around, and Apex threw him something. Oh, look. Fucking Christmas.

Lucan caught the gun he'd given the male and didn't check to see how many bullets were in the magazine. He just popped off rounds as his mate did the same—while Apex jumped in the back of the car and moved those two injured males down in their seats.

"I'm out of bullets," Rio said.

This was announced just as Lucan squeezed his own trigger and came up with a big, fat nothing. And the guards were no dummies. The instant there was a breather in the ammunition shower coming at them, they got their lead back on, the Monte Carlo now functioning as a bunker, all kinds of metallic drumroll making Lucan wonder how long it was going to take for that gas tank to get hit and light them all up like a Roman candle.

Given what Kane had already been through, there was no reason to volunteer the prisoner for another BBQ.

He looked at his mate. "You have to drive out. It's the only way—"

The shattering of safety glass was an explosion of sparkles, everything going disco in the moonlight as the window of the open rear door got hit at just the right angle. Jumping on his mate, he covered her with his body.

And heard the shouts of the guards.

They were getting ready to advance with all guns blazing.

Lucan unsheathed that knife again. Closed his eyes. Breathed in deep.

"I love you," he whispered in her ear.

She twisted around and grabbed his arm, her eyes wide with fear. "No, you don't go up there."

"Fresh out of options and you know it. When I give you the chance, you take it and get them all out of here—"

"I'll go."

As the male voice interrupted, the two of them turned their heads to Apex.

Considering the source of the offer, Lucan was as stunned as if the Gray Wolf herself had appeared from out of the ether and announced, *I'll take it from here, boys.*

Lucan opened his mouth—

Right as the screaming started up on the road.

◆　◆　◆

One by one, they came on stretchers.

Back at the prison camp's makeshift clinic, Nadya stepped aside as guards brought in her new patients, one after another after another.

And even though the uniformed and heavily armed males were in charge, they waited for her to indicate where to and which bed.

She had heard talk that they were mercenaries, but they obviously had some care for each other. Or maybe they were just worried what the head of the guards would do to them if there were no more guards for her to be head of.

Seven beds. That was all Nadya had. Well, six—

"No," she said sharply. "You may not put him there."

Not where Kane had lain. Never.

When there was no more room—that she would allow—she directed the incoming to an empty stretch of shelving.

"Pull those two vacant sections together. Suspend the stretchers between them, so that their horizontal supports form a kind of bed frame. It's the best we can do."

The guards didn't hesitate, didn't question. The ones that were empty-handed followed her orders, hefting that which would have been dead weight to her across the floor, and arranging the banks of shelves just as she'd prescribed. And the system worked, the stretchers turning into hammocks.

"We need to put them higher so I can duck beneath them—"

Two more patients were brought into the storage room.

She nodded to the makeshift bunk. "Over there—no, wait. Not him. I need to see . . . him."

The guards brought the second of the males over, and Nadya regarded the injured as if from a vast distance. As a result of a neck wound, the front of his uniform was stained with fresh blood, his loose, black, many-pocketed shirt like a sponge that wasn't doing a very good job. Below the belt, there was another gunshot in the thigh, and some ancillary injuries at the knees.

His face was pale and streaked with dirt and blood. His eyes were closed. His mouth was lax, the fangs sheathed and flashing white in the midst of the pink foam that had bubbled up out of his throat.

He was an utter stranger whose face she would never forget.

"Put him over there." She pointed to Kane's bed. "He will go there."

After they placed the patient where she told them to, the males stood around, like robots looking for assignments.

"Where are my supplies," she demanded.

"They're coming," one of them answered.

"Go get them now and bring them to me. Some of these males are dying."

After the guards ran off, their footfalls disappearing down the concrete corridor outside, she went across and stood over the patient she'd put on Kane's bed. Her hands shook as she pulled the shirt collar away from the throat. The anatomy was ravaged, veins and arteries cut, the windpipe exposed. His breathing was bad, uneven and ineffectual because of the tear in the airway.

He had only a minute or two left to live.

As if sensing her presence, he opened his eyes. One was bloodshot from some kind of impact, a fist or perhaps a blunt object.

"Help . . . me . . . ," he whispered.

Reaching out, she gently lifted his head. Slipping the pillow free, she lowered him back down in place, his cervical column now flat, his throat no longer compressed in any way.

Nadya stared at him, taking note of the hair color, the complexion . . . the name badge on the front of his uniform.

"I know who you are," she said softly.

His mouth opened as he tried to breathe better, his tongue clicking as fresh blood dribbled down onto the sheets she had washed with such care.

"And I know what you did."

With that, she covered his face with the pillow and put all her weight into holding the seal in place. As the guard's torso jerked and his arms flailed, as his heels kicked at the foot of the bed and his hips twisted back and forth, she pictured Kane's face.

While she killed the guard who had taken him away with such harsh hands, taken him to his certain death.

When all movement ceased, she eased back and lifted the pillow. The male's eyes were trained on something up above him. Perhaps the Fade . . . but she prayed it was *Dhunhd*.

"May you rot in the earth," she said in the Old Language.

CHAPTER SEVEN

As Apex had volunteered to go up and distract the guards, he'd been ready to fight. He hadn't had much of a plan, but considering he'd found what appeared to be a steak knife in the back of the Monte Carlo, he was just going to balls-to-the-wall it and keep the guards busy long enough for Lucan and Rio to get the show on the road, so to speak.

Plus he really felt like killing something(s).

And he'd figured when the guards took him down, which they would because they had superior firepower, especially when compared to his absolutely-no-firepower, at least he could die with the knowledge that he'd done some damage on the way out.

Except now there was screaming up there. What the hell from the screaming—

Straightening from his crouch, he got a gander at . . . a massacre up on the road. The guards had stopped their vehicles in a tight row, the better to provide cover, and in the glow from all those headlights, six or seven of them were flailing around, trying to run, but getting dragged back into whatever was happening. Most of the action was out of view, but he could smell the blood—

Some kind of fragment flew up into the air, its arc bringing whatever it was into Apex's orbit. After the thing landed on a bounce in the dirt, he glanced down. It was a hand, severed at the wrist, the gristle a glossy set of streamers for the opposing-thumb-and-then-some whole.

Fuck it.

As Lucan yelled for him to stop, Apex bolted for the fight, jumping across the hood, landing on the shoulder, and racing up to the cracked asphalt. Rounding the first vehicle, he—

Stopped.

A mere five feet away, on the pavement, a wolf was savaging the chest of one of the guards. As the male tried to beat the animal away, he got nowhere with that—and then there was no way he was defending himself against anybody: That set of canine hardware got past the shredded uniform and into the pecs, the sternum, the stomach cavity.

Like the shit was a meal.

"You want some beer with that?" Apex muttered as he looked past the funeral-in-the-making.

There were four other guards in various stages of lunch meat, the ones still on their feet soon to be on the ground, the ones on the ground soon to be immobile.

The immobile ones soon to be consumed.

Lowering his dagger hand and his pointy little steak knife, he stayed where he was, because why ruin somebody else's party—but more to the point, holy fuck he was in pain. Getting blendered in a rollover was not conducive to being all hale-and-hearty, and as he took a deep breath, one side of his rib cage lit up like it was hooked to a car battery.

So yes, he stayed off to the side.

The gruesome deaths didn't bother him. As a hired assassin, you better not be squeamish, and even though he'd been a prisoner for a while, it wasn't like that camp had been Shangri-La. If anything, it had made him even harder.

And then it was over. Nothing left to kill.

The aftermath of such violence was as always so quiet and strangely peaceful: Dripping. Subtle shifting. Twitches.

Like after a thunderstorm, nothing but damage and rain drops left.

Although in this case, there was a lot of panting. One by one, the wolves lifted their bloodstained muzzles and set their sights on him. So yup, hello, boys, he lifted his knife, such as it was, into position. Because by all means, face off against a pack of carnivores with something better suited for a hamburger—

"Now what, Cousin."

Apex glanced over his shoulder. Lucan had come up behind him, and the male was making a show of keeping his gun down by his thigh. Good job only the pair of them knew that there was no lead left in the chamber of that autoloader.

When he looked back to the other wolven, he witnessed the change that he had heard about, but had never seen up close and in person— and it wasn't anything that he'd expected. Instead of some agonizing contortion, the wolves assumed humanoid form in a sudden burst, their fur retracting into their skin, their torsos expanding, their arms and legs breaking out in a smooth series of shifts. And when they stood at their full heights, curls of white smoke released into the thin air off their shoulders as if the energy required to alter was the combustion kind.

What do you know, they were all still bloodstained.

Apex marked each one with his eyes, moving sequentially from right to left, memorizing them. No surprise, their features were cataloged more easily in this form. As wolves? They'd looked the same with their white, gray, and brown fur—

He stopped at the last one—and not just because there were no more to take visual impressions of.

The male at the end of the lineup was especially broad of shoulder and tight of waist, the inverted V of his torso balancing his powerful thighs and calves. With white hair and what appeared to be pale blue eyes, he was both ethereal—and, with all that muscle, very, very corporeal.

And he was hung like a . . .

Well, yes, a horse, as the saying went. Which, considering the sonofabitch had just been a wolf, felt inappropriate. Too many farm animals.

Especially as Apex was staring at the guy's cock.

To maintain a decorum he didn't actually care about, he ran his stare back up over the abdominals, past the pecs . . . and to the face.

The male was staring back at him.

"Callum?" Lucan said. "You going to speak? Or is that blood all over you yours and you're about to cardiac-arrest on us—"

Off to the right, one of the uniformed bodies twitched. It was such a small movement, the kind of thing that could just be part of the parasympathetic nervous system shutting down for good. But as Apex's eyes shifted over—

"Gun!" he barked as he leaped into the air.

While everybody else took cover, he threw himself at the guard and led with the tip of his blade. Just as the male who was covered with blood sat up and pointed his weapon at where the white-haired wolven had been standing, Apex grabbed the wrist, slammed it into the asphalt, and struck the center of what should have been a corpse's open wound of a chest cavity.

The steel went where Apex wanted it to, directly into the heart.

But he was a guy who took pride in his work. Always had.

And something about the idea that the fucker could have killed that wolven made him cranky.

Giving into his fury, and in spite of his busted ribs, he continued to stab, and stab, and stab—and then as he yanked the knife free again, he took that gun out of a very non-resistant grip.

After that, things got a little hazy, but he dimly noted the scent of gunpowder overpowered all the fresh blood in his nose.

Unlike Lucan, the guard had plenty of bullets left in his chamber.

✦ ✦ ✦

All things considered, Lucan could not be surprised about the carnage. Apex had always had a nuclear switch, some level over and above what any normal male brought to a fight. And the fact that in this instance, what he was doing was more a case of mutilation of a corpse didn't seem to matter.

The unhinged SOB stabbed that dead guard with some kind of knife, the arms and legs flopping each time a new entry was made, the blood splattering his prison tunic and loose brown pants until it was like he had joined the leaking artery club.

When it was finally over, the prisoner just stayed where he was, straddling the hips of the mess, his own chest pumping, his blood-speckled face something out of a nightmare.

"Good job," Lucan muttered. "He's *really* not coming down for breakfast now."

The vampire looked over and there was a lack of recognition that, for a moment, was concerning, considering what he'd just done. But then Apex blinked, dismounted what was left of his prey, and seemed to wait for some kind of direction.

Like he was a hollow shell.

"Come over here."

Lucan's words seemed to reach him, and Apex walked over and turned back around so he was facing the wolven as they uncoiled from their defensive crouches.

Meanwhile, Lucan's DNA pool only cared about their kin. In the tense silence, as he was stared at, all he could think of was . . . how much he did not want his mate to get tangled up in this family reunion. And given the noses of his cousins and his clan, they'd sniff out Rio's scent on his clothes in a heartbeat, even with all the nostril-distraction going on.

It was killing him not to look over his shoulder to check on her position. But he didn't want to get her targeted. Rio was smart, well trained, and had experience with shoot-outs. He had to trust that.

Callum came forward. Not a surprise. He was the most dominant of the wolven on-site, and they would submit to that authority.

Meanwhile, Apex's focus was trained on the male like he hadn't run out of an interest in turning things into pincushions.

Lucan reached out and squeezed the guy's biceps. "Don't."

The reality was, if he wanted to get his mate and fellow prisoners out of here alive, a battle with the other wolven was not the path of least resistance. It was the path to the graveyard.

And something was bothering him.

Why had the wolven attacked? It made no sense. They had no reason to take on the guards, no role within the prison camp—other than framing people and tossing them in there.

Callum stopped about five feet away. "Lucan."

The name was hoarse as it left his lips—and then . . .

The wolven lowered himself onto his knees, his naked form resplendent in the glow of the headlights. Dropping his head, he shifted onto one hip. Stretched his legs out. Then rolled to the side to lie faceup on the asphalt with his palms on the bones of his pelvis and his legs crossed at the ankles.

His eyes stared up at the heavens.

Until he closed his lids.

Lucan's chest got tight—and abruptly, his grip on Apex's upper arm was no longer to keep the guy from doing anything aggressive, it was to help with his own balance.

A wolf never offered his belly to anybody, especially if he was undefended.

Unless it was his family . . . and he was seeking forgiveness.

By presenting the kind of atonement that, if it was refused, would lead to his own death.

Lucan didn't speak. He couldn't.

Instead, he took two steps forward. When his cousin's eyes re-opened, he thought about the murder he'd been framed for, and the years he'd spent in that prison, all because he'd been born a half-breed. As if he'd had control over that.

"I have hated you for decades."

Callum's pale blue stare gleamed. "I don't blame you. My father ordered us, but that's no excuse. It was wrong."

Lucan thought about those fantasies he'd had as he'd lain in that hard bunk, behind bars. Then he glanced at the other four wolven. They were all standing still, their hands clasped behind their backs, a signal that they would not interfere. No matter what Lucan did.

Glancing over his shoulder, he checked on the Monte Carlo. Rio was standing in front of the bullet-riddled hood, her arms crossed over her chest, her body braced.

Lucan smiled as he refocused on his prostrated cousin. "You're fucking lucky I met her because of that hellhole."

On that note, he extended his palm—and when his relative took what was offered, he pulled the other male up . . . and held him close.

Callum shuddered as the scent of tears wafted up between them. "My conscience has never forgiven me those actions."

"Good." Lucan cradled the male's head as it dropped down. "That's a fitting punishment."

CHAPTER EIGHT

Several hours later, Kane awoke to the sound of burbling water and the smell of fresh-cut pine and good earth. As he drew in breath, he had the sense that his body had been carefully tended to. He was not pain free, but he did have enough distance between his sensory receptors and his brain's capacity such that he could try to assess where he was.

His eyes opened. He expected to see the night sky, for he was certain that he was out of doors. Instead, there was some kind of draping over him, and not far above his head, but rather close to, by merely six inches.

Somewhere nearby, a fire crackled, and the flames cast yellow and orange flares across the sheeting. He wondered about the water, the flow like a small stream that traversed rocks, the chatter friendly. Welcoming.

"You wake."

The voice was female, but he could not tell what direction it came from. Rather, it seemed to be all around him. Perhaps inside of him? But that was not possible.

What kind of drugs had they given him back at the prison camp?

"Where am I?" he asked, not really expecting an answer. He wasn't sure he was conscious, and if he was, he didn't trust that voice was real.

"You are on the mountain. You are safe."

Unexpected tears speared into his eyes.

"It is all right," the voice told him. "You have been through quite a trial."

Was she referring to finding his *shellan* murdered, or when he'd been framed for the death, or the centuries in prison? Or the escape itself?

"May I inquire something?" he said hoarsely.

"Yes, of course."

"Are you real?"

There was a chuckle. "Yes."

"Am I out of the prison camp?"

"Yes. You are here with Lucan's clan, on our territory."

"Are my people okay? Lucan and Rio? Apex. Mayhem . . ." The male had been so injured. "Is Mayhem—"

"They are all well and safe. They're being fed and watered by Lucan's family. Amends have been made and accepted, the rift that was someone else's tear mended by what is left of the perpetrators of the crime." There was another soft chuckle. "I do believe Callum, as intractable and arrogant as he is, has had quite a humbling."

"Are they safe? My . . . friends."

Given that they were out of the prison camp, it seemed wrong to use the term "prisoner," and what a relief.

"Yes. And so are you."

He paused and gathered his thoughts. "What year is it?" When she told him the date, he frowned. "Is that in human years?"

"Yes."

Kane's math on how long he'd been in the camp was a revelation, and he was tempted to ask her if she was sure. "I thought I was in there for . . . much longer than I had been. I lost count of the time."

"That would be expected."

"Who are you?"

"I am a friend Fate has seen fit to provide you. And you're with me now because it is time for you to choose."

"Choose what." He lifted his good hand and wasn't surprised that he couldn't hold the slight weight up for longer than a heartbeat or two. "What am I choosing."

"Whether you stay or go."

"I didn't know I got a vote in that," he muttered.

"We are in a unique situation, you and I. I have something that I can offer you, a rejuvenation of sorts. There are some . . . unusuals to the commitment, but given your situation, I have a feeling they may be worth what you get in return."

A breeze entered whatever room he was in—no, it couldn't be a room. Unless it was made of windows and all were open.

"You're in my private quarters," the voice explained, as if she read his mind. "It's a bit of a tent, a bit of a hut. This is where I live."

He closed his eyes, weariness catching up with him. As he felt his strength ebb, he thought back to another disembodied voice that had kept him going. Under all the robing, Nadya had seemed mysterious and formless to him, too.

His lids popped open. What about her?

"You are dying," his host proclaimed.

"No."

As the word exploded out of him, hazy memories of a guard all but ripping him off the bed he had been lying on were so vivid, he remembered the male's face with all its satisfaction, as if the domination was enjoyed. Nadya had begged the guard to stop. Pleaded.

He had pushed her aside and she had fallen hard on the concrete floor.

"I want to see them," he demanded. "My friends. They need to go back and—"

"What if you could take care of that female yourself."

Even though Kane heard the words, he could not comprehend the statement: "That is so absurd as to be cruel."

"No, it is not." The voice seemed closer now. "Your heart is going to stop in approximately eight minutes. You must decide what you want to do. Live or die."

"I am past resuscitation, there is no breath you or anybody else can give me."

"There is something else."

"Like what?"

Abruptly, a surge of strength entered him, the source of which was unclear—unless it was true that there was a kindling before death, a final flare of coordination and impulse: He sat up. On his own.

And as his face caught the draping, he pulled its fragile weave off of—

A coffin. A pine coffin.

How fitting, and he told himself that his eight-minutes-left needed to be spent ordering the others back to the prison camp. Nadya had done nothing more than treat him, but what if the guards thought she'd been in on the breakout?

The veil was pulled free of him, and what he saw was a source of great comfort: an older female, who was not a vampire, was sitting cross-legged next to his final resting place, her hair in great platinum waves spilling over her shoulders, her dress deep red and beaded with a pattern that was somehow both symmetrical and free-form.

"Welcome to the mountain," she said as she balled up the shroud that had covered him.

"Where are my friends?"

"You have six minutes and change. Tell me what you want to do. I am offering you life—or you can die and go unto the Fade to see your *shellan*."

"I have no choice—look at me," he snapped. "So I need my friends to—"

"I shall tell them, of course. Whatever you wish."

As she fell silent, her eyes stared back at him, challenging his decision.

"I don't know what you're offering," he countered.

"I offer you life. All you have to do is host some energy."

"Energy?"

"It's what you're losing because your vessel is so compromised. The energy I'm referring to needs a place and it will heal you if you allow it to stay."

"Like I'm an electrical cord," he muttered.

"No, like you're a lamp."

"That makes no sense."

When she just stared at him, he dropped his eyes and looked down at himself. The burns on his chest were open, weeping, bloody in some places, debrided in others. And in the midst of the raw damage there were flashes of white, his rib bones, his sternum. Down below, his lower body was utterly shriveled, with no muscle left.

Flaring his hands, he held them up. He was missing some of his fingers on one side, and when he turned over what would have been his dagger hand, he had to swallow a surge of bile. The flesh of his palm had disappeared, the inner workings of things completely exposed.

"Are you sure you want to go unto the Fade?" the female asked. "When you are so worried about another who needs you."

"My *shellan* waits for me on the Other Side."

It was more a defiant protest than any statement of fact. But who was he arguing with? This ancient female . . . or himself?

As if she were prepared to settle the debate they weren't putting to words, she rose to her feet with the grace of a younger female. Padding across to a steamer trunk, she opened the lid and rifled through some contents. The mirror she brought back seemed like something that had been passed down, its glass wavy, its frame pitted. And yet given the reverence with which it was held, it was clearly cherished.

Kane reached forward with his ruined hands. When she just shook her head, he thought, but of course she was right. He wouldn't be able to hold it up in all likelihood, and moreover, why would she want his bloody stumps on her prized possession.

"Take a deep breath," she murmured.

"How do you know I haven't already seen my reflection since the explosion?"

He wasn't surprised that she didn't answer him. But given that he hadn't actually gotten a gander at himself, he did inhale as she suggested, even though he doubted it was necessary—

Kane's heart stopped and his lungs turned to stone. Strips of flesh hung off his chin, and one eye had no lid to speak of—which made him wonder numbly how he managed to turn off his sight. He had no mouth, just the whites of his teeth spearing into his gums, and his nose was nothing but two holes into his skull, what had once been shaped by cartilage and bone burned off.

He had almost no hair.

For some reason, of all the damage, the scruffy baldness, the patches of exposed skull, were the hardest to see—or perhaps his mind simply refused to grapple with what people had been looking at when they had sat next to his bed.

"Where have I gone," he said hoarsely. "Why . . ."

Well, he knew why, at least when it came to the explosion. He had taken his restraint collar off, breaking the seal and igniting the charge so that two deserving souls who were in love could have a future.

A lifetime with the one who mattered most.

As he shifted his eyes to the old female, the expression on her face seemed odd to him. Then again, she was a stranger.

And he was in proper shock.

And . . . he was dying.

"Is that what you really want?" She kept the mirror in place. "To go unto the Fade."

"It is all I have wanted for the last three hundred—two hundred years, I mean."

How could he have lost track of time like that. He'd been so sure he'd had his calendar correct, the years, months, and nights catalogued to the point of obsession. Then again, intensity of thought did not equate with accuracy, and he'd started with the vampire calendar, not the human one, and had never bothered to reconcile the two.

"All I have wanted is to join my *shellan*," he said dully.

The female tilted her head, as a dog would if they had found something of interest. "Look in your heart. What do you see?"

"Will you please lower that mirror. I cannot bear it."

As his image disappeared, he wished he could die in the same way, just one moment here, the next gone. And then . . . the Fade.

"I see my *shellan*," he said roughly. "In my heart."

"Do you."

"Of course!" With the exclaimed words, he started coughing, the effort to clear his throat, or maybe it was lungs, such that the world swam around and he gripped the sides of the coffin to stay upright. "I want to be with her."

"Very well then."

That the female seemed saddened was just another part of so much that made no sense. What business was it of hers? He didn't even know who or what she was—and he suspected it might well be a case of "what."

Plus she most certainly was keeping things from him.

"Lie back," she said. "It will be over soon."

Another round of coughing fisted his ribs and revved his internal body temperature such that a roaring fire lit within him. Releasing his hold on the pine box, he put his destroyed hand over his chest, as if that would help. It didn't. When he was finally able to catch a breath, the rattle in his lungs was such that he was reminded of the game he had played as a young, marbles in a leather bag, crackling aggies—

For no reason at all, his eyes went to where his hand had been on the side wall. His blood had seeped into the fresh, untreated pine, the print strawberry red and smudged.

He thought of when he had first woken up from the explosion. His mind had been fuzzy, but he had been able to remember being in the

Hive, that communal cave, up on the platform where the prisoners were disciplined. With stinging clarity, he had recalled pulling his collar off, his body shaking from what he was doing, his hands nearly fumbling the thing as the little red light on the back clasp had started blinking. He had relived the way he'd looked at the Jackal and Nyx, both chained to the thick trunks, about to be tortured. Then he'd felt once again the brilliant blast and the furnace of heat.

He'd had no idea how he had survived, or who had gotten him out of the Hive—and in confusion, he had turned his head . . . and seen a fully robed figure whose face was obscured by a hood.

"Nadya," he whispered as he came back to the present.

"You are a male who takes his duties very seriously." The old female moved closer to him. "I have heard of the Fade, you know. We wolven have our own tradition for the afterlife, yet I have always believed it is congruent with what vampires believe. All of us go to the same place— and all of us take our burdens with us."

As Kane felt another wave of coughing come on, he tried to sift through her words for the true meaning, for what she was hiding from him—and then it didn't matter. The memory of Nadya sitting beside his bed, and singing softly to him, and then getting up to bring him food, bandage changes, water, whatever he needed, took over his consciousness such that it was all he could see.

Though he had tried not to stare at her infirmity, he had often speculated about the cause of her difficulties. She had never spoken about them, however, and he had never asked. Instead, their discourse had focused on what she could do to bring him comfort, and what his mumbled responses were.

He had never seen her face. But he knew her scent and her voice as if they had been familiars for centuries.

She was still back in that prison.

"My *shellan*," he said. As if to remind himself where his priorities were and had to be.

With that, Kane lay back down. If there was any purpose to him, it had to be the reunion with his mate. He was a gentlemale who had been raised properly, after all. But more than that, if there was wrong to redress, it had to be his failure to protect Cordelhia.

"Our conscience is part of our eternity," the old female said. "And burdens that cannot be shifted grow heavier. By the moment. By the hour. By the year, the decade . . . the century."

"As if I do not know that," he snapped back. "I have been under a pall since I found my mate bled-out on her bed. Do not speak to me of burdens—"

"Then why would you add to your suffering voluntarily." The old female lifted her lined palms. "It is true there is much you have not chosen. But this weight is one you may choose."

He closed his eyes. Eye. Whatever.

"How many minutes left," he asked roughly.

"Two, now."

"Will you tell Lucan that he must go back for the nurse."

"If that is what you wish, to put in harm's way a couple whose future together—"

"Will you please stop talking," Kane groaned. "And what the hell can I do in this condition."

Closing his eyes—eye—again, he told himself that as grateful as he was to Nadya, he was not responsible for her, not in the way he was to a mate. Cordelhia had to be first.

He had not been there when she had most needed the protection of her male.

He would not forsake her again.

"Let me go," he said, unsure of who he was talking to.

Resolved to his fate, he exhaled what little breath there was in his lungs . . . and prepared to fade unto the Fade. In the quiet, his wheezing grew louder and louder, and yet there was something else inside the hut. Something . . .

It was the burbling brook. Behind the ragged sounds of his respiration, the rushing water continued to flow, but it was growing in volume. Once soft, the river became all that he could hear, as if the water was closer by. And getting closer.

As if it had legs and was walking to him.

Then again, maybe it wasn't water, but the coming of the Grim Reaper to claim what was left of Kane's body.

How could Nadya have poured any effort at all into such a hopeless case as himself, he wondered. She had never faltered in her faith in his survival, however. Not once.

And she had never left him.

CHAPTER NINE

It all came.

Everything Nadya had asked for, each drug, all the supplies, even food and water, and more blankets and proper cots, arrived in a steady stream. The guards were good packhorses, coming in laden with duffels and baskets or rolling in carts. They also continued to take direction very well. She created an inventory system quickly, ordered the males around, and got the new provisions to her clinic sorted. Then she asked them to remove the body of the dead guard and dismissed them to get to work.

"One more suture and we're done," she murmured to her patient.

When there was no response, she glanced up. The guard whose thigh wound she was stitching closed had his eyes shut and his hands resting on his bare stomach. She had had to cut his clothes away because there had been blood all over him, but his nakedness was just a necessary part of taking the inventory of his condition. He had no injuries to his privacy, and no doubt, assuming he survived, that would be something to rejoice over. The laceration on his head had been severe, however, and she had worried whether he would pull through. So far, so good, though.

Down on his leg, her last stitch was at the base of a ragged wound, and as she tied a knot and clipped the string, she graded her handiwork. The injury had been a tearing of some sort, as if the leg had gotten caught, and in the pulling free, the skin had given way. The bruising was extensive, the swelling getting ever worse, the redness under the skin already going to purple.

"But you're going to live," she murmured as she wiped everything down with peroxide. "We have to be positive."

After she had triaged all the guards—with him being least acute, which was why she was treating him last—she had parceled out pain relief in pill or shot form, and settled in to deal with what she could. She had worked as fast as her hands would allow, and as her back began to ache and her limp grew more painful, she ignored her own discomfort.

The fact that it had taken a full squad of guards being injured to get the kinds of prescriptions and bandages she needed made her angry. Back when they had been at the subterranean location, she had once gone to the Command and begged for things to cure, to ease, to help. She had never asked again. Some lines walked were too dangerous, and how could she do any good at all if she herself was dead?

Ever since they had been relocated to this abandoned hospital, she had had a lull in her patient volume because so many had died during the evacuation as a result of the stress and the travel. But she knew there would be more who'd come to her, there were always more, and so she had claimed this storage room as her own clinic. After the Executioner, who had been the prison camp's second-in-command, had assumed the leadership role, he'd been far more pragmatic than his predecessor. He'd recognized the financial interest he had in ensuring his workforce could do what he required of them. He had known that unless more inmates came in—which, for whatever reason, they were not—he needed to take better care of those he had.

So he'd allowed her to maintain the clinic.

Which was now full of guards.

After bandaging her set of stitches, she got up off the hard floor and disposed of the detritus of wrappings. Then she limped over to a cart full of fresh bread loaves, knots of cheese, and plastic bottles of water. In quick succession, she fed herself, hydrated, and felt little improvement in terms of energy. What kept her going? Her promise to herself, forged long ago.

She would let no one die or suffer if she could alleviate what ailed them.

As she brought the water bottle back to her lips, she emptied most of what was in there, the chemical tint from the purification system stinging the sides of her tongue. For a moment, she longed for a taste of purity, of something that quenched the thirst not just by adding H_2O to her system, but by—

Pivoting around, she looked down the row of beds. Then regarded the guards that had been moved out of the stretchers suspended between the shelves and onto the cots.

Her patients were lying like logs, none of them moving except for breathing. There was only one who was facedown, due to lacerations on the backs of his legs and his buttocks, but the rest she could check their faces to see if they were awake.

One was staring over at her from the far end.

His lids were cracked just a bit, so it was hard to tell if he was feigning sleep or that was as far as he could open things. But his eyes were definitely on her, and as she pivoted to set the water bottle off to the side and then turned back, his focus remained.

Hobbling over to him, she leaned down. "Do you require aught?"

The male had some deep lacerations across his upper body, throat, and face, the kind that were characteristic of a knife fight. She had stitched them up, but the one down his jaw was probably preventing him from speaking.

"Your pain medicine should be working now."

His eyes shifted over her shoulder.

Nadya stiffened as the presence who had arrived registered. "Greetings."

She turned around. The head of the guards was standing in the open doorway, looking down the rows of her wounded subordinates. When she got to the final bed, the one that was empty except for a bloody pillow and some smudged sheets, she cocked a brow.

"Yes," Nadya said. "There was a loss. But he was dying as he came in, and the supplies I required had not been brought to me."

The female came forward. "Indeed."

Nadya remained where she was, and when the head of the guards was before her, she tilted back because there was such a height difference between the two of them.

"I want to see your face," the female said.

"Why."

There was no reply. But a long arm reached forward—

Nadya slapped a hold on the wrist. "No."

"What are you hiding under all that fabric."

"Nothing that will affect my ability to take care of your males. And that is all you need to care about."

There was a tense silence, and it went without saying that the female could do what she wanted physically. She was ten times stronger.

"Thank you for the supplies," Nadya said stiffly. "They are very much appreciated. But they confer no rights on your behalf."

"You're not as meek as you make out."

"And you need me. Unless you want to service their bedpans and ensure that you don't overdose them when it is time for their medications again, you better leave me to do my job."

The head of the guards twisted her arm such that Nadya had to release her hold.

"One of them dies," the female said, "and I will kill you myself—even if I have to find someone else to do your job."

Nadya inclined her head. "You were quite clear the first time."

◆   ◆   ◆

In the midst of the sound of the river he could not see, Kane could find no clarity at all.

As he lay there with the seconds ticking by, the sand running through his last-hour hourglass, he had expected relief with his decision made. When that didn't come, he decided resignation was more what he needed to feel. Finally, he just waited, once again, to see the white landscape he'd heard about. Surely, that white door would be rushing up to him soon, the knob prepared for his palm.

He did not see white. He saw dark brown.

It was a memory of robing the color of mahogany. And then, as if his mind's eye was a camera lens that widened, he recalled the clinic with its lineup of empty, precisely made-up beds, and its forest of shelving, and the dust-covered boxes and long-forgotten items and the chipped desk. It was all so makeshift modest, so threadbare and worn. But it had been created by Nadya to care for others with limited supplies, and with that noble purpose, it was a palace.

He had never thought to ask her how she had ended up with the rest of them, for it was impossible to imagine her as a criminal. No one with that good a heart could hurt somebody—

Kane opened his eyes. "I have to go back for her."

The old female in the red beaded dress smiled at him. As if she had known all along he would change his mind.

"I can't leave her in that hell," he said roughly.

"If you choose to stay, you will not be as you are—"

"Hurry."

"—you will be changed forevermore—"

"*Hurry.*"

"You will not be the same—"

"Whatever it does to me, I don't care!" Less than two minutes left, nearly a minute to go. "Just do it!"

The female nodded. "I am so sorry."

There was no reason to ask what for. Kane didn't care. He just didn't want to run out of time—

All at once, the coffin's walls fell away, and as he looked to the side, he saw the stream that ran through the hut, its rock bed snaking around the fire—surely it was not going under the flames?—the dark gray stones gleaming and mysterious where the water coursed over them. Though nothing struck him as particularly miraculous about the little river, he couldn't look away, and the longer he stared, the more he realized that there was no bottom to the tributary. In fact . . . it wasn't a river at all. That was not water.

It was a metaphysical divide that seemed to penetrate deep into the earth—and the fire suddenly struck him as odd as well. The flames had no kindling or wood to feed their hunger. As with the not-real-water, they seemed to just exist.

"The energy that needs a host is a fundamental and comes from the center of everything," the old female said as she stepped to the end of the coffin.

No, there was no coffin. He was lying directly on the ground, not even on the handspun rug, the earth underneath him neither hard nor soft. And with the connection between his broken body and the soil, the unnerving charge that vibrated up from beneath him passed directly into his flesh—

The river was suddenly under him, a diversion instantly rerouting its flow, and yet he felt none of the rush nor any dampening. Instead, he was suffused by warmth and an easing of pain that was not drugs, but something far more elemental, as if his nerves were being brushed with compassion and calming as a result.

"It has accepted you," the old female murmured. "This is good."

As if her pronouncement started some kind of process, he began sinking, or maybe the level of the energy was rising; either way, as he looked down at his body, he was in the river now, the flow, now dark as night, coming up and over his knees and thighs, his hips, his chest.

"Be not afraid—"

The black rush claimed him, the submersion as if he were drowning, a weight upon him compressing his body under the—

Snakes.

The flow was not water, and it was not raw energy, it was hundreds of black vipers . . . a thousand of them . . . an infinite number.

A burst of fear animated him, but as he tried to sit up, he was trapped, held in place by the slick serpents that coursed over him. Instinctively, he struggled to shove them off, kick them free, his body bucking and twisting. The reptiles just continued to slither over him, coating his corporeal form, a teeming blanket that moved against him as if it were trying to find a way inside.

In the midst of his panic, he somehow looked outside of the vipers, and what he saw of the old female made as much sense as the river of snakes. Her face had become youthful, her beauty glowing with an otherworldly beneficence, sure as if that which appeared aged was but a mask, and that which was underneath was the true, infinite essence of her.

And as if she had waited for him to look up, she stepped free of the body she had presented herself to him in, becoming nothing but a glowing shape that had a hazy form and the contours of a female, although no true substance.

As her ghostly hair swirled around her like platinum flames, it was as though a wind source from within the earth was finding her and her alone. "Be not afraid."

Why was it when someone said that to you, it always made things worse—

Her "arm" extended out five, six, seven feet, until it entered into the flow of serpents, the life-force that was her penetrating the tangle of vipers . . . and coming back out with something in her grip. The long black snake emerged tail-first from the twisting mass, and as the female pulled it free, its tremendous length wrapped around her all the way up to her shoulder, the movement so sensuous, so accepted and expected, it was a gesture of familiarity.

And then came the head.

The triangular apex of the serpent swung around, its red reptilian eyes locking on Kane. A black tongue licked out. Retreated. Trolled out once again. Then the head reared up.

"My dear friend is in search of a host." The female came closer, floating over the earth as opposed to ambulating in the conventional sense. "You will find him a most hospitable guest, although he will do some redecorating. I don't believe you will mind that, however."

Kane's heart started pounding. "Host?"

"You will get the rejuvenation you require. He will get a chance to see the world again. A fine bargain for both sides."

The old female was talking, Kane knew this because sounds in her intonation were entering his ears, but he could comprehend none of her words. Staring into those reptilian eyes, a disassociation took him over, removing him from everything but that ruby gaze.

The viper began to weave from side to side, and Kane found himself echoing the sway, until they were moving in synchronization . . . side to side, side to side.

The lower jaw dropped and the fangs descended. The tongue retracted—

The great head reared back and hinged open, exposing long, sharp fangs.

The strike happened so quick, quick as a gasp, and yet his mind recorded the swing and the piercing contact over his heart in slow motion. It was like the culmination of a dance, a to-and-fro that claimed him, and in the aftermath, he looked down at his chest.

Two rivers of blood streamed down the raw burn wounds—

Kane gasped and arched. Then his head fell back and he crashed into a free fall, into the stream of snakes, which claimed him now in a different way.

He was one of their own.

The seizures came in waves, rattling his teeth, stiffening his every muscle, nearly cracking his spine in half as he spasmed. And as his lips opened, something entered his mouth, entered him. Choking, he fought against—

Another viper barged in, going down his throat, curling in his gut. He screamed and tried to breathe, but there was an endless number that followed. As his stomach bloated, he thought he was going to throw up, and still they continued to penetrate him, his mouth stretching wide.

No more room, he was going to blow apart—

The vipers broke out of his gut and speared into his torso, curling around his organs, distending his skin—and then they filled his arms, his legs.

When there was no more territory to take over . . .

. . . what he had felt coming arrived.

Kane screamed again as he blew apart, his corporeal form disintegrating into the ether, no part of him left intact.

CHAPTER TEN

Home again, home again, jiggety-jig.

As Lucan stared into the flames of his clan's central fire pit, he had no idea where the hell he was. Okay, he knew he was out of the prison camp. He knew he was on the mountain. And he knew that his *shellan* had made it out of the fighting alive, that Mayhem was resting, that Apex was okay, and that Kane . . .

He glanced over his shoulder at the Gray Wolf's hut.

Kane was under the matriarch's care.

But that was where his yup-I-got-it ended. Then again, was there much else that mattered?

As the banked fire snapped and crackled in its seat of crisscrossed logs, and as the sweet smoke spun around to tickle his nose, he remembered being in the original prison camp, and lying back on his hard bed, cradling an old cassette player to his chest. As Duran Duran played over and over again, he would stare up at the rough rock ceiling above him and think of this exact moment right now.

Sure as if this was a destination some part of him knew he would return to.

He had had so many dreams of this circle of logs around the flat stone hearth, the conifers tall and fluffy above him, the earth padded with fallen pine needles, the boulders that peeked out of the ground stalwarts that had survived the advance and retreat of glaciers millions of years ago. And the funny thing was, no matter how much he had changed, the setting was just exactly as he remembered it, the cave entrances hidden, the females out of view for safety's sake; the males front and center, prepared to defend the territory; the elders out on the overlook, sharing stories, at peace with the present because they lived in the past.

As the wind shifted around again, he looked up at the sky, following the soft smoke curls and heat tendrils up to the stars that twinkled, bright as penlights, in the velvet-dark heavens.

"You okay?"

At the whispered words, he tightened his hold on Rio's hand. "I don't know. I think so?" He glanced over. "I'm glad you're here. I didn't even think I'd get a chance to show you this place."

Rio looked out into the trees, the firelight playing over her face. "It's so peaceful."

"And it's safe."

Because the irony of ironies was that this tranquility would be protected by bloodshed, if necessary. Back after the run-in with the carloads of guards, when Lucan had accepted his cousin's submission in front of those dead bodies and free-for-the-taking SUVs, he had known that this was where they should go to recover and figure out all the what-next. And Callum didn't have to suggest it or offer an invite. What was the clan's . . . was all of the clan's—and it looked like he was back in the family.

Wiping his eyes, he cleared his throat and looked across at Callum. The male was sitting down, it was true, but his powerful body was no more at rest than any predator's. Though his eyes were mostly on the fire, he was constantly monitoring the perimeter, as were the other wolven.

Lucan had to hand it to the hardheaded sonofabitch. The guy had thought things through when it came to defensible positions and evasive maneuvers. After gathering all the guards' weapons and what little was left of the ammo, they had taken the vehicles about four miles away and run them off a cliff into a ravine one by one. Then the wolven had taken his dead cousin's body and dematerialized to a location at the base of the clan's mountain, while Lucan had driven as fast as he dared in the Monte Carlo to meet them there.

Talk about shitty garages. The structure had looked like it was only a sneeze away from collapse, but that was only on the outside. The interior of the place was a miracle, fully stocked with everything you'd need for an evac, an attack. A meal. A nap. A holdout for several weeks.

It even had an underground bunker and an escape route.

Stashing the sedan, they'd removed and destroyed the two restraining collars, put Mayhem and Kane on stretchers, and then they'd collectively muscled the two males into the acreage. The trail was not one Lucan knew, which made him suspect it had been carved out especially for the bolt-hole, but the environs were instantly home, from the pine scent and the soft earth, to the trees looming as if in protection of the innocent, the injured, the lost, and the needy.

The journey into the heart of the clan's territory had been forty minutes on foot, and those who hadn't had their hand on a stretcher grip were armed to the teeth and guarding the trail from ahead, from behind, from the sides. And some of the wolven had assumed their four-footed forms, because they could be faster over the—

Abruptly, Callum rose to his full height. As everyone turned in his direction, he just shook his head and walked off to the west like it was a call-of-nature thing.

In deference to Rio, the wolven had clothed themselves while in their two-footed forms, and there hadn't been any issue raised that she was a female among them. He appreciated the deference and the decorum, and supposed it was a sign of how much he had moved on that he found the sequestering of the clan's females and young so strange and uncomfortable. In fact, he wasn't even sure any of them were on the mountain at all.

Well, what do you know.

Off to the left, Apex's eyes followed Callum even as his head didn't move and his body didn't shift. It was hard to know if he didn't trust the wolven or if he just wanted to kill the male on principle. Apex was weird like that. He had his own moral standards, and if you tripped one of them? Like betraying a family member, even if amends had been made?

Big problems.

But as with where the clan's females were and whether or not Apex was going to do something stupid, Lucan didn't have the energy to get involved.

"What is she doing to Kane?" Rio asked softly. "The old woman."

The fact that the Gray Wolf was neither a woman nor old in the conventional sense didn't seem like things worth correcting, and he wasn't sure what to say about the rest. If he replied with an "I don't know," it was a half-truth that sat badly. But he didn't want to freak her out—and he reminded himself that he wasn't exactly sure what was going on inside there—

The scream coming out of the hut was what he had been waiting for, what he had feared . . . and also been hoping to hear.

He glanced at Apex and prayed that the male stayed put. If there was a wild card in all this, it was that vampire, but things had been explained to him—as much as they could to an outsider, that was—and he'd eventually allowed Kane to be sequestered alone with the Gray Wolf. It was the aristocrat's only chance, although it was one thing understanding that on an intellectual level, another thing to hear the sounds of it all.

Except it looked like Apex was staying where he was, his hands locking together and his elbows getting planted on his knees, like he was keeping his body in place by force.

Closing his eyes, Lucan remembered when he'd been growing up on the fringes of the clan, the whispers about the rejuvenation and the speculation about what exactly transpired in the hut the kind of thing that was spoken about in hushed tones. It had been generations since it had been done, and as he glanced around at the assembled wolven, the other vampire, and his human woman, he realized that the group of them were witnessing a piece of history, a wondrous event that would be passed down to their progeny, becoming that which was spoken about in quiet, reverent voices around late-night campfires, always in private, like not everybody knew—

From out of the darkness, Callum reentered the circle of firelight, and he threw his head back and let out a howl, the sound not made by the throat of what appeared to be a man, but that of the wolf that lived in every molecule of his body.

One by one, the other male wolven rose to their feet, drew in deep breaths, and released calls that rose in volume until the screaming of the vampire in the hut could not be heard at all.

The chorus of howls was the most beautiful sound in the world to Lucan, the kind of thing that turned his body into a tuning fork and made his vision go blurry from emotion—

As he felt the hold on his palm tighten, he looked over at Rio, and when she nodded, he knew what she was telling him, but wasn't sure whether he should—

His body made the decision for him, releasing his hold on his mate's hand and rising up on its own volition. As he lifted his eyes to the sky, he pulled in a great breath, smelling anew the pine and the fresh smoke and the scents of the lake down below.

Lucan joined his wolf call with the others of his kind.

As tears rolled down his cheeks, he felt a release in the center of his chest, a sweet, wonderful wholeness permeating him.

Even as he worried about what the hell was going to come out of that fucking hut.

◆　◆　◆

Surrounded by howling wolves who looked like regular Joes, Apex sat on his log seat with the fire tanning his face and his ass going numb. In spite of all the racket the males were making, he ignored them.

He only cared about what was happening to Kane.

Running a hand down his face, he massaged his jaw—because it was the only part of him that didn't hurt. Everything else was either aching, swelling up, or scabbing over, to the point where each of his feet had a separate heartbeat and his head was like a balloon that was only loosely tethered to the top of his skull—

Okay, that screaming was doing his nut in. Jesus, what the *fuck* was she doing to him?

That old female in there gave him the creeps. Yeah, sure, she was supposed to be all homey-*grandmahmen*-looking, but anyone who fell for that shit needed to develop their survival reflex a lot better. One look into those gray eyes and his balls had tried to climb back into his pelvis—and he hadn't wanted to leave Kane with her.

What, like she was a healer? Bullshit. If she was some kind of nurse, then he was the Earnest Rabbit. The Able Bunny? What the hell did the humans call that thing with the dumb basket and all the eggs.

"Here."

As something appeared right in front of his face, he slapped a hold on a thick forearm and bared his fangs.

Standing over him, the white-haired wolven with the pale blue eyes, who'd prostrated himself in front of Lucan like he was Fido looking for a Milk-Bone and a belly rub, smiled in a wicked way.

"I'm offering you a cigarette, not shoving a gun in your face. Relax."

Apex pushed the arm away and went back to staring at the hut. As the silence around him re-registered, he became dimly aware that the screaming had stopped and the woofers in the group had dropped their howling routine and dispersed.

How long had Kane been in there?

"About an hour." The wolven sat down next to him on the log. "By the way, your friends just went to bed. They're over there in the tent. They told you so, but I didn't think you were tracking."

"They're not my friends."

"Oh, really." The male shook a cigarette out of a red-and-white pack and lit up with an old silver lighter. "Then why did you work so hard to defend them."

When Apex didn't reply, an exhale was sent in his direction. And he ignored it, too.

"Ah," the wolven said. "So it wasn't about my cousin and his mate or the other guy. It was about getting that burned male out of the camp. I'm Callum, by the way. Pleased to meet you."

A hand was extended, but Apex ignored the palm in the hopes it would discourage conversation. And talk about survival instinct. He shifted his eyes up to the sky to check the position of the stars. Dawn was coming, although they had some time left—

"You don't talk much, do you."

As the wolven just stared at him, he got the impression that if he didn't say something, the bastard was just going to sit there for the rest of the night. Or maybe eternity.

"You're doing just fine with your own chatter," he muttered. "I'd only slow you down with responses."

"Who is he to you? The male."

"Nobody." He grabbed for a cigarette. "And I don't smoke."

To his credit, the guy—what was his name, Callum?—didn't even pause at the contradiction. He just flicked a flame up and held the lighter forward. Bending down, Apex had to cup a hand around things to get a good burn, and then he was exhaling long and slow.

"What did she do to him," he demanded. "That old broad."

"Why do you care if he's nobody. And show some respect."

"Fuck you."

"Tough talk from someone smoking one of mine."

"You want it back?"

When there was no answer, Apex turned and looked at the male. As the features of the face registered one by one, starting with those incredible, icy blue eyes, it was like seeing a painting come to life . . . or maybe a sculpture. The wolven was just that beautiful, his features strong and even, his shoulders broad under the flannel shirt he'd put on, his jeans-covered thighs powerful. And that white hair. The stuff was so thick he didn't even have a part. It just seemed to grow in waves and settle off his high forehead.

What would his blood taste like on the back of the tongue?

Flushing, Apex dropped his eyes to the cigarette he didn't really want and refocused on the real priorities. "If that old lady kills him—"

"You're going to what? Go in there like a hero? Avenge some guy who's a nobody to you?" The wolven gestured in the direction of the hut with his cigarette. "What a Samaritan—and hey, you're welcome to have at it. I'll even give you a gun. A knife or two. You want a grenade? *Boom.*"

As he flared the fingers of his free hand, his chuckle was the kind someone made when a toddler threatened to take a car and drive away because they had to eat their carrots before dessert.

Except then "Callum" suddenly wasn't laughing. He straightened up on the stupid fucking log and looked really goddamn serious.

As Apex went to glance at what had caught his attention, the male grabbed on to his face. "Shut up," the wolven snapped. "Listen to me. He looks like your friend, but he's different. Do you understand me? He's *not* the same anymore. You need to respect that."

Apex jerked out of the hold and burst to his feet. But when he saw what had come out of the hut, he . . . didn't have any fucking clue what he was . . .

Some version of Kane was staring out across the encampment, his eyes vacant, his face showing no emotion. He was naked, which wasn't a surprise. But he was whole, which was the kind of shocker that made a vampire's brain freeze up.

Somehow, some way, Kane's injuries had healed, his skin now healthy and covering a musculature that the prisoner hadn't had even when he'd been relatively well. And he even had his missing fingers back.

On a blind flail, Apex grabbed on to something to steady himself. The fact that it was the wolven, Callum, was immaterial.

"He only looks like who he was," the guy warned.

"Shut up."

Pushing himself free, he stumbled forward, and as he approached Kane—or whoever it was—he couldn't believe it. No more burns. No more raw skin. Nothing but a perfectly unmarred body, all that muscle backed up by the erect carriage of someone who had never been hurt, never been ill, never been anything but totally whole his entire life.

The urge to run and embrace the prisoner was so strong, he started to jog on his aching feet. Yet when he got into immediate range, he slowed. Then stopped.

The face was the same. But the eyes were different somehow, even though they were the same silver color, set in the same sockets.

Maybe it was because they didn't look at Apex, they stared right through him, as if it wasn't a case of the male not recognizing him, but not even noticing him.

In spite of the fact that he stood directly in front of the guy.

"Kane."

He spoke the name with the kind of hoarse entreaty he was god-damn glad no one else was around to hear—

All at once, like sense had been slapped into him, Kane came awake, his eyes blinking, his head jerking back, his heavy shoulders and long arms bouncing as he jumped. And then he properly focused at Apex.

"Oh . . . my God," he said.

The voice was the same—and then those arms were around Apex and holding on so hard, there was no breathing. But that was okay. Who cared about that.

Apex shook as he embraced the male carefully. Except then he realized, he didn't have to think like that anymore. Tightening his grip, he stared out over Kane's shoulder at the red hut . . . and the old female who was standing off to the side, looking like her handiwork had come out even better than she might have hoped.

Who the *fuck* was she, Apex wondered.

CHAPTER ELEVEN

All Kane could do was hold on to Apex. That was it. But it wasn't because his balance was bad. Or because he was losing consciousness. Or because he was in pain or weak or dizzy or nauseous.

No, he felt like he had traveled a vast distance, as if he'd been gone a full decade. It was as though he had embarked on a trip and gotten lost somewhere along the way—and however much he'd been sure he'd never return to his fellow prisoners, to the world as he knew it, by a miracle of unfathomable origin, he had.

The closest thing he had to compare was the trip over from the Old Country all those years ago, and even that failed to properly encompass the dislocation and confusion he had. And dearest Virgin Scribe, the second he'd seen a familiar face, he'd become overcome with gratitude and amazement—

He shoved Apex back, his brain sharpening abruptly, his urgent mission helping him prioritize. "I need weapons. I need guns and ammo and—"

"*Kane.*"

At the sound of his name, he stopped. "What?"

Apex was still tall and built like a wrestler. And his hair was still all but shaved. And his lean face was as harsh as always.

But his expression was strangely bleak: "Kane . . ."

The male reached out a shaking hand, and his fingertips, dirty and bloodstained from fighting, trembled as they hovered above Kane's chest—as if Apex couldn't bear to touch the flesh. Or maybe didn't believe it was real.

The sight of those skipping, tripping, almost-touching-him fingertips made him take a look at himself properly.

"Oh . . . ," he whispered.

All at once, sensory perceptions flooded into his awareness: He was standing up on his own two feet, and the earth under his bare soles was cool and prickly from fallen pine needles. He was physically whole, no longer covered in gruesome, weeping burn wounds. He was also physically strong, his body prepared to do what he demanded of it, with plenty of energy banked and ready for use.

But more than all of that . . .

"I have no more pain," he said roughly.

He twisted around and looked back at the hut. The flap that had been pulled to the side by the old female was back in place, barring entrance—and he had the sense that he would never be welcome in there again. She was also nowhere to be seen.

He was on his own.

Putting his hand up to his head, he tried to remember what had happened in there. When nothing came, not how he'd been brought inside, not what he and the old female had spoken of, certainly not whatever had come next . . . he felt a strange relief. It was better not to probe, he decided.

He refocused on Apex. And in a voice that held a kind of aggression he didn't recall ever having had before, he said, "Weapons. Now."

"What happened in the hut," Apex said.

"Leave it."

With a quick shift, Kane's eyes tracked a movement behind the male, and he flared his nostrils, testing the scent. The wolven who had come forward was an imposing presence, and unusual-looking with his white flowing hair. Yet Kane recognized him. He had been part of the rescue group.

"Do you have weapons," Kane demanded. And as he spoke, he recognized that his directness was rude, bordering on offensive . . . but he just didn't care. "Can I take some weapons from this camp? You've got to have some guns."

The wolven stared at him without blinking. "You don't need them."

"I don't have time for this bullshit." He glanced back at Apex. "Where's the stuff you had in the car you put me into. I heard gunfire—"

"Where do you think you're going?"

"Why the hell are you asking that question?" As Apex recoiled once again, Kane couldn't be bothered. "Look, someone just needs to get me a gun and then I'm out of here—"

"And clothes. You need clothes, you're naked."

Kane looked back and forth between the two males. Both were staring at him like he'd sprouted another head, and he wasn't sure who had pointed out the naked to him.

"I'll take whatever I can get."

After a moment, the wolven cleared his throat. "I have clothes, and weapons. But what no one has is much of the night left. Dawn is coming fast."

"I'm not worried about that."

"You should be." Apex cursed and stamped off. Then turned around. "What are you doing. You're free from the camp. I don't know what happened in that goddamn hut, but you're . . . back, somehow. Why the *fuck* would you pick a fight to get back in there."

Kane stared the male right in the eye, aware that a strange feeling was coursing through him. "What does it matter to you," he said in a low, warning voice.

Apex marched right up. "Because I've got to go back if you do, and I'm fucking free now, too."

Kane glanced at the security collar that remained locked around the male's throat. Clearly, it had been deactivated. "It's not your fight. It's not your problem."

"She's just a nurse—"

Kane's dagger hand snapped out and locked a hold on that throat. Baring his fangs, he said, "Loyalty is not earned by station. Something you'd do well to remember, considering where you came from."

Apex recoiled as if he'd been punched in the jaw. And then he stammered, "Who the fuck are you."

Kane dropped his grip and pivoted to the white-haired wolven. "Clothes. Weapons. I'll find a way to pay you back, but I'm done with the talking."

◆   ◆   ◆

Callum flared his nostrils and breathed in. He had little frame of reference for what the male's scent had been before the Gray Wolf had summoned the Viper unto him, the desperate male unwittingly offering himself up as host so he could get a return to health.

The guy had no idea what he'd signed up for.

"Come," Callum said. "I'll kit you out. And then your friend and I will join you to get . . . whoever the nurse is."

"I'm not looking for your help."

"Well, you've found it, vampire, and the price of what you need is that I come with you and so does he. The choice is yours."

There was a split second of direct eye contact—and Callum found himself taking a step back. That silver stare . . . was not right.

But then the male shrugged.

"It's your funeral." The vampire looked at his friend—or whoever they were to each other. "Yours, too."

"This way," Callum said as he started for the tree line.

When he passed by the shelter that had been loaned to Lucan and his female, he expected the vampire to stop and check in with his fellow prisoner, the one who had worked so hard to free him. His nose would tell him exactly where the half-breed who had risked his own life was lying in recovery—

There was not even a pause.

Callum's den was located in a cave, the entrance of which was camouflaged by a fall of boulders. As he came up to the way in, he glanced over his shoulder. The two vampires were tight with him, and he wasn't surprised when the one who'd been granted a miracle in exchange for a curse barged right past him, like he owned the place.

Callum stopped the one who'd been called Apex. "Wait out here."

Fangs, sharp and long . . . and sexually alluring, at least on Callum's side of things . . . made a fast appearance. "The hell with that."

"Stay here. Please. Unless you want to assess whether he's physically capable, and if he isn't, tell him he needs to wait a full day before he should go anywhere?" When there was no response, Callum said dryly, "I thought so. Let me handle this."

As he pushed against the vampire's chest, he expected a fight, and he wanted one. It would be an excuse to feel that hard body as they went down to the ground.

"I won't let anything happen to your friend," he vowed.

"That's not your job."

The testy comeback made Callum smile. "So territorial. I guess vampires and wolven have something in common—"

"Fuck you."

Callum's eyes traveled to the male's mouth. "Is that an invitation." He leaned in. "Or a demand."

Under other circumstances, the expression on that harsh face would have been frickin' hysterical.

"Surprise," Callum whispered. "And if you have a secret you need to keep, that's okay with me. I can be discreet when it suits me. Now wait here, please. If he starts throwing rocks at me, I'll duck and run."

Pivoting away, he followed the curve of the cave's neck, until the belly of the underground cavern presented itself. The glowing oil lantern in the far corner illuminated the stark furnishings, the shadows thrown by the bedding pallet, the stacks of folded clothes on the card table, and the ammunition and weapons boxes long and indistinct. The yellow light also traveled over to the naturally heated spring, the mountain-made pool gleaming at the very rear of the den.

"Do you care what I take," the vampire said as a statement, not a question.

"No. Whatever you want."

The guy made quick work of getting a shirt and pants on, and good thing they were of similar build—now that an extra fifty pounds of muscle had been added to that mystically revived body.

Aware that he was staring, Callum went over and opened the first of his weapons trunks. It was funny. The fact that he never used the locks had never registered before. The clan's territory was respected, and even so, it was never, ever undefended. Even during the day.

But suddenly, he felt a threat was close by.

He glanced back across the cave. The vampire was pulling on Callum's favorite jacket, something else that was a revelation: He hadn't known he had one until somebody else's body was in it.

"What kind of gun do you like," he said as he refocused on the locker's click-click-bang-bang contents.

"One that shoots."

"Picky, picky." He took out a .357 Magnum. "We are kind of old-fashioned around here."

"How so."

"None of that autoloader bullshit."

"I don't even know what that is."

Cocking a brow, Callum tossed the gun into the air while the guy was working the favorite-jacket's buttons—and he wasn't surprised when a hand whipped out into thin air and caught the grip on the fly. Only after a steady hand was already locked on the weapon did the vampire look down his arm—and as he stared at what he'd caught, he frowned.

"Not your type after all?" Callum murmured. "Or just checking the weight."

For a moment, the male didn't move. But then he seemed to snap out of his astonishment. "Ammo."

"Right here." Callum tossed a suede bag across, the bullets inside chiming on the fly. "But you won't need any of this."

The vampire hooked a palm around the satchel and buried the loose load in the outside pocket of Callum's jacket.

"Aren't you going to check what's inside there?" Callum murmured.

"I trust you."

"You don't know me."

Those eyes narrowed. "You're afraid of me. You're not going to fuck this up because you'd don't know what I'm capable of."

Callum blinked. A couple of times. Then he shrugged. "I also don't like blueberries, harmonicas, or cats. Is there anything else we need to discuss?"

"You said I won't need a weapon." The vampire looked down at the gun. "Why."

No reason to go into that right now, he thought. "I'm coming with you, remember?" Callum put up his palm as those strange eyes refocused on him. "And it's not your decision."

"I'm not saving you."

"I wasn't aware I'd asked you to. And you know, you're kind of a dick, no offense. Were you like this before?"

The vampire checked the Magnum's cylinder. Gave things a spin.

And then he pointed the hand cannon right at Callum's frontal lobe. On the business end of the trigger, there was absolutely no expression on the male's face, the only outward sign that there was anything unusual going on a slight twitch of the right eyebrow.

"*Boom,*" the vampire whispered. As if he had overheard the conversation at the fire pit.

Justlikethat, the male dematerialized out of the cave.

Callum sagged and lowered his head. As he patted around for his cigarettes, his hands shook, and he ignored that. Even when he dropped the first coffin nail he took out of the pack.

Just as he lit up, Apex barreled into the den, looking like he was pre-pared to break up a bar fight—or a glory hole.

"Shut up," Callum growled. "And he just left. We've got to go get him. Here."

He tossed over something that spit out bullets. Who the fuck knew what it was. Then he took a couple guns for himself and prayed that what he grabbed in the way of extra ammo fit anything either of them had.

Stalking past the vampire, he knew he should have dematerialized right away, but he couldn't concentrate. He needed some fresh air, along with the nicotine.

And as he rounded the cave's passageway, he thought . . . he was going to lock up those fucking guns as soon as he got through what was left of this night.

Assuming he made it through, that was.

What the *hell* had the Gray Wolf brought back.

CHAPTER TWELVE

As Kane re-formed for the third time in a row, it was into a thicket of undergrowth, the vines and bushes clawing at the someone-else's-pants he had on as his body once again became corporeal. Breathing in through his nose, he—

"Finally."

Setting off in a northeasterly direction, he followed the scent of concrete, rot, and vampire, and with his target identified, he moved with a deadly purpose, crushing the weeds under the boots he'd borrowed, shoving branches out of his way instead of moving around them. As he went along, he had the strangest sense of bifurcation, as if he were watching himself from a distance even though it was his own legs churning, his own heart pumping, his own eyes scanning the environment for threats.

In the back of his mind, he knew something wasn't right. But he kept going because he couldn't worry about—

Dearest Virgin Scribe, he hoped he ran into guards.

With the thought occurring to him, he felt his fists curl up and his shoulders flex. The urge to fight was so natural, it didn't even dawn on him that he had never before, not once, looked for conflict in anything. Especially of the physical kind.

If only he had felt like this the night Cordelhia had died.

"Focus," he muttered as his head whipped to the left.

There was nothing but shadows that didn't move, the ambient light of the night sky neither highlighting nor obscuring anything.

His other attempts to get downwind of the prison camp's new location had been an inefficiency he'd had to tolerate. He hadn't been conscious enough to track the location as he'd been driven away from the abandoned hospital, and walking directly up the road they'd escaped on was just volunteering for a bullet to the chest. The best he could do was triangulate through this scruffy forest of—

His head jerked to the left again, his instincts firing for a second time. He had the gun tucked into the waistband of the wolven's pants, even though there was every reason for him to have it at the ready because if he was going to fight something, he wanted it to be close, and very much in person—

The wind changed direction and that was when he caught the scents of Apex and the wolven. They were on the property, but they were not near him, and that was fine.

Better that they stayed away.

The chain-link fence appeared about thirty feet later, and instead of dematerializing through it, he took some running strides and jumped onto the links, clawing a hold into them, yanking his body up. He made no attempt to be quiet about the ascent, the metal-on-metal clanging the kind of thing that surely functioned as an alarm.

Up and over, dropping down, landing on the boots in a crouch.

Now he took out the gun. This urge to punch and kick was all well and good, but not if it got him killed before he found Nadya.

The weight of the weapon was heavy in his hand, and he glanced down. "Magnum."

The word came out of him, even though he had never seen a gun like this before.

"Callum."

That was the name of that male with the white hair and the blue eyes. But how did he know this? He hadn't read the wolven's mind. Had he heard it spoken by somebody? Or was he phasing in and out of amnesia?

Now was not the time for this.

Jogging forward, he kept low and his eyes began to move in a pattern he recognized only because he didn't control it any more than he did his arms and legs. His body, and all its components seemed like . . . something that had been aimed at the camp.

As a weapon would.

It was as this thought occurred that the great, gloomy monolith appeared on the horizon like something out of an Edgar Allan Poe story, the center core anchoring two enormous wings of open loggias. The exterior was discolored from what had to be a hundred years of weathering, gray stains drooling down from the slate roof, the brick appearing wrinkled as a result of the vertical stripes. The structure was still solid, however, nothing listing or crumbling, proof that back then builders had constructed things to last. He had overheard that humans had first used it as a hospital for tuberculosis patients, the afflicted set out on the five levels of porches to take the air, the dead removed out the back via a subterranean body chute. After that era, it had housed the insane for a time, and then later, the site had been abandoned.

Assessing the front entrance, with its steps rising to a set of inset doors of considerable, if faded, majesty, he quickly moved on to the banks of windows on either side. The sashes were all down, but the occasional pane was broken, not that it mattered. All he had to do was get close, confirm the interior of one of those rooms, and dematerialize in, as long as there was no steel mesh. Or he could go off to the wings on either side. The open porches would be safe to re-form on and he could navigate downward.

Or maybe the roof was where he needed to start.

Except then what. Once he was inside, he had no idea where to go. Or where to locate Nadya.

Reaching into the banks of his memory, he tried to remember where the guard who had taken him from his bed had dragged him to. His awareness at the time had been hazy, and he had passed out, only to come to at the terminal of a long corridor. There had been guards, and Apex and the others, and—

A rustle of leaves behind him had Kane pointing the gun at the sound before he looked over his shoulder.

Apex was standing there, still in his dirty, bloodstained prison togs, the tunic and loose pants so worn and thin they were nearly transparent. As the wind blew in, the ghostly garments moved against his body, turning him into a specter, and this seemed logical. As aware as Kane was, he hadn't scented the male. Or sensed him.

If it had been a guard, with a weapon, Kane would probably be dead.

"We go right in the front." Apex nodded at the grand portal. "The rear is where the drugs come and go, and that's where the guards will have to be. We took a lot of them out on the way to the exit, so the head of those males is going to have to prioritize her staffing. Besides, this whole level is blocked off. We'll be safer."

Between one blink and the next, Kane had an image of a tall, powerfully built female in a black uniform. He had no recollection of her face or coloring particularly, but the muscled body he could recall in detail— and he would recognize her scent anywhere.

"I want to go in the back," Kane said as his fangs descended. "Besides, if this floor gets us nowhere, why waste the daylight."

"Because I know a way to sneak down and where to go from there. Plus this is the only way I'm going to take you in and you need me."

"The hell I need you."

"I know this fucking place like the back of my hand, and you're lost in there. Unless you got up out of that bed and had a wander no one noticed?"

As their stares clashed, Kane had to remind himself that the male before him was an ally who was being reasonable. Not an enemy. And in the back of his mind, he recognized that Apex, for once, was not the unhinged one.

"Where's the wolven?" Kane asked as a way to derail the focus. His own focus, that was.

Apex looked around the scruffy acreage surrounding the hospital. "He's here somewhere."

Kane started marching for the heavy double doors, like they were an adversary he could punch. And when his arm was snagged in a hard grip, he bared his fangs, and kept right on going.

Apex's voice was sharp. "We don't want to kick the hornet's nest right away. That's not going to help."

"I thought you liked to fight." Kane yanked free and reached for one of the tarnished brass handles. "And that you—"

The door opened wide.

The white-haired wolven with the powerful body was on the far side, looking like he was already tired of saving the day. "Welcome back, Kotter."

Kane blinked. "Who?"

"Guess you don't watch a lot of TV in this place."

"How the hell did you get in?" Kane flared his nostrils to test the interior scents that were wafting out into the night. "Don't answer that, I don't really care—"

"Open window."

"Aren't you a genius."

Kane barged past the wolven—*Callum*, his brain supplied—and did a quick survey of what appeared to be a lobby. The open area had a high ceiling and many overturned chairs. A reception area was off to one side, running down a wall, and as he looked at the slots for folders, and places for mail, he could sense the orderly way things had once been run.

"This way," Apex said as he headed for one of the corridors that radiated off the central core.

Kane made sure he was ready with the heavy gun, and even though his body was roaring for a fight, he recognized that he had to control himself. He wanted to start shooting already, to bring all the guards to him, to pick them off one by one or in pairs, until the blood flowed on the threadbare and dusty carpeting.

But Nadya was the point of this.

And what was wrong with his thinking that he had to remind himself of that?

On that note, he let Apex lead them into an unremarkable room, one that had peeling ceiling paint, and a broken chair, and a window that looked out over the back parking lot.

"How is this going to help us?" Kane demanded.

"That is a dumbwaiter." Apex pointed at a square panel that was inset into the wall. "The shaft leads down into one of the drug workrooms. I know the layout, so no, you dematerializing to there isn't an option. You'll re-form in the middle of a table and die."

"I'm not staying here."

"You want that nurse dead? Fine, fuck around. Go right ahead—what the *fuck* is wrong with you."

Kane couldn't understand what the problem was. Then he glanced down at the space between their bodies. A hand and forearm that he vaguely recognized as his own were holding a gun out, the muzzle pressing into Apex's abs. The safety was not engaged. There was a bullet ready to go. And his finger was tense on the trigger.

Off to the side, the wolven watched, one hand markedly down at his side. Kane didn't need to see anything directly to know that there was a gun in that grip, one that was just as big as the Magnum the guy had lent out.

"Who are you?" Apex whispered. "This is not you."

Kane retracted his weapon. Then he turned it around and offered it to Apex, handle first. After the male took it, he blinked and put his free hand to his head. "I don't know . . . who I am anymore."

"That I believe," Callum said grimly.

◆   ◆   ◆

Down in the clinic, the guard who Nadya had triaged last, whose thigh she had stitched up as her last bit of needlework, was feeding from a female who had been brought in from the outside. It was clear they were mated, the pair's eyes clinging to each other's as the wrist was offered and accepted. Though they didn't touch other than the connection of mouth to vein, they didn't have to.

The love between them was obvious.

As soon as the female had been brought in, Nadya had stepped back into the forest of the shelves, and taken cover in the midst of the dusty left-behinds. The *shellan* had been like the others who had come to service their males, in this case blond, but in any event, fresh from the world beyond the prison, dressed in blue jeans and a dark sweater, her body and hair washed, her throat perfumed, her face made up.

On one level, none of the mates had been remarkable, their attractiveness of no particular note. And yet to Nadya, they were extraordinary, a reminder of something she had not seen or experienced in what felt like a lifetime.

Reaching up, she touched the hooding that covered her face. Then she shied away from thoughts of her own past—and instead focused on the other reason these females were of such fascination.

She was shocked that the guards were mated. That they were capable of warmth and relationship. Of common decency.

Based on their behavior in the camp, she would have assumed them all as cold and cruel as the female who led them. But seeing them look with tear-filled eyes at the females in their lives? It exposed sides to them she didn't expect, and couldn't understand: When the first *shellan* had come in, she had been struck by an urgent need to rush forth and save the female in some way, ensure that she was not there under duress, protect her.

Yet it had all been voluntary. More than voluntary.

Feeling like a voyeur, she looked away from the couple because they should be granted privacy, and noted that many of her patients were already recovering and some were even leaving. In the last four hours—going by the watches she'd taken off the guards' wrists—three of the males had transitioned out of the clinic. Their healing was . . . incredible. Then again, it had been a long time since she had been around healthy vampires, who were properly fed both in terms of good food and blood.

And she supposed the fact that two of what she had classified as the most critically injured patients had been among the first out the door meant that her treatment decisions had been appropriate and successful.

Closing her eyes, she braced a hand against a shelf ladened with laundry soap flakes, the boxes of which had faded and were coated with dust. With a groan, she stretched her back and didn't get far with it given the way her body was—

"Come with me."

Jerking to attention, she looked over her shoulder. A guard had marched right up to her, looming with aggression in his black uniform and all his weapons. She didn't recognize him specifically, but there were so many kitted out in the same clothes, with the same short haircut, and the same sharp stare, that they were interchangeable.

Nadya faced the male. "I can't leave the clinic. I have patients—"

He took her arm in a hard grip and didn't make any accommodation for her immobility, shoving her out of the storage room until she lost her footing and fell just past the doorway. Nadya cried out as her legs went loose under her, but he didn't stop. He just grabbed whatever he could under her robing and kept going, dragging her down the concrete corridor.

Just as had been done with Kane. At the end.

"What did I do?" she demanded. "What have I—"

He jerked her and she caught a scream of pain in her throat. He wasn't going to tell her, anyway. The head of the guards had given a command, and he was executing it, and maybe he didn't even know.

"Would you treat your female this way?" she grunted.

"You're not a female to me. You're not anything."

Nadya gasped, even though she shouldn't be surprised. That really was the answer, wasn't it.

When they got to the stairs at the end of the hallway, he set her back on her feet with such roughness that pain shot up her calves and into her knees. On the ascent, she did what she could to stay upright, gathering her robing so she didn't trip, trying to stay on her feet because the alternative was so much more agonizing. It was hard to track what floor they were on, the landings a blur as the subterranean levels were climbed.

After what seemed like an hour of hiking, she was pushed through a door, and as she got a hazy look at what was ahead, cold fear replaced all other sensory inputs.

Down at the end of a long corridor of closed doors, a towering wall seemed like the only thing in the whole world. Added as part of the build-out that had occurred before the prison camp's population had moved to the location, it was raw and unpainted, swaths of plaster marking the seams of unpainted gray panels. But none of that mattered.

It was the stains.

Brown stains had seeped into the matte gray, felt-like surface, and though the swaths of discoloration were varied in saturation and shape, there was a pattern. They were between sets of pegs . . . where the prisoners being punished or controlled were chained.

The guard prodded her, and she stumbled forward. Any time she slowed, she was poked in the back by what felt like a finger, but she suspected was a gun. As she passed by the closed doors, she could smell the drugs, the chemical sting in the air making her eyes water—and she thought about the prisoners who were forced to sit at tables and add compounds to raw cocaine and heroin, and then package the powders into saleable units. For hours. For no pay and little food.

At the wall, the guard's hard hands spun her around and put her back against the plaster and the felt. Chains seethed with a metal chorus as her wrists were locked on the wooden pegs. She didn't fight him. There was no way she could overpower the guard in any way that would work in her favor, and she was already bruised and fighting for breath from pain.

As the guard stepped back, there was a pause—perhaps he expected her to beg him for mercy, or at the very least ask him why again—

The knife came out of a holster at his waist, and as its blade caught the light with a flash, she began to tremble.

Leaning into her, he put the sharp edge to her throat, the hood's folds providing no protection at all. Underneath her robing, she closed her eyes and realized she had always been waiting for death to come to her, but as a far-off kind of thing. She had lived through an attempt on her life already; she'd assumed old age would get her—

The male jerked his arm, the blade slicing through the hood.

"No!" But she wasn't begging for her life. "No—"

As he peeled the folds back, Nadya ducked her head and leaned to the side, chasing the covering until it was gone. And then the lights were too bright for her eyes. Turning her face to her shoulder, she did what she could to hide herself.

"Jesus . . . Christ," the guard whispered.

When he stepped back, she wanted to tell him to stop staring. But she couldn't speak.

And then someone approached.

The footfalls were heavy, the pace quick, the arrival imminent. Nadya guessed who it was, and was not wrong.

The head of the guards stopped next to her male with the knife—and for a moment, all she did was stare.

"My hood," Nadya said hoarsely. "Please . . . give it back to me."

The other female cleared her throat. "You know why you're here."

"No, I do not." Nadya squeezed her eyes closed, as if she could make the world go away if she just didn't see anything. "Why."

There was more silence, but she wasn't going to solve that problem. It would just be a waste of energy.

"You killed my guard," the female in charge said in a low voice.

"I most certainly did not. You will find all your males doing well, with several having already left—"

"No, the one whose corpse was removed. I have an eyewitness."

Nadya frowned into the shoulder of her robe. "Then he doesn't know what he saw—"

"You put a pillow over my guard's face and suffocated him."

"I did not." Nadya shifted her eyes over, until the image of the taller, stronger, dark-haired female entered her vision. "So do whatever you will with me—"

It happened so fast. The female grabbed what little hair Nadya had and yanked it, nearly snapping her skull off the top of her spine. As she cried out, the harsh face came close to her own.

"You should be *very* afraid of me."

Nadya pulled weakly against the pegs, chains rattling softly. "I am afraid of you, but there is nothing I can do. I am not strong enough to fight anyone or anything. Therefore I must accept what happens."

She met the other female's eyes—and was surprised to find a certain removal in them, as if the camp's new leader had taken a step away, even as the distance between the pair of them was unchanged.

"Who did this to you," came a quiet inquiry.

"He's dead."

"Who *ahvenged* you."

Nadya blinked slowly. "I did. I took care of things . . . in my own way."

The other female shook her head, and then her expression hardened. "You should have lied to me."

"Why?"

"Because you just admitted you've murdered before." The female's eyes narrowed. "Not what I'd lead with if I were bargaining for my life."

"You're going to kill me anyway."

And besides . . . the only thing Nadya had felt like living for was dead and gone. What did she care what happened to her now? Something about losing Kane had stripped her of whatever connection she had with the world.

Even though he had never been hers.

The sound of the knife being drawn out of its sheath was a ring of metal like a note sung, resonant, high-pitched, lingering in the still air.

The head of the guard's face did not change as she brought it up. "At least you know what I must do. What is taken from me, I must redress."

"What is your name?" Nadya asked.

That got a brow arch. "I don't need a formal introduction to use this weapon. And if you're trying to make some kind of connection, it's not going to save you—"

"I don't need to be saved and I have no regrets." Abruptly, she dropped the act. "That guard who died in my clinic, he dragged a prisoner who was suffering from burns all over his body off that bed like he was a piece of meat. He showed no concern for the suffering. He enjoyed it, actually."

The female looked bored. "Nurses shouldn't be *ahvengers.*"

"And guards shouldn't be murderers. Neither should you. If you want to keep order, that's one thing, but when was the last time anyone stepped out of line."

The blade came up right to Nadya's eye. "It is going to be such a relief to get you to stop talking."

Nadya closed her eyes again. "And it will be a relief to have nothing left to say."

CHAPTER THIRTEEN

Following the whole who-are-you/who-am-I confrontation, Kane stepped away from Apex and the wolven. As he paced around the room, he was aware that the light was coming soon, and that him losing his shit was just going to slow down everything. But he was having trouble controlling a sudden, roiling panic.

What had happened in that hut? With . . .

The old female, he remembered with a sudden clarity. Yes, he had been with someone, someone who had been a guide of sorts. She had offered him . . . what. An opportunity. Yes, she had—

"Kane?"

As his name was spoken, he looked at the two other males. They were standing back at a discreet distance, watching him as one might a caged, dangerous animal—as if they were assessing whether he was going to attack them.

"That is not who I am." He put his hand over his heart. "I am . . . not this."

"Okay . . . I know." Apex glanced around. "We've got to get moving. And I'm going down there."

There was a pause, as if each one of them was recalibrating themselves and returning to the mission, stepping away from whatever tipping point had been narrowly avoided.

Apex cleared his throat, and his voice got stronger. "I still have my prison uniform on, maybe they'll think I wasn't part of the escape."

"Really?" the wolven drawled. "In those clothes, you look like you slaughtered a cow in the basement before you went on your little walk."

Apex talked over the male. "I go out into the corridor, hit the stairs at the far end, and get down to the clinic at the lowest underground level. I isolate her and remove her out the back through the body chute. That's where you meet me. Go down the hill from the parking lot. It'll be about two hundred yards. You'll see the train tracks and the chute's entrance."

The male's face was composed to the point of being a mask.

"All right," Kane said. "Go, and be safe."

Apex stayed where he was for a moment, as if he'd seen a ghost. And then he turned away to the panel that was set into the wall and lifted it up.

Kane went to ask the wolven if they could stay for a little bit to make sure—

"Shit." Apex leaned into an internal chamber. "Steel. I can smell the fresh metal." The male retracted his upper body out of the tight space. "They've wrapped the dumbwaiter with all sorts of mesh. No dematerializing down there."

Apex stood with his hands on his hips and his eyes staring into the dark hole in the wall like he was hoping for some kind of magic solution.

"We've got a real problem if I have to go a more direct route," he muttered.

"The wolven and I can be your backup," Kane pointed out.

"No, you need to take care of the nurse when I evac her and he's no help."

The wolven popped his brows. "Excuse me?"

"You don't know the layout of this place."

"Fine, but I have skills, and by the way, your tone was objectionable."

"So the next time I point out the obvious I'll give you flowers."

"I prefer white roses to red." Callum leaned in, his eyes becoming hooded. "Write that down, will you. I don't like repeating myself—"

Lights pierced the window and flared across the wall, the icy white glow split into squares by the panes, the swing of the illumination from a vehicle turning down the lane.

Kane moved silently across the dusty floor to look out. Down below, a guard parked and got out of a big, boxy vehicle with darkened windows. The male was twitchy, glancing around the broad open area and the cars parked grille-first into the building.

All at once, everything changed for Kane.

"He has no one with him," he heard himself say.

Closing his eyes, he gathered himself to dematerialize through the glass—

The hard grip on his arm took him out of the trance he needed to briefly shed his physical form, and he pulled at the wolven's hold. "I'm going down there, and getting keys to this place—"

"Bite him." The look in the male's eyes was strange. "Don't use a gun. Bite him."

The male did have a point. No sound that way, although Kane wasn't a fighter.

He couldn't worry about that, though. He *wouldn't* worry about that—

He had nothing to worry about.

As a rush came over him and his body began to swell with strength, he shut his eyes again and scattered into his molecular form, traveling easily through the window. Down on the asphalt, he re-formed at the far side of the guard's vehicle and he wasted no time. Striding around the back bumper, he—

Set upon the vampire from behind.

Once again, his body was taken over, the animation emanating from somewhere inside of him that was nonetheless not intrinsically him:

Clapping a hold on the side of the guard's neck, he slammed the male face-first into the side of the vehicle. The impact made a sharp, declarative sound, and riding a surge of aggression, he shoved his hand down to the male's hip and came back with a gun, the weapon tight in his palm. Slipping off the safety, even though he shouldn't have known where it was, or how the weapon operated, he—

Another set of headlights flared, but they were still in the distance some.

The guard moaned and tried to recover his balance.

Bite him.

As if on command, Kane's fangs dropped down, and he hissed as he jerked the head back to expose the throat. With a quick strike, Kane bit the male from behind, burying his canines deep in the veins and sinew. The gasp was not a surprise, and it was quieter than the discharge of the gun he'd taken would've have been—

The spasming didn't make sense.

Against Kane's body, the guard began to thrash and buck, and the seizures were so unexpected that he spun his prey around.

The male's face was beet red and sweat was beading up across his forehead and above his lip. Eyes that were wide were going bloodshot, as if they were flooding from some kind of hemorrhaging, and his breathing changed pattern. As the wheezing started, high-pitched and panicked, the guard went for his throat with his hands—as if he were attempting to clear a constriction.

Kane glanced toward the ever-brightening light source coming around the building. Then he looked back—

"What the *fuck*," he breathed.

The front of the guard's uniform was covered with blood, the flow from the bite so great, it was pumping out in surges. Kane had a dim thought that he must have hit an artery—no, it was too much blood. Grabbing hold of the guard's hair, he pulled the lolling head back to see what was going on . . . with . . .

The strike mark was . . . liquefying?

"Dearest Virgin Scribe."

The skin and the anatomy of the neck were being melted away somehow, denaturing before his very eyes. And as the breakdown continued, the blood flowed to the beat of the heart.

Everything was dissolving, even the bones of the spinal—

Flop.

As the head separated from the body, the latter dropped to the ground by the vehicle's back tire, and Kane was left holding the former. The eyes, so wide the whites were showing, stared back him, the lid of the one on the left twitching such that it appeared to be winking.

Like this was all one big fat joke.

"I told you. You don't need a weapon."

Kane wrenched around to the wolven, who'd dematerialized down to the pavement and was standing with his hands on his hips.

"Did I do that?" Kane asked. Then he corrected himself. "How . . . did I do that?"

◆　◆　◆

Apex re-formed down by the SUV just as a guard's body went loose and hit the cracked asphalt like a deadweight. Because that was what the male was: Alive no more than a minute ago, and now an inanimate corpse but for the involuntary muscle contractions. One bite and the bastard had gone down.

There were questions to ask.

"Now's not the time," Apex said as a box van came around the corner of the building.

They all ducked—well, he and the wolven did. Kane was still standing there like a tool, holding the decapitated head like it was a trophy that he didn't want, his eyes locked on the guard's as the neck continued to disintegrate.

Apex grabbed the idiot's free arm and yanked him to the ground. "Jesus! You wanna get killed?"

As Kane looked over in confusion, the box van pulled in on the far side of the SUV. Apex glanced to Callum—no wolven. The male had taken off somewhere.

Maybe he'd seen a squirrel.

"Listen," Apex whispered. "I need you to focus."

When the male just blinked, Apex grabbed the head by the puss and thanked God they were downwind of the guard who was getting out from behind the van's wheel.

Slapping a hold on the side of Kane's neck, he jerked him close.

Staying quiet, he tried to communicate with his eyes: Now. Do what you did, *now*.

There was a sudden flash of recognition, as if something within the guy responded to exactly the demand that Apex was attempting to send through the thin air between their faces.

After which Kane's expression changed, a dark intent coming over him.

The male rose up and turned away, moving in total silence around the back of the SUV. The sounds of what happened next were music to the ear: Gasp. Grunt. Another flop onto the pavement.

The scent of fresh vampire blood blooming in the air.

Apex left Kane to it, and leaned over the guard. The weapons strip took seconds because he just transferred the belt holster onto his own waist. Then he looked over his shoulder at the rear of the hospital.

The exit he'd evac'd Kane out of was locked with a keypad combination that Mayhem knew, but Apex had never bothered asking for. No way to infiltrate there. There was another opening, however.

Apex glanced back down at the guard. "And I do have a knife. Thanks to you."

Taking the blade out, he shifted his position to the male's right arm.

Moving down to the wrist, he yanked up the uniform sleeve, flattened the palm, and placed the knife directly over the wrist joint. Putting his shoulder into it, the cut went quick, the crack reminding him of a whip's call.

He picked up the hand and turned it wound side up so the leaking wasn't that bad.

At that moment, Kane came around the back of the SUV. There was blood on his chin and another head hanging from his grip. He didn't look surprised, though. He seemed pretty damn satisfied with himself.

"What did you do with the body?" Apex asked.

"Stripped the weapons and rolled it under the van."

Apex blinked and rose to his full height. "Don't take this the wrong way, but I love you."

Kane nodded to what Apex was holding. "If you needed an extra hand, you could have just asked for help."

"Funny. Very funny."

With a grunt, Apex rolled the body of the first dead guard under the SUV. Then he threw the head in there with it, a basketball that bounced against something and clanged into the undercarriage.

"We're going that way." Apex pointed to the woods on the far side of the parking area. "And no, I don't want to debate it. That's how we're getting in."

Leaving Kane in the dust, he figured the guy was welcome to beat his head against the entrance to those private quarters, or to try to get in through the first floor they'd been on, but the guy wasn't going to get far. The underground levels of the building were as secure as a bank vault.

And daylight was coming fast.

Just as Apex came up to the tree line, he heard approaching cars, and a quick glance over his shoulder informed him that not only had Kane decided to follow-the-leader, but the wolven had showed up again—and the male had easily four times the number of weapons he'd brought with him.

Guess he'd been busy taking out threats Apex hadn't sensed and certainly hadn't seen.

Turning away, Apex disappeared himself into the trees, and the other two were tight on his heels as a pair of vehicles came around to the rear of the building. Looking back again, he was glad they were downwind and therefore their position was somewhat secure because the shit was going to hit the fan. Vampire noses were so precise, it was easy to tell the difference between fresh blood, as in minutes or moments old, and anything that had been spilled an hour or two or five ago. This new set of guards was going to know that the killings had just happened, and conclude that either someone else had escaped or somebody was trying to get in.

"We're almost there," Apex muttered as he pressed on through the trees and scrub brush.

It took no distance at all to start the decline, and as the terrain took on a steep angle, the foliage got thicker. Shoving branches out of the way, Apex ducked and weaved, and when his boots skidded, he used the tree limbs and trunks to catch himself. The scents of earth and greenery irritated his nose, reminding him that for all his singular focus, there were always things getting in the way. Always things in his fucking path. Always obstacles.

Eventually, the slope poured itself into a flat plane.

"Are these the railroad tracks?" the wolven asked as he pointed to the twin lines of rusty steel.

"No, they are the trailheads of destiny." Apex double-checked the path they'd come down, but he would have scented anyone riding behind them. "This way."

He took them to the right, following the train route that was overgrown enough to have trees sprouting in between the tracks. About two hundred yards later, an open area with a loading dock appeared, its overhang providing cover, but also such a saturated darkness that even vampire eyes were going to struggle—

Click.

The flashlight beam was discreet and exactly what he needed. But the fact that the wolven was on the business end of the glow was annoying. Especially given the waft of the male's superiority.

Which Apex shouldn't have thought was appealing, in an annoying kind of way.

"So that's why you took the hand," the wolven said.

Apex followed the beam to the lock pad that was mounted by a reinforced steel door. Without comment, he went over to it, his body obscuring the illumination. Holding out the guard's palm, he had to get the position correct.

Vampires did not have fingerprints, but that wasn't how it worked. Right at the base of the palm, in the fleshy part below the thumb, each one of the guards had gotten some kind of implant. He had no idea how the technology functioned, but he had seen them wave whatever the hell it was over the readers at the loading area at the main building. The head of the guards had started the practice within the last week, although not all the doors were secured by the system yet.

Apex swiped the palm. And when the pinpoint red light did not turn to green and there was no unlocking, he wondered if blood flow was required. The palm was getting cold—

The grinding reverberated through the steel panel, making a sound that fortunately didn't travel far, and as the seal on the entry was broken, the whiff that came out was of concrete, old oil, and death.

Too impatient for the automatic opener's slow pace, he yanked the heavy weight wide, and gave the wolven's flashlight a vista to pierce. The ascent was at a stiff angle, a pair of trolley tracks disappearing up the rise. An old cart was locked onto the tracks at the base of the incline, its high sides brokered by locked flaps that could be lowered by—

Between one blink and the next, he saw bodies tangled in its grim belly, the dead humans shriveled in their own skins, having wasted away. The vision was accompanied by a pungent smell he recognized as the full fruition of that which he initially scented as the door had been opening.

Bringing his hands up to rub away the image, he poked himself in the eye with the guard's middle finger and almost dropped the palm. But the grinding into his sockets did nothing. Lids up or down, what he was being shown didn't change.

"Apex?"

He didn't know which of the two said his name. Probably Kane. Who the fuck cared.

"Gimme a minute."

Sagging against the concrete wall, he felt a dampness seep through the thin tunic he had on, and he tried to tune in to what the cool wet felt like on the crest of his shoulder. Sometimes, if he could hook on to something that was real, he could bring himself out of it. But that didn't always work—and until the vision decided to move on, he was stuck where he was, blinded by something that had happened in the past, the stain on the landscape the kind of thing that never washed out, but was never seen or sensed by anyone but him—

"What's going on, mate?" the wolven asked softly.

"You guys go up the chute, I'm right behind you," Apex said.

Kane took off, running up the concrete steps that paralleled the body car's tracks. The guy might not have had any idea where he was going, but all he had to do was get to the top—and there was a lock on the door up there, so he wasn't going to go start biting people and melting them all willy-nilly.

"Mate?"

"I'm fine. Let's go."

Except Apex's body refused to follow commands. But it was always like that, when the dead forced him to see their corpses. And fucking hell, he could do without that smell, the sweet stench of decay making him choke.

Flailing around inside his skin, he clapped his eyes on the wolven. "What the hell are you waiting for."

There was a pause. Then the white-haired, blue-eyed wolven replied, "You. I'm waiting . . . for you."

CHAPTER FOURTEEN

On the ascent, Kane's legs were moving like pistons, his thighs pumping as he ascended a grade that was almost a total vertical. As his breath inflated his lungs and exploded out of his mouth, he had a thought in the back of his head that this shouldn't be possible. Even before he'd been burned, he would never have moved up stairs like this.

An image of the guards' throats dissolving and the bodies dropping free barged into his mind.

Good thing he reached the top of the body chute. Behind him, the thin beam of the wolven's light started jerking back and forth, reminding him of a butterfly's flight path. It didn't take long for the other two to join him.

The guard's hand came in handy for a second time, and Apex was careful as he opened the vaulted door. There was no need for directions. The smell that entered the chute was that of the clinic—and Kane's body moved on its own, shoving the other male aside.

So close. He was so close to Nadya—that scent of disinfectant was unmistakable, and it was emanating from the left—

Two guards rounded a corner in the dim, rough-walled corridor, and he ducked back into the chute, closing the door so that there was only a slit to look out of. As the uniformed guards talked back and forth, their voices were hushed, and waiting for them to go by took self-control he barely had.

Somehow, he managed to hold himself in place—and then he slipped out into their wake. He jumped the one on the left, grabbing the guard's head and wrenching it to the side with so much violence, the vertebrae cracked as they powdered—and he had the presence of mind to catch the male before he fell so there was no flopping noise.

Apex was right behind him, taking care of the other one, his knife penetrating the guard's temple as he turned to look at his cohort. It was over so fast, Kane was aware of a feeling of letdown. Which was not right. Who the hell wanted to engage in combat?

They dragged the bodies into the chute.

"Let's get changed," Kane said as he whipped off his shirt.

He wasn't sure where the idea came from, but it was suddenly an urgent solution to a problem he wasn't aware of consciously tracking.

"You two take the clothes," the wolven said. "Something tells me I'm going four-footed soon."

In the thin light beam, they made quick work of the togs. The fit should have been loose, Kane thought, as he pulled off a large pair of pants and shirt that seemed three sizes too big. Yet when he got the uniform on his body, he was constricted in the shoulders and the thighs.

"Good idea," Apex said as he tucked his new shirt in.

No hats, which would have been helpful, and they already had gun belts. Callum took one of the spare holsters, and after he cinched it on, he glanced up and down.

"Just so you know," he said, "you both lucked out with the short hair. You two could pass for guards, you really could."

On that note, they filed out of the chute one by one and he glanced around. The hallway had a bare concrete floor and rock walls that were streaked with groundwater seepage, and absolutely no guards.

Kane started running.

When he got to the former storage room, he skidded on the concrete as he wheeled in through the open door.

"Nadya?" he called through the rows of shelves.

Bursting out on the far side, he jerked to a halt. The beds . . .

. . . were nearly full. There were only two vacancies, and one of them
was the berth in which he had lain. But that wasn't what he cared about—
and neither were the guards who had been tended to over on some cots.

"Nadya," he said sharply.

He looked all around, even though he knew by the scents of the
males and the blood, and the clearly-nothing-fresh of Nadya, that she
wasn't in the clinic. With a curse, he went over to the nearest patient,
noting the precise bandaging, the care that had been taken to clean him
of the dirt and blood, the way the guard was in comfort in spite of his
injuries. Then he glanced over to the desk. There was an array of drugs
and supplies that he had never seen before. While she had been treating
him, and Lucan's Rio, she had made do with what she could find.

But of course, guards were more important than prisoners, so
human-grade medications and supplies had been brought in.

He refocused on the patient. "Do you know where the nurse is?"

He willed those eyes to open, and as he waited for a response, he
glanced over at the bed where he had been. He could recall the pain as if
it was something he could pull back into his own flesh, like a pall that
still hovered around in the air, free for the grabbing if you were dumb
enough to volunteer for it. Then he pictured the brown robes, sitting at
his bedside, his nurse's kindness and compassion like a blanket to tuck
around himself.

And that was when he realized why he hadn't died. Nadya had been
a tether that had kept him on the earth, the way she touched him with
such care, and spoke to him, and listened to him as he mumbled, all ties
that had bound him to the present . . . and kept him out of the Fade.

A penetrating guilt went through him, and unable to bear its implications, he marched the length of the room, going all the way to the far
end. But like that would change anything—or make Nadya come back

from wherever she was? As he passed by the beds, he assessed the other males who were under her care. Then he glanced down at himself, picturing the whole flesh that was under the stolen uniform—

"You are not one of us."

His eyes shifted to the patient in the last berth down the row. The guard's eyes were trained in Kane's direction, suspicion gleaming out of them.

"Where is the nurse," Kane demanded.

"She'll know. The head of us will know you're not—"

Kane was on the male in the next second, slamming his palms into the pillow on either side of the guard's head, that injured body jumping in response.

"*Where is she,*" he gritted out. "*The nurse.*"

The guard just shook his head, his eyes widening, although it was clear that he feared whatever his leader would do to him more than whatever was facing him now.

The gun came forward before Kane was aware of taking the weapon out of his waistband, and he put it into the male's nose, shoving the barrel so hard, the guard groaned.

"I will paint the wall with your brains," Kane said grimly. "Tell me where the nurse is."

"They took her."

The answer came from the patient in the bed next door, and Kane's head jerked to the side. "Where."

"They think she killed one of us." The male shook his head slowly and winced, like any movement hurt him everywhere. "I don't believe . . . it. She . . . saved me. She saved . . . all of us. Don't know . . . who you are . . . but don't . . . hurt her."

The glistening in the guard's eyes reflected the light from overhead.

"—Kane?"

Someone was saying his name, but he couldn't look away from the other guard.

"She saved me, too," he said hoarsely.

"The Wall," the male whispered. "That's where they'll take her. And they're going to work fast. You need to go now."

"Fuck," Apex said.

Kane wheeled around. "Where is the Wall."

◆　◆　◆

Mounted like one of those Victorian bugs set on pins.

That was what she was, Nadya thought as she stared into the eyes of the head of the guards. They were unusual eyes, with flecks of yellow in the darker base, and the dilated pupils seemed like black holes to swim in. To die in.

When the female brought her dagger up higher, the blade winked as it caught the light.

"You will spare me the pain when you kill me," Nadya said softly. "I was defending the male I love. You lost one of your guards, but I lost him. There is justification."

"What makes you think I care about love."

"You are alive, not dead. That is why."

For a moment, the female seemed frozen where she stood, even though she was such a source of power in the world they lived in, god-like in her influence.

"I will spare you nothing," she said grimly. Then she frowned. "Why don't you have a restraint collar on?"

"Because I came here voluntarily."

The head of the guards laughed. "Why the hell would you do that?"

"I wanted to be of service to the female who saved my life. She took care of the prisoners, and I learned everything I know about healing from her."

"Aren't you a saint—"

Footfalls sounded out. Coming fast. Closing in.

Nadya turned her head as a guard shambled in from around the corner, his distraction and gait nothing like the coordination that the males usually displayed, his uniform partially untucked. There was blood on him, and it was fresh, going by the scent.

His leader lowered her knife. "Shut up," she told him. Then she pointed the tip of her weapon to the door that was centered among the sets of pegs. "In there. Both of you."

As she walked over to the entrance to some kind of interior, she was confident that she would be followed by her two males, and that was precisely what occurred. The door was closed smartly. It was a surprise it was not slammed.

Releasing a ragged breath, Nadya sagged, the chains that kept her on the pegs biting into her wrists. Her bad leg was aching, and her heart was skipping beats, especially as she looked down the long corridor and saw how far away the stairs were. But as if she had a chance of getting free? Even if she could pull her hands out of the steel links, she couldn't move fast enough to get to that stairwell, and where did she think she was going? The old prison camp had been a series of underground tunnels; there had been ways to get in and out if you knew how.

This new one had locks controlled with technology she didn't understand and certainly couldn't get past—

Down at that far end, the stairwell door swung open, and a guard appeared, no doubt coming to report further on whatever was happening. Some kind of threat . . . or an escape? For a moment, she entertained a fantasy that Apex somehow got Kane out, that true medical aid was being rendered to her most precious patient. But she knew that was not—

The guard froze as he focused on her. And then he broke out in a run, coming at her with a speed that didn't make a lot of sense. Unless, of course, it was because he had been summoned urgently.

Except . . . the male slowed down. And then stopped.

Turning her head away, she braced for some kind of aggression.

"Nadya . . ."

As her name traveled the distance between them, she was confused, and not because he knew what she was called . . . it was that voice.

"*Nadya.*"

This isn't possible, she thought as she shifted her eyes to the guard.

What she saw defied reason. Defied everything that she knew of the way the world functioned.

"Kane?" she whispered.

The male started toward her again, his feet stumbling, but his balance was caught readily by a body well equipped to respond to any demand. And the closer he got, the clearer the picture that didn't make any sense became. Her brain could not reconcile his mobility, the clear skin of his jaw and throat, the regeneration of his hands, his hair . . . with everything she knew of him and his burns.

And then she realized what he was seeing.

Lowering her head as far as she could, she squeezed her eyes shut. "Don't look at me."

"Nadya . . ."

"Is it really you?" She asked this even though his scent was like the sound of his voice, unmistakable. "How is this possible?"

"I'm going to get you out of here." In her peripheral vision, she saw him test the chains. "I need to cut these."

He looked around and cursed softly. Then he put his hands on his hips—

"Keys." He grabbed at the belt of weapons around his waist. "I have keys!"

Kane yanked the jangling ring off its mount, and as he leaned into her, she caught his scent again. Drawing it down deeply into her nose, she noticed that it was slightly different than she remembered. Then again, no wounds. He was . . .

"What happened to you?" she breathed.

Kane—or what appeared to be a version of Kane—shook his head. "I don't know. And that's the truth. But we can talk about it later."

She could feel his eyes searching her, and hated what he saw. Which was a sign, she supposed, of how attached she had grown to him.

"Please. Stop staring," she begged.

Bending forward, he went to work on the lock on the links, his fingers moving so swiftly as he tried key after key—and when the chains dropped free, he immediately shifted to the other side. When they also went loose, she started to collapse and he gathered her, pulling her against him. His body was so solid, his muscles flexing as he held her easily.

"I've got you," he said as he picked her up. "But we have to go fast."

"Wait, wait." Extending a hand to the floor, she tried to reach her hood. "I need—"

He swooped down and grabbed the fall of dark fabric. Giving it to her, he started striding off as she yanked the cover back into place. As her face was draped once again, her breath was an unpleasant blasting of heat, and she thought of how good it had been to breathe more freely, even if she had hated revealing herself.

Even though she'd been about to die.

Looking around Kane's bulging arm, she focused on the stained wall, and wondered how much longer until the head of the guards came back out. "Hurry."

He began to run, and as they zeroed in on the stairwell's doorway, she found herself praying unto the Scribe Virgin. So close, so close . . . but the danger seemed to magnify as they covered more and more of the distance.

Down at the exit, Apex swung the steel panel open and urged them on, his frantic hand motions as if he could remove obstacles out of their way—

The head of the guards emerged back where the pegs and the stains were.

"Run faster," Nadya hissed. "They've seen us."

At which point, the head of the guards shouted and drew a gun.

Later, Nadya would wonder the hows of everything that happened next, but she knew the "why": In a split second, she pictured Kane getting shot in the back, and she could not let that happen.

Moving with a desperation that meant she ignored the pain, she shoved her hand down under Kane's arm, got the gun that was on his hip out of its holster, and lifted the weapon up over his shoulder. She was so weak that she had to use two hands, and after she flipped the safety off, she just started pulling the trigger without bothering to aim. As a bullet exploded out of the muzzle, and another, and another, Kane put another surge of speed into their escape—and the head of the guards ducked back behind the door.

Nadya shot again and again, the discharges hitting the wall, picking off pegs and putting holes in the stained gray panels. Sweat broke out across her forehead and she struggled to keep the gun up, but fear gave her what she needed.

And then they were in the stairwell.

Apex grabbed the weapon from her just as her hands lost their grip, and he quickly reloaded with a clip from his own gun belt.

"Smart thinking," he said to her as he shoved the muzzle back out the door. "Take the hand! Go to the chute!"

"I have the key," someone said. "To one of the vehicles down in the lot. We can drive out!"

Everyone glanced at the male who spoke up. White-haired, and very definitely not scenting like a vampire, he was dressed in a flannel shirt and blue jeans, with a flashlight in one hand and a large gun in the other.

Before he could say anything else, a barrage of bullets sprayed the door Apex was at, pinging off the steel, shattering the wired glass window. The male braced the thing closed and winced, sure as if the lead was going into his own body.

Kane ducked down. "Can you dematerialize—Nadya, can you—"

"No," she said grimly. Then she gripped his massive shoulders and looked at him through the hood. "Leave me, you're free—"

As more bullets hit that metal panel, he shook his head. "As long as you're in here, I am not free."

At that moment, the world seemed to stop and she stared at his face. In the raw light from overhead, she still couldn't believe her eyes.

"Who did you feed from," she whispered. "The Scribe Virgin Herself?"

There was a brief pause, as if the guards down at the other end were reloading, and Apex jumped up, cracked the door—and pulled his trigger again.

"Go!" he barked. "I'll hold them as long as I ca—"

He didn't get a chance to finish. The white-haired male with the flashlight and the car key locked a hold around his chest and hauled Apex right off his feet.

Kane took off up the stairs, taking the steps two at a time. When he got to the next floor, which would be the first that was aboveground, he couldn't reach the handle on the fire door with her in his arms and he stamped his boot like he was impatient with waiting even a moment. Apex and the other male were arguing as they arrived on the landing, but the former paused long to yank the handle—

"Fuck," he muttered. "Centralized locking has been engaged, and there's no reader for the hand. Stand back."

Kane turned to the concrete wall and sheltered her with his body as Apex discharged three bullets at the juncture of the door and the jamb. Then he pulled the panel open.

The alarm that went off was loud enough to wake the dead.

Meanwhile, right under them, what sounded like an entire army flooded into the stairwell, the clamoring boots, mix of scents, and waft of gunpowder the kind of thing that spelled deadly defeat.

"Don't even think about staying here to cover us," the male with the white hair said. "I picked you up once, I'll do it again."

Apex grabbed his arm. "Get them out. That's all that matters. *Please.*"

Kane didn't wait for them to sort things out. He started running again, Nadya catching the door as they were the first across the threshold into the hallway. As she glanced around his arm, gunfire was exchanged, but she couldn't track who was shooting first, Apex and his friend or the males in uniform.

Did it matter, though. They were out-gunned, outmaneuvered, and dawn was coming fast.

There was no way this ended well for them.

CHAPTER FIFTEEN

Kane was all adrenaline as he burst out onto the first floor of the central building. After a quick orientation, he went to an open doorway on the left and prayed he was facing the rear parking area. And that there was a window. And that the guards were new recruits with bad aim. And . . .

There *was* a window at the far end of the narrow room, and he quickly surmounted an obstacle course of broken office furniture and ceiling debris. When he got to the intact panes of glass, he considered how to keep a hold of Nadya and get the sash up—

A body streaked by him, went airborne, and solved the problem by crashing through the frame and shattering everything. As a waft of fresh air broke through the moldy stink of rot, Kane leaned out of the hole.

Down below, the wolven sprang up from a crouch and spun around. Holding his arms out, he yelled, "I'll catch her. Come on—drop her to me."

As gunfire continued to echo around in the stairwell, Kane looked at the female in his arms.

"It's the only way," he said.

"You can just save yourself," Nadya said. "Really, you can."

The hellfire chaos of bullets began to come down the hall, suggesting Apex had changed position—or been killed and the guards were trampling his dead body to finish their job.

Tilting out of the hole the wolven had made with his body, Kane extended his arms. On the ground, the other male sank into his thighs, bracing for the catch.

"Get ready," Kane said. And wondered who he was trying to prepare.

His heart was in his throat as he let her go. And time halted as she dropped. She was so fragile, she wouldn't survive a—

The wolven made a new friend for life as he snatched Nadya out of the free fall, swinging her around so that the landing against his chest was as gentle as possible. And after Kane logged a permanent memory at the flop of her thin arms and emaciated legs, he hopped up on the sill and free-fell himself.

Landing in a crouch, he didn't have to ask the other male for what he needed. The slight load was transferred, and then the wolven took off for the lineup of vehicles. For a split second, Kane glanced up at the building. In the darkness, the discharges from the guns were brilliant flashes, and the sounds of gunfire were a staccato snare drum.

He set off running after the wolven.

When they got to the car, the other male knew what to do with whatever small device was in his hand, lights flashing at the four corners of the vehicle as all the locks were disengaged. While Kane piled into the rear with Nadya, he had a thought that this was what Apex had done for him, stuffing his broken body into a lifeboat that had four wheels.

The wolven didn't waste a second. He started the engine, slammed the gear shift back, and then they were off, exploding into reverse. The squeal of the tires was followed by a lurch that was so violent, Kane rebounded off the door he'd shut, and he did what he could to keep Nadya from flying loose and getting knocked out.

"Take this. It's fully loaded."

As a gun was tossed into the back seat, Kane caught it just as another screeching sound screamed in his ears and they shot forward. The lane ahead was illuminated by the headlights, and he measured the distance and direction. There were no meaningful conclusions to be drawn, however. He didn't know where they were going. Where they could go.

"I have a place," the wolven said. "Five miles from here."

"Go faster."

There was a corresponding increase in the engine roar, and soon enough, they were off the property and on a road that was better maintained.

Shifting Nadya around in his arms, he breathed in to see if she was bleeding.

"Are you all right?" he asked hoarsely.

"I think so. But Apex—"

The rumble on the roof was like something dropping out of the sky and landing on top of the vehicle, and immediately the wolven started wrenching the wheel back and forth like he was trying to lose whoever or whatever had attached themselves up there.

Damn it.

It was a guard. It had to be—one of them had dematerialized onto the roof. Cursing some more, Kane trained the muzzle of the gun upward, covering Nadya's ear with his forearm. Just as he was about to pull the trigger—

"Don't shoot!" came the holler over the din. "It's me!"

"Apex?" Kane yelled back.

The wolven glanced upward. "Hold on tight, vampire! I can't stop!"

There was a final surge of speed, as if the male behind the wheel had stomped his foot and demanded all of what was mechanically possible out of the engine. Outside the windows, the forest that crowded up to the road whizzed by in a blur, and as they rounded a curve, he caught sight of a vehicle that had been involved in a crash. There were bodies next to it, lying in the road.

The wolven drove past the wreckage—and over some of it.

"Are you okay?" Kane asked again softly. When there wasn't a reply, he felt a stab of fear. "Nadya?"

"Yes. I think so—yes."

Kane glanced behind them. When there was only darkness in the road, he told himself they were going to make it.

But he wouldn't have bet much on that outcome.

◆ ◆ ◆

For Nadya, it was such a whirlwind, from getting thrown out of the building to being caught by a stranger. And then the car ride.

Her mind couldn't keep up with it all, and she felt like that was a good thing. The risks were too obvious; she had heard the gunfire and smelled the acrid smoke of the discharges back at the prison camp. And now felt the lurching of the vehicle they were in, and heard the yelling among the males.

So she wasn't sure how to answer the question that Kane kept posing to her, and decided to just go with the reply that would make him feel a little better. Besides, what was really bothering her the most didn't have anything to do with the guards or the mortal threats.

What she was really struggling with was that he'd seen her. That revelation, which she had never intended, seemed more traumatic than the very obvious risks of this escape. Rescue. Whatever this was—

"Nadya . . ."

The way Kane said her name, with such compassion and sympathy, was the reason why she hid herself away, his pity the worst possible reminder of how bad she looked. And it was even more terrible because it was *him*. She just wanted to look how she'd been before for him. Which seemed so superficial given they were speeding away from the camp with a male on top of the car and at least a half a dozen guards free to come after them.

She glanced at Kane. As the world rushed by, he was still staring down at her, and she thought of what it had been like to sit by his bed, safely under her robing, hiding and yet feeling whole because he had been so broken.

"What happened to you?" she asked quietly.

The driver spoke up over the roar: "It's not much farther."

As if he had misunderstood the question.

When the car went around a tight turn, Nadya grabbed on to the front of Kane's stolen uniform, and his arms tightened around her. The corner was so sharp, she was sure they would roll over—they did not. Somehow, the vehicle righted itself and continued on its course—

The brakes were hit and they went into a fishtailing skid, the sedan dead-ending in a dusty swirl.

"Get out!" The male at the wheel wrenched around. "Take these keys. I'll be back for you at nightfall—this car likely has a tracer on it so we're rolling a lot of dice right now. I have to get it good and lost."

Kane did not hesitate. He took the keys, opened their door, and gathered her as he would any kind of delicate package.

Carefully.

The moment they were free of the car, she looked up to the roof. Apex was gone, not anywhere that she could see or scent. There was no time to ask where he was—and it was likely the white-haired male did not know any more than she or Kane did.

With spinning tires, the car tore off in reverse, as if the driver knew there wasn't time enough to turn around. In its wake, more loose dirt spooled up into the night air and a faint whiff of gasoline lingered.

"He's right," Kane said. "If they kept collars on us, they definitely put locators on their vehicles. Come on."

As if she were walking beside him instead of in his arms.

At first, she was too distracted by how it felt to be so close to him. To have his scent in her nose and the beat of his heart under her cheek. To be held with such strength. But as he paused to put a copper key into a copper lock, the hunting cabin registered: Single-story, falling down, the kind of place that had been abandoned for far longer than the prison camp's tuberculosis hospital. Indeed, except for the dead bolt, the place seemed utterly worthless, gaps in the exterior boards, the windows cloudy, the roof sporting a crumbling chimney.

The interior was just as bad, the floorboards cracked and sprung, no furniture around, dust on everything. There was also no bathroom, just a stretch of chipped countertop with a sink that was rusted out, and no appliances, only a gap in the cupboards where a refrigerator might have been.

Both of them looked at the gaping hole in the roof at the same time—and that was when the glow registered. With everything so frantic, she hadn't noticed that dawn's arrival was imminent . . . but now, through that wide-open aperture, the subtle shift from the deep black of night to the prodromal gray of day was alarming.

"There has to be an underground hideout. Callum never would have sent us here—"

"Lights!" Nadya said. "Through the trees. Someone is coming."

A dance of illumination sparkled, the sets of headlights piercing the landscape and strobing as the trunks and branches broke up the beams' penetrations.

Guards. It had to be.

"Goddamn it," Kane muttered as he spun around.

Nadya glanced to the empty hearth and entertained a brief and unsatisfying idea that they could hide in the chimney. But what else could they do? They were sitting ducks, for both the guards and the dawn. If they lived through the former, they were certainly not living through the latter.

"I feel like this night is never going to be over," Nadya said under her breath.

Kane slowly lowered her to the flooring. "Can you stand on your own?"

"Yes."

"Stay behind me. I'm going to do what I can."

Reaching up, she touched his face—and something about the contact made both of them go still. "Please leave me?"

"Never."

Unexpected tears flooded her eyes. "You have nothing to repay me for."

Car lights washed the front of the cabin, and with the door open, the dark interior was bathed in false illumination as bright and dangerous as the sun.

"Thank you," Kane said roughly.

"For what?"

"Taking care of me. You eased me."

"I didn't have any medicine to give you."

"Your presence was balm enough." He was careful as he brushed the hood as if he were stroking her cheek. "It was you more than anything that gave me relief."

His eyes burned with such emotion that she struggled to comprehend what was in his face, in his heart.

"How can you look at me like this?" She moved his hand away. "You know what I am."

She tried to turn away, but he gently moved her chin back. And then with steady hands, he slowly lifted the hood. She was so shocked, she didn't fight him.

"I see your soul," he said. "That is why I find you beautiful."

Tears fell from her eyes as no more than twenty feet away, the guards got out of their vehicles, the unlatching of the doors, the crunch of combat boots on the ground, as alarming as gunshots.

"Please leave," she whispered urgently.

Kane shook his head. "That's not how this is going to end."

With that, he lowered his lips and softly brushed her own. As she gasped, he arranged the hood back in place and looked away to the males who were outside.

The change in his face was so total, he became a stranger even as his features remained the same: Violence, dark and powerful and evil, transformed him. And then he picked her back up and moved quickly. Going over to the hearth, he set her in the corner, facing away from the door.

"Do not move from this position. Do not look." When she didn't reply, he said, "Nadya. You don't look. Swear to me."

It went without saying that there was no reason for any vow because they were both going to be killed—or worse, taken alive.

Inclining her head, she said, "I swear."

He touched her shoulder for a moment, the gentle contact at odds with his expression. And then he was gone, striding out of the open door.

She knew the instant the guards saw him. They started yelling and shooting. As Nadya began to tremble, she turned into herself even more, tucking her knees up to her chest as best she could, holding on to herself . . . trying to disappear—

The scream was that of a male, loud and deep.

Nadya squeezed her eyes shut under the hood. Kane's death had finally come, and unlike before, now it was because of her, instead of in spite of her best efforts.

The shaking was so violent, she felt as though she were being torn apart, but it wasn't fear. In the corner of the abandoned hunting cabin, in the dust and the aged disintegration of the place, she wept for everything that she had hoped for in her heart during all those hours of nursing Kane. She wept for all that he had suffered.

But mostly she wept because he'd almost made it out alive.

And whole.

The cruelty of some destinies was infinite.

CHAPTER SIXTEEN

Death stalked life, sure as if it were a fleet-footed predator.

Yeah, no shit, V thought. But come on. The whole maternal/fetal death thing for vampires was downright rude.

Stepping out of the subterranean tunnel and through the back of the training center's supply closet, he had to turn sideways and squeeze his way along. A new delivery of printer paper had arrived and the stack of six Hammermill boxes was exactly not the kind of obstacle course he was looking to work out on. On the far side, he entered the office proper, and paused by the desk to light up a hand-rolled. Then he pushed open the glass door.

The facility's main thoroughfare was a concrete corridor that ran from the escape hatch at one end to the parking area and the road out at the other. Branching off its broad pedestrian highway were all kinds of state-of-the-art, from the gym, locker, and weight-lifting rooms, to the shooting range, swimming pool, and classrooms.

And then there was his wedding gift to his *shellan*.

When he and his Jane had come out of the throat punches Fate had thrown at them, he had gained a kick-ass partner—and delivered to his brothers exactly the sort of on-site, dedicated doctor that they had long needed.

After all, Havers, the species' healer, while clinically sound, was a fucking numpty who had a list as long as his arm of bad ideas. Like trying to kill the King and tossing his own sister out on her ass just before dawn for dating a human. And then there was the bow tie bullshit, and those tortoiseshell glasses. Who did he think he was, Clark Kent with a stethoscope?

Sure as shit he was able to leap to tall conclusions about a person's worth faster than a speeding aristocrat.

So yes, the Brotherhood had needed a fine doctor. And V's fine surgeon had needed a place to treat her patients with the best technology, and the right complement of rooms, and everything his Jane would ever need to do her job to the very best of her considerable ability.

V stopped, exhaled over his shoulder, and looked down a lineup of closed doors. There were a couple of exam rooms, an OR that was packed tighter than a toy box with equipment, and a number of recovery berths. And they had a staff now to go with it all. After he and Jane had designed and built out the spaces, she'd been joined by Manny Manello, M.D., her old boss out in the human world and V's now brother-in-law, as well as Ehlena, Rehv's mate, who was a nurse.

The brothers were lucky to have all of them.

Checking his watch, he was surprised the appointment had gone on as long as it had. But he had no experience with possibly-gestating-female-vampires, and that was something, thank God, he was going to stay in the dark about. Doc Jane, in her ghostly form, couldn't have young, and besides, she was more interested in her work than rearing any kind of next generation.

Focusing on the first of the examination rooms, he couldn't speculate about what was going on inside. He didn't have to. The Jackal had been brought in about thirty minutes ago with his female to see if she was pregnant, and talk about no FOMO. V didn't envy the guy in the slightest. You have this female you really care about, who's the center of your world—and then the creator of the species throws a shit pie at you: Hey, you can service your female during her needing, and be the only thing that eases the suffering cravings, but the booby prize is you might knock her up and kill her.

Thanks, Mom, he thought as he ashed into the palm of his leather-gloved hand.

No wonder most couples, most of the time, just treated the fertile time with drugs nowadays—

The door opened and the Jackal came out. The guy was tall and trim, in the way aristocrats tended to be, all that fine breeding creating a body *habitus* that was attractive without being too muscled. And you could tell the guy and Rhage were related. The ocean blue eyes and the bone structure were the same—although the Jackal wasn't permanently cheerful like Hollywood was.

Then again, few things outside the Times Square ball on *New Year's Rockin' Eve* were.

The former aristocrat stopped short. Cleared his throat like he was trying to control his emotions.

"Just spit it out." V took another drag on his cigarette. "It's a safe space here—I think that's what they call it, right?"

V personally preferred unsafe spaces, but tomato/tomahtoes.

The Jackal waited until the door had completely eased shut behind him. "She's not pregnant."

"And you're relieved, but don't want her to know."

"She was hoping to be with young." The Jackal leaned back against the corridor's concrete wall. "I mean, she really wants one, and you know, what else could I do? She went into her needing and . . ."

There was the temptation to point out to the guy that at least he had a good decade off from any further discussion on the subject, but V didn't want to pile on. Besides, chances were good his sense of superiority, which came from never having to worry his mate would die on the birthing bed, would come through in anything he said.

"So." The Jackal smoothed the front of the plaid work shirt he wore. "Thanks for coming down and meeting me."

Somehow the guy made the jeans and that lumber-sexual shit look like something out of Butch's couture-drobe. Then again, the Jackal had the posture of a prince, and that elevated even the most common of threads. Hell, you could probably throw a hazmat suit on him and it would look like something Tom Ford had put together.

"Is there something to eat around here?" the guy said. "I'm starved."

"Yeah, come on."

Closing his gloved hand around the ashes, V led the way down to the cafeteria. Even though the Brotherhood had suspended the training program for future soldiers, the mess hall was kept fully stocked—first, because the brothers needed fuel before and after workouts, and second, because Fritz needed something else to look after.

'Cuz running a five-star-hotel-standard private home occupied by the First Family, the brothers and fighters, their mates and young, as well as a dog and a cat, wasn't enough on his plate.

As they came up to the breakroom, V held the door open. "After you."

With an expression of wonder, the Jackal drifted into the tiled expanse of free vending machines, snacks, sodas, and candy like he'd never seen food before. There was also a serve-yourself counter with fresh fruit and other good-for-you's that V always completely ignored. And a hot plate center that was currently not open for business.

As the other guy wandered around the calorie load, V poured himself a cup of hot coffee and grabbed a cruller. Parking himself in one of the dorm-decor armchairs, he snagged the remote off a coffee table and hit the volume on the TV in the corner. A crack-of-ass local news reporter was prattling along about God only knew what, but it was better than the silence.

A good ten minutes later, the Jackal came over with a tray laden with all kinds of munchie-crunchie. As he sat down, he seemed to deflate. Then again, he'd used a lot of energy in the last couple of nights, which explained the get-in-my-belly.

"Doc Jane told us that they used to not be able to test for pregnancy so early," the male said as he cracked the top on some high-test Coke. "Amazing what medical science has done."

"Yeah."

The "ahhhhhhh" that came out of the guy after he threw back half the carbonation should have been used as an ad for the Real Thing.

"Your *shellan* was so good to her," he said. "Afterwards, they were talking about Nyx setting up an Etsy store for Posie, her sister. I figured it was best to just leave them to it. What do I know about handmade jewelry, you know?"

Just get to the point, V thought as he polished off his cruller.

"Yeah," he said.

Overhead, the news anchor started reporting on the burglary of an upstate store of some sort, a field reporter standing in the dark in front of a twenties-era mom-and-pop.

The Jackal continued to eat and talk, and V let him go, making random *uh-huh* sounds when there were pauses in the prattle. It was clear the guy was working off his anxiety, and hell, after V had lived with Rhage for as long as he had, he was used to being backdrop while someone sucked back five or six thousand calories.

But the entire time, he was wondering when the real reason for all this was going to be brought up—

"So have you?"

V stabbed his third butt out in a conveniently placed ashtray. "Sorry, what?"

"Found the new site of the prison camp."

Finally, V thought as he sat forward in the padded chair.

"No, not yet." And the guy must know this from his own half brother. "Actually, it might be worth going over this with you again. When you were in the prison camp, do you have any memory of the Command talking about where the new location was going to be? Or anybody discussing it? Like some of the guards, maybe?"

The question had been asked before, but you never knew what someone would recall out of the blue—and V was getting desperate.

Not in a good way.

The story of how the aristocrat had ended up in that cesspool had been a bummer. The Jackal had been framed for deflowering a virgin and sent up the proverbial river for life. Destiny had given him a way out, however, as well as one helluva jackpot in his female. But the shit he'd been through lingered—you could tell by the shadows in those baby blues.

"No, I'm sorry." The Jackal stared across his tray of ultra-processed dopamine releasers. "I don't remember that female talking about it—and I've been racking my mind. As you know, she and I had . . . well, we had a certain tie. But I didn't spend much time with her."

Certain tie = they'd had a son. Except that didn't need to be said out loud, if the guy wasn't comfortable remembering who his offspring's *mahmen* had been. And who could blame him.

"It's okay." V took a sip of his coffee. "Maybe something will come to you later."

Refocusing on the TV, he watched the reporter motion to the store behind him again and he had to wonder what had been stolen. Certainly not computer equipment. The business looked like the kind of place where receipts were still written out by hand and prices were punched into a cash register that didn't require electricity.

V cleared his throat. "We just need some kind of break in the case, so to speak. Pardon my Columbo."

"I want to be in if you find anything."

Ah, V thought. So this was the why of the meeting.

When he didn't respond, the Jackal tore the wrapper off a Snickers bar, but he didn't bite the thing. He used it as a pointer, angling the chocolate-covered hangry-cillin at V. "Those males and females in there . . . I was one of them. They were the only people in my life for a very long time. I want to be part of their liberation."

"You've mentioned this before."

There was a pause, and then the Jackal said, "That's not anywhere near an I'll-call-you."

"Will you look at the time." V got to his feet with his coffee. "I'll see you later."

"I've earned the right to help with the evacuation."

"Is that why you texted me? Like I'm a gatekeeper or something."

"You're the holdout. Everybody else wants me there."

Oh, so there'd been a vote taken. Great.

"At this point"—V turned away—"I have absolutely no idea how we're going to find the place. So it's a moot fucking point."

"I know who is a prisoner and who's a guard. I know the way the place works."

V glanced back. "Unfortunately, I think it's going to be very obvious who is who and not because the latter are wearing uniforms. And you know the way the *old* place works. You don't know shit about the new location, starting with where it is. You're well-intended, but you're un-trained, unexperienced, and you have a son and now a *shellan* who need you. I get the loyalty, but I can't get behind the risk assessment. Sorry."

Leaving the male to sort the Cheetos from the Cheerios, V walked back out into the corridor before he said something he was going to feel slightly bad about—and then get really annoyed he was wasting any energy on regretting. Goddamn civilians. Always with the bright ideas.

But whatever, he was not about to jeopardize his own life or the lives of his brothers just to help the Jackal through his survivor's guilt.

That was a burden the guy was going to have to put down on his own.

CHAPTER SEVENTEEN

The element of surprise could work as one hell of a preemptive strike.

As Kane stepped free of the hunting cabin, he didn't hesitate, not even for a second. He dematerialized directly onto the guard who'd just gotten out of the passenger seat, and he bit the bastard on the side of the face.

The instant he struck, the male screamed, and as Kane jerked back, he took the skin and meat of the cheek with him. Spitting everything out, he shoved the guard to the ground and jumped up onto the roof of the vehicle—just as the driver emerged from the interior.

A gun swung up and sent a bullet Kane's way, but as he somersaulted over the other male's head, he was a target missed. He landed hard in his borrowed boots, grabbed the guard's head from behind, and yanked back. As balance was lost, more gunshots went off toward the sky, and Kane caught the wrist that controlled the weapon. With a vicious snap, he broke the forearm bones, and when the screaming started, he took that gun.

Pointed it at the male's face.

And pulled the trigger.

The bullet went right through the forehead, and the body jerked, arms and legs flopping, mouth falling open, eyes wide and instantly sightless. He let the guard fall to the ground and jumped over the hood. For a split second, he couldn't go any farther. The male he'd bitten had half a face, the bone structure eaten away under where his fangs had penetrated, the roots of the teeth exposed, the nose nothing but a pair of black holes. One eye was gone entirely, and the disintegration was spreading.

Kane turned back to the cabin and thought of the wolven.

"I won't be gone long," he called out to Nadya. "Stay where you are!"

"Kane?" There was a pause. "Kane!"

"No time, stay where you are!"

Jumping behind the wheel, he remembered what he'd seen the others do. He planted his foot on something down on the floor—the engine roared. That wasn't right. He punched his foot into the other pedal. There was nothing. Locating the shifting rod, which was in the center between the seats, he found it frozen in place—until he punched at the pedals again. As the gear wand became freed, he wrenched it all the way back.

The car went forward.

Not what he wanted, but he made it work. Yanking the wheel around until it was tight to the left, he herky-jerked the car in a circle, heaving, ho'ing. Punching at the pedals. Lurching.

When he had a clear shot out the lane to the road, he ran over the driver as he shoved his boot into what made the car go. Skidding, slipping, drifting from side to side, he mostly kept on the twin paths that had been worn into the ground, and when he got to the paved double lanes they'd been on, he made a turn that was as close to ninety degrees as he could make it.

The glow in the east was gathering real momentum now, and he had to hold his arm up over his face to keep his eyes even partially open. As another vehicle came toward him, a horn sounded, loud as the kind that he remembered being on steam trains. His instinct was to wrench the wheel to the right, but he knew that he'd end up deep in the bushes and the trees—and he was still too close to the hunter's cabin to ditch the vehicle. He held on tight and kept straight, inching over to make room, catching a quick glance at the furious human as they passed.

Glancing up to the little mirror mounted on the front window, he saw the other vehicle's red lights keep going, that blaring noise getting cut off.

He kept going, too.

The burn of the sun's first rays on his face and upper body made him remember being in the clinic's bed, and the memories of Nadya made him focus through the pain. As he continued to surmount the road, as miles went beneath the wheels, he controlled things better, managing the speed and the steering with greater competence. Signs appeared off to the side, but he couldn't read them because his bloodline had thought that the languages of humans were beneath his kind. They'd always had *doggen* for English translations.

As the sun's rise grew even more relentless, his eyes began watering such that he could barely see, and wiping them repeatedly didn't help. The only good news was that the guards would be under the same conditions he was.

And then he simply couldn't go any farther.

Looking to either side of the road, he saw nothing but tree line, no glowing lights, no drives into the forested acreage. He extended his right foot as far as it could go, and the engine responded as he demanded, his speed increasing. As he rounded a bend and came to a straightaway, he closed his eyes, took a deep breath—

And spun the wheel hard right.

At the very moment the vehicle shot off the road, he dematerialized out of the interior, sending himself off in a scatter, beelining for the hunting cabin. With every foot of distance he covered in the ether, his strength got sucked away by the arriving day—and he had a thought that he had waited until too late.

Except then he knew he was in the right place, his sense of direction undiminished by the sunlight.

Re-forming with momentum, he came back into his physical body in a run. As he barreled forward, racing in between the two bodies on the ground that were already smoking from the sun, he took a leap at the hunting cabin's open door, going parallel to the ground with his arms outstretched. He meant to land in a roll, but he was too busy looking to the hearth, to the far corner.

She wasn't there—

With a thunderous bang, he landed facedown, and there was no skidding because the floorboards were rough. Cursing, he didn't care as the breath was kicked out of his lungs and one of his hips sang with pain.

Twisting on his side, he looked around.

Nadya was gone.

✦ ✦ ✦

Back when that wolven had been driving away from the prison camp like a bat out of hell, Apex had had to dematerialize off the roof of that car. Strong as he was, he hadn't been able to hold on anymore, and when the wind shear had peeled him free of the panels, he'd let himself go. For a moment, he'd just hung in midair, the rushing wind keeping him aloft, his eyes trained on the infinite sky above the earth.

Too bad that coast couldn't last.

And the pursuing car full of guards was going to be the worst possible landing pad.

Closing his lids, he dematerialized just as he felt a bullet nick the side of his leg. The strike wasn't enough to slow him down, but he didn't have a destination.

So when he re-formed, it was . . . anywhere.

No, that was a lie. It was back at the fortified garage, the one the wolven had taken them to, where they'd gotten the stretchers for Kane and Mayhem, and more ammo and weapons.

Checking the exterior out for a second time, he found it such an unassuming structure, and he approved of the camouflage. And back when they'd be reconnoitering, before they'd headed up the mountain, the wolven had given them all the combination, so he let himself in.

Standing over the battered Monte Carlo, he replayed the escape as he breathed in the gas and oil fumes that still lingered, thick as if the car had just been driven. On a hunch, he bent down. Yup, something was leaking, like the vehicle had joined the injured ranks along with the rest of them.

With so many near-misses, they shouldn't have made it out at all.

Where the hell was that wolven?

Not that he'd come here to wait for the male or anything.

As the skin on the back of his neck tingled in warning, he glanced out the milky glass of the window over the work bench. He was going to have to hunker down for the day and here was as good a place as any. He could only hope Kane and that female were okay wherever they were.

Looking around, he spaced for a second about how to get underground. Then he remembered the wolven going over to that bench and flipping something under the upper shelf—

"Thank fuck."

As he repeated the male's actions, a wooden toolbox nearly the size of a car left its seat and swung aside to reveal a set of stairs. There was no sound from its well-oiled hinges, no clue that it was anything other than it appeared. Lights went on when he began to descend into the darkness, and at the bottom, he was greeted by a sight that had stirred him the first time: Stacked against the smooth concrete walls, in boxes, bags, and various containers, there was an arsenal of weapons and ammunition. Dried food in drums. Water jugs. Flak jackets, winter coats, and snowshoes. Medical supplies.

It was all so well thought out, so organized, so useful, needed, and valuable.

The male who had assembled the collection of necessaries was a clear, practical thinker who wasn't going to be taken unawares. He was prepared. Thorough. Defensive when he had to be, aggressive when it was warranted.

Looking away, because in a weird sense, Apex felt like he was ogling the wolven himself even though he was just checking out the stuff the guy had, he measured the shower and toilet, which were out in the open, and the two cots that were off to one side.

But the admiration came back. If he had designed a space for a bolt-hole, he couldn't have done a better job.

Behind him, the toolbox slid back into place, and he heard the catch of the copper lock. Glancing up, the steel mesh that covered the ceiling and the walls shimmered, and there was a flap of it that could be secured over the opening of the stairs.

That wolven was a damned mastermind.

Within moments, the resonant silence became as dense as the earth itself, and eventually, the shower in the tiled corner drew his eyes and held them.

As he went toward it, he passed by all the jackets that were hung on pegs—and stopped halfway down the lineup. Glancing around, even though he was alone, he leaned into one of the down coats that was camouflaged to look like leaves. His nostrils flared as he breathed in, and the scent that registered was a spice that he had done his best to shut out.

Except who was he hiding from down here?

Closing his eyes, he drew the wolven's scent deep into his lungs and held it there. Something about the combination of spruce and fresh air made him feel warm under his skin—and like he could have happily blown ten or fifteen years of his life just standing at the parka and inhaling through his nose.

But because that was pathetic, even with no witnesses, he forced himself to keep going down the aisle that was formed by all the supplies. As he went along, he took off the guard's uniform, starting with the gun belt, which he tossed on one of the cots. The bloodstained shirt was next, then the boots and the pants. He let it all fall wherever it did, noting that if the clothes had been his, even if it had just been that tunic and loose pants, he would have treated them better out of habit.

Fuck those guards, though, even if it was only the uniform of a dead one.

By the time he got to the showerhead, he was buck-ass naked and braced for cold water and rotgut soap. Reaching to the handle, he—

The instant he made contact with the stainless steel, an electric shock went through him and he saw the dead, like a hologram overlapping reality. It was a male . . . hanging from the bolted-in fixture above, a brown belt around his throat . . . his naked body against the tiled wall, his legs extended straight out at an angle with no bend at the knees . . . the heels planted on the floor, the toes fanned out.

The eyes were open in the gray, frozen face, the dark-blond hair falling over the forehead, over the shoulders.

With a hiss, Apex retracted his hand and shook his head.

When he looked back again, the vision was gone—and stayed gone as he tried again to turn the water on.

Pivoting away, he put his back to where the body had been and set about clearing his mind by letting his head fall into the cold spray. When the temperature started to warm, he was so surprised, he stepped out and double-checked that everything was working. It was.

He put his palm out.

"Oh . . ."

The warmth was enticing, and he thought how fucked up it was that even though he had been involved in multiple skirmishes with armed weapons tonight, as well as a car accident, an amputation, and topped that off just now with a dead body sighting . . . he was scared of getting back under the rush.

One thing he had learned was that it was easier to stay uncomfortable.

What hurt was when you let your guard down, and then had to re-enter hell.

The burn on reentry was never, ever worth whatever eased you.

CHAPTER EIGHTEEN

O ver here! Quick!"

Just as Kane was losing his mind, as he'd decided that Nadya had been picked up by a second set of guards, or had run off for safety because she was horrified by what he'd done out in front of the cabin, just as he was about to run out into the gathering dawn to try to find her—

The urgent male voice wheeled him around sure as if he were a puppet.

Callum, the wolven, was peeking out of a panel in the floor. "Come on! I got to get out of here. I have no more time than you do."

Kane scrambled across the rough floorboards like he was being chased, and as he hit the stairs that had been revealed, the wolven traded places, jumping free of some kind of subterranean hideout.

"I'll be back at dusk," the male said as he slammed shut the panel.

Bump, bump bumpbumpbump.

Kane didn't pay much attention to the wolven running off overhead. He only cared about skidding down the steps. As he bottomed out on his butt, he looked up and saw the only thing that mattered at the moment: Across a shockingly well-kitted-out interior, on a sofa that was strewn with fluffy pillows, Nadya was sitting up at attention, her hands gripping her hood and robes, her body trembling.

Kane stayed where he was for a couple of reasons. One, it was possible he'd broken his ass, literally. Two, he didn't want to rush at her, which was all he felt like doing. And three . . .

"Hi," he said.

"Hi," she whispered as she gripped the sofa arm like she was going to stand up.

"No, let me come to you."

He got to his feet and walked toward her. The underground quarters were narrow, but long, and accommodated a small galley kitchen for food preparation, a water closet with a door, and furniture that, if measured against his standard of living prior to the prison camp, was casual, but compared to where they'd both been was palatial and beautifully clean as well as color-coordinated in blues and grays. There was even a proper bed, located behind the couch Nadya was sitting on.

"Callum said this is his personal retreat," she explained. Then she blurted, "Are you hurt? I heard you scream out there—I thought you were dead."

She covered her mouth over the hood with one hand. And then the other.

As he reached her, Kane lowered himself to his knees. In the lights that were mounted on the ceiling, Nadya's draped form trembled and he wanted to take her into his arms, but he wasn't sure where the boundaries were.

"I'm fine. I'm here. We're safe."

"Are we?"

"Yes, I promise." *At least for right now*, he tacked on to himself.

As they fell silent, he didn't know what to do next, but then she stopped his heart.

With a shiver that transmitted through the robing, she lifted shaking hands to her hood . . . and slowly moved it up and over her head.

Her stare remained lowered as she revealed herself to him, but then she looked at him, and for the first time, he saw her eyes properly. Her irises were a swirl of blue and green and brown, the combination of colors so unusual, he had never seen it before. And in the center, in the black pinpoints of her pupils, he saw an eternity—

"You don't need to cover yourself," he said roughly. "Not around me. You're beautiful."

Her eyes returned to her lap. "How can you say that."

"Back in the clinic, I was uncovered before your eyes. Did it affect your opinion of me?"

"But we are not the same anymore."

"Yes, we are."

He searched her face, cataloging the ropey scars that distorted one eye and half her nose and all of her cheek. He suspected the damage continued below the robing because the side of her throat was marked as well.

"Nadya . . ."

Rising up, he sat beside her on the sofa, put his arm around her, and eased her against him. Though her body remained stiff, she did tilt in—yet he had the sense that, though they were close to each other, they were miles apart.

"I'm going to keep us safe." As the words came out of him, he looked over to a lineup of weapons in a glass-fronted cabinet mounted on the wall. "Don't worry about that."

And that was when it hit him.

"We're out of the camp." His voice was rough as he tried out the syllables, letting his ears test them for truth. "We're not in there anymore—"

As he turned his head to look around some more—marveling, really, about the liberation—he caught his reflection in that gun cabinet's glass.

What stared back at him was at once a stranger . . . and someone he could recall seeing all of his life—well, at least before he went into the prison camp. After that date, there had been no mirrors anywhere.

"Kane?" she whispered.

He had some vague notion that his body was getting off the couch and moving across to the cabinet, but he wasn't tracking his own movements. He was too busy looking at himself, and as he came up close to the glass, he touched his own face, feeling nothing but smooth, healthy skin as he let his fingertips drift down his cheek to his jaw. Then he stepped back and stared at his torso. As he extended his legs, they worked perfectly, the muscles strong and coordinated, the knees flexing without pain, the bones underneath willing and able to support the load of his upper half should he need them to.

And underneath his skin? A humming of power that should not have been foreign, but felt like a revelation.

Turning away from himself, he felt helpless. Which made no sense. He should be jumping up and down and celebrating.

But none of this made sense. All he knew was that Apex and the others had gotten him out of the camp, and then someone had interceded on his behalf, and then . . .

"Yes," Nadya said softly. "That's what you look like now."

"I find this . . . impossible to believe."

He shook his head and walked around the cramped space. As he went up and back, he thought of the manor house he'd been given by his intended's bloodline. There had been that horse path that had skirted the back meadow, the one he had taken his trotters on. He could have used its length and calming vista right now.

Except then he found himself in front of a stove and refrigerator. Though they were modern appliances, he recognized what they were from when he had worked in the prison camp's kitchen, and he knew how to use them.

He would also benefit from a different focus right now.

"Are you hungry?" he asked.

"I don't know."

Kane smiled a little. "I feel the same way. I'm willing to bet that the wolven has something to eat here—"

"Kane."

"Yes?" When she didn't answer, he turned to face her. "Tell me. Whatever it is."

"I want to know what happened to you." She held up her hands. "I'm not formally trained in medicine by human standards, but I have apprenticed for years. And the healing that you have gone through, in a matter of hours, defies reasoning. Where did you go and what was done unto you."

◆　◆　◆

Nadya was so used to being covered that the absence of her hood made her feel too light, as if she would float away if she didn't hold on to the cushion beneath her. She was also shocked she could face Kane at all.

But she had other things that were foremost on her mind. And given the way Kane had looked at himself in that glass? He was as shocked as she was.

"I expected to you to die," she said softly. "Every night when I would first check on you, I would brace myself to find you unresponsive. And now you're strong and whole, and perfectly healthy."

Kane opened his mouth. Closed it. "Are you hungry? I am."

As if he hadn't heard her. As if he hadn't just asked her that.

She was not surprised as he turned back to the kitchen area, and as she watched him move, she remained so confused. It was him . . . and yet not Kane at all.

He opened the refrigerator and took out a carton of milk to check the date. "Still good. I guess the wolven stays here regularly. Oh, look, an apple. May I please feed you?"

Nadya opened her mouth. Hesitated. "No, thank you."

As he pivoted around again, he frowned. Then he came back over to her. "May I give you my vein?"

"Oh, no." She put her palms up as she flushed. "No. I am fine."

In the silence that followed, she became achingly aware of the height of him as he loomed above her, so vital, so healed . . . so beautiful in a masculine way.

When he sat back down next to her, he put his elbows on his knees, propped his chin on his linked hands, and stared at the floor.

"I don't know what she did to me." He shook his head. "All I know is that I came awake in her hut, and she told me she could save me."

"Who was she? A healer?"

"No, she was something else entirely. She was mystical, she was . . . well, it sounds crazy, but she was of another world." He held up his forefinger to emphasize the point. "That I am very sure of."

A tingling ran down Nadya's spine. "Was it the Scribe Virgin?"

"I don't think so . . . but I'm not sure I'd know as I've never met the species' creator before." He shrugged. "She didn't introduce herself, so maybe she was."

"What did she say to you?"

"She offered me a resurrection. But then . . . I can't remember what happened. It gets hazy for me after that."

He held his hands out, turning them palm down and splaying all ten fingers. Then he flipped them over as if he couldn't believe what he was looking at.

"All I knew for sure was that I had to get back to you," he murmured. "It was all about going into that hellhole and bringing you out."

Nadya's throat tightened. "You didn't need to save me."

He glanced over at her. "And you didn't need to save me. So we're even, aren't we."

As she stared back at him, she realized that they had been intimates when she had been tending to his body. Now, they were all but strangers, and she couldn't imagine him naked.

Then again, maybe that was because of what he was like now.

"I took care of you because it was the job I declared for myself." She tried to clear the lump that was making talking difficult. "You were my duty, so you owe me nothing—and before you say it, no, I wasn't the one who really healed you. It was whoever you were with when you were gone, and that is the truth."

"Well, my truth is that I am a male with honor, and after everything you did for me, I wasn't leaving you in there." He crossed his arms over his chest. "And I should like to take you to your family at nightfall. Your loved ones will be missing you."

"There are none who miss me."

Kane frowned. "What of your bloodline?"

This should not hurt as much as it does, she thought as a lancing pain went through her sternum.

It was a while before she could find her voice, and she hated the weakness inherent in the reedy syllables she spoke.

"I left my *mahmen* and sire. After . . . my difficulties."

As a surge of anxiety rippled through her broken body, she, too, was seized by a need to move, even though she had long ago learned that everywhere she went, there she was. No true escape was available for her, which was why Kane's chivalrous mission to free her from the prison camp was always going to be in vain. Her ruined body formed the bars she languished behind, her past the warden of her incarceration.

Her physical location was immaterial.

"Tell me," he said in a low voice. "What was done to you."

CHAPTER NINETEEN

Callum almost didn't make it out of that hunting cabin in time. It wasn't that he wouldn't have spent the day guarding that wounded female, if he'd had to. But when her male showed, it was a case of three was not a party.

Besides, he wanted to go check on That Vampire.

The one with the bad attitude.

You know . . . just to make sure the guy was okay. With all the shooting and car rolling and other fun and games, one couldn't be too sure that somebody like him might not need resuscitation of some sort. You know, chest compression. Assisted breathing.

A hand job.

And Callum was a fine Samaritan, the very model of a servant to others. Hell, he'd even put on a nurse's uniform. He had the legs to carry off a skirt, assuming thick calves and muscled thighs were what the vampire was attracted to.

As he re-formed at the foot of the mountain, he rushed into his garage's interior, for once forgetting to double-check that he hadn't been followed as he entered the place. Except daylight was here, and he was out of energy. Wolven of his clan didn't turn into torches like vampires did in sunshine, but his strength would get drained very fast, and he had no intention of feeling like he had the flu until the next full moon could recharge him—

Callum halted. Sniffed the air. Started to smile.

Shutting the door, he went over to the workbench and released the trigger on the toolbox, then beat feet around the old Monte Carlo as the staircase was revealed.

"Don't shoot," he said as he jumped down and the cover slid back into position. "I own this . . . place . . ."

Over in the shower, That Vampire was facing away and under the warm spray, his hands braced on the tile on either side of the fixture, his thick arms bowed, his back rippled with muscles. His head was down, the force of the water focused on the nape of his neck as if he had an ache there.

Well . . . what do you know. Callum suddenly knew something about aches—

As if his presence registered, the male he couldn't look away from twisted around. The torsion in his torso made all kinds of things flex and bulge—with the flexing happening over at the shower, and the bulge being Callum's department.

That Vampire's eyes narrowed, and then they went for an up-and-down travel. When they stayed at Callum's hips, he felt like someone had started a hot shower over his own head.

Looked like a candy striper uniform might be in his future after all.

And under the theory that it was better to apologize than to ask for permission, he walked forward, passing by the jackets that were hung on pegs, the extra supplies and weapons, the snow boots and the gas cans.

In the back of his mind, a familiar internal warning bell went off, but he ignored it.

It was beyond time to move on, he told himself.

When he came up to where the flooring switched to white tile, That Vampire turned back to the spray and pushed his hands through his short dark hair, sloughing the water off his head. As he arched back, his shoulders flared and his ass tightened—and Callum decided that, Gray Wolf's presence up on the mountain aside, there absolutely, positively was a god.

And then the male turned around. The pivot was slow, and what swung to face Callum was the kind of thing that was worth getting sore knees for.

That Vampire's erection was a dumb handle that needed a good handshake, and far be it from Callum not to properly introduce himself.

"How did you know I was here," the vampire demanded.

And people thought romance was dead, Callum thought dryly.

"Where else were you going to be."

"I didn't come here because of you."

"I don't mind being your last option." He pulled his shirt out of his waistband. "As long as you don't mind being mine."

One by one, he undid the buttons starting at the bottom, splitting his heavy, long-sleeved flannel shirt up the center, exposing his abdominals, his pecs . . . his throat, because they were supposed to like that, right?

And hey, the fact that it was a vampire was going to make this much easier. Yeah. This was the way it had to happen. The only way it was going to happen.

Callum let his shirt fall to the ground, and he inhaled sharply as that hard, aggressive stare went over his upper body. When his hands went to his fly, he paused.

"You know what," he murmured, "I think I'll let you do this part. With those fangs of yours."

Stepping onto the tile, he had his boots on and didn't care. He didn't care about anything—until he glanced up at the showerhead. For a split second, he lost his connection to the sexual charge, images he had worked hard not to see every waking minute taking over.

"I'm not going to beg you for it."

The deep, tension-filled voice refocused him. And even still, he had to clear his throat. "Fine. The begging can come later."

Pushing aside everything but the vampire who was currently under the water, Callum stepped into the spray, and the second the other male's powerful body shuddered, he knew he was doing the right thing—for the both of them. And then he touched the slick, smooth chest, running his hands down from the collarbones to the pecs . . . to the abs. The rain sounds of the water got very loud as he did it again, feeling the muscles, the warmth, the skin.

"What do you like, vampire?"

When there was no answer, he glanced up to that face. The male was staring down at Callum's fingertips as they traveled over his body, and the expression on his face was one of . . . wonder.

As if this was a revelation.

Except that couldn't be true.

Closing the distance between them, Callum tilted his head and put his mouth to the side of the vampire's throat. His reward was another shudder, and he took that as a green light. He kissed the collarbone, running his canines over the curl of bone. Then he sank into his thighs and nuzzled the sternum. The water that fell on the vampire tasted of the male and he licked at the droplets, catching them on his tongue, swallowing.

He glanced up to make sure he wasn't misreading anything.

Nope. They'd both opened this book to the same page.

The eyes that were always so aggressive were open wide, the vulnerability in them the kind of thing that no doubt revealed more than the male would have wanted—except he was so caught up in what was going on that his defenses were down.

More with the descent of his mouth, until Callum was at the hip bones, the graceful arch of the male's pelvis accentuated by a flare of muscle . . . that, when he followed it, brought him right where he wanted to go.

And yet he took his time, his lips drifting slowly to his destination as he got onto his knees. Well, what do you know. He was the perfect height.

Stretching his arms around the male, he stroked the ass he had admired. Then cupped it—and opened his mouth wide.

As he sucked that erection down, the response was violent, the vampire bucking into a thrust that pushed his arousal even deeper into Callum . . . whose lips stretched to accommodate the girth. And the withdrawal was just as immediate, the pelvis jerking back, the suction making the male moan and thrust again.

All Callum had to do was hang on and catch a breath when he could.

The pumping went from slow to fast, and when he looked up as the vampire looked down, their eye contact was a huge part of the out-of-control.

It went without saying that things didn't take long.

As the male got closer and closer to a release, he lost the ability to keep those burning eyes of his open, and then the orgasm tackled him. With a powerful arch, he reached up and back, grabbing on to the showerhead, holding tightly as his cock released into Callum's mouth, the hard length kicking and contracting, spilling a heavy load, as if it had been a long, long time since any pleasure had been had—

Callum froze as he focused on the way those hands gripped the stainless-steel fixture mounted into the tile.

The break with the here and now was a body blow, and he tried to close his own eyes so he could keep connected to this present that he was enjoying so very much. But he couldn't maintain the link. As he swallowed, and swallowed again, he was numb as he looked at that grip.

The water hitting his face took care of his tears.

Good thing, too.

The vampire wasn't the only one with things to hide.

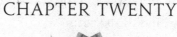

CHAPTER TWENTY

H ere. Have an apple slice."

Sometimes, all you could do for someone was the simplest thing, either because that was all you had to give or that was all they could afford to take. And as Kane sat back down on the sofa, he held a piece of a bright red apple out to Nadya, wishing he could take his question back. Her past was not something she owed him.

"No, thank you," she said.

He wasn't surprised when she didn't take what he offered. On his side, he was both hungry and nauseated, a one/two punch to the gut that should have been incompatible. Maybe eating something would help. Probably not.

Putting the section into his own mouth, he switched the paring knife back to his dominant hand and cleaved off another wedge. As he chewed the crisp, sweet flesh, the silence in the living quarters was as heavy as a solid object, and he wondered if—

"It was an arranged mating," she said roughly.

He'd intended to play it cool if she spoke. He failed at that miserably. His head shot up and around so quickly he felt the strain in his neck.

She cleared her throat. "I come from nothing, and his family—they were more prosperous than we were so it was a step up for me and my parents. Or it was supposed to have been." She shook her head, her unusually colored eyes focused on the mid-distance in front of her. "He never let me forget that, either. He was a male on the rise, he used to say. He was really going places. I was supposed to be grateful, go along for the ride, and keep my mouth shut."

Kane knew versions of this story very well, and he thought of his aunt. He thought of Cordelhia. He thought of his own parents' beliefs. Nadya might not have been in the *glymera*, but the fundamentals were the same, females leveraged as assets to bolster a family's fortunes, real and imagined.

"No one asked me what I thought or what I wanted." She looked at him directly. "My *mahmen* and sire were not bad people. They did honestly believe they were doing the right thing, and I went along with it even though I was screaming inside because their expectations became my priorities. The male did not love me. I did not love him. And in the back of my mind, I wondered what exactly he was getting out of it. I was not a beauty of note and we had no money. Why would he bother?"

There was a pause. "But I was not supposed to find out the basis of it all. That was supposed to be a secret."

Kane sliced another piece off the red apple, and he was surprised as she reached forward and took it directly from the blade. There was a cracking sound as she bit into what he had cleaved off the whole— and he was struck by an urgent need to feed her everything in that refrigerator.

He wanted to hunt for her. Provide for her. Fill her belly and have her take from his vein—

"This is good," she said. And as he just stared at her, she held up what was left of the slice, like she thought she'd confused him. "The apple?"

"There's another." He pointed to the icebox with the knife. "If you want more after we finish this."

Preparing another slice, he offered it, hoping she would take it as well. Instead, she sat there and stared at what she had bitten into, the semicircles of her teeth a pattern through the sweet flesh.

She continued in a steady voice, as if she were girding her courage to get through the story. "It turned out my father knew that my intended's sire had been having an affair. That was not unusual, but the assignation was with another male. I believe the term is blackmail? So, yes, my mating was arranged, and there is, built into that concept, a certain lack of free will. In my case, however, there was straight-out coercion to get the *hellren* to show up."

Kane shook his head. "How did you find out?"

Nadya put the rest of the slice in her mouth. "I overheard my father arguing with my intended's sire. It was right before the ceremony. My intended had disappeared the previous night, and his sire was making excuses for the delay in his son's appearance. But my father . . . well, he was determined his daughter was going to make a good match and he went through his scheming all over again." She shook her head once more. "I heard the whole thing . . . how my father, who was a builder, went to get his tools at the detached garage he'd been working on and saw the sire together with the male. My dad had been prepared to go to the young male's bloodline, and he was sure he'd be believed because he was an honest male of worth who had a reputation for fair and upright dealing. He told the sire that no one was going to be surprised, but everybody was going to talk about it, and that the male's *shellan* would surely leave him.

"And that was when I realized that my father hated the male for his infidelity. In addition to giving our family a leg up by association, the mating was a punishment because every time the sire saw me, he would think about what he did—and there would be no way of avoiding me. I was due to move in with their family." She took a deep breath. "I wasn't a blessing, I was a curse on both my prospective mate and the sire. The former was being forced, the latter was being coerced."

You aren't a curse, he thought. *Not at all.*

"What happened next?" He held out another slice. "Did your in-tended show up?"

Kane was relieved when she accepted the piece.

"Not that night, no." She shifted herself around. "But he came and found me a week later. I don't know if he'd learned the truth about why the mating was happening or whether he decided he was just going to get out of the arrangement any way he could."

"What did he do," Kane said—and mostly kept the growl out of his voice.

"I, ah . . . it was in the nineteen eighties. I was volunteering at a human library because I had access to all those books about medicine I couldn't afford to buy. I'd always wanted to be a nurse, you see, and I just wanted to learn. I was in charge of the last shift, and that meant I did the sweep of all the floors and locked up everything at midnight. I al-ways left through the back door because I could dematerialize out of the shadows from there and he knew that. He was waiting for me."

Kane closed his eyes. "What happened."

"As I locked the dead bolt, I turned around and he stepped out next to me. I was so surprised to see him, I just froze. And that meant, when he threw the acid at me, he had good aim—"

"God*damn* it—"

"—and it was as I put my hands up to my face and started to scream . . . that he threw the salt at me."

Which was why the scarring was permanent, Kane thought grimly. Vampires could heal back to their original state under most circum-stances, provided that they were otherwise healthy and well-fed, and that the injuries were not as severe as his burns had been. Surgical scars, puncture wounds, gunshots . . . all of it could regenerate.

Unless there was salt involved. Salt sealed up the imperfections, making them permanent.

"I tried to get away from him." Nadya made rolling motions with her arms like she was panicked and off-balance. "I was up on a set of steps. I couldn't see, I was in pain, I was worried that he had more acid.

I spun around and fell. I broke my leg when I landed and I've never screamed so loud in my life. I was just ... screaming."

Nadya sat there for the longest time, shaking her head, lost in the attack. "I clearly remember him standing over me. He was ... shocked. But what did he think was going to happen? And then my father showed up. I wasn't allowed to drive a car because I was a female, and my father always dropped me off and picked me up at the library. And it was as I was lying there that I realized I was the message back to my father. My injuries ... were the message back to him that he shouldn't have tried to force the sire and the son like that. Anyway, that's the story, and that's how I ended up in the prison camp."

"Wait—what? Why were you blamed and sentenced for what he did?" Kane sat forward, like there was someone in the underground hideout he could take the injustice to. "How does that make any sense—"

"No, it wasn't like that. My father immediately took me to a nurse who was of the species. My injuries were so severe, I had to stay with her, and she attended to me as if I were her own. As I got better, she started teaching me about taking care of patients. She was very kind to me, very generous with her knowledge. She was just starting her decline of old age, and I know that she was happy to have someone to pass on what she had learned over a lifetime."

"But where were your parents?"

She shook her head sharply. Then had to clear her throat. "I made the nurse tell them I had died. That I couldn't handle the pain and that I took myself out unto the sunlight and there was nothing left of me."

Kane lowered his head. "Oh, Nadya—"

"It was better than them having to see me all the time. My father was consumed with guilt and regret, weeping at my bedside. It seemed kind of ironic that I became the curse for him as opposed to the sire of my intended. I just knew, if I went home, he'd never be able to move on and neither would my *mahmen*. At least if I were dead, they could grieve and find some kind of a new life."

Kane couldn't imagine any part of the situation she'd been put in. "And where did you go after you were with the nurse? I still don't know how you ended up in the camp."

"After I was as healed as I was going to get, I continued to stay with my mentor, but I kept hidden from everyone. Around the time I developed some stamina, she started going to the prison camp to treat the sick and injured. I wanted to go there with her because I needed to do something to be of use to someone. I always went draped, of course, and it became something we did together. It saved me, the purpose I found therein." There was a silence. And then she accepted another apple slice from him. "Under her instruction, I took care of so many different males and females, and I got to be a really good nurse. When my mentor finally went unto the Fade, I assumed all her duties, and as her house was left unto her relations and I had nowhere to go, I began to stay in the camp."

"Where is the male who hurt you?" As Kane heard the hard tone of his own voice, he tacked on, "I mean, is he anywhere in Caldwell?"

Do you have an exact address? he thought.

"Well, there was this one prisoner . . . who was so kind to me."

A spear of jealousy made Kane imagine going after two different males, and given his aggression, he wasn't surprised she ducked the question about her intended.

"And . . . ?" he prompted.

"It was about ten years ago." She folded and refolded her brown robing in her lap. "He was dying and I helped ease his suffering as best I could. He was old, but had once been so vital. We got quite close, and perhaps because I was missing my family, or lonely, or whatever, I told him what had happened to me. I told him everything. He's the only other one who saw what I look like . . . aside from now you."

As she fell silent, he absorbed the honor she had paid him, to remove her hood, to share of herself in the most vulnerable way.

Nadya looked at him sharply. "I need to be honest with you, even though it will affect what you think of me."

"Nothing could affect—"

"Allow me to rephrase that. It *should* affect what you think of me."

He glanced around, measuring the clean and tidy space, with its comfortable furniture and its kitchen and its little bathroom. Even though they were out of the prison camp, he felt as though they had returned to its confines once again, to the point where he could smell the stink of the place, the dirt and the filth and the old sweat remerging in his sinuses.

But that was the power of the camp, wasn't it. Even free, neither of them had been truly liberated because of what they had seen . . . and what they had done.

"Keep going," he murmured. "Please."

"I used my intended's name." She shrugged. "It was just in relation to my story. Or at least I told myself that. But if I'm honest? I think I knew who the old male was . . . and what he might do if he ever got a hold of my intended."

"You said the older male was dying, though. Surely he couldn't have *ahvenged* you?"

"He went unto the Fade soon thereafter and I thought that was all." She took a deep breath. "But about five or six nights later, I returned to my berth, the place where I slept. There was a . . . I found a knot of cloth on my pillow."

Kane waited for her to continue. When she didn't, he said, "What was in it?"

"A signet ring. My intended's." She seemed to hang her head. "The old male? I had heard he was . . . how do you say it, an enforcer? And it's hard for me to admit this, but yes, I knew he had contacts outside of the prison. I mean, the guards themselves deferred to him, and brought him things. He told me once that I was like a daughter to him."

"You're not responsible for that male's choices."

"I believe I am, actually." Her hand hovered over her chest. "My heart was unclean when I told the story. I embellished nothing, but . . . I did give my intended's name. I had learned to hate him, you see. Over the years. He had decided to destroy my face so that he would not be judged for not following through on the arrangement and so my father would be punished for the blackmail. I mean, if we had been aristocrats? My father would have ended up in the prison for what he did, but because of our station as civilians, my intended took matters into his own hands, with no consequences except the ones I bore."

"You don't know what actually happened with the ring."

"You think my former intended, who I hadn't seen for ten years, who no doubt had heard I was dead, infiltrated the prison camp, found my berth among all those tunnels, and left his ring there? His single most precious possession, the gold ring that was his grandfather's?"

Kane rubbed his face. "I don't know."

"Yes, you do. You just do not want to see me for what I am."

"Don't tell me how I feel, okay? That's my job."

She looked down at her hands. "You need to take me back there."

"*What?*"

"To the camp." With a shaking hand, she touched the scars that ran down her face. "I live there."

Kane blinked. And then couldn't find the words. "You can't be serious," he blurted.

"That is my home, my purpose." When Kane just stared at her, she made a move to get up—and promptly waved him off when he leaned in to help her. "What did you think was going to happen once you 'rescued' me. I have nowhere to go."

"Your parents—"

"Are dead. They were killed in the raids about three years ago. My father had taken work at one of the grand houses of the aristocracy as a handyman. My mother joined him as a maid. The *lessers* . . . attacked the estate and my parents were locked out of a safe room by the family. They were . . . slaughtered."

Kane closed his eyes. "I am so sorry, Nadya."

"I found out because . . . I overheard some of the males who were doing the drug deals down in Caldwell talking about the raids. They mentioned specific houses and I knew where my sire and *mahmen* had gone to work because, back when I was living with the nurse, I would return to their house to check on them from afar. When they moved out, the new family in our home gave me their forwarding address. That's how I found out the name of the mansion. That's how I recognized the name when I heard the males say it."

Her voice cracked at the end. And then she lowered her hands into her lap.

"I am grateful for what you did for me. But I will go back to the prison camp because that is all I have."

Kane cursed. Because he didn't know what else to do.

Then he sat forward on the sofa. "Look at me. Nadya. Look up, at me."

When her focus shifted to him, he braced his palms on his knees. "You were about to be killed. When I found you? You were mounted on that wall like a piece of meat, and they were going to kill you. If you want to fall on the sword of your guilt, or whatever it is? That's your business. I'll take you back myself. But you'll be dead before I'm off the property."

She blinked. A number of times.

As tears came to her eyes, he cursed again and got up to walk away, but where was he going? When he found himself standing over the sink, he ran some water and splashed his face a couple of times. There was a roll of soft paper by the basin, and he dried himself off.

Then he pivoted around and leaned back against the counter. He tried to imagine taking her back to that abandoned human hospital, with its underground cruelties and its drug dealing and all those guards.

He'd thought she wouldn't last without protection before. Now she was on the guards' list of things to do. He might as well drive her up to the Fade and drop her off in front of that white door.

"Why do you care so much," she asked.

It was on the tip of his tongue to say that he didn't know, he really didn't.

Instead, the truth jumped out of his mouth: "I couldn't save my *shellan*. I guess I've decided to try to save you."

CHAPTER TWENTY-ONE

The following evening, after night had fallen, V was in the Pit, sitting in front of his Four Toys and playing with his mouse. Which was not as sexy as it sounded. His dick's nickname had nothing to do with any of the thirty-eight or more species in the genus *Mus*, so, yes, he was actually moving his wireless palm puck around in circles.

"You coming to First Meal?"

His roommate was talking as he came down the hallway from where the bedrooms were, and as Butch stepped into the living room, the former homicide detective was dressed for the field. Instead of as someone from the cast of *Bridgerton*.

Fucker might have had a narrow wardrobe when he'd been human, but he'd been making up for the deficit ever since. He had more clothes than the Metropolitan Museum had art. Unfortunately, most were in the hallway that led down to their cribs. Every time V had to leave his and Doc Jane's room, he felt like he was in the last thirty feet of a car wash. The fact that he hadn't taken a flamethrower to the threads proved how much he loved the guy.

"Hello?" Butch said. "You in there?"

"I think we need to start at the beginning."

The cop's brows popped up over his baby hazels. "Well, considering that involved Fritz asking you all to kill me out behind the house because he didn't want to bloody his rugs—I mean, do we *have* to go back there?"

"Har-har."

V watched his arrow make the perimeter around the Firefox window he'd opened to the *Caldwell Courier Journal*'s website. Then he switched over to his Microsoft Outlook. "Why the hell is there so much spam. I spend my fucking life sending things to my junk folder—and every fucking night, it's a new crop dusting. Like I've ever ordered anything from Wayfair?"

"Oh, that was me."

"I beg your pardon?"

"Shoe sorter. You know the ones you hang on the backs of closet doors?"

V sat deeper into his chair. "You already have one of those."

"I'm going to hang the new one on the wall. Like it's art."

"Jesus."

Butch made the sign of the cross and went over to the leather sofa. "So, what are we going back to the beginning on."

"Finding the prison camp. We need to follow the drugs again. That's the income source for the place, and no matter where they are or who is in charge, they will keep that business going. Even if they change the packaging, we'll be able to track them down somehow."

"Did Wrath outlaw the camp?"

"Saxton's still working on it. He's dotting t's, crossing i's."

"Isn't that the other way around?"

"And you think I struggle with a sense of humor."

Butch rolled his eyes. "Well, I do think you're right—not about the alphabet, though. The drugs are all we've got, so let's head out into the field now. Marissa's already at Safe Place working, and I heard Doc Jane leave earlier—she's at the clinic, yeah? We can skip First Meal, grab some Arby's, and go."

V shook his head in awe. "You complete me."

"I know. And I had you at Arby's—although that shit has to level up to get to Taco Bell's gastric distress standard. I'll never understand why you eat it."

"Old habits die hard." He clicked out of his email, grabbed his phone and texted Tohr. "I'll let the boys know what we're doing."

"I'll weapon up."

Butch disappeared back down his hall of fancy-dancies, and it was hard not to thank—well, not the Scribe Virgin because she wasn't around anymore, and V sure as shit wasn't going to be grateful to Lassiter for anything other than that fallen angel moving out of the mansion . . .

Fine, he'd just thank the Creator for having that male in his life.

With that thought, V stood up and began gathering some hand-rolleds and—

With a frown, he leaned down to the monitor. The *Caldwell Courier Journal's* website was a subscription service he disdainfully paid six bucks a month for, and he'd been trying to figure out how to cancel the goddamn thing. For all his IQ, he couldn't remember the email address he'd used to create the account eight years ago, or what credit card he'd put in, and with the password lost inside his computer somewhere, it was just too fucking much work to either break into the stupid site itself and cut the vampire charge or go into the weeds of his absolutely-not-an-Apple tower to track the account shit down.

Plus all he really read the thing for was the relationship advice column—not because he cared about the stupid crap the humans wrote in about, but because he enjoyed crafting responses in his head that were considerably more direct.

But as he bent over and reread the *CCJ's* splash page, for once he wasn't focusing on the annoying monthly bill or the Ann Landers stuff.

He was looking at an article about that break-in he'd seen on the news when he'd been with the Jackal in the training center's cafeteria.

"You ready?" Butch asked.

"Hold on a sec." V scrolled up and did a full start-to-finish on the reporting. "It was a pharmacy."

"I'm sorry?"

As his roommate came over, he pointed to his screen. "Last night, upstate, someone broke into a pharmacy in Leczo Falls, New York. Ransacked the place."

"Yeah, and? They were probably looking for oxys or something."

"They took more than that, though."

"So they wanted some Mountain Dew and a bag of Doritos along with their federal felony charges. Mmmm, tasty."

When V just stared at the website, like he was somehow going to pull out extra details from between the glowing lines of typey-typey, Butch put a hand on his shoulder.

"Are we going to Leczo Falls, by any chance?" his roommate asked. "Maybe you'll tell me why?"

V glanced at the brother. "If you were running a prison camp, and you had just moved it how many miles away? Wouldn't there be casualties you'd need to treat? Or what if there was an escape and the wrong people got hurt? You'd need medicine."

"But how do you know what they stole?"

"It's all here. Bandages, tape, surgical gloves . . . that's not just oxys." V pointed to the lines in the article and shook his head. "Little town upstate. Not many prying eyes, lots of land and privacy, but it's next to an exit on the Northway for transporting product. Come, it's not that farfetched—and even if they didn't steal from the town they're in, they'll be somewhere close."

Butch shrugged. "Well, it can't hurt to head up there. God knows we have nothing else to go on, and the drugs will always be waiting for us in Caldwell."

"You got that right," V muttered as he grabbed his holster off the floor to arm himself.

"Only problem is it'll take forty-five minutes to drive there. You need backup."

"No, I don't—"

"What if you find the prison camp." Butch shook his head. "Sorry, but safety first, and I'll tell on you if you don't take someone else."

"What are you, five? And since when have you become Tohr." When the brother just stared back at him, V rolled his eyes. "Fine. And I know who I can ask."

As he took out his Samsung again and sent a text, the former cop cleared his throat. "Can I ask you something?"

"No, I don't know why Lassiter is still hanging around when he could be cooling his jets in my *mahmen*'s Sanctuary." As the response V wanted came back on his phone, he strapped his weapons belt around his waist. "Come to think of it, maybe I need to install a TV up there."

"That wasn't the question."

V reached down for his leather jacket, picking up the dead weight with his gloved hand. "I also can't comment on Rhage's calorie count. Simple mathematics states infinity has no limits, but he tests those boundaries on the regular—"

"Why is finding this prison camp so important to you?" Butch put both palms out, all calm-down-hothead. "I'm fine with it. Whatever you want to do is good and I've always got your six. But you're pushing hard on this."

V pulled his jacket on and went through his pat-down ritual. Ammo, check. Lighter, check. Hunting knife, check. Daggers—

Shit. He'd forgotten his dagger holster.

He took off the jacket and let it fall to his chair, the thing landing in a series of dull thuds as the poke-and-tickle of weapons inside of it settled. Reaching down for the black-bladed weapons he had made himself, he pulled the straps of their mounting onto his shoulders and around under his arms. The securing of the holster was such second nature that he didn't have to look down. He could stare into his room-mate's eyes while he tightened it properly.

"I grew up in the war camp," he heard himself say. "I didn't choose to be there. It was a fucking horrible place. If what the Jackal's told us is true—that a lot of those prisoners were tossed in prison because the aristocracy wanted them out of the way for their own goddamn reasons? Then that's bullshit and we need to get the ones that aren't criminals out."

His roommate nodded. "Fair enough."

V glanced back at his screens.

"That's the point," he murmured as he pulled his jacket back on. "It hasn't been fucking fair, and what the hell good are we if we can't fix shit that's wrong."

As he headed for the exit, Butch chuckled. "Look at you, caring about your fellow man. Vampire. Whatever."

"Don't get it twisted." V held open the way out. "I still think people are stupid."

"Oh, good." Butch stepped through into the night. "Otherwise, I'd mistake this for an episode of *Black Mirror*."

CHAPTER TWENTY-TWO

Down under the decaying hunting cabin, Kane spent the daylight hours sitting on the floor, propped up against the wall, within view of the bed behind the sofa. With that couch functioning as a footboard, he couldn't see much of Nadya as she slept, but going by her breathing patterns, he figured she must have gotten at least a little rest.

There had been no shut-eye for him, and the weird thing was, he didn't feel tired. That buzzing under his skin, that seething, churning energy, was a constant, banked for now, but ready and hungry for . . . anything, really.

It was a reminder of how long it had been since he had had any level of health.

And he remembered the moment he lost it.

Putting his hand out, he looked at his palm, went back in time, and recalled pouring that drink at the libation cart in his study. Thinking back on it now, he couldn't recall whether the sherry had tasted off. He'd been so consumed by Cordelhia's impending needing, those hormones of hers calling a response in him that grew ever more distracting, that he hadn't paid any attention to what had rolled over his tongue.

But it clearly had been poisoned.

He'd had that first glass.

Followed by the other.

After that . . .

Wincing, he rubbed his eyes as if he could wipe away the image of his Cordelhia up on that bed, her blood dripping off her lax hand, pooling on the floor. He'd had the same vantage point then as he did now, looking up to see the dead body.

And then he'd heard that scream.

Cordelhia's *mahmen* in her fine silk-and-fur overcoat, standing in the open doorway of the chamber, screaming in horror—

◆ ◆ ◆

"You have killed my daughter! My daughter is dead!"

Kane tried to get up from the floor. But as he pushed his palms into the finely woven carpet, his arms refused the burden of his torso and he slapped back down onto his face.

When he turned his head to the side . . . he saw the bloody knife in his hand.

His first thought was that it was not his hand. Then he thought it was not his blade.

And finally, he realized it was not a knife at all.

It was his letter opener, the one from his desk down in the study, the one made of sterling silver, which bore the crest of his bloodline . . . the one he'd been given after he'd survived his transition by his sire.

The dagger-shaped object had been missing for a couple of nights.

And now, it was back, and his hand was upon the bloody length, his fingers wrapped around the miniature sword's hilt.

In the back of his mind, he noted that his beloved's mahmen was still screaming, but he was trying to remember how any of this had come to pass—and grappling with the reality that if the female in that formal cloak and dress had thought there was any sign of life in her progeny, she would not be yelling incomprehensible things at him, but rather calling for help from the staff—

A male was shouting now, and in Kane's delirium, he thought for a moment it was he himself. But no, someone else was in the doorway, and they were drawing the mahmen back, turning her face into his shoulder.

Cordelhia's brother shifted their mahmen out of view, and then he came in and grabbed Kane, dragging him off the floor. The blows came from every direction, pummeling his head and chest, and then he was thrust across the room. His lack of coordination meant that the momentum carried him onward, his weight pitching headfirst, his feet failing to keep up. His shellan's dressing bureau stopped him, and he caught his reflection in the mirror stand for a split second before the impact of his body wiped everything off its surface.

Crashing, now, but the sound was distilled through the cotton wool that his head felt packed in.

"You killed her!"

Kane was yanked back to his feet. And as he looked to the bed, he couldn't breathe. The blood . . . was everywhere.

"Cordelhia—"

Her brother's face thrust into his own. "Do not ever utter her name again. Ever!"

The slap came from the right, and the contact of the hard palm on his face was so violent, he spun around, or mayhap the room was spinning, he did not know. As his balance left him, he hit the wall across from the bed, the oil painting of his female's favorite wee terrier falling from its mount.

Kane's knees went out from under him and he sank down to the floor. "I did not kill her! It was not me!"

Cordelhia's brother snatched something off the needlepoint rug, and as the male lunged forward, the sterling silver blade of the envelope opener caught the lantern light, flashing with a wink.

Kane rolled onto his back and presented the front of his throat. "Kill me! Kill me now! I do not want to live without her—"

The words stopped the other male, and there was a moment of suspended time. Then his female's brother fell to his knees. He was panting, his chest pumping beneath his finely tailored clothing, his flushed face a horrible facsimile of what it normally appeared to be.

The letter opener trembled in his hand. But it steadied as he raised the tiny sword over his shoulder, the arc of its sharp point angled so that it would pierce Kane through the center of the chest.

"Kill me," Kane moaned as he tore his shirt asunder. "Kill—"

"No!" Abruptly, the other male leaned forward and made a fist. "No! You will live with what you have done, Kanemille, son of Ulyss the Elder."

Her brother slashed his arm down and the blow to the head finished what the delirium had started. Kane lost consciousness, his final awareness the scent of his tears mingling with the copper bloom of her blood and the . . .

. . . smell of the earth.

No, that couldn't be right.

Firstly, he surely must be dead, so why would he be smelling aught? And secondly, if he were alive, he would be at his home, so why would he be smelling dirt if he were in Cordelhia's bedding chamber?

And there were other things in the air: A wretched rotting stink. Mold. Old fabric. His own blood. Verily, he was no longer at his estate.

Unable to assess his surroundings, he performed an accounting of himself: His mind remained sluggish, his hearing was phasing in and out, and his eyes refused to open. Farther down, his belly was both sour and empty, but he could not worry about that—

"Aye, yer in rough shape."

The voice was close by, and as the words registered, he was unsure who was talking. He had a thought he should lift his lids, but his head was pounding and his face felt swollen—therefore, he did not believe it was possible.

"I beg your pardon?" he mumbled.

"Ah, so yer a posh one. I fig'd by the looks of yer—and who dropped yer off." There was a shuffling, as if someone was moving around on packed earth. "Yer'll be needin' to take cover, gov'ner."

With sloppy thoughts, he attempted to remember what had happened after Cordelhia's brother had struck him that last time. He had the sense that there had been a passage of hours. Perhaps even a day and night cycle.

"Where am I?" he asked.

When there was no answer, he tried again to open his eyes. And when he was unable, he had a thought that he would lift up one of his hands—but alas, his arms did not seem to be of function.

"Yer in the prison camp. Yer were dropped here at dawn yest. Yer cannae stay here. There be people yer needing to stay away from."

Prison camp? Wherever was that?

"Yer best be moving, gov'ner. Yer caught here, they'll be takin' yer to the Hive. Yer be an exemplification."

He had to get out of here, Kane thought. He had to find whoe'er was in charge, and explain his situation, and tell whoe'er would release him that he was being held under false pretenses. Then surely they would return him unto his freedom and he could set about speaking properly with Cordelhia's bloodline. After all, he had a funeral to prepare, and there were doggen and servants to settle.

And a murderer to find.

Someone had planned the death. They'd removed his envelope opener from his desk—and chosen it with purpose as something, in a house full of items and art that had been gifted unto him, identified as his own possession. Then they had put some kind of substance into his sherry, in the decanter from which he, and he alone, partook. And just before he had collapsed—

The sound. Outside the study.

Somebody had come unto his study's window, as if they had been waiting for him to drink and be o'ertaken by whate'er had been mixed into the sherry.

And then he had fallen to the floor and seen the boots.

After which, he had woken up in Cordelhia's bedchamber.

The image of his mate having bled out on the bed ushered in a wave of pain that broke through his numb confusion, and as he breathed in, he smelled her blood again and recalled the scent of her fertile time. How had this happened? Just a fortnight before, he had come home to find her and the doggen celebrating the anniversary of his birth. And now she was dead and he was . . .

"Are you awake?"

The stranger's voice was a bit more urgent now, and Kane found it difficult to ascertain whether it was male or female. At first, it had been male, it seemed, but now there was a female lilt to the syllables. A rather different accent as well.

How had his life come to this—

"You're moaning. Are you hurt?"

"Yes," Kane said. "My mate is dead. And I did not kill her—they put me in the prison, and I did not—"

"Kane?"

How did the prisoner know his—

✦   ✦   ✦

Kane came back to the present with a full-body jerk, the shock of reorientation such that for a moment he had no idea where he was. He knew it wasn't the chamber of his murdered *shellan*, and he knew it wasn't the prison camp, but other than that—

"Kane."

His head snapped up. On the far side of a sofa, on a bed that was quite wide, a draping of blankets appeared to be speaking to him—

"Nadya?"

As her name came out of him, all was set to rights: The escape of the night before. The hut with the silver-haired female. The viper . . .

He frowned and tilted his head. Between one heartbeat and the next, an image came to him, bubbling up from the amnesia that had locked the memories of the night before out of his reach.

"Viper," he whispered.

"What did you say?"

Just as quickly as it came to him, the memory was lost. Like a curtain closing, whatever glimpse he had been offered zippered itself tight, no more to be seen, no more information available.

To the point where he couldn't even remember what he'd spoken.

"Sorry," he said as he rubbed his face. "I'm . . . so sorry."

As he muttered to himself, he had no idea what he was apologizing for. And then something dawned on him.

He was free.

He could find out who had killed Cordelhia.

The mystery could finally be solved.

With that realization hitting him, a lethargy claimed his body and mind, sucking him down into a darkness that was so complete, he wasn't just sleeping . . . he was owned by the void.

CHAPTER TWENTY-THREE

From over on the bed, Nadya couldn't look away from Kane. He was sitting on the floor, his legs stretched out in front of him, his arms resting around his middle, his head tilted down with his chin on his chest. He had been talking under his breath, and with his half-closed eyes, she hadn't been sure whether he was awake or not.

When she'd said his name, he'd glanced at her, mumbled a word, and then apologized. But he hadn't been talking to her, not really, and now he was gone again—although she knew where he was in his head. She had heard the story before, while sitting at his bedside for all those hours at her clinic, his subconscious churning over events that would not, could not, be changed, no matter how many times he went through what had happened.

The death of his Cordelhia. The night that had derailed his life. The way he had ended up in the camp.

He'd said something else at the end now, though. A word she hadn't quite caught, and had never heard him say before in connection with his history.

And now he appeared to be fully asleep, his frown intense, but his breathing deep and even. Staring across at him, she still couldn't believe his appearance, and she finally had to look elsewhere because she felt as though she were invading his privacy because he was unaware of her focus.

Glancing around, she was astonished at how everything was so neat and quiet—in contrast to the prison camp, especially the former one that had been a rabbit warren carved out under the earth.

Then again, the difference was the safety, not the silence or cleanliness.

It had been so long since she had not slept with one eye open. Part of it was the security of this hidden place, but more of it was Kane. His presence was a declaration of protection, and though she had not expected to find any rest, she had even dreamed during the day—and not had nightmares for once. In fact, in her repose, she had been back as she had once been, with flowing hair, and limbs that worked, and a future ahead in the human library.

And Kane might just have walked up to her front desk with a book in his hand . . . and warmth in his eyes.

"Stop," she whispered.

Fantasies were not what she needed right now. What she needed was . . .

A real bathroom, with running water.

Yes, that was it.

Shifting around, she moved over the top of the bed to the far side, and gingerly put her bare feet down to the floor. The carpeting was soft, just like the bed had been, and both were a reminder of creature comforts, things she had taken for granted and then not known for what seemed like an eternity.

As always, she was careful settling her weight on her bad leg, giving the knee and ankle joints an opportunity to accept what she was requesting of them. When she was ready, she took the blanket she had slept on with her and limped across to the bathroom, shutting herself in. There was a tiny light plugged into a socket, the glow like a firefly mounted on the wall, and she was relieved she didn't have to turn on anything harsh.

For a moment, she just stood between the white porcelain sink and the shower stall, and when she had trouble connecting to where she was, she put a hand out in either direction, feeling the pattern on the frosted glass door and the cool smoothness of the basin.

Then she reached in and started the shower, used the toilet, and removed her robing. It was impossible not to look down at her knobby knees and her bony calves as she tested the water. The acid attack had only impacted her face, neck, and some of her upper body, but that broken leg of hers, which had healed so badly, was going to be an equal problem for the rest of her life.

As she considered her frailty, her mind took her back to when she'd been chained to the pegs on that stained wall, the guard cutting the hood off and then staring at her as if she were a carnival exhibit he was determined to get his money's worth of before the curtain closed.

Stepping into the shower, she shivered at the gentle fall on her skin, and for a moment, everything was too comfortable, too much as it had been before the acid attack—especially as she looked to the tiled wall and saw on a little shelf twin bottles of shampoo and conditioner. There was also a bar of soap still in its wrapper.

"Dial," the logo read.

Her hand shook as she reached out and opened the soap's folds of foiled paper. It was a small bar, an individual-use one, and it was orange as a mandarin. The smell was not pleasant, but nor was it offending to the senses.

Palming the bar, she created a froth by rolling the square over and over again under the water, and when there was a sufficiency, she took the suds to her face and her neck. The nerves in the skin that had been burned by the acid no longer functioned, and it had taken her time to get used to the one-sided nature of the sensations, only the ridges on her forehead, cheeks, and jaw registering on her hands, nothing else making any impression on her face.

The fragrance swelled as she continued to wash herself, including the top of her head and the straggled patches of hair. The shampoo and conditioner were just not warranted: She didn't have enough or in good enough shape to worry about that.

How had she let Kane see her like this, she wondered.

Finished with her ablutions, she turned to the spray and tilted her head back as far as it could go—which was not that far. And then, she had to get reasonable.

Kane was right.

If she went back to the prison, she was as good as dead. That head of the guards was going to get her pound of flesh for that guard Nadya had killed, and it was going to be a very painful death. And if she died at the hands of that female? She was making a mockery of the risks Kane had taken to come back for her.

But she had not lied when she'd told him she would go back because she had nowhere else to go. The prison camp was a terrible place, but she had a routine there. She knew what she had to worry about, what she should be scared of, and where to go if she was in danger. And sometimes comfort could be found in the predictability of the unpleasant. It was easier than evolving past her grief and anger, for sure, and besides, she had been out of the human-dominated world now for forty years. Things were going to be very different than she remembered.

She wasn't sure whether she had the energy to assimilate into all the modernity.

Where would she go, though?

Turning off the shower, she stepped out and debated whether to use the towel that was hanging on a rod mounted by the sink. The white terrycloth length was folded perfectly, and she didn't feel as though her body deserved the disturbance of its careful arrangement.

As she turned to the sink, she discovered that even though she'd been preoccupied as she'd entered the bathroom, she had nonetheless placed the lid down on the toilet and precisely folded her robing, her loose tunic, her underthings, and her leggings upon it.

None of it was clean, and as she lifted the tunic, the whiff of the prison camp lingered in the cloth like a stain.

Unable to bear the smell, she wrapped herself in the blanket and stood over what she had worn, wondering where she could find replacements. The fact that she had no options for something as basic as clothing was chilling, and she felt the pull to return to what she knew, the delusion that she could somehow hide herself amid the more structured arrangement of the new prison camp a tantalizing lie.

"You are a coward," she said.

Riding that condemnation, she gathered everything she had to her name, and carried the small pile over to the door.

When she opened things, Kane was sitting on the couch at the foot of the bed. He had his head propped up on his fist, his elbow on the arm of the sofa, his body in a relaxed arrangement that belied the strength he had somehow gathered within his previously injured flesh.

He looked up. "Hi."

"Hi." She indicated the bathroom behind her. "They have soap and hot water."

"That wolven is a good host."

"He is."

She glanced around and intended to make a comment. Instead, she fell silent.

"It's after sunset," he said. "The wolven is coming back here soon. That's what he told us."

"Then you should wait for him, yes." Nadya held her clothes even tighter. "And I . . . well, I don't know where I'm going, but you're right. It can't be back to the prison camp."

He exhaled in obvious relief. "Oh, blessed Virgin Scribe. Listen, you can come to the wolven clan's territory. Mayhem is still recovering there, and I'm sure they'll give you a place to rest and—"

"They're strangers who owe me nothing. I can't impose on them."

"Then where will you go."

"I'll figure something out." As she dropped her stare, she could feel his frown as if it were a gust of dissatisfaction. "I can take care of myself, you know."

"Nadya—"

"And you? Where will you go off to?"

As a wave of exhaustion crept up on her, she leaned against the doorjamb and thought back to the apple they'd shared sometime around dawn. She had to eat properly before she left—and then she realized that not only was she not very mobile, she had not been able to dematerialize since she'd been wounded.

Cursing herself, she detested the helplessness—

"When was the last time you fed?" Kane asked. Then he put up his hand. "Please . . . just answer the question. I don't think either of us has the energy for any more arguments."

✦   ✦   ✦

As Kane waited to see if she was going to answer him, it took everything he had to stay where he was on the couch. Over in the bathroom doorway, Nadya was looking as though she was ill from fatigue, and as he imagined her setting off in the dark, alone, unarmed and unable to protect herself, his stomach turned.

Which was why he'd asked her the intimate question.

"I'll eat before I go," she said. "I was just thinking that very thing, actually—"

"I'm not talking about food," he cut in darkly. "And I know you fed me back at the clinic."

When she looked over sharply, he nodded. "You opened your vein with your own fangs and put your wrist over my mouth. The taste of you was the first thing that I remember that wasn't pain. Come to think of it, it was the only thing that did not hurt me."

She lowered her eyes to the bundle of clothes that she was holding tightly to her chest. "I did not know you were aware."

"I'm only alive because you shared of yourself." He cleared his throat. "So will you let me replenish you?"

"You already saved my life." She fiddled with the blanket she'd wrapped around herself. "So your perceived debt to me has been repaid. We're even now."

"Well, if that's the logic you want to use, you have to allow me to repay the gift of your vein, too. It is only fair, do you not agree?"

In truth, fairness was the last thing on his mind. He was just flailing around for any argument that would get her to agree to feed from him. Vampires had been designed by the Scribe Virgin to require the blood of the opposite sex to maintain optimal health. Feeding was not an every-night kind of thing, but it had to be done on a regular basis, and going by her obvious exhaustion, it had been a very long time for her. Also, he was worried about her lack of resources and contacts. Her parents were gone. That nurse who had been her mentor, too. She was all alone.

So if not him, who? Although . . . when he even hypothetically considered her at another male's vein, that strange side of him, the one that had come to the fore when he'd been determined to rescue her, lit up with aggression.

To the point where he needed to get a hold of himself.

"Look, I would give you money," he said grimly, "but I have none myself. I would ask you to stay with me, but I have no home. I have no clothes, no shoes, to offer you. The only thing I can present to you is what you yourself gave me—and please, don't argue that you're not my responsibility. That's not the point."

At least not from the way she saw things.

As she fell silent, he studied her, and when her scars and her baldness registered, he thought of how much he wasn't aware of either. It wasn't that he didn't see her disfiguration and hated what it represented. It was that he saw through the damage.

Attraction was physical. Connection was soul to soul.

"I don't like to rely on others," she said softly. "I don't like to be in debt."

He frowned, wondering if there was something else she was worried about. And then he thought . . . well, of course: "It won't be sexual. I promise you."

She laughed in a short burst. "Oh, that I know. I would never think you'd . . . well, anyway."

"I mean, you can trust me."

"I've never doubted that either." After a beat of quiet, she lowered the bundle of clothes she'd held against her heart. "It has been forty years."

Kane blinked in confusion. "I'm sorry, what did you say?"

"I haven't fed since I was hurt."

Shaking his head, he leaned forward. "But that isn't possible."

"It's the truth. I'm very careful to conserve my energy, and besides, with my leg, I can't move very well. Ever since the acid attack, I've been kind of suspended, neither living nor dead. A ghost that wanders among the living, I guess. So it makes sense that I wouldn't require feeding."

"You're not a ghost." He roughly yanked up the sleeve of the shirt he'd taken off that guard at the camp. "Come over here. Use me and help my conscience—be my salve, by taking my vein, so that I know, as we go our separate ways, you're as strong as you can be."

He laid his forearm along his thigh and just stared at her.

Forever passed in the silence between them.

And then she slowly approached and put her clothes down on the opposite side of the couch. "I'll leave when it's dark enough."

Is that a "yes"? he wondered.

Except how was he going to leave her? They had spent so much time together back in her clinic, his suffering stretching the moments and minutes into years and decades. The idea that he would not see her after this, that she would go off, on her own, and he would never know how her life went, made him ache all over.

As Nadya sat down, he knew she was shaking, and he told himself to stay in the present.

This is a "yes," he thought.

"I am just so tired," she whispered.

"I can help." He moved his bare forearm closer to her. "Take from me. It'll make you feel better, I promise."

The blanket shifted as she lowered her head, and he hated how frail she was, how thin her shoulders were, how hollow her collarbones.

"It's going to be okay," he said. "I promise."

What the hell was coming out of his mouth, he wondered as he extended his arm so that it was in her lap.

But she didn't bite him.

With a tingle in his upper jaw, his fangs dropped down. It was clear he was going to have to get this going, and that was fine with him. Anything . . . for her.

Except just as he was going to score his own flesh, as she had done for him in her clinic, something hit the inside of his wrist, a droplet.

A tear.

"Oh, Nadya."

"We'll say goodbye after this." Her voice was firm as she wiped her eyes like she was clearing her emotions away, too. "We go our separate ways."

He cursed under his breath. "I don't know why that's so important to you—"

"Because I know what you're going to do now."

"Excuse me?"

She retucked the blanket a little tighter as she looked over at him. "I know what you're going to do as soon as we're finished. You're going to go and find out who killed Cordelhia."

A cold wash went throughout his body. Was it shock—or something else? "How, ah, how do you know about her?"

"You spoke of her in your delirium. So I'm very aware of what happened after you were drugged by that sherry . . . I know what you woke up to, and what happened next . . . I know everything you lost."

Kane cleared his throat. "I wasn't aware I was so verbal with all that."

She nodded. "You told the story over and over again. It was as if your mind was churning over the events, trying to create another outcome from the fact pattern. I've done this myself so I know what it's like, the obsessive rethinking, reimagining. It changes nothing, and yet you do it—"

"I didn't kill her."

"Oh, I know that." Her eyes were direct. "Unprovoked violence is not in your nature, not even with a stranger, and much less someone you love as much as you love her. That's why I need to go my own way, you see."

Kane shook his head. "No, I don't see. At all."

Nadya took a deep breath. Then she smiled in a stiff way, the false expression the kind of thing somebody does when they're attempting to camouflage a vulnerability with nonchalance. "I can't watch you *ahvenge* another, even though it is not only your right, but a sign of how much your *shellan* meant to you."

"You don't have to worry about my safety. I'm going to be careful."

"That's not the deepest why, I'm afraid."

As her hand went to her eyes once again, he caught the scent of more tears, fresh as an ocean breeze. He wanted to reach out for her, to ease her in some way, in any way, but he knew she would move out of his reach.

"Nadya—"

She straightened herself and folded her hands in her lap, like she was gathering some kind of physical strength from the composure. "I have come to care for you—and not just as a patient or a friend. I suppose it doesn't reflect well on my character, professional or otherwise, but we cannot change our emotions. We can only endure them." Her hand brushed her cheeks with impatience. "So yes, that's the truth of why I must go. I find being reminded of your love for another an intolerable pain, and how stupid is that."

Kane just sat there for a moment, his mind replaying her words and trying to make sure he'd heard them right.

"I didn't imagine it," he whispered.

"Imagine?"

"I felt the warmth of you. All along. I used to anticipate it. After you would work around the clinic—cleaning and moving things—you'd come sit with me and I focused on you to try to get out of the pain. You were my lighthouse in the darkness. I used to get so impatient for you to finish what you were doing and come back to me."

"I didn't know you were so aware."

"Of you, I was aware of everything."

Abruptly, he thought of Cordelhia, picturing what he remembered of the way she looked and scented, dressed and spoke. The memories of his blond, waifish betrothed were not as sharp as they had been back in the beginning of his incarceration, the details of her dulled as if his recollections had been worn down by too much examination.

And then he remembered the choice he had made the night before: To stay alive and help Nadya, rather than go unto the Fade to be reunited with his mate.

"You ask me how I can bear to look at you." He shook his head. "I became attached to you when I couldn't see. Those feelings don't go away. Your scent, your voice, your care for me were what saw me through, and what defines you for me."

As she seemed surprised, he fell silent—until words left his mouth without any forethought, a truth shared because it had bubbled up within him and had to be expressed: "I had to come back to you for the same reason you feel the need to go now."

He could sense her shock as a charge in the air.

But then she composed herself. "It's not uncommon to think you have feelings for someone you see as your healer."

"And maybe it's just you. Maybe it's not about the nursing . . . and all about you."

When she just looked away, as if she wasn't going to argue with him because the truth was too obvious, he had no idea what to say or do about any of it.

So he extended his wrist.

"Take my vein for any reason you want to justify to yourself," he said. "I don't care about the why. If we're going our separate ways, I want you to be as strong as you can be. It will help me construct a future for you that I can be at peace with."

In the silence that followed, the details of the living quarters they were in, from the blues and grays of the rug, to the plain walls and the comfortable furniture, became super-sharp in the periphery, as if his mind were recording everything about Nadya with such intensity, even the background around her was drawn into the intense focus.

"Thank you," she whispered.

"For what," he prompted, when she stopped there.

"Your vein."

With that, she lowered herself, and he felt the brush of the blanket's fringe on his forearm first. Then came her small, cool hands, so gentle, so soft. Closing his eyes, he let his head fall back. As his breath began to pump, a tingling went through his body from the anticipation of the sharp points scoring his—

Her bite was slow and gentle, to the point where he worried she hadn't seated her mouth properly—but he knew the instant she began to draw against him. There was a pull upon his vein and then she gasped deep in her throat and her hands tightened on him.

The drinking was very restrained, as if she were determined to cause him no discomfort. Except there was no way she could hurt him.

Actually, no . . . that was not true.

His free hand lifted because he wanted to draw her closer—and as his arm hovered in the air over her bent shoulders, he wondered how this had happened . . . how he had become attached to another other than Cordelhia. What did that matter, though.

Like their parting, it was something he could not change.

And she was right. He had a purpose to carry him onward, and vengeance was no casual thing. He just wished she could believe that, if not for *ahvenging* his murdered *shellan*, he would have begged to stay with her.

But if not for Cordelhia, he wondered if Nadya wouldn't have asked him to stay.

He couldn't not *ahvenge* his mate, however. And anyway, it was clear that Nadya didn't believe what he'd said to her.

So after this feeding, they would part, and if there was any fairness in destiny, he was going to kill someone if it was the last thing he did.

And he had the sense . . . it probably would be.

CHAPTER TWENTY-FOUR

Thanks to the newscast's footage about the burglary in Leczo Falls, Vishous was able to re-form safely in the middle of a picturesque town square, right behind a white gazebo that looked like it had been used in any one of the Kevin McCallister movies. As he glanced around the park-like public lawn, he checked out the line of nineteen-twenties-era storefronts across the street.

There was a diner, a clothing boutique, a grocer's, and a butcher's. Also a flower shop and a mail place.

And the pharmacy.

Had he been here before? V wondered. Because he had the sense he'd seen the layout somewhere, even before some parents had left a nine-year-old behind at Christmas.

"Well, if this isn't a gingerbread village. Looks good enough to eat."

As the female voice registered behind him, V smiled in the dark and turned around. His blooded sister, Payne—also a product of the truly toxic union of the Bloodletter and the Scribe Virgin—was standing tall in all her black leather, her shitkickers planted in the grass, her lean and powerful body set, but not tense. With her long black hair braided, and no makeup on her face, she looked beautiful and deadly.

"Hey, Sis," he said.

"I was surprised to get your text."

"You told me you wanted to be more involved."

"I'm not complaining." She put her palms forward, all chill, brother. "I did have to tell your boss that I had to reschedule our sparring session, depending on how this goes."

V winced. "So you made Wrath's night, huh."

"He took it as well as could be expected."

"Did he light something on fire? Or just steam from the ears."

"It was over text, so I can't comment on anything other than the words he used. The tone and whatever else he felt were mercifully absent."

"He says you're the best partner on the mats he's ever had."

"There he goes, making me blush."

The King had lost his eyesight completely a couple of years ago, but he'd kept his hand in the fighting game, even though to his immense dissatisfaction no one would let him out into the field. His life was just too precious to roll any kind of dice with, and besides, considering the straight-up killer he'd been for most of his adult life, he'd already run out of luck in battle.

"So, what are we doing here?" Payne glanced around. "Other than reenacting *Back to the Future*."

V snapped his fingers. "Oh, shit. That's what it is. Rhage was watching Marty McFly the other night, and I came in during the skateboard scene. That's where I've seen this town layout before."

"It sure is picturesque."

"Ah, but the big bad world has come to Leczo Falls. Someone's been doing a little breaking and entering over there."

McTierney's Family Pharmacy was on the corner, the plate glass windows of the three-story, wedge-shaped brick building hand-painted with the name in old-fashioned gold leaf. In contrast to all the Norman Rockwell, however, the door was marked with police caution tape and there was an evidence seal at the jamb.

"Come on," V said as he indicated the way forward. "That's our crime scene."

"Oooooh, I've always wanted to play Jessica Fletcher."

"You're going to need to be a lot shorter and get a wig."

"Also learn how to type."

The two of them set off, heading around the gazebo and onto the public square's sidewalk, then stepping into the road. Everything was neat as a living room, no litter around, nothing collecting at the storm drains, not even a stray newspaper page wafting on the breeze. It was like the place had been vacuumed and dusted.

Going up to the pharmacy's glass, he cupped his hands and leaned in. "Looks like the investigation is ongoing. No cleanup yet, and that has to be a city ordinance going by how tidy the frickin' park is."

Thanks to the peachy glow of the streetlamps, he could measure the mess, all kinds of products on the floor, bottles broken, boxes strewn about, display shelves pushed over. It looked like a bar fight had relocated to the pharmacy's interior, a couple of three-hundred-pounders with Bud-melted brains throwing sloppy punches as they danced like polar bears.

"You want to tell me why we care about a human pharmacy that looks like it's been in a blender?" his sister asked.

"Let's go around back. And it's because I think whoever broke in here might be tied to the prison camp."

As he nodded off to the right, Payne led the way down the other side of the building, moving silently over the sidewalk in spite of her steel-toed boots.

"You and Manny doing good?" he asked as he checked across the block. But not a thing was stirring, not even a proverbial mouse.

"We're great, thanks. He's a fantastic male. I'm lucky."

"*He's* lucky."

She glanced over. "We're both lucky, how's that."

When she turned back to refocus on what was ahead, her Lara Croft braid swung back and forth across her tight waist. The fact that she'd mated a human had been as miraculous as the fact that she'd gotten out of their *mahmen*'s private quarters up in the Sanctuary where she'd been kept in suspended animation, like a Barbie collectible, instead of a living person.

"You'll let me know if you have any problems with him," he said.

And mostly kept the growl out of his voice.

His sister stopped and turned around. And she didn't wait for him to come up to her—she marched to him like the pair of steps he would have taken to get to her were an impermissible delay.

"Back off, V. We don't have any problems, and if we did, I'd handle it myself. Our mates may work together, but I don't need my brother in my relationship."

Meeting pale eyes that were as sharp as his own, he had an uncharacteristic urge to throw out a hug. Instead, he smiled. Honestly smiled.

"Roger that," he murmured.

With a nod, like he'd made the only reasonable choice in Payne's mind, she kept going, and so did he. And as they came around to the rear of the pharmacy, there were no cars in the shallow parking lot—and check it out. More neat-as-a-pin: Even the dumpster that was set by the rear door sparkled, its perfect paint job as if the stuff had been slapped on fresh during the day, no bumps or dings in the side panels, either.

The dumpsters down in Caldwell looked they had terminal acne and a case of the punching bags.

"I think I know why humans move up here," he muttered as they approached the pharmacy's back door. "Go figure, it's more civilized in the sticks."

"Do we care about this seal?" Payne asked as she pointed to the orange eye-level sticker that had been affixed on the juncture at the jamb.

"Not in the slightest. They can have a field day getting thought up about it being broken tomorrow morning. That's not our problem."

His sister willed both the dead bolts free, and she palmed up one of her guns as she opened the door. The whiff of laundry detergent, dryer sheets, dish soap, and shampoo was a fake meadow in the spring, and they both sneezed at the same time.

"What are we looking for?" she asked.

"I don't know."

He walked in behind her and glanced around. Then went over to the coupon flyers that had been Scotch-Taped around the enclosed drug-dispensing area. "Two for one, the vitamins. And a ten percent off diabetic supplies."

"This was not a professional job." Payne leaned down over a humidifier that had lost whatever battle it had been in. "Too much displaced, too inefficient. Or they were professionals and just didn't give a shit."

"I vote for the latter."

He stepped up onto the raised floor behind the counter, where the cash register and the expensive things like blood pressure cuffs, thermometers, and insulin testers were mounted on the wall. No cigarettes. Those were at the front of the store at the other register with the candy and the magazines.

The kicked-in door to the segregated drug-dispensing area had been a flimsy barricade at best, separating the rest of the store from the prescription medications by only a panel of particleboard painted with the same logo that was on the glass of the front windows. Routing around its cockeyed recline, he entered the thicket of shelves. The bottles and boxes that had been discarded by the burglars as undesirable were a debris field made up of Johnson & Johnson, Pfizer, and AbbVie products; bending down, he rifled through and recognized some of the generic names, as well as some of the branded ones.

"It's not someone looking to cook up meth." He glanced over at the organized lineup of Sudafed and other decongestants. "The ephedrine and the pseudoephedrine weren't touched."

He quickly kept sifting through what was on the floor. "Xanax. Other benzos. They left behind what would be a fortune on the streets."

"What am I looking for exactly?" his sister asked as she joined him.

"Penicillin. Tell me if you find anything like amoxicillin, ampicillin—anything that ends in 'cillin.' Also, sulfa drugs. Z-Paks. I think they took all of it."

Payne threw her braid back over her shoulder. "You should have brought my *hellren*. He would have been—"

The creaking sound of the rear door into the store brought both their heads up. With a coordination that came from training and in-stinct, as well as shared DNA, they both palmed up and pointed their guns at whoever was making the colossal mistake of entering through the back way.

"Great," V muttered. "Just when we needed some company."

CHAPTER TWENTY-FIVE

Back at the underground hideout beneath the hunting cabin, Kane's blood was the most beautiful wine Nadya had ever tasted. As its nourishment slipped over her tongue and traveled down the back of her throat, a compulsive need to take more and more made her swallow faster and faster. Even as she told herself to go slowly and be careful not to drain him, instinct took over—until her blunt nails were digging into his forearm, and her fangs were all but chewing on him, and the gnawing hunger in her got worse, instead of better.

He didn't stop her.

To the contrary, she felt a gentle cupping of her head. When he should have been telling her to disengage, he was urging her to his wrist, even though there was no way to be closer to it.

For some reason, him wanting her to keep at it just made her even more hungry, and not only for the nutrients. Indeed, heat was kindling in her belly and traveling to her extremities, the waves warming her arms and legs, her hands and feet. It was such a contrast to how she normally felt, making her realize how cold she usually was. How frigid. How frozen—

A moan escaped her, vibrating up her windpipe even through the drinking. As good as this was, though, she really had to stop. She had to pull back. She had to . . .

The thoughts disintegrated as her starvation took over again, nothing but the feeding mattering, not even Kane's life. She was a servant to her biology, to her decades of denying her needs, to the reality that she had been near death for the entire time she had been in the prison camp.

For as long as she had been wounded.

The heat was extraordinary, awakening her from the inside out, filling her with a vitality that was so great, she wasn't sure she could contain the energy within her body. The sensation was as if she were swelling within her skin, growing larger, filling out. Every part of her, each cell, down to her very molecules, was starting to vibrate with life long dampened by—

The trembling came upon her from out of the blue, and at first, she thought it was just a shiver, a shake, that would pass. Instead, it was an entire storm of shivering and shaking, so violent that her lips began to slip against the puncture wounds.

And then she lost contact altogether.

Desperate as she was, she lurched forward to reestablish the bite. But suddenly, she couldn't control her body. As much as she wanted to lean in, she couldn't—

With a sudden spasm, her spine arched on its own, her torso curving back with such force, she fell away from him. As her vision swung up to the ceiling, her arms extended out from her shoulders on their own and her legs pushed stick straight from her hips.

Her next awareness was of being on the carpet at Kane's feet. The seizure owned her in the same way the hunger for his blood had, her body not under her own control, her vision jerking about so that she couldn't focus on anything, her reflexes going haywire as she flopped around, a fish on the bottom of a boat. As she continued to spasm, speaking wasn't an option, her molars clapping together,

her mouth both lax and gritted as it alternated between the two extremes—

Kane's face appeared above her, but she couldn't communicate with him, and though his mouth was moving, she had no idea what he was saying.

Grabbing on to the front of his shirt, she tried to—

A scream curdled out of her. And then another.

"*Nadya.*"

Something about the way he said her name made her come to a sort of attention. Through chattering teeth, she attempted to speak.

"Nadya . . ."

"I don't know . . ."

"Nadya. Drink this."

Is he insane, she thought. She had already taken so much from his vein. With more determination than actual follow-through, she fought whatever he sought to put to her lips, her sloppy hands batting away—

"It's water," he said roughly. "Drink it. It's too much of a shock, the blood—I should have limited how much you had. Dearest Virgin Scribe . . ."

He forced her to take some of the water, but the little she managed to get past her lips did nothing. The inferno inside her body continued to rise, doubling and then redoubling again, no longer warming, now consuming. She was burning, incinerating, eaten alive by the power of his blood.

The blanket was ripped from her, and as her scrambling hands tried to pull it back over her nakedness, he shoved the wool weight out of her reach.

"N-n-n-n-nooo—"

"Nadya, I've got you. Here. Come here."

She felt his arms go around her, and then she had a sensation of being lifted. He was carrying her somewhere—outside? To the colder air? Was it dark? She didn't know, she couldn't think, she wasn't . . .

The scent of the Dial soap broke through the seizure. She was in the bathroom?

The sound of rushing water answered that.

"This is going to hurt," he said in a loud voice, as if he were yelling at her in hopes of getting through to her, "but we have to get you cooled. No—don't fight me—don't—*Nadya*. Stop it."

He got into the shower with her.

Kane carried her into the stall, and held her under the spray, though surely it must have been cold for him as well.

"Hang on, Nadya. I'm going to take care of you. Just stay with me . . ."

◆   ◆   ◆

A good ten miles away, in the bolt-hole under the crappy garage, Callum got up for the night by getting up to his feet from the floor. He was fully clothed and his boots were laced tight, but then he'd slept fully clothed with said boots on. He'd also slept sitting up.

Or not slept, as the case was.

Turning his head, he looked down the long, narrow space. At the end of the lineup of cold-weather coats, the vampire was in the same position he'd been in at the base of the stairs. They hadn't said a thing to each other during the daylight hours. Then again, Callum's mouth had done enough before they'd gone their separate ways, hadn't it.

Time to wakey-wakey, he thought as the male didn't rouse from his chin-on-chest prop-up.

"It's dark now, vampire," he announced in what he intended to be a brisk voice. And what do you know, he did a pretty good impression of briskness.

When there was no response, he walked down and stood over the male. "Are you alive?"

Well. If the guy was dead, this was most unexpected, and surely not his fault. Coitus-related deaths typically occurred at the moment of orgasm, the pressure of the pleasure blowing a gasket in the heart—or directly afterward, when the exertion overtaxed a lax cardiac muscle. But ten hours later?

"Hello?"

The utter stillness in the vampire was eerie. He did not appear to be breathing, and he sure as hell wasn't moving. But his eyes . . . they were in fact open, little slits under the lashes allowing sight, and blinking at a nearly imperceptible rate.

He was focused over on the shower, which was weird. As far as Callum was aware, there were absolutely no Chippendales can-can'ing in the corner. No pinups, either. Nothing but tile, really.

"What are you looking at?" he asked.

It was a long moment before that face turned his way, and the male's expression was remote. "Who died there."

With a shake of the head, because clearly he didn't hear that right, Callum said, "Excuse me?"

"There." The vampire's arm lifted and he pointed to the shower. "Who was the male who died there."

Callum felt the blood drain from his face. "No one."

"You lie. I can see him. He's hanging from the showerhead by a brown leather belt. His hair is dark blond and he has an earring in one ear. Who is he."

It was a while before Callum could find his voice. "No one."

"So that's what the blow job was about." The vampire looked over. "You wanted to do something to wipe that memory away. Did it work?"

"How . . ."

"Did it?"

"You're lying. You don't see shit." Callum walked up and back, and then made a show of inspecting one of the parkas hanging on a hook. "And I'm going to go check on your friend and that female back at my hunting cabin."

"Guess it didn't work, then."

Where the hell was all the air in this place, Callum wondered as he pulled at the loose collar of his flannel shirt.

"Are you volunteering for another try, vampire?" he heard himself toss back. "I don't think you have the guts, frankly."

The other male shifted his boots under him and rose up to his full height. "Tell me who he was really, and I'll give you my answer of how I see him."

"I'm not interested in your answer."

"Then why'd you ask."

With every back and forth, they were taking a step toward each other, the distance disappearing until they were standing toe-to-toe. The vampire was slightly taller, so Callum had to tilt his head back to continue meeting those eyes.

"I'm glad that wasn't personal," the vampire said.

With a frown, Callum tried to figure out what the hell the male meant. But whatever, he wasn't going to ask—"What wasn't personal?"

"You sucking me off. I'd rather it was about something else."

The vampire turned away and went over to the shower. As he stood there, Callum braced himself for the bastard to reach up and put a hand on that fixture, just to dangle the pain in between them.

Instead, he only stared at it

"How do you see . . . things." Callum focused on the showerhead, too. "There's nothing there."

After a pause, the vampire shrugged his powerful shoulders.

"I don't know the why or the way, I only know the what." The male looked back and smiled with an edge that made him seem positively evil. "Which was how I ended up in the prison camp."

Callum frowned. "I don't understand. You killed someone, and then saw them? Isn't that overkill?"

Chuckle, chuckle, Callum thought to himself.

"Oh, yes, I murdered somebody."

Callum checked his watch even though he didn't have to. But he needed to do something other than stare down to where he had found his lover that hot August night two years ago.

"Who did you kill?" he asked.

"The male who butchered my *mahmen*." As Callum recoiled, the vampire shrugged and turned back to the shower. "He came in and robbed her. We didn't have much, but he took the mead, the pewter, and her life. Then he hid her body. I walked into our little house and I saw the image of her on the bed." There was a pause. "She was unclothed—"

"*Fuck*—"

"—and I never did find her body. I think he left her out for the sun somewhere. But I knew what I had seen because I'd had the visions ever since I could remember, and they are always right."

"How did you know who . . ." His *mahmen* had been violated, too? "I'm so sorry—"

"He marked her. On her stomach. I couldn't think of where I had seen the pattern before—but I definitely recognized it. A year of searching later, I found him. He'd been the blacksmith until the drink got to him—and killing my *mahmen* was what sobered him up again. The mark was how he kept track of the horseshoes he made." The male paused. "He was back in business when I found him, so I killed a productive member of the village we lived in."

"What did you do to him."

"I took a hot branding iron and I disemboweled him with it." The vampire shrugged again. "An aristocrat who lived just outside the village threw me into the prison camp. He was fussy about his horses, and I think he cared less that I'd murdered the male than the fact that the hooves under him were no longer shod as he liked. As for the camp, at that point, it didn't matter where I was. My family was gone. What did I care."

"What of your sire?" Callum pushed a hand through his hair. "Were there no cousins, no one in your bloodline to defend you?"

"I never knew who my father was. It was just my *mahmen* and me.

She was a laundress, I worked in the fields for the aristocrat who put me in the camp. It was a simple life." The male rubbed his thumb over his eyebrow. "But the prison was good for me. I got to kill there. Often."

Callum popped his own brows. "Just for sport?"

"I considered myself the best kind of vigilante."

"And what kind is that?"

"I took out a lot of trash. We'll leave it at that."

With a nod, Callum murmured, "I actually don't have a problem with that."

"It wouldn't matter to me if you did. You asked about the visions, and here we are." He glanced to his left, to what certainly appeared to be bare tile. "He did it to get back at you for something, didn't he. The male who hung himself here."

Clearing his throat, Callum tried to show no emotion. "You can't see that."

"But this is your personal space, right? It smells like you, and all the clothes are in your style. You were the one who brought us to this place and gave us things from the garage upstairs . . . the stretchers, the weapons. So he came here because you'd brought him here before—probably to get away from it all, whatever all there was to get away from. But then something changed between the two of you. He returned and left his body as a fuck-you. Didn't he."

Callum turned away and blindly went over to the coats. He had no need for one, though, so he just rifled through the puffy-tufties.

"I'm going to go check on your friend." He walked over to the stairwell and put his forefinger on the reader, knowing damn well he'd get the number combination for the keypad wrong if he tried to punch it in. "Are you coming? Or not."

Overhead, the toolbox trundled off to the side, exposing the garage above. The scent of motor oil and fresh night air rolled down to his nose, and he breathed in deep.

Putting his foot on the first step, he said over his shoulder, "As you like to say, what you decide doesn't matter to me."

CHAPTER TWENTY-SIX

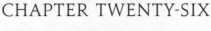

Talk about too much firepower for the situation.

As Vishous and his sister leveled a pair of forties at whoever was entering the back of the pharmacy, he was prepared to make a Rorschach test out of the fucker. Except instead of a *lesser*-like fighter, a shadow who operated like Rubber Man, or a human looking to steal what was left, a little old man waddled through the door and stopped dead when he saw the two guns pointed at his head.

His palsied hands lifted above his straggly-cap of white hair. "Hello?"

Like this was a cocktail party written by Stan Lee and he'd just met the bad guys in the story.

V got into that mind real quick, shutting down any bright ideas— because while he didn't mind shooting humans who got in his way, he'd prefer not to have the heartburn that would come with popping some- one's grandpa off to his royal reward.

"They don't know who did it," V said as he started to go through the man's memory banks. "They have no leads. This is the owner, but his son's the pharmacist now—"

When he stopped, his sister glanced over. "What. What's wrong?"

V shook his head. "It's hard to make sense of what's in there. His mind . . . it's gone."

"He has amnesia?"

"No, he's got . . . holes in his memory. He has pieces of the present, but not a lot to go by."

The past was solid, though. There were all kinds of very distinct memories from the fifties and the sixties, back when there had been an ice cream counter, with banana boats and milkshakes . . . then later, they'd served French fries and hamburgers. But the good ol' days hadn't lasted. As the town's population had thinned out, the food service part of the store had been replaced by grab-and-go groceries and home goods. Now the building was pretty on the outside, thanks to a federal grant for small towns, but the business's finances were hanging by a thread.

"Why are you back?" the old man asked. "Did you forget your medication?"

"No," Payne answered gently. "We didn't. We're sorry we bothered you."

"Oh, it's no bother. I'm happy to help you." The old guy went over and flipped a switch. "Don't know why the lights are off. They're on now, though."

As the fluorescent boxes in the ceiling flared, the wan illumination of the security lights was blown away, and the chaos of what should have been order was exposed in a glare.

"So what are you looking for tonight?" The old man stepped by Vishous and got firm. "Sir, I'm going to have to ask you to move out from behind the cash register. It's store policy."

Vishous put his gun back in his holster and shuffled around the guy. Down on the floor proper, he glanced around, taking note of a bank of empty shelves.

"Were you just driving by?" Payne asked the owner.

The old man's answer was a ramble that started back in nineteen seventy-two. As he described the house he and his wife had moved into with their sons, and the options the developer had given them for the kitchen, V went to the aisle that had been completely cleared out. Bending over, he picked up a box of surgical gauze that had been stomped on.

All the wraps and the tape, the pads and the Ace bandages, in the pharmacy were gone. And when he went to the next set of shelves, the hydrogen peroxide, the alcohol, and the distilled water were also wiped out.

V headed back to the ramblin' man and his sister. The way Payne was looking at the guy was intense, and when V tapped her on the arm because there was nothing else to do here, she didn't look over.

Fine, whatever; he could wait. He was more convinced, rather than less, that this robbery was tied to the camp; he just had no concrete evidence and no idea how to connect it to the new location.

"So you go walking at night?" Payne was saying.

"It's hard to sleep."

"And does your family know where you are?"

V tilted his hip against the counter, and took out a hand-rolled. As he lit up, the old man looked over sharply.

"There's no smoking in here."

As V cocked a brow, he went back into that feeble brain—"*Ow.*"

Payne flared her eyes, all "don't make me kick your shine again." Then she turned back to the old guy. "He's putting it away. And please, keep going."

Except the old man just stared off into his store. "What happened here . . ."

"I'm really sorry." Payne reached out and took his hand. "Can we call someone for you?"

He seemed to come back to attention at the contact, and as he looked at her, he frowned. "You're back."

V frowned and cut in quick, "Yeah. We are. Did you see us before?"

"You were here the other night. I came in as you were leaving."

"What did we look like?"

"Like you." The old guy seemed confused. "And you were taking things and putting them in the van out back. Two vans."

Patting his own chest, V said, "We were dressed in black, yes? Did we say anything to you?"

The old man frowned and then weaved on his feet. As he put a hand to his frontal lobe and winced, there was a whole lot of "ding-ding-ding, we have a winner" in V's head.

Vampires, he thought. And they'd scrubbed his memories.

"Okay," Payne said, "thank you. You've been really helpful. But who can we call for you?"

"My son, Ernie Junior," the owner mumbled. "He gave me this . . . to give to people . . ."

An arthritic hand reached into the pocket of his loose pants and he took out a laminated card. Payne handed the thing to V. Then she just stared at the man.

"I'm really sorry," she whispered.

V snagged his Samsung and dialed the number. And sometime between the second ring and when a guy answered, he realized what his sister was thinking of doing.

Opening his mouth, he intended to tell her no. Then he looked on the wall behind the cash register, above the displays of those blood pressure cuffs and the blood sugar testers. The lineup of photographs started black-and-white, ended in faded colors, and the lot of it was a documentation of the aging process at work. The constant was the store, while the owner progressed through the eras of his life. Most of the images had been taken out in front, and there were other people in them, men in suits who looked like politicians, women in hats and dresses and cat-eye glasses.

The first and the last pictures were with a woman standing at his side, and like him, she went from somewhere in her early twenties to something north of seventy.

"—hello?" a voice said over V's phone. "Who's there?"

At the prompting, V refocused on the man in vivo, the elderly, confused old guy who had sundowner syndrome, and whose dementia or Alzheimer's or whatever it was took him back to his true North, this store.

"I've got your father," V murmured. "He's at the pharmacy."

"Oh, God, not again—" There was a muffling, and then the son said to someone in the background, likely his wife, given the female voice, "Dad's out again . . . no, I know—I know, we need to get him into a home—"

"We'll stay with him here," V cut in. "Until you come."

The man put the phone back into place at his mouth. "Sorry—thanks. Hey, who is this?"

"Just a passerby. My sister and I saw the back door open and the lights on."

"He does this a lot. He needs to be in a memory care unit."

"Like I said, we'll wait here and keep an eye on him." God, why was he volunteering to stay in this drama? "Unless you want us to call the cops or something."

"I am the cops. Local sheriff. Anyway, I'll be there in five minutes."

"We got 'im."

"Thank you—what did you say your name was?"

"Vinnie Sanguerossa." As V ended the call, he glanced over at his sister. "You shouldn't be fucking around with this. I'm telling you."

When she glanced over at him, he was pretty sure the look on her face was what people saw on his own when he was telling them to butt-the-fuck-out.

"Mr. McTierney?" she said as she refocused on the human.

"Yes, honey?"

"You're going to be a mess," V muttered as he checked the time. "You do this and it costs you."

"Close your eyes for me, will you?" Payne stepped in closer. "That's right. This isn't going to hurt, I promise."

"Not him, it ain't." V took out a hand-rolled and put it between his front teeth. "I'll be outside while you're saving the world. 'Cuz I'm not allowed to fucking smoke in here."

Walking through the partially open rear door, he took a deep breath of the night and then lit up. As he leaned back against the brick building, he looked across a farm field and then along the rear entries to the other stores in the row.

Behind him, in the pharmacy, Payne was talking to the old man, murmuring so quietly V could only hear the rhythm of the syllables, and then there was a gasp, a sharp inhale. Hard to know which one of them it came from—

A flare of light pierced out between the door and the jamb, and he braced himself for what was coming next. Three . . . two . . . one . . .

The release of energy fully opened the door, the nuclear-bright illumination turning the empty parking lot to daylight for a split second. And then the panel closed with a clap.

Vishous shook his head and flexed his gloved hand. Underneath the black leather, there was a weave of lead, and without it, anything his glowing curse came into contact with would be destroyed—people, places, things.

Just another gift from his *mahmen*.

In contrast, Payne's inheritance was not destruction, but regeneration. It was not free, however. Balance had been the Scribe Virgin's watchword, except for as it applied to herself, and accordingly, there was a price and a payment that came out of Payne's hide every time she used her "gift."

As for why she would waste it on a human? That was her choice. Just like she had chosen to heal her *hellren*'s racehorse, and decided to keep George, the King's service dog, alive and well for the next couple hundred years.

Which was a public service. Who the hell wanted to live with Wrath if anything happened to that golden.

Jesus, Armageddon would be a better time—

A gold and brown municipal SUV with bubbler lights on the top came steaming down the back road, its tires squealing as it angled into the parking lot and slammed to a halt in front of V. What got out was a taller, thinner, younger version of Mr. McTierney, and V pulled a quick glance behind him to see whether wiping out the memory of a brilliant, mystical light was going to be on the night's hit parade.

Nope. It had faded.

"Vinnie?" the guy said.

"Yeah, hey, Ernie." V exhaled and offered his gloved hand to the guy. "How you doin'."

"Doing good. How you doin'."

Well, weren't they all Soprano-tastic.

They shook, and the guy started in with the he-does-this's again. And fucking hell, not that V tended to give a shit about anybody else except for his short list of besties in the mansion, but you had to feel for the son. He looked frickin' exhausted, like not only was he getting a reg-ular diet of these nocturnal wanderings, but the waking hours weren't much better when it came to Dad-management.

"Thank God you came along when you did. Couple of nights ago, he walked in on the burglary."

"The place does look a little torn up."

"I don't think we're going to find 'em. I should have put up cameras in the back a long time ago, but things like break-ins don't happen in Leczo Falls. Not usually, at any rate. We were lucky he wasn't hurt. I guess they were on their way out when he got here. He knew enough to call me, though—he took out the laminated card you found in his pocket and dialed my number. It was a miracle. Lately, he doesn't even recognize me."

As Ernie McTierney kept talking, V let the guy go. What the hell did he care—he wanted to finish his cigarette anyway, and it wasn't much different than having a TV on in the background.

"He's here, but he's not, you know?"

"Yeah." V nodded back to the store's closed door. "So you got any leads on the break-in from your dad?"

"He was talking a lot about soldiers, but he lost a brother in Vietnam, so who knows. Mostly he's forgetful, but sometimes he sees things that aren't there. And what are the chances a platoon of Army guys pulls up here to steal a bunch of antibiotics and Band-Aids."

"Nothing else is gone? Fucking weird."

The sheriff cursed under his breath. "That's what I said. Anyway, I'll go get Dad."

At that moment, the back door reopened, and the elder McTierney stepped in between the jambs. As he stared across at his son, the old man seemed at a loss for words.

"Hi, Dad," Ernie said with utter exhaustion. "I'm here to take you home."

The father couldn't seem to move.

"Dad, it's me, remember?" In a lower voice, the guy muttered, "Of course you don't—"

"Ernie?"

The son's eyes came up. "What did you say?"

"My God . . . Ernie."

The old man closed the distance on a shuffle, and he grabbed on to the shoulders of the adult his child had become like they hadn't been in the same country for a decade, holding his progeny still so he could have a proper look at his boy.

"Dad?" the sheriff said with wonder. "What's going on?"

"I don't know." The old man shook his head. "I have no idea."

The sheriff glanced around. "I think we better get you home—"

"Wait, because I don't know how long this is going to last. I need you to know . . ."

"What, Dad?"

"I'm so proud of you." The old pharmacist searched the face of his son.

"You're such a good man. And I know it hasn't been easy with me, especially since Momma died."

"Dad . . ."

"Come here."

As they embraced, V looked away and put his hand-rolled out on the heel of his shitkicker. Tucking the butt into his ass pocket, he figured he might as well go and deal with a family reunion of his own.

Slipping through the back door, he glanced around. The pharmacy was empty—

Down on the floor, his sister's boots were sprawled out on the far side of the counter, and he shot around to her. "God*damn* it."

Payne was faceup and out cold with her eyes open, her skin as pale gray as the linoleum under her.

Kneeling down, he lifted her head and settled it in his lap. "Payne, how we doing."

But like he didn't know the answer to that?

When there was no reply, he took out his phone and started texting with one hand. At least Butch was already on his way in something they could transport her back to the training center with—but Manny was going to be hysterical.

"Oh, my God, is she okay?"

V glanced up. Ernie Jr. had come in, and his dad was right behind him, the latter looking around his store as if he hadn't seen it recently, and remembered nothing about the burglary.

"My sister's fine. Just a little fainting spell." '*Cuz she regenerated your pop's gray matter.* "We'll be out of here soon."

"The robbers," the dad said. "Did this."

Even though V didn't want to go in and mess around any more with either one of their minds, he knew he had to clear them out before Butch got here. Tapping into the son first, and then the father, he sent them off to that sheriff-mobile, their memories of two vampires checking out the pharmacy's burglary hidden from their consciousness as if they had never come here.

As they exited and the SUV drove away, he looked down at his sister. Payne's eyes were starting to blink. Thank fuck.

"Hey," he said. "You're back."

"Kind of." She tried to sit up and didn't get far with that. "Where is—"

"They just left. And before you ask, yes, Dad was looking like he was back from wherever he had been."

"I don't want any bitching from you." She cleared her throat, but still spoke weakly. "I don't regret anything, even if I need an evac. That's torture, to have someone right in front of you even though they're all but dead and gone. I had to help because I could. Sometimes . . . you have to do what you can to ease suffering. It's the way I live with the gift our *mahmen* gave me."

It was right on the tip of his tongue to tell her she was so much more important than those two humans and whatever fate had in store for them. But then he remembered the father coming out of the back of the pharmacy, and how the two had hugged it out.

"It's okay," he heard himself say. "You should have seen the way that sire looked at his son."

He thought of their own pops, the Bloodletter. And the war camp V had been left in.

"I would have given anything for a father like that." Goddamn, he needed another cigarette. "So, yeah, kind of makes it all worth it as long as I get you back to the clinic safely."

"Do we have to tell Manny?"

V smiled. "Yes, and you're going to have to feed as soon as we're back."

"I'm fine."

"Oh, okay, good. So how about you stand right up now and dematerialize back to Caldwell." He put his hands out to the sides, all go 'head. "Just do you, hard-ass."

There was a heartbeat of silence. "I hate you right now."

He chuckled. "I love you, too, Sis. And whatever, you did the right thing."

"Oh, my God. Did you just say that?"

"No, you're delusional. Now, close your damn eyes and rest up so you can deal with your male."

V's phone started ringing and he checked the screen. "Oh, look. Manny's calling right now. I'll put him on speakerphone, unless you'd like to keep this private?"

"No," she said with a wince. "He's likely to be less hysterical if he knows you're listening to him . . ."

CHAPTER TWENTY-SEVEN

In spite of the cold rush falling on them both, Kane could feel the waves of heat coming off of Nadya's body. The blasts were so strong that the rhythm of them was apparent, the surge and fade like a heartbeat.

"Hang on," he said for what surely was the hundredth time.

He had her directly under the showerhead, the faucet handle set on C, the water pressure mercifully strong. But he wasn't sure it was making any difference at all. She felt just as volcanic as she had when he'd brought her in here at a dead run.

No, at a *fast* run.

There was no using the "d" word. Not now.

The fact that he didn't know who to call or where to go for help was truly terrifying. He didn't mind being on his own when his life was the only one he had to worry about. But she was clearly in a medical crisis of some kind, and he had no fucking clue what to—

The sense that they were no longer alone cranked Kane's head around and he bared his fangs over his shoulder, prepared to attack if he had to.

The white-haired wolven in the open doorway to the bathroom was staring into the shower with a look of horror on his face. And as his nostrils flared like he was testing the air to judge a scent, he had to grip the jamb to keep his balance.

"You fed her. Jesus Christ . . . you *fed* her."

"Will you shut the fucking door! She's unclothed!"

"Her naked is the least of our problems."

The door slammed shut and Kane had a brief impulse to punch a wall. That faded quickly, though.

"Nadya, I'm going to put you down, dearest one."

Bending over, he set her on the clean tile floor, right over the drain, and when she couldn't keep herself upright, he laid her down on her side. She looked desperately ill, her body with its stiff joints and thin limbs the kind of thing that surely did not have much more life left in it.

In spite of the heat inside of her, she was horrifically pale.

"I'm just outside," he told her. "I won't be gone long."

He took one lingering look at her, and then he snapped into action, prowling out of the bathroom and closing the door behind himself. On the far side, he leaned back against the panels to keep her protected, even though neither of the males now in the living quarters made like they wanted inside.

The wolven was pacing up and back, as if in his mind, he was doing some calculations that spelled out the doom of the earth's population.

In contrast, Apex was standing at the base of the stairs in total stillness.

His eyes were alive, however, and they were locked on Kane as if he couldn't believe something or another.

"Of course I fed her." Kane looked down the narrow space at the back of the wolven's head. "It's how vampires work—"

The male spun around and jabbed a finger. "Not you, and not anymore."

"What the hell are you talking about—"

"You killed her, you asshole. You fucking killed her!"

"She hasn't fed in decades!" Kane didn't bother to keep his voice down. "The seizures are because her body has had an influx of nutrients, and we need to get medical help—"

"No! She can't handle what's in your veins!"

"It's just blood—"

"Not anymore!" The wolven marched up and went nose-to-nose. "You're not who you once were. You are not you anymore!"

All at once, an image came back: Kane was in the hut . . . with the female with the long gray hair. She was telling him that he could be saved, but that he . . .

Kane looked back at the bathroom door he was guarding with his life. With quiet intensity, like he could force reality to meet his standards if he just willed it enough, he repeated, "She just hasn't fed in a long time."

"No, she drank poison."

A sudden suffocation stole all of the breath out of his lungs. Maybe all the air out of the quarters.

Glancing down at his wrist, he saw that he was still bleeding from the puncture wounds she had made. With a sense of utter unreality, he brought the wounds up to his mouth and braced himself.

Closing a seal around the leaks, he ran his tongue over his flesh. Then he tasted for himself what she had taken into her body—

A terrible sense of dislocation took him over, transporting him outside of his body, taking him far away even as he stayed exactly where he was.

Lowering his arm, he swallowed the unfamiliar taste, the foreign . . . utterly different . . . taste of his own blood.

He thought of biting those guards, and what had happened to them.

"What the fuck did that old female do to me?" he said numbly.

"What you asked for."

"I didn't ask for this."

"You agreed to it." The wolven pulled his hands through his hair. "Jesus."

With a combination of panic and dread, Kane turned his head again, and as his ear came up against the door, he listened to the fall of the water; what did he need to—

"I have to take her to the gray-haired old woman." He looked at the wolven. "You need to help me get her to that female."

"She's not going to help you—"

"Yes, she will. This is her fault."

The laughter that came out of the other male was the nastiest thing he had ever heard. "Sure, I'll bring you back to the mountain. And you can tell her the blame's all hers. Let's just see how that goes—"

When the male abruptly stopped speaking, Kane looked toward the stairs. Apex had palmed a gun and was pointing it at the wolven.

"You're taking him to that old female. Right now."

Kane glanced back at the wolven. Instead of looking scared or even defiant, he assumed a bored expression.

"That's a helluva way to ask nicely," the male said in a dry voice.

◆ ◆ ◆

As Apex trained his gun on the male who had given him the best blow job of his life about twelve hours before, he really wanted to shoot the wolven. He was praying—*praying*—that the motherfucker would do something stupid. Which was saying something for an atheist.

If only the guy'd say something like *Fuck you, I'm not taking you anywhere.* Or maybe he could attack Kane.

Or play a terminal game of hard to get by rushing for the exit.

The idea that that male knew both Apex's secret and his past was creating a cognitive dissonance that couldn't be reconciled. Why the *hell* had he gotten to talking? It was no one's fucking business what he saw or where, and it certainly wasn't a good idea for him to be blabbering about anything that had to do with his *mahmen* or why he'd ended up in the prison camp.

And yet all that had come out.

But that wasn't the worst part. That dead guy? The one with the brown belt around his throat?

Apex had really wanted to know about that male. He'd been hungry for the details—in a way that made no goddamn sense. What did it matter to him and his life who had hung himself where and why.

"Let's go." He motioned with the gun. "You said you have a car hidden on this property. Do you have a stretcher, too?"

Kane spoke up. "I'll take her in my arms. For however long I have to, I'll carry her."

The wolven lowered his head like he was hoping there was another way, any other way. Then he shrugged. "This is not going to go well."

"What makes you think we're having fun now," Apex muttered.

Callum seemed to snap to attention. "Excellent point. Let's head out."

With a nod, Kane disappeared into the bathroom and closed the door. A moment later, the water was cut off, and Apex looked back down at the other male.

"Is the nurse going to live?" he asked.

"No."

"What's in his veins?"

"Death." The wolven paced around, his long, lean body churning under his camouflage clothes. "It was supposed to be an old maiden's tale, something that was blown out of proportion to scare the young—a deal made with the dark forces, a resurrection with a price . . . a curse hiding behind a gift."

Apex marched down to the male. "You were the one who took him to that fucking hut." He punched the guy with two fingers, right in the pec. "You fucking did this."

The wolven bared a set of fangs that were long as stakes. "He made the choice."

"Without knowing what he was getting into, right? That's how it works—it's a false decision because the landscape is a fucking lie."

"You wanted him to live." The wolven punched back with the same fore- and middle finger combo. "You asked me where to take him, and it was the only hope you had for your lover."

Don't say it, Apex thought. *Don't—*

"Too bad you didn't take yours to her."

As his words dropped, the face in front of his own went sickly white. "You fucking asshole—"

The door to the bathroom opened and Kane came out carrying a small bundle wrapped up in a towel.

"Can we hurry?" he said.

The wolven put both palms up in the air, sure as if he had a weapon against his back. "Sure. Fucking fine. Let's go."

With a choppy march, the guy went to the staircase and ascended out of the private quarters, and Kane was right on his heels, skipping every other step.

Apex glanced around at the private quarters, and had an odd thought: They were really cozy.

He wasn't used to thinking about comfort.

Tossing that idiot thought aside, he followed along and became aware that Kane wasn't the only one who had gone through some kind of metamorphosis. He didn't feel anything like himself either as he emerged into the hunting cabin.

Just as he cleared the entry, the panels of the floor moved back into place, sealing the way down. For a split second, he glanced at the hole in the roof and imagined the deadly sunlight pouring in.

"Are you coming or not."

Feeling like he was in slow motion, he turned to the wolven who was in the doorway of the cabin. The male was looking down at the rough planks of the floors, his boot tapping, his impatience sparking the air.

As Apex approached the exit, he could see outside to where Kane stood with his precious cargo. But he didn't put his focus there: He only had eyes for the wolven who was right in front of him.

And that was a huge change, wasn't it.

CHAPTER TWENTY-EIGHT

The trip back up to the wolven clan's mountainside territory took forever, but as Kane rounded one of the last turns in the trail with Nadya in his arms, two familiar faces were coming down toward him: Lucan and Mayhem were side by side in a patch of moonlight, the icy blue illumination making them seem like specters.

But they were alive.

As they rushed forward to greet him, he felt a surge of joyful reunification, and his steps quickened. Except then they stopped and just stared at him.

"And greetings to you as well," he said as he had to keep on going.

He knew there were things they wanted to ask him, but now was not the time—and even if it was, he didn't think he could answer the questions they had. He couldn't even answer his own.

On that note, he couldn't really think straight at all. His mind was churning over the implications of what he had done under the guise of helping his female. That he hadn't known feeding her was dangerous was bullshit.

But really, he should have guessed. He had seen anatomy disintegrate as the result of his bite. He just hadn't been thinking properly—

No, he thought as that final turn in the trail presented itself. His problem was that he'd been thinking too much about other things.

Like a fantasy future that could not be.

As he entered the clearing with the crackling fire pit and its circle of log benches, he looked off to the side. The hut was right where it had been, and he felt a surge of relief. This was going to be okay, he told himself—the old female was going to fix this. She was going to take care of everything.

On the approach, he started to jog, but when Nadya moaned, he slowed down. The hut had its flap down, and he tried to visualize the old female in there, by the fire, by the stream—

His feet faltered. *The stream.*

Just as the thought entered his mind, the heavy bolt of cloth covering the shelter's entrance was swept aside and the one person in the world he wanted to see emerged.

The white-haired female stepped out. Tonight, she was in sunflower yellow, her hair braided into a thick rope that lay down the front of her.

Her eyes did not go to Nadya. She just stared into Kane's face.

When he opened his mouth, she shook her head. "I'm sorry, but I can't help her."

"Wh-what—you have to." He held his arms out in desperation, and then captured the edge of the towel he'd wrapped his female in to keep it in place. "I need your help."

"There is nothing I can do—"

"Please—she's dying!"

"I cannot—"

"You can save her, like you saved me!"

The old female shook her head. "There is only one of the energy, and you were chosen to be asked. After which you chose to accept."

Kane opened his mouth to argue, but then the heat emanating off of Nadya's fragile body refocused him.

"Please," he begged. "Help her."

The old female reached out and moved part of the towel back. When she saw what was under the covering, she went still.

"Who hurt this child?" the mystical female whispered.

"He's dead."

"Good."

The old female softly stroked Nadya's cheek. "Bring her inside."

"Thank you," he said as he ducked down.

Inside the hut, he went to the pallet he'd been on—

No, it had been a coffin. He'd been lying in a coffin.

Shaking his head to clear it, he knelt and laid Nadya out on the blankets. "Here you go. You're safe and we have aid now."

Then he fell back on his ass and tried not to lose it.

The old female put her hand on his shoulder. "You care for her very much."

"She helped me."

"She is your healer."

He nodded and brushed his fingertips over the patches of soft hair on Nadya's head. "She's the reason I'm alive, and when she was looking so weak, I gave her my vein—"

"You did *what?*"

Glaring at the old female, he said, "Okay, so everybody else seems to know this. Great. You'd think it would have come up in conversation last night."

"You *fed* her."

Kane rubbed his aching eyes. "Here's an idea. Next time you do what you did to me? Lead with a helpful tip like that."

"Poor, sweet child." The old woman touched Nadya's scarred face. "And she's so hot."

"I put her in the shower. You know, under the cold water, to try to cool her down."

"You did the right thing with that."

He caught the female's arm. "Please, help her. You owe me this and you know it."

✦ ✦ ✦

With a sense of awe, Callum stood off to the side with the vampires as their friend disappeared into the Gray Wolf's hut with the female. And while the other males spoke in hushed voices, he wanted to yell at them to shut up and pay attention. Pay some respect.

They had no idea what a rarity it was, that the Gray Wolf presented herself as corporeal, that she welcomed anybody into her place of repose. That she was willing to be of aid.

But then that was his clan's spiritual tradition. Not the vampires'.

"What the hell happened to him?"

It was a hot minute before he realized he was being addressed, and as he swung his eyes away from the Gray Wolf's shelter, he wasn't sure what to tell his cousin, Lucan.

"It's true, then," the male prompted. "The Viper has taken him."

"Not taken him. He *is* the Viper. They are one and the same now."

The vampire he didn't know, who'd been injured the night before, paced the periphery, the kinetic energy in that body bubbling, boiling, but not aggressively. He just couldn't seem to stand still.

Callum glanced around, looking for his male. Not that the guy he'd given a blow job to was his. That Vampire had been there a moment ago.

"So it wasn't just a myth," Lucan murmured.

"No, it wasn't, Cousin." Callum glanced back at the tents. "Where's your female?"

"Still sleeping in there."

"You can stay here, you know. For as long as you want."

Lucan nodded. "Thanks, but we have work to do."

"Do tell."

"We're going to go back to the camp. We need to free everyone."

Well. If that didn't get a wolven's attention. "You're serious?"

"We are."

"And what are you going to do with all those males and females?" Callum glanced at the hut again and wondered what was going on inside it. "I mean, how many of them are criminals?"

"Not many. Not all." His cousin glanced at the other two former prisoners. "But first, we wait to see if Kane is okay."

Translation: *We wait to see if he loses his shit after his female dies because he tried to save her with his vein.*

And people thought destiny didn't have a sick sense of humor.

"Well, looks like you've got yourself a situation, Cousin." Oh, hell. Why couldn't they get a break. "Anyway, good luck with that—and you're welcome here. Always. If you'll excuse me? I gotta take care of some stuff."

It was a lie, of course. He had nothing to do but wait around, like everyone else, to find out if the vampire female died. Or rather . . . to see how long it took her to die.

As he passed the fire pit, there was a flare of warmth and a brief waft of woodsmoke, and then he was on the far side. The rest of the clan were out doing their nightly things, living their lives, passing among the humans if they wanted to. The dens here were one among several places for his kin to live, and with that hotel being built across the valley and the threat it had created, he wasn't surprised things were so quiet.

It was a blessing, actually. The good thing about wolves was they were pack animals. The bad thing about wolves was they were pack animals. Strangers, even if they were invited into the territory, tended to make people uneasy.

Especially if the Gray Wolf was on the premises.

Ducking into the entry of his cave, he willed the torches mounted on the stone walls to flare. As light licked across the narrow, uneven passageway, he followed the turns out of habit, his mind back at the garage's underground hideout.

"How does someone see the dead?" he muttered. "What, you just walk into a place and they're standing there with a Hello, My Name Is on? Theresa-fucking-Caputo of the bloodsuckers. Goddamn."

When the belly of the cave unfurled itself, he stopped and looked around. The bed was nothing more than a cantilevered platform covered with furs, and his trunks and supplies were right where he'd left them. In the back, the natural spring, which was heated through some geological mystery, burbled along as usual. The fire pit was cold, the ashes from when he'd been there the day before last.

Nothing out of place. So why did he think it had been redecorated?

That fucking vampire really needed to get out of his head.

Callum undressed quickly. He always kept changes of clothes on the mountain, in case he needed them, but he didn't think of this cave as his home.

He'd used the garage hideout as a fuck palace and munitions dump.

The hunting cabin was his I'm-trying-to-be-classy place.

And he had a bog-standard, nearly human, basement apartment with a TV and Internet access for when he needed to connect with the outside world he really couldn't be more than an observer of.

Because, hello, to him *An American Werewolf in London* was a documentary, not fiction.

It would be nice to have a proper home.

Before he got into the spring, he took a couple of lengths of wood, set them in the fire circle, and willed them to light. As cheerful orange and yellow flames set up shop on their source of spruce-sustenance, and the filaments of smoke rose up and dispersed into the cracks in the rock ceiling, he felt like he wanted to scream.

So he went to the water.

Lowering himself into the pool, he found the weightlessness soothing, and he pulled himself around to his favorite spot, the smooth contours of the naturally sheared stone like a seat honed just for his body. Letting his head fall back, he watched the play of light.

That *fucking* vampire—

Sure as if he had called the very male into existence, a figure that resembled the one he couldn't get out of his mind for too many reasons stepped out of the passageway and into the cave proper.

Callum lifted his head. "Is she dead then?"

They were going to have a tiger by the tail if anything happened to that female.

When it happened, that was.

"No."

As the male stared across the fire, Callum became very aware that he was naked in the spring. "So what are you doing here."

When there was no answer from the guy, he tightened his own lips. "That was a bloody cruel thing to say, you know. Back at the hunting cabin."

"I know. That's why I came."

There was another pause, and then the vampire crossed his arms over his chest. As his jaw worked like he was trying to chew his own molars to stubs, Callum felt the resolve to hate the bastard ease up a little.

"What the hell is your name, vampire."

"Apex."

Callum threw his head back and laughed. "Oh, they named you right. Top of the food chain, ready to eat anything, you are." As he righted himself, he narrowed his eyes. "So are you here to apologize, then."

"Yes."

More silence. And Callum lifted a brow. "Well, get on with it, mate."

"I'm . . . sorry."

"And?"

The vampire, Apex, frowned. "I said it. I apologized."

"That's it? *I'm sorry?* That's all you've got."

"What else is there? That is the very definition of 'apology.'"

Callum tilted his head to the side. Then he lifted his forefinger. "Question."

"What."

"When was the last time you apologized to anyone? Or are you so 'Apex' that you just don't bother with courtesy and consideration?"

"Mostly, I kill people who are in the way."

"Ah, so we're not well versed in the common practice of apologies. Right. Well, let me explain something to you, predator. Usually there is context around the two words you've staked your claim upon. There is an explanation, a promise to do better, perhaps a plan to improve oneself."

The vampire narrowed his eyes. "You want all that? Really."

As the vampire stood in the firelight, dressed in that black uniform he'd taken off a dead prison guard . . . he was really quite sexy, his short hair, his glowing eyes, those broad shoulders and strong body the kind of package a wolven didn't get to see very often.

And this awkward apology, sheepish thing was pretty frickin' cute.

Abruptly, the soft water that moved with a natural current no longer felt like something to bathe in. It felt like hands on his body. Lips . . . on his body.

Caressing him in places he very much wanted this predator standing in front of him to get into.

"Actually, forget the apology," Callum drawled. "I quite fancy something else from you."

"I don't sing. I don't dance. And I can't read."

"I was thinking of something else entirely." He crooked his finger. "Come here, predator. I'll tell you what I want from you—or show you, if you prefer."

CHAPTER TWENTY-NINE

Inside the red hut, Kane shook his head at the old female. "No, no. Not me, *you* have to help her."

He smoothed his hand over Nadya's forehead again. She was even hotter than she had felt on the way here, yet her skin was as dry as the desert. On her face, he could understand how the scarring might prevent perspiration, but the same seemed true of her extremities where she hadn't been hit with the acid.

"On the contrary, it is up to you and you alone if she is to survive," the old female said. "You are the one who can draw the heat away from her. Lie down beside her, and put your naked flesh onto hers."

"That will just make her hotter!"

There was a pause, and the expression on the mystical female's face changed. But he didn't care if he offended her.

Just as he was about to point that out, she looked over her shoulder to the exit. "Not tonight. Surely not tonight."

"Madam," he said sharply as he tried to be both demanding and respectful. "I need you to—"

"Stay in here," she said urgently as she refocused on him. "And do as I tell you. You must put your skin upon hers—"

"It's not going to work—"

"Then watch her die—it is your choice!"

The old female's tone got through to him like a slap in the face, and he felt his brows pop up. "All right . . . I'll do that."

Not that she seemed to hear him. She went to the hut's flap and lifted it partially. As she leaned out, he had a thought that she was testing the air for scents, but he wasn't sure.

Turning around, she met him in the eye. "You must stay in here. I can protect you if you are under this roof. If you leave, you are on your own—and she will definitely not survive. It is your choice."

Then the female ducked out. What happened next . . . Kane wasn't too sure about.

The walls of the hut began to flutter, as if there was a wind swirling around outside, and then there was a vibration that came up through the earth, the kind of thing that entered him through his contact with the ground and traveled up his own body.

After that, everything went translucent: Sure as if a brilliant light were being shined on the exterior of the structure, the heavy fabric seemed to disappear, a red fog replacing that which had been solid.

Which was how he saw the old female change shape just outside the shelter.

One moment, she was up on two legs; the next, she went into a contortion, her shape changing until she was down on four paws.

As she threw back her head and howled, the eerie sound went into his bones and he looked down at Nadya. Things had taken a very paranormal turn, and that was saying something, considering he was a vampire—

An internal voice cut in: *If you leave, you are on your own—and she will definitely not survive.*

For a second, he was confused about its origins, but then the message truly sunk in.

"Nadya," he said, "I need to lie with you."

He started to remove his clothing, and as he bared his torso, he could really feel the heat rising from her, sure as if he were in front of a fire. Moving faster, he kicked off boots, peeled socks, pulled off his pants. No undergarments.

Staring down at his sex, he gave it a quick pep talk to not get peppy. This was medicine, he told the damn thing.

"I'm going to lie with you now."

She moaned a little and moved under the towel. "Kane?"

"Yes," he said urgently. "Yes, it's me."

"Help me . . ."

"I will. I have to lie down with you."

Nadya lifted her arms up, rolling herself back and forth on the pallet. "Here I am."

Gritting his teeth, he shifted down and stretched out next to her. Immediately, she settled against him, her body like cozying up to a rock that had been baking in the sun, the dry heat warming him as if, sure enough, his flesh was a sponge for it.

The ragged sigh she let out suggested that it wasn't all in his mind, that what the old female had told him to do might work.

"I'm just going to get us sorted," he said awkwardly as he moved arms, shifted legs, positioned them better.

And that was how, for the first time in two hundred years, he came to be naked with a female.

No, that wasn't quite right. Cordelhia had never been fully nude the few times they had been together. She had always declared the need for her modesty by retaining her silken nightgowns, and of course he had wanted to honor whatever made her feel more comfortable.

Besides, though he had wanted further closeness from his *shellan*, he had never been sure whether that was just the nature of sexual acts—or whether it was specific to his mate. Not that the answer to that would have mattered. He had just wanted Cordelhia to be happy, whatever that entailed.

"Shhh," he said as he ran his hand up and down Nadya's shoulder.

He wasn't sure whether he was trying to calm her . . . or himself.

This felt wrong, to lay with another female.

It also seemed very, very right—

Just outside the red fog of the hut, he heard another howl—after which there were voices, males talking with urgency back and forth.

They were under attack, he thought. From who, though?

That was yet another question that did not require an answer. Not right now, at least. He could only hope that Apex, Lucan, and Mayhem would help the wolven.

"I've got you," he whispered as he closed his eyes.

The heat that entered his body was unrelenting, to the point where he was convinced that he was going to have more burns. But as long as Nadya came out of this somehow, any suffering on his part would be worth it.

◆　◆　◆

Inside the wolven's den, Apex stood on a precipice, and the temptation was to jump into the rather miraculous natural basin that, given the steam rising up, had some kind of underground source of heat: The male in the undulating water was staring up with an invitation that was unmistakable, and the urge to get in there with him and find out what else could happen when they were in private was irresistible.

"Your name is Callum."

The wolven nodded. "What have you been calling me in your head? I'm just curious. To me, you were That Vampire. Capital *T*, capital *V*."

"I haven't been calling you anything."

"You sure about that? Even when you weren't sleeping today."

Apex took a step forward. "I didn't have to give you a name."

"No?"

"I just remembered what you looked like down on your knees in front of me."

The vibration that purred up and out of the male in the pool was an enticing sound if Apex had ever heard one—and then Callum's hand disappeared under the churning surface of the water. As he bit his lower lip with sharp white fangs, his eyes glowed.

"What are you doing, wolf?"

"Would you like to see, predator?"

Oh, fuck, yes. "Show me."

The male rose up from whatever ledge he was sitting on, and in the firelight, the muscles of his shoulders and chest gleamed, the droplets of springwater falling from the contours of his torso. But not everything was easy to see. The level in the pool was such that Apex was merely teased by the sight of a strong hand wrapped around a shaft that was long and hard.

As the wolven stroked himself, his forearm flexed and relaxed, the veins popping, the strength erotic as fuck.

"Do you like this, predator."

"Yes . . ."

"Good. I like you watching"—the male's breath caught—"me."

That hand moved faster, and Apex started to feel the stroking in his own cock, as if by some alchemy, the touch was transferred across the distance between them.

"Tell me . . . something . . . predator . . ."

God, he couldn't think. He was consumed by watching the water level flirt with the hand job, the revelations and obscuring a peep show that made everything more captivating.

"What," Apex breathed.

The wolven stopped what he was doing—a total travesty of nature in Apex's view.

"You've never been with a male before, have you."

Apex opened his mouth. Closed it. Then figured, fuck it. "No, I haven't."

The smile that came back at him was slow and very, very satisfied. "How fun. I look forward to this even more."

With that, Callum began jerking himself off properly, the pump hard and fast, the head of his cock breaking out of the surface of the pool, the wolven's head falling back, his lips parting, his rib cage expanding and contracting—

The orgasm was delicious, kicking come out into the pool, and Apex had an irresistible urge to jump in and capture it all, swallow it down, feed off the release.

But he didn't move. Even as his eyes consumed the pleasure and his mind swirled with anticipation, just as his body hungered to spin the wolven around, push him face-first over the lip of the pool, and mount him from behind—

His ears were hearing something that wasn't right.

Off in the distance, there was a howling, the sound loud enough to carry down the passageway to this private fuck cave the wolven had very clearly put to good use before.

And then came the shouting.

That got Callum's attention. His head snapped back to rights and he looked toward the head of the rock tunnel.

"What is it?" Apex demanded as he got out his gun.

"Hunters. Motherfucking hunters."

Sure as if a switch had been thrown, the wolven shed the mantle of passion and hopped out of the pool, pulling his pants back on and going for a cache of weapons.

"They're from that hotel that's being built. They come at night into the territory and try to pick us off in the dens, but at least most of us have other places to live, with this being our sacred community space."

The male checked the bullets in his gun. "All we can do is defend what is ours and bury the bodies. What we do not need is them finding out about our real truth as wolven."

Callum turned and started for the passageway. When Apex fell in behind him, the male paused and looked back.

"What are you doing?"

Off in the distance, there were more howls.

Apex leaned into the guy. "Didn't I already tell you? I'm very, very good at killing things."

There was a split second of silence.

Then that wolven with the magic palm and the perfect body sealed his lips to Apex's.

"That's a rain check," the male said roughly. "And also, a thank-you."

CHAPTER THIRTY

As Callum emerged from his den, Lucan was already running to him sure as if his cousin had come to get the four-pawed cavalry activated.

"They're hiking up the trail," his cousin said. "And it's not hunters."

"The guards from the prison?" Callum glanced back as his predator stalked out. "They found us?"

"It's not that hard. We had other things on our minds than remaining strictly hidden. My mate's staking out behind here. We need to get positions ready—"

A bullet whistled by and pinged off a vein of rock.

"Fuck," Callum said as they all ducked.

Another howl floated up in the night air from somewhere on the left, and Callum knew which wolven it was by the ascendency of notes.

"How many," he demanded as they hustled behind his den's outcropping of boulders.

From out of nowhere, Mayhem, the twitchy one, re-formed. "A dozen or more guards in tactical gear. Guns have silencers on them. And the last guy in the lineup is pulling an empty sled, like they expect to take live hostages with them."

Another bullet ricocheted off some rock and then *pfft*ed into the dirt about a foot from Callum's head.

"Who the fuck are they shooting at?" Lucan muttered as he stationed himself next to his *shellan*.

"They're trying to draw us out," the human female said. "Classic move. They're banking on us not being able to hold fire, and want us to waste ammunition and show our positions. And we're going to do neither."

The woman was solely focused on the trail's entry into the clearing, her eyes narrowed, her gun up and braced against a vee in the stones. She was ready to defend turf that technically wasn't hers.

Except the enemy coming at them was personal, wasn't it.

Shit. With that human among them, they could dematerialize and leave her to die. They had to stay and fight.

That was his last cogent thought.

Like someone hit the go-button, there were suddenly discharges coming from nearly every direction, pieces of tree trunk going flying, lead slugs hitting rocks and sparking, tufts of dirt being thrown up. As the scent of pine quadrupled in the night and he started to return fire, a bullet sizzled right past his ear.

From the opposite direction.

"They're behind us, too," he announced as he swung around.

The good news, if there was any, was that there was a natural trench in the landscape and they were in it, so there was some coverage from the rear. And at least everybody got the memo, half of them continuing to defend the front of their position, while he and Apex began pumping off rounds into the lineup of pines behind them—

Someone was hit. He smelled fresh blood of the vampire variety, but there was no time to worry about who and how badly. Fortunately, next to him, Apex was still shooting in a slow circle, sending bullets out into the trees—

There was a brief shout, a barking order, and then shadows moved from positions, the guards closing in. As the wind came around, Callum smelled the scent of vampires amid the acrid burn of gunpowder, the fresh dirt, and the night air.

They needed more ammo. More weapons.

And with his den's supplies run out, there was only one way to get it all.

The hard way, that was.

✦ ✦ ✦

From his cover in the trench, Apex could track the figures dodging from trunk to trunk, and he was not surprised to see all those familiar black uniforms. He should have known the guards would find them. Maybe there had been locators in the uniforms that no one had been aware of. Who the fuck knew—

"I'm going for more ammo in my garage."

Cranking his head around, he glared at his wolven. "No, you're staying here. We don't know how many more are on the mountain, and we need—"

"Don't get dead, predator. I have plans for you later."

And that was that. The reckless motherfucker just disappeared into thin air.

"Are you kidding me?" Apex said into the absolutely nothing next to him.

A bullet biting his shoulder brought him back to reality, and he resumed panning rounds of gunfire into whatever was out there—

"Lucan!"

The sound of Rio's panic turned him around. Great. Fucking wonderful. The woman's mate had collapsed onto his side, his hands pushed into his groin, which suggested two possible injuries, both of which were fatal, just in different ways.

In one, he had his femoral artery perforated, and was bleeding out.

In the other, he'd just been castrated.

Lucan's female shoved her weapon at Mayhem and the guy double-barreled his shooting, sending God only knew how much lead out in front. And as she tried compression to stop the bleeding, Apex also continued to pull his trigger.

Until his gun was emptied.

After which things went silent behind him. With a quick glance over his shoulder, he met Mayhem's eyes. The male shook his head once.

He was also out of bullets.

"Sonofabitch," Apex muttered as he got prepared for what was coming.

Fucking hell. Unless that wolven pulled off a miracle and got back here in the next thirty seconds, they were going to be captured and dragged off the mountain.

Either on their feet in collars and cuffs.

Or in body bags.

CHAPTER THIRTY-ONE

I t was a dreamscape.

As Nadya felt the furnace inside her begin to lose some of its heat, she was so relieved that a floaty disassociation finished the job of lifting her up and away from the pain. Suspended on a bed of soft air, with time stopping altogether, she was content to just let the tension funnel out of her joints and limbs.

The absence of stiffness was such a shock, she was compelled to move herself—and that was when she discovered she was not alone.

Except she already knew this.

"Kane . . . ," she whispered.

"I'm right here."

More relaxation now, and she told herself to open her eyes and look at him, but her lids were so heavy. Besides, why fight anything. For once, she was without discomfort.

And she was with him.

And . . . he was really, really naked.

So was she.

Nadya discovered all this as she arched her spine, her bare breasts coming against his bare chest, her nipples peaking at the friction—as well as the knowledge that they were lying down without the complication of clothes.

"What happened?" she murmured. "Where are we?"

This had to be a dream, right? Surely this was a dream.

"We're safe."

"Were we in danger?"

"You don't have to worry about anything."

As she felt his hand stroke her head, she had a moment of anxiety as she pictured him passing his palm and fingers over the patches of stubble. Except assuming this was a playground set up by her subconscious, she decided to just pretend she had hair again. Not long hair, as it had been, but some kind of regular growth up there. Maybe a halo of short, soft curls?

"How do you feel?" he asked.

"I feel . . . amazing." She stretched again, and had to admit to herself that she did so in a deliberate manner—so that her nipple ran up what had to be his sternum. "Really amazing."

His breath caught, as if he had felt exactly what she had wanted him to. And then a shudder went through him.

To encourage this fantasy to go further, she moved her leg, bending her knee in such a fluid way, it was unfamiliar, normal function having been absent from her experience of ambulation, of living, for so very long. And of course, because she wanted it to, she made sure that her knee happened to go in between his.

So that the inside of her thigh stroked up the inside of his.

"Nadya . . ."

For a moment, she was worried he was telling her to stop. But then his strong, broad palm slipped down her shoulder and onto her back, making a swoop that ended on one of her hips. When it started its return trip up, she twisted her torso in a manner that would have been completely impossible before—in a manner that brought her breast directly into his pec.

"Oh, God . . ." His voice was strangled, but in a good way, his yearning clearly tightening his throat. "*Nadya.*"

"I love the way you say my name like that."

"How am I saying it?"

"Like you're hungry."

With a boldness that came from this being some kind of dream, she decided to do a little exploring of her own, her hand moving over the muscles of his arm, feeling his corded strength, his long bones. He was built so differently from her, everything hard and unyielding, and she liked that. She wanted that. Nothing soft, all of him hard . . . so he could enter her.

Moving her hips forward, she felt the bump of his erection, and the heated length was a brand she didn't mind the burn of. Especially as he sucked in a breath.

"Is this okay?" she asked.

"Are you fucking kidding me."

At his dry response, she had to laugh. And then nothing seemed particularly funny as he eased onto his back, giving her his whole body to explore. Tucking her head into his throat, she ran her hand down his pecs and onto his heart. Then she kept going, feeling the ridges of his abdomen.

Skirting to the side, his hip bone was a graceful arch, and the expanse of his thigh was thick and streaked with muscle that flexed under her touch—

He caught her hand, stopping her as she went to move up to his sex. "Nadya. Are you sure you know what you're doing?"

"Yes . . ."

"Open your eyes, then."

She thought about that. "No, because then this would be real." As she felt him pull back sharply, she shook her head. "I don't want to be who I am with you. If it's like this, if it's a dream . . . then I can be whole. I want to be like that."

Tears came to her eyes, and as they soaked her lashes, she wondered if he might not get his wish. If she had to raise her lids so she could wipe away the old, familiar pain—

"You are whole to me," he said softly. "Open your eyes."

Bracing herself, she lifted her lids—and there he was for real, the male she had never dared fantasize about in this way, even though she'd wanted to. With a shaking hand, she reached up and touched his face.

"You're really here?"

"Yes."

She glanced past him—and felt a measure of relief. The odd red fog that surrounded them was utterly implausible, and she took solace in it. So this actually was a dream, even this part that felt like he—

"Thank you," he said roughly.

"For what?" she murmured as she ran her hand over his shoulder.

"Touching me. Wanting . . . to touch me."

"How could I not want this?" She kept going onto his smooth chest. "You're beautiful."

There was a strange pain in his face, a darkness in his eyes. But as he shook his head, she had a feeling he was getting rid of it, closing a door firmly.

"I want to kiss you," he said.

"So kiss me."

She tilted her chin up, lifting her mouth into position, and he lowered his head to hers. The brush of his lips against hers was soft, a velvet warmth, tantalizing and comforting at the same time.

"More," she murmured as he went to pull away.

Kane smiled. "More?"

"Yes."

Their words were simple, the syllables neither quick nor slow—yet every response was charged with a powerful electricity that brought along with it a great heat, a volcanic heat—

His hand captured her breast and she arched into him, her moan getting swallowed by him. And when he explored her, teasing her nipple with his thumb, stroking the weight of her and moving on to the other side, she found a rhythm in her hips so that she stroked him as well.

Stroked his erection with her pelvis.

Between her legs, her sex grew swollen and wet, and every time she moved against him, the warmth there redoubled. But it wasn't like before. This kind of heat was nothing painful. It made her feel alive.

And . . . beautiful.

Spearing her hands into his hair, she held on to him, giving herself fully to what was happening between them: the teasing exploration, the promise of release, the security of knowing that this beautiful male did not judge her as less than.

But instead saw her as worthy, exactly the way she was.

✦   ✦   ✦

As Kane stared into Nadya's eyes, he was aware of something in the back of his mind, an alarm going off, quietly and persistently. There was a problem he needed to worry about. Something urgent . . .

"I love that you want to touch me."

The words jumped out of his mouth and shocked him because they revealed a truth that was complex—and he kept the second half of it to himself: His *shellan* never had wanted to. And, dearest Virgin Scribe, there was a big difference between duty and desire.

Nadya's touch was like a sunrise, and it brought good warmth. The healing kind.

He had a thought that he had more things to say, but then he was kissing her again, reveling in the difference of being with a female who wanted him. Maybe needed him. And didn't that take his attraction to the next level.

To the soul level.

The next thing he knew, his lips were on the side of Nadya's throat, but when she tilted her head to offer him her vein, he knew that was not a good idea. She seemed to have rallied. He just didn't know for how long, and he wasn't taking chances.

Besides, there were other places he wanted to put his mouth.

Her breast was a soft, creamy swell, unscarred and smooth, the nipple taut and ready for him to capture it. So he did. Sucking the flesh in, he rolled it with his tongue, circling, circling, before latching onto it again.

Beneath him, she was arching even more, her body so fluid, her chest inflating as she had to pull air into her hungry lungs. With his free hand, the one that wasn't propping him up to keep him from crushing her, he explored the other side of her breasts, feeling the contrast of her skin between the tip and the contours, pinching gently the nipple, rubbing at her.

He had all the time in the world and no time at all, both desperate and patient. Which seemed to fit this strange plane of existence they were on: It was as if they were neither here nor there, not dead, certainly, but not alive, either, in the conventional sense—

He was supposed to be worried about something.

The conviction was so strong, he lifted his head and looked over his bare shoulder. The red fog that surrounded them, and gave the impression that they were floating, seemed like an impenetrable boundary, no way to get in or out of it. And yet he remembered something about the exit being right over there, at the flap.

"Kane?"

Blinking, he shook his head and refocused. "Hi."

"Are you all right?"

"I need . . . something is out there, something dangerous."

"Where are we?"

"On the mountain. I think. I don't know." The old female, he thought. "She told me . . ."

What had she told him? The gray-haired female had told him—

"Stay here," he blurted. "That's what it was. I have to stay here with you."

And yet that didn't sit right. He just couldn't seem to recall why, as if his memory was like the landscape on the far side of the foggy boundary. Too far away to read.

"Well, I'm glad you're here."

Forcing himself to leave the ether alone, he looked at the female who was lying naked in his arms. "I want . . . you."

"Then take me," Nadya said.

CHAPTER THIRTY-TWO

Under the Fuck-It rule of warfare, when you were out of ammunition and in a position that was not offering sufficient coverage to be considered even remotely defensive, and when no backup was making an appearance, there was only one thing left to do.

You took the pin out of your aggression-grenade and did something so outrageously stupid, the enemy was briefly frozen in disbelief.

"I'll take care of this," Apex said to no one in particular.

Where was that fucking wolven?

"Where are you going?" Rio shot back as she looked up from Lucan.

"Out for a stroll in the woods."

"Apex—"

Closing his eyes, he dematerialized into the field of battle, re-forming behind the only guard who'd stayed in the same position. The rest of them moved around, shifting from tree to boulder to tree. Not this guy.

Mr. Static was either shitting his pants at his first combat experience. Or he was wounded. Or maybe he just liked the view.

In any event, Apex was on him before the bastard knew it, a sharp blade opening a barn door in his carotid artery while at the same time leaving his windpipe nonfunctional. No more high or low notes for him.

Catching the body when it started to slump, Apex laid it on the ground, stripped the weapons, and waited.

Three . . .

Two . . .

One—

Another guard was in a forward position about twenty feet over. Leveling the muzzle of the handgun he'd just taken, Apex waited for the flash after the other trigger was pulled—and then he discharged a bullet of his own at the target that revealed itself: There was a strangled yell, and then the oh-so-lovely sound of a sack of potatoes hitting the ground.

With a quick check of the magazine, he confirmed he had seven bullets in the chamber. Not enough. Keeping his eyes on what was in front of him, he patted down the bled-out guard, feeling the body heat still radiating from the torso, and he found—

"Toss the weapon and hands up or I shoot you in the head."

Apex cursed and considered trying to dematerialize. Until he felt the precise circle of a gun muzzle on the back of his skull.

"I'm waiting," the guard snapped.

As Apex pitched the handgun, the loss of ammo stung just as much as the loss of the weapon itself, and then he put his palms up in classic stickup fashion. The clink of handcuffs was a musical sound, and he felt his right wrist get taken in a rough hold and cuffed with steel. But he didn't care about that. He was waiting for the spin-around.

Because, really, somebody needed to welcome the sonofabitch with a head butt.

The second his body was sent for a little turn, he—

The gun was shoved right into his face, with such force it bent his nose. The guard was not one he recognized, but then it wasn't like he'd gone to a cocktail party with any of the fuckers.

"If you make me shoot you right now, prisoner, you won't know whether your friends made it out of here alive."

Well, guess that was why the bastard was taking his time with that left-wrist thing.

As the guard nodded a signal, there was a rustling from behind the boulders, and as Apex glanced to the sound, he saw Mayhem and Rio being marched out of that foxhole behind Callum's little pool party location. There was a pair of guards with them.

Lucan was being dragged by his arms and appeared to be unconscious.

"You fuck around with me," the guard said, "I will order all three of them shot. Right here and now."

Apex cursed in his head. Yes, they'd been outnumbered, but goddamn it. And it went without saying that they were being taken back to the camp and would be used as examples of what not to do.

Those pegs on that stained wall were going to have a new set of body weights to hold in place.

"Let's move them out," the guard said. "Do we have the all-clear—"

As the question was cut off, Apex didn't pay attention. He was too busy running probabilities on escape ideas—and calculating how many coffins were likely to be required with each scenario.

And then he realized the gun being pointed at him was gone. So was its guard.

Apex looked down.

Well. This was unexpected. The male in the uniform appeared to have spontaneously ruptured his entire throat: Glossy red blood was everywhere.

The question was who had done the handiwork with the knife.

The two guards who had daisy-chained Mayhem and Rio started shouting, and it was with a feeling of total unreality that Apex watched as something came out of the darkness and went for their throats.

It was not a vampire, that was for sure. It was more like a tree trunk that had suddenly taken on a life of its own, moving with a sinewy grace. Attacking with deadly accuracy.

The mountain itself defending her own.

Both of the guards dropped to the ground, one after the other.

And then Rio threw herself over Lucan, putting up her handcuffed wrists like she was prepared to use them as battering rams to protect him.

She was clearly far more scared of whatever was roaming around the darkness than of the guards and the prospect of being taken back to the prison camp and tortured to death.

What the *hell* was out there?

CHAPTER THIRTY-THREE

For Callum, the descent to his garage at the base of the elevation was lightning fast. Even though his wolven side wanted to run, he dematerialized to the supply hideout, and the second he arrived, he went down to the gun closet. After draping himself in bullet delivery devices of various calibers, he accessorized with enough ammo to wage a siege on a military installation.

The trouble started when he reemerged and made sure the bolt-hole was secure. As he stepped out of the garage, he caught the scent in the air.

Blood.

And it was one of his own.

He tracked the scent into the woods a couple of hundred yards, and he found the slaughtered wolven just off the side of the trail. Sinking down on his haunches, he closed his eyes briefly . . . and then scented the corpse's fur.

Vampire.

Not a human poacher.

It was definitely a guard, but how in the hell had they found this place? There were thousands of square acres, and they just happened to show up here? Bullshit. Glancing back in the direction of the garage, he wondered where the tracer was. A piece of clothing? Or had they done something subcutaneous to the prisoners that they didn't know about?

With a shaking hand, he touched the still-warm flank and whispered an incantation to the Gray Wolf to see the male safely to the sacred grove. Later, he would come back and take care of the remains—

The sound of two males talking floated over on the breeze, and he had to make a decision: Stay armed and on two legs to track them . . . or increase his senses and ability to travel.

He had no choice but to keep going with the weapons.

Dematerializing up about three hundred yards, he re-formed behind a large pine and was goddamned grateful he knew every tree on the mountain. When that got him closer, but not in range, he moved forward once again—

And got too close.

As his corporeal form reappeared, he was right next to two guards, both dressed the way the ones at the prison camp had been. The fact that the males were on his land at all, killing his kind, felt like a condemnation of what he and his two cousins had done when they'd framed Lucan at the demand of the elders.

They should have known better.

Now wolven were dying because they'd brought the prison camp to the mountain.

His other side demanded expression, but he choked down the pounding fury in his veins. Taking out a laser-sighted handgun, he turned off the red beam and leveled the muzzle. In the moonlight that filtered down, he aimed for the one on the left.

When he pulled the trigger, he willed the bullet to go into the plane of the male's cheek, and sure enough, as if the lead slug were remote-controlled, it entered just under the eye. The sound of the discharge got the attention of the guard's partner, but the amount of time it took for him to get out his gun and try to triangulate where the attack had come from was too long.

Callum picked him off like he was a tin can on a fence post.

As the guard joined his little friend in perma-repose, Callum went dead still, stopping his breath—he would have stopped his heart if he could.

There were more sounds up ahead.

It was too dangerous to dematerialize—if there had been other guards within any kind of sightline to the pair he'd killed, he might get popped himself.

He was silent as he shifted through the pines, grateful that with the harsh winters, there wasn't much undergrowth to trample on.

His wolven side would have been much better. But again, he couldn't leave the arsenal behind.

Why the *fuck* hadn't he kept more provisions on the mountain?

Because it had always been a peaceful, protected place.

Except for the human poachers, of course—and they were easy prey, very different from a professionally trained and armed force, trying to get their prisoners back—

Callum.

Just as he heard his name, his boot landed on a dry stick, and the cracking sound was loud as a mortar going off.

And when he turned his head to see who had called for him, a bullet hit him square in the chest, knocking him off his feet.

As he landed on his back, he tried to lift his weapon so he had a chance at defending himself. His arm wasn't working—and every breath was like getting stabbed in the sternum. Turning his head to the side, he coughed blood and thought . . .

Wow, so it ends here.

He'd always known he'd die on the clan's land—he'd never once anticipated living into any kind of old age. Still, it was a shock to realize that what had seemed like something far off in the future was happening right this moment.

He was dying.

He supposed that he should be thinking of his family, from his parents, who had long since passed, to his hundred or so siblings that had been born, lived, and died, over the last two centuries.

Instead, the only thing on his mind was his vampire.

Would his predator come to this spot sometime, after his soul was gone from his body, and see him lying here?

They had had so little time—

The approach of his killer was mostly silent, but not completely so, confirmation, not that he needed it, that whoever had put a bullet in him was not well versed in working their way through a wooded envi-ronment.

A pair of black boots entered his line of vision, and he followed a set of legs up to a lean torso.

It was a female, and she was staring at him with a detachment char-acteristic of people who killed often and not always with provocation.

"I was aiming for your heart," she said levelly as she looped her rifle over her arm. "My goddamn sight needs to be calibrated."

❖ ❖ ❖

After Kane had heard gunshots and left that red hut, he hadn't been aware of vacating his body—or being tossed out of it, was more the case.

But he was back now, and as he felt his bones accept his weight, he licked his lips and tasted blood. Then he looked down in confusion. A guard in a prison camp uniform was dead at his feet. And there were a couple of others in the same condition close by.

"Kane."

He turned around. Apex was standing next to him, the male streaked with blood, a set of handcuffs hanging off of one wrist. And that was when the scent of injury registered. Somebody, one of theirs, was badly wounded—

Lucan was laid out on the pine needles, Rio arched over him, her cuffed hands pushed into his groin.

"He's bad," she said. "We need to get a doctor."

Kane looked over his shoulder for the hut, just to make sure Nadya was okay—

What the fuck.

Where was the hut?

"Hold on," he said as he started to bolt back to where it should have been.

Well aware there could be more guards on the mountain, he all but jumped over the fire pit, except when he got to the hut's location . . . nothing.

And that wasn't all. The riverbed was dry and there were short-stack bushes rooted in earth that was undisturbed: No rushing water, no campfire, no shelter. It was as if nothing had ever been there.

What the hell?

He'd been making love to Nadya, treating her body as it deserved, reveling in the fact that she had not been doing some duty, but rather enjoying him as well . . . when he'd heard the gunfire. The sounds of bullets being exchanged had been far off, but very real, and the idea that his fellow prisoners or the wolven who had taken them in were in trouble had clawed into his consciousness.

That was when he'd seen the flap door. From out of the red fog that surrounded him and Nadya, the exit presented itself as if his change in awareness had created the portal. He had said something to Nadya, something like he'd be right back, and she knew what he was doing.

She had heard the gunshots, too.

And then he was out of the shelter, naked as the day he was born, the sense that he had been away for over a year making him look around to re-catalog the surroundings. But nothing had changed because it had been mere moments—

"Kane!"

Rio was coming out of the woods in a scramble, tripping over her feet, her face pale. "Where's Nadya? She's a nurse—"

"I don't know—"

Except as he turned back to the dry riverbed and the thatch of vegetation, a leg appeared from what seemed to be a split in the landscape. And then, sure as if she were stepping through a set of drapes, his female appeared, the towel she had been wrapped in once again around her body, her eyes wide like she didn't understand what was happening.

For a split second, Kane froze. Something was different about her . . .

"We need your help," he mumbled.

But she was already looking at the human woman who was running toward them. "Who is injured?"

Andjustlikethat, his female went rushing by him, ready to do what she could. As she passed, she gave his hand a squeeze, and it felt like he was following his destiny as he ran in her wake. When they came up to Rio, he listened with half an ear as she explained what had happened and gestured wildly to where Lucan was lying.

It wasn't that he didn't care that his fellow prisoner was injured.

He couldn't stop staring at Nadya.

She was moving differently. More than that, though, her hair . . . seemed thicker on her head—and when she glanced back at him, the scars on her cheek appeared to have faded, the uneven ridges less pronounced.

"—Kane!" She waved a hand in his face. "We need you to find some medical supplies."

All at once, his hearing came back to him, and he nodded. Of course. Medical supplies. He'd go find—

"I think I know where we can go."

He turned to Apex. "Tell me."

"The garage, at the base of the mountain. It had a stretcher, it had other stuff. It's our only chance, assuming some wolven doesn't show up in an ambulance. Here. You take these."

Weapons were pressed into his hands, and then the male took a step back. "I'll go get the supplies. I know how to get into the place."

There was a split second of suspended animation, as if both were waiting for the other to say something; then Apex was gone, and Kane was running up to his female and making a report.

"He's going for what you need. He knows where to find . . ."

He stopped talking as he looked down at Lucan. The male was dying, and everyone knew it. He could tell by the way Mayhem was desperately trying to stop the bleeding, his two huge hands pressed into the male's groin, his face a stark mask of pain, even though he was not physically injured. Meanwhile, up at Lucan's head, Rio was at her mate's ear, talking to him, urging him not to go.

As if the choice was his.

And in the center, Nadya was probing the male's abdomen, like she was looking for more injuries.

Giving Apex the job of getting supplies had been the right thing to do.

Kane wanted to be here when his female lost her patient—and Rio lost her love. And as he stood over the sad tableau, he felt himself getting sucked back into his past . . . picturing Cordelhia in her bedchamber, all her blood out of her veins and staining the fine silk covers and woven blankets that her family had included with her mating payment.

When a wave of dizziness came over him, he threw out a hand and caught his balance with the help of a tree branch—

Something moved about fifteen yards away into the tree line.

Narrowing his eyes, he subtly turned his head. "I'll be right back."

With a quick shift, he ducked down and jogged in the direction of the disturbance. He'd thought it was down near the ground, only appearing to be higher up because of a rise in the earth. He was right.

It was a guard who had sustained a gunshot wound to the head. The neat little entry wound at the temple was very no-muss-no-fuss that was nonetheless very lethal—just taking its time to kill the male. The bastard was still moving, his hands making circles at his sides as if he were trying to paddle himself out of the Grim Reaper's reach.

Kane knelt and thought about the fact that someone he knew very well and cared about a great deal was dying on a similar countdown.

Capturing one of those rotating hands, he yanked up the sleeve of the uniform, lowered his head, and bared his fangs—

At the same time he struck the flesh he had revealed, he reached up and slapped a palm over the guard's mouth so the howl of pain didn't travel far. And then he retracted his bite and watched.

As the flesh began to be consumed by some invisible, hungry force, Kane shook his head and wondered why he needed the confirmation.

Then he thought of Lucan's cousin staring at him with wide eyes, telling him he didn't have to worry about weapons.

Glancing through the trees at Nadya as she did what she could for a dying male, he focused on her hair.

The patches were disappearing because new growth was overtaking them, the baldness filling in before his very eyes. And her face was even smoother than it had been when she'd first appeared to step through a slit in the fabric of time and space.

As he fell back on his ass and put his elbows on his knees and his head in his hands, he stared at the guard's arm as white bone began to show through the red meat of the muscle and sinew. And then it was all bone, nothing else.

With the infection or whatever it was continuing to spread, Kane counted the passing minutes by how the back of the hand turned to a skeleton's, and the nail beds were consumed, and finally the bones fell loose to the weave of pine needles in the same orientation they had just been connected in.

A deadly mystery.

He once again looked at Nadya.

That may well be a saving grace.

CHAPTER THIRTY-FOUR

Callum had been here.

That was Apex's first thought as he burst into the garage. All he had to do was take a deep breath and he could catch the fading scent of the wolven with the talented mouth and hands. The male had come for weapons, not medical supplies, however, and as Apex hit the trigger to send the toolbox off its seat, he prayed it wasn't going to take him long to locate the first aid shit down among the parkas and other provisions.

Actually, he prayed that that wolven would suddenly show up again, although that was less about the needle-in-a-haystack stuff and more about just wanting to confirm for himself that sonofabitch was still alive.

With the stairs exposed, he jumped down into the bunker and ransacked the otherwise neat and tidy arrangement of everything. He was looking for something with a red cross on a white background to it—come on, there had to be a duffle, a box, a collection, fucking anything that could help someone with a mission critical leak.

Nope. He found ammo, booze, more ammo, guns, knives, ropes. Dried food. Water. Gasoline.

The more time passed, the rougher and more desperate his hands got until he was pulling parkas off hooks and sending them flying, the Gore-Tex birds failing to stay aloft in spite of how many feathers were stuffed into their quilted panels. And then he hit a lineup of steamer trunks, but he found only clothes that had long sleeves and lots of pockets—

The sting on his hand was like he'd clutched a swarm of yellow jackets, and he whipped his arm back out of the soup made of pants and long Johns. A quick check on his palm and nothing was bleeding, swelling or abraded.

Frowning, he scooped out the contents of the trunk—

The brown belt was on the very bottom, crammed into the back corner. Made of what felt like cowhide and with a hand-tooled buckle, it was a utilitarian object as exotic as a sock.

He had to drop it, the sensations were so uncomfortable.

As the length bounced and the buckle rattled, he looked over to the showerhead. The image of the body was still there, and he didn't need a close-up comparison to know that what he had found by mistake was what had been used by the male to kill himself.

"Fucking hell."

Bracing himself, he picked the belt up and put it back where he'd found it. Then he shoved the clothes back in, ignoring the fact that he'd messed them all up.

There'd be time later to fix that.

Maybe.

Up on his feet, he looked at the dead male. "You know where the first aid kit is?"

He didn't expect an answer. He didn't get one. The dead never talked to him, which was the good news. Just locking eyes with them was enough, fuck him very much.

Turning away from the shower, there was nothing else to go through.

Well, shit. Lucan better hope for a miracle.

＋ ＋ ＋

As Nadya assessed Lucan's thigh wound, she knew they were running out of time with him. The blood loss had slowed, thanks to a vampire's natural healing capabilities, but it was not stopping. Not by a long shot.

"I need a belt."

"Here." Mayhem swiveled around and began undoing what was around his waist. "Take mine."

She grabbed what he held out. "And a knife."

One appeared right in front of her and she didn't bother wasting time to figure out who had given it to her. She cut through the pants that Lucan had on, slicing most of the leg off. Then she pulled the fabric up the thigh, slipped the belt around the muscle, and tightened it until the flesh swelled up around the leather length.

Making sure the constriction was between the heart and the wound was critical, and Lucan was lucky that he hadn't been hit any higher up. If he had been, there would have been no way to tourniquet the injury.

She looked at Rio. "He needs your vein." As the woman's eyes bulged, Nadya talked over the questions that were coming. "Yes, I know you're a human, but he's bonded to you. Your blood will give him a burst of energy because of the way he responds to you. It's a quick fix, but it's all we've got. We need him to hang on until . . ."

There was no telling when the "until" was going to arrive or what it was going to look like.

"I'll do it," Rio said. "Whatever he needs."

The woman pulled up her sleeve and extended her wrist over her mate's lax mouth. But Lucan wasn't strong enough to bite. He'd taken a turn for the worse in the last two or three minutes, and it was doubtful that he was going to be able to break the skin, much less latch on.

"You can use this." Nadya handed over the hunting knife. "You just have to open the vein yourself."

Rio's hand shook as she took the hilt of the blade, and when she looked down at the inside of her wrist, the color went out of her face so that she was almost as pale as her male was.

"Here." Nadya gently took the knife back. "Would you like me to help you?"

"Please. And hurry."

The petrified courage on the woman's face was the definition of love itself: Though she was absolutely terrified, she was not going to allow herself to turn back, not when she could save the one she loved.

For a moment, Nadya pictured Kane's face—his new one, not the old one. Then she said softly, "Look at him, focus on him. You won't feel a thing if you connect with how much you love him."

Rio's eyes shimmered with tears and one crystalline drop escaped, pooling on her lower lashes and then falling down her cheek. She was impatient as she brushed it away.

"Do it."

Nadya nodded, and waited as the woman took a deep breath. Then she put the blade to the bones that were so close to the skin, and penetrated the flesh running parallel to them.

The blood welled immediately, and Nadya rushed the source of energy to Lucan's mouth. "Talk to him. He needs to hear your voice. Tell him to drink."

"Lucan? Honey, it's me." The woman smoothed his hair back from his forehead. "I want you to . . . swallow? Okay? I need you to swallow."

Rio looked up for confirmation that that was correct, and when Nadya nodded, she continued speaking in the same quiet but firm voice.

And that was all they could do with what they had: The blood was pooling on his lips, right under his nose. He just had to open his mouth and take it down. Whether he could or not, was up to Fate.

As Nadya let herself fall back into a sit upon the soft padding of the pine needles, she thought of her mentor.

Do what you can with what you have, whenever and wherever you are.

Memories of the prison camp came back to her, and none of the images were good. She saw males and females who were half-starved, ill, injured, all of them being forced to package the drugs that were brought into the camp for distribution down in Caldwell.

"Is he going to make it?"

Mayhem put the question out there as blood trickled off of the sides of Lucan's closed lips.

"I hope so." Nadya reached out and stroked the sides of Lucan's windpipe. "Swallow, Lucan. If you want to pull through this, you have to swallow."

Her voice was so sharp and demanding that it cut through the crooning of his mate.

And sure enough, that was what did the trick. The male responded to the command and gurgled—and then took everything that had gathered around his tongue down into his gut.

It was not going to be like it would be if the blood were of the species. But it was what they had for where they were, and his bonding for the woman was going to turbocharge the strength it gave him.

"Just keep feeding him," she said.

Glancing over her shoulder, she wondered where Apex was with those supplies. Although what Lucan really needed was an operating theater and a surgeon who could delicately reattach the severed artery.

"Stay with us, Lucan . . ."

"Honey, I need you to swallow—"

From somewhere off to the left, Kane suddenly reappeared, and as he looked at her across the dying wolven's body, he had the strangest expression on his face.

Nadya stared up at him, and worried that he thought she wasn't doing enough. *I'm sorry*, she mouthed.

For what? he mouthed back.

As she considered her options, she didn't know, she really didn't.

No, that was a lie.

She had fallen in love with him. Sometime, over the last twenty-four hours, she had gone from teetering on the edge to free-falling into thin air.

And her gut told her it was going to mess everything up.

Assuming they made it off the mountain alive.

CHAPTER THIRTY-FIVE

Down in Caldwell, a good twenty feet under the earth in the training center, Vishous was standing outside the treatment room his sister had been delivered into. He wanted to light up, but she had an oxygen feed, and although the chances of things going fireball with the door closed between them was low, he really didn't feel like adding to the fun and games that were already rolling out tonight.

So instead, he just held on to the hand-rolled—his last that was prepared—like it was a blankie and he was fucking two years old.

Maybe three.

On the far side of that closed door, he could hear Doc Jane and Manny talking in low voices, and he took that to mean that things were going downhill.

"Hey, you want some?"

He looked over. Butch was coming out of the cafeteria, an open can of Coke in his dagger hand, a bag of chips in the other. Hard to know which one he was offering, but it went without saying he would give either away.

Once Butch was in range, he planted his firm ass on the concrete corridor's floor and put the can to the side.

"Sour cream and onion," V murmured as he went over and sat with his buddy.

"Yup."

When the open bag was offered, V shook his head and decided to hell with it and lit up. As he exhaled, he realized he hadn't really been worried about combustion. He just hadn't felt right about enjoying any-thing while his sister was in rough shape.

And hey, if his roommate could dive into a Lay's bag, he might as well bust out his Bic.

"How's she doing?" Butch asked as he munched.

"Not so hot." V stared at his lit tip. "She needs to go to the Sanctu-ary."

"Have you called Lassiter."

"I keep hoping he'll just show up. But I'm working through my feel-ings about that."

"Deep breathing?"

"Convincing myself I don't need to punch something." God, he was such an ass. "But you're right."

Rolling onto one butt cheek, he took out his cell phone and locked his hand-rolled between his teeth. As he texted, he tried not to sound as desperate as he was getting—and then he wondered what the fuck was wrong with him. Like his sister's life was worth less than his precious ego when it came to that angel?

Hitting send, he set the phone faceup on his thigh. "He'll get back to me."

As he and Butch both stared at the closed door, he wondered whether he could take her up there himself, and then remembered that his mate and Payne's wouldn't let her leave before they had done a thor-ough assessment of her physical condition.

"Who'd she heal?" Butch asked.

"Old guy. Who worked at the pharmacy."

As he recalled the way the father and son had embraced, he wondered why life seemed determined to show him clips of family wholesomeness when he had no interest in it. He so wasn't looking for Tim the Tool Man Taylor to come and make his little Jonathan Taylor Thomas feel better about things.

Aware that he had mixed up the reference, he quit it with the trying to find metaphors.

"I was right, you know," he said. Because sometimes, when you were feeling shitty, getting superior about something even when no one was competing with you for top dog made you feel better. "Whoever broke into that pharmacy went there with a purpose."

"As a former cop, I can tell you that nine out of ten crimes are committed with a purpose."

"Is that like nine out of ten dentists recommend?"

"If you're talking about fluoride, yes." Butch put another chip in his mouth. "And do you need a Snickers?"

"No, I'm actually most myself when I'm hangry."

"Remind me why I live with you again?"

"Because I can fix the wireless router when it goes out."

Butch held up his forefinger. "Oh, right. It's coming back to me now."

"Anyway, whoever broke into that pharmacy needed medical supplies, not shit to cook up dope with. That was the reason."

"We're never going to find that prison camp."

V frowned. "And you're the one who wears the Jesus piece."

"I'm just saying, if they want to stay hidden, they will."

"Not acceptable." V picked up his phone and went to the Internet. "They're going to need a place big enough to house, what, three or four hundred people minimum—underground or in a sufficiently stable structure to protect the prisoners from daylight. It's going to have to have some mod cons so that they can conduct business. Like they'll need cell phone access or at least a landline. Rudimentary electricity and running water. A perimeter fence and guard stations."

"So they'd want an abandoned prison, for example."

"Exactly." He continued typing. "Because the chances of them finding another underground facility like the first location? Very small."

"There isn't one in New York State. Vacant prison, that is."

"How do you know."

Butch pointed to his own chest. "Cop, remember."

V frowned at the results he got. "There isn't an abandoned prison, by the way."

"Do you ever listen to anybody. Like, ever?"

"We need to look at other places. An abandoned museum. Old mansion. Sports complex, library, city hall."

"Well, that'll narrow it down, if you're looking through the entirety of New York State. Sure. How many are there, like, a thousand or two?"

"Think positively."

Butch crumpled the bag. "This coming from you?"

Both of them looked up at the same time. Then they turned their heads to the left.

Lassiter, the fallen angel, was stepping out of the glass-fronted office, and as he came down to them, his long strides covered the distance with an impressive alacrity. And, hey, he wasn't in pink zebra print today. Surprise!

"How's she doing?" the angel asked.

For once, his blond-and-black hair was pulled back, and he was super serious. Which was a little like Mr. Bean trying to give a TED Talk. You just kept waiting for the guy to go off on a tangent that involved putting his head in a Thanksgiving turkey.

V shook his head. "She needs to go to the Sanctuary and heal up there."

"The recharging will help." Lassiter glanced at the closed door. "They're in with her now? The docs."

"Yeah."

"I can wait."

"Please don't. She didn't look so hot."

Lassiter bent at the waist in a bow. "I'll take care of it right now."

V opened his mouth to say something. But then he closed it as the angel went through the door and the panel shut in his wake.

It was hard to be a douche to the guy when he was actually helping. Even though Payne had done the healing thing before, and had fallen into similar states of molecular exhaustion, it seemed like there was some kind of cumulative effect on her, each intercession on her part taking her closer to an edge nobody wanted her anywhere near.

"What the hell happened to that angel," Butch murmured. "It's like he's running out of battery strength."

Shaking his head, V went back into his phone. "Betty White did die. Maybe that's why he's in a decline."

"Yeah, that's got to be it. The last thing we need is more turnover in that role. I wonder who he would turn your mother's job over to."

"Not me." V started thumbing through results of his Internet search. "I am not in the running for that thankless position."

"You don't want to be in charge of the Other Side?"

"Fuck no."

"Oh."

"You sound disappointed." V glanced over. "But you know the Scribe Virgin, and then Lassiter, and then whoever is next, can't play favorites when it comes to the hard graft of destiny. That's not how it works."

Butch took a draw off of his soda. "Oh, I wasn't thinking about pulling rank like that. It's the closet space."

"Excuse me?"

"Payne told me that your mother had the mother of all closets in her bedroom up there. I figure I could use some of them. Or, you know, most of them."

Cursing, V went back to the search. "You're a sick man."

"And there are twelve seasons of weather in Caldwell. Jus' sayin.'" Butch tilted his head all the way back and finished his soda. "Here. I'm done with this. You can use it to ash in."

As the male set the empty red can between them, V had to smile. That was the thing with your best friend. They knew when you needed somewhere to tap your cigarette before you did.

They were also the type to sit outside a hospital room, when you were shitting your pants about your sister but didn't want to admit that to anybody, and talk to you about anything but what was really on your mind.

"Thanks," V said as he took his hand-rolled to the little hole.

"Anytime," his roommate replied.

CHAPTER THIRTY-SIX

Apex re-formed back at the wolven's clearing, ready to get some advice from Callum about where they could go for medical supplies. As soon as he was corporeal, he caught the scent of vampire blood and followed it around to where he'd left the drama.

Well, what do you know, Lucan had a belt on. And they were trying to get him to feed, his female's wrist over his mouth.

"I didn't find anything," Apex announced as all kinds of faces turned to him. "Where's Callum."

"He hasn't been back yet," Kane said. "So there wasn't anything down there?"

"Oh, there was shit. Just nothing that's going to help, not unless you think he's going to need a parka to shovel snow in or some target practice."

"Goddamn it—"

Apex took the other prisoner's arm and urged him out of range. "So Callum hasn't been back?"

"No. There haven't been any wolven around, actually. They seem to have scattered."

"Fucking cowards." Then again, was it really their fight? "What are we going to do with Lucan?"

Nadya rose up and came over. "He's stabilized a little. But he's either going to lose his life or that leg. We've cut off circulation to it completely, which has stemmed the blood loss, but the tissue is going to start dying soon—and there's no way I can operate on it. Even if we were in a sterile environment, that's way beyond my abilities."

"Where's the nearest human healer?" Kane asked.

When there was no answer from anybody, Apex realized he was looking at two people who had as much knowledge about the environs as he did.

"We need to go find a human," Kane announced. "Get into their brain, find something that way."

Apex's eyes went out to the valley below. He had no idea what time it was, but that didn't matter. They were going to be scrubbing memories whether or not they had to wake a man or a woman up to raid their brain.

"You two need to go," Nadya said.

"No way—"

"No fucking way—"

Nadya dropped her voice. "If there were still guards on the mountain, they would have attacked by now. It's more likely that whatever's left of them are steaming down the trail because you eliminated so many and they're in retreat."

"Or they're getting reinforcements," Kane cut in.

"From where? How many have you killed in the last twenty-four hours?" As that shut her male up, the nurse kept going. "You need to stick together. Rio's a trained shooter. Mayhem is good with a gun. I'll keep Lucan as stable as I can. We have to split up if we're going to get him the help he needs."

Kane broke off and did a little walk around like he was losing his mind and didn't want to speak until he was sure he had himself under better control.

"We can move you into Callum's den," Apex said. "You'll have your back against the wall, but it's a single access passageway and we can leave you with enough guns and ammo to kit out a small army."

"Dearest Virgin Scribe," Kane muttered.

"He's going to lose that leg," Nadya said. "It's already turning blue at the toes. He needs a real doctor."

Apex looked at the other male. And when things continued to be tense and silent, he glanced at Nadya—

And did a double take.

The female was looking . . . well, she had a full head of hair all of a sudden. To the point where it was brushing the lobes of her ears, the baldness completely gone. And her face had smoothed out, no more of the skeletal bones and scarred skin.

In fact, she was almost radiant, the kind of female that people would glance at, and then keep staring toward, because she was pleasing to the eye.

Apex looked at Kane and thought of the shape the nurse had been in when they'd brought her up here to the hut.

"Fine," Kane announced. "But I don't like this."

Holy crap, Apex thought. What the hell was in that male's veins?

Whatever it was, it had both nearly killed the female . . . and resurrected her.

◆　◆　◆

Before Kane dematerialized down into the valley below, he stepped against Nadya and dropped a kiss to her mouth without thinking about it. And as she kissed him back, he liked the sense they were both on the same page with things.

At least one part of the night wasn't going badly.

"We have to move him," Kane said to Rio. "If both Apex and I are leaving, Lucan needs to be in a more secure area."

The female, who still had her wrist to her mate's mouth, just nodded in a wan way.

"And you need to stop feeding him," Nadya said. "Before we have two people needing transfusions."

Too right, Kane thought as the woman tried to stand up and wobbled.

"Let me bandage that up," Nadya said as she looked around like she expected there to be supplies available.

It was the kind of knee-jerk thing healers did. Except there was nothing.

"Come on," he said. "I'll take his head."

Apex stepped in to heft up Lucan's feet, and then they were all moving in a group. The relocation involved a squeeze through the entrance to the passageway into Callum's den, and then some narrowing twists and turns that meant they had to slow down or risk knocking Lucan into hard things that were not going to help.

Inside the den, they settled Lucan on the pallet across from the natural spring basin while Mayhem started moving in the weapons they'd taken off the guards. Thanks to the gun belts the males had been fitted with, there was plenty of ammo, and Kane started to feel slightly better about things as Rio went through the various guns and handled them with complete confidence.

And then it was time to go.

Drawing Nadya aside, he stared down into her eyes. There were things he wanted to say, but there was no time, so he just stroked her hair and her neck—

Hair.

With a sense of wonder, he touched the lengths that were just below her ears. But as he went to say something, she interrupted him.

"Just come back safe with a plan."

"I'll come back to you, I promise."

As something warm bloomed in the center of his chest, it had nothing to do with what she looked like. It was the fact that she was willing to endanger her own life to save a male she owed nothing to.

Just like she had done everything she could to save Kane.

"You are the strongest female I have ever known," he said.

Actually, he really wanted to tell her he loved her, but not like this. Not like now.

"I'm not," she whispered. "I promise you, I'm not—"

He kissed her again, but deeper this time, his tongue slipping into her mouth. As she arched against him, he was at once peaceful and fully aroused.

"I won't be gone long," he said against her lips.

Then he forced himself to break away and nod to Apex.

The two of them left without another word, and as they made their way out the narrow passage, Kane had a sudden, very clear thought.

Whatever was inside of him? However violent it was? However much he didn't understand it?

He was glad he had the damn thing.

Anything to be able to protect his female—and increase the probability he had not just lied to her.

CHAPTER THIRTY-SEVEN

By mutual agreement, Apex dematerialized with Kane back down the mountain to the garage. As they re-formed in shadows thrown by the low angle of the moonlight, they were not far from the road that wound its way around the base of the mountain.

Too bad it was in the middle of the night, Apex thought. The chances of finding a human out in this kind of rural area were small.

"There was a village," Kane volunteered. "South of here. I could see it from the clearing."

"It's our only shot."

They nodded and dematerialized again, re-forming and then ghosting out in increments to close in on a cluster of little houses and shops by the side of a riverbed. All of the windows were dark, even in the gas station, and for a second, Apex wondered whether the structures had all been abandoned. But no, there were cars with tires that were not flat, and other signs of life like tended-to bushes and trees, and paint that wasn't peeling, and shutters that sat right in their mountings.

"Any one will do," Kane announced as he walked over to a yellow clapboard house with bright white trim.

The guy walked up onto the porch and peered in a pane of glass. A second later, he disappeared inside.

As Apex waited, he scanned the environs . . . and pictured Callum moving among the humans in the village, buying groceries after dark, filling a car up with gas across the road, maybe opening a bank account with falsified documents. Clearly, the humans had no idea there were wolven in their mix—

What was the story with his lover who'd killed himself?

If he'd kept the belt, it hadn't just been a one-night stand. No, it had been someone he'd cared about. Somebody he'd maybe even loved.

So what had happened?

"I've got an ambulance coming—"

Apex spun around. "What?"

Kane put his hands out, all relax-buddy. "Sorry. I had one of the humans call what they referred to as an ambulance for us. We'll get the medics to go to the garage and bring Lucan to them. Whatever has to happen, happens there. We can't take him to a human hospital, not with all those prying eyes and daylight coming. It's just not an option. This is the best we can do."

"You scrubbed them?"

"Yes, and we'll take over the medics as soon as they pull up. They're coming to this address."

"What's the ETA?" Apex asked.

"They said fifteen minutes."

Apex made a show of looking left and right, but his mind was on other things. "When they get here, you can go back and be with your female, and start bringing Lucan down. I know you're itching. I would be."

Kane glanced over. "Yes, I am."

After a moment, Apex took a deep breath. "You can say it, you know."

"Say what?" But then the male dropped the feigned ignorance. "I, ah, I was really grateful for your company, back when I was burned and in the clinic. I'm not sure I ever understood why you sat there so much . . . but it helped me for certain."

"Yeah. I probably should have left you alone more."

"No, it really mattered to me and my recovery."

With a flush, Apex thought about the hours he had spent by the male's side, as Kane had lain there, on the verge of death.

The truth was, he'd fancied himself in love with the former aristocrat for years beforehand. There had just been something attractive about the fact that Kane had always retained a humanity in that god-awful place. In spite of the dirt, disease, death, and hopelessness, he had been a cut above.

Which was why, when the male had taken off his tracking collar and the explosion had happened back at the Hive, Apex's one and only thought had been saving him. He had gotten Kane out and then made sure that Nadya, who had been a source of healing, had attended to him as soon as possible.

It had been such rough going in the beginning, those wounds so raw and pervasive, it was as if there had been no skin left on the male's bones.

"Thank you," Kane said. "For helping me find my way to Nadya."

"You would have done the same for me. For anybody." He cleared his throat. "And I'm not in love with you anymore."

He sensed that head whip around, and had to smile. "Does that make you uncomfortable? Sorry."

"Ah, no. I had wondered. I mean, you were kinder to me than you were to anybody."

Apex thought of Callum, of his visceral attraction, the urge he had to fuck the guy so hard, for so long, that neither one of them could walk right.

"I wasn't really in love with you," he said. "I just thought I was."

"Well, I'm flattered."

Apex smiled again. "Anything I can do to make you feel better about yourself."

The other male's chuckle floated over on the breeze. "Any chance that wolven, Callum, was the one who clarified your emotions?"

His self-protective instinct was as finely tuned as always, so he opened his mouth to set a hard line. But then he thought . . . fuck it.

"Yeah," he murmured. "I think so."

◆   ◆   ◆

For a night that had otherwise proved to be full of bad surprises, finally, *finally*, something went right. As Kane settled back against the garage's interior wall, he couldn't believe that the plan he'd thought up had actually worked.

One hour and fourteen minutes.

And thirty-eight seconds.

According to the strange, glowing digital clock in the back of the ambulance, that was how long it took for them to get the healing vehicle to this fake-sagging structure, carry Lucan down the mountain, and stuff him, the two medics, Nadya, and Rio into the vehicle.

There had been no room for anybody else, and Rio, even though she was the mate, had to sit in the front and watch from there as the three people with medical know-how went to work.

The pair of human healers had been a stroke of dumb luck. The driver had actually come out of the Army with field trauma experience as a nurse, and her partner had likewise been in the Marines as a medic. Though Kane had not known what either of those titles meant, though he could certainly extrapolate on the first, what he was certain of was that Lucan was in good hands.

As they waited for news about how the treatment was going, Kane got up and paced around, and Mayhem propped himself in the corner and went to sleep.

Apex, meanwhile, stayed perfectly still by the exit. Like he'd been flash frozen in a harsh winter.

Only his eyes moved, and they just went from between two fixed points: The concrete floor at his feet and the toolbox in the corner. Back and forth.

At first, Kane didn't catch on. But then he realized . . . that wolven, Callum, still hadn't shown up.

Glancing at Mayhem, and finding the guy twitching like a retriever curled up in front of a fire, Kane went over to Apex.

"None of the wolven have come back," he murmured to the male. "He's probably wherever his people are."

"Oh, yeah. Sure. Uh-huh. Yup."

The former prisoner clearly had no idea what he was saying.

"Why don't you go out there," Kane offered. "Look around. Maybe you'll find where they're hiding—or, hell, go to that hunting cabin. He's probably there hiding out."

An abrupt relief came into Apex's eyes. "Are you okay here?"

"This is as good a shelter as we can have—also, not only did I not see any guards moving around when we were up on the mountain, the bodies were where we left them, so they haven't come and collected their dead. I think we made a dent in their numbers." He squeezed the male's shoulder. "Go. You're too distracted. Settle your mind and come back after you find him."

Apex glanced at the ambulance. Then looked back. "Okay, thanks."

After a moment where they just stared at each other, Kane got the shock of his life as Apex drew him in for a quick, hard embrace. And then the other male was off, slipping out of the side door.

In his absence, Kane checked the gun he had in his hand. Yes, the bullets were still in it. And even though Mayhem was asleep, he knew that male could go into a defensive position in a moment's notice.

As there continued to be no sounds that were suspicious, no scents, either, he let the male sleep. They were all overtired, and undernourished, and running on nervous energy. But they were alive.

They were *alive*.

Focusing on the back of the ambulance—which had the word "AMBULANCE" spelled out across the rear doors in bold red letters—he wished he could affect the outcome that was evolving inside the vehicle. He'd gotten a glimpse of what kind of treatment bay it of-fered, and there was equipment in there that he had never seen before—a reminder of how far things had progressed while he had been incarcerated.

In a surge of optimism, he envisioned himself and Nadya living in a small place, which happened to be kitted out as the quarters under the hunting cabin were. Together, they could explore the world around them and get up to date. They could be properly mated and find a col-lective purpose. They could live out what days and nights they were given, side by side.

Perhaps even with young.

The fantasy instantly became so real and detailed that he began to smile to himself, the future nothing he had dared to dwell on before be-cause it had only promised suffering and sadness.

Now things were different, and not just because he was whole.

Not just because . . . Nadya seemed to be healing as well.

"Old female," he murmured. "I think I made the right choice—"

The rear doors of the ambulance swung open and Nadya leaned out. She had pale blue skintight gloves on her hands that were covered with fresh blood and there were specks of it on her clothes.

"I think we've done it," she said with an exhausted grin. "I can't be-lieve it, but I think we've saved him."

Kane was out of his lean and going to her before he had a conscious thought, and as he captured her face in his palms and brought her mouth to his, he had the sense that her news validated his version of what was ahead for them.

All good things.

Only good things.

As he pulled back from her, he stared up into her face. "I am so proud of you. So *damned* proud of you."

When she flushed, and turned to the blond human woman and the gray-haired human man behind her in their blue uniforms, he let her tell him that it was really the experts. But the respect that the medics showed her as they discussed their collective patient told him so much more than her self-effacement allowed.

Then again, he already knew how good his female was at what she did.

"Listen," she said, dropping her voice. Then she glanced back and urged him a little closer. "They actually opened his wound up—and repaired the damage. The artery had begun to regenerate by the time we got in there, so Lucan played his part, too, likely because he fed from Rio. But he's not totally out of the woods. I want these two to stay overnight here. They have monitoring equipment that will help ensure we know what's going on, and their skills are materially better than mine."

"Whatever you think is best. Whatever you want."

"I think we can concoct an excuse in their minds. I know that it can be dangerous to tamper with memories other than short-term ones, but—"

"We'll make it work. Okay?" He kissed her. "I will make it work for you."

The tension eased out of his female. "Thank you. I don't want to lose him now, not after everything we've done."

"I couldn't agree more," Kane murmured as he pressed his lips to hers once more.

And then he did it again. Just because he wanted to.

Just because he could.

CHAPTER THIRTY-EIGHT

It was sometime during the early hours of daylight that Nadya felt comfortable enough to go down to the subterranean bolt-hole and use the loo. The two human medics were sound asleep in the front seats of the ambulance, the fact that they could rest so easily sitting up and facing the inside of a garage testimony to exactly how tough-minded they were.

She especially liked the woman, who had been the one to operate.

There were things still to learn, Nadya thought as she flushed. And wasn't that wonderful.

As she cleaned her hands with an antiseptic wipe, a quick glance around showed a lot of messy clothes strewn about, as well as provisions and survival equipment. The chaos didn't bother her. It was going to take so much more than some wrinkled shirts and upended boxes to dampen her spirits. She felt like she could fly, even as her feet stayed on the ground—

Nadya froze. Then she went forward on numb legs.

Across the way, hanging from a hook, a flat pan with a high finish was facing bottom out, and it just happened to be angled toward her.

The reflection in it was fuzzy, nothing like that offered by a mirror, but it was enough.

Dearest Virgin Scribe . . . it was enough.

As Nadya stared at herself, she thought surely there was some kind of distortion at work, some sort of . . .

With a shaking hand, she reached up and touched her face. Then she furiously felt around her cheeks, her jawline, her forehead. She went up and touched her hair, feeling the growth that had come in, the length—

"Hi."

She wheeled around. Kane had come down the steps and was on the last one, staring across at her as if he didn't know what to do.

"How did this happen to both of us?" she demanded.

"I don't know," he replied. "I wish I did."

Nadya turned back to her reflection. *Her* reflection. As in the one of the female that she had been before the acid attack.

"It's so . . ." When she trailed off, Kane came up behind her so that she could see his face as well. "I'm back."

Before she knew what she was doing, she turned and threw her arms around him and held on hard. As she squeezed her eyes closed, she thought it was absurd to think that what she saw now—what she once again saw of herself—was who she had always identified as even after the attack. Because she had been scarred for longer than she had been unmarked.

But then she had had her face stolen from her. And though her insides had remained the same, the outside world would only see the crippled stranger she'd become.

She had hidden herself to avoid the pain of what she had lost.

"I want you to know something," Kane said, his voice rumbling up through his chest. "You were always whole to me."

She eased back and looked up at him. Then she touched his face. "And you were always a gentlemale of worth to me."

As her eyes went to his lips, she wanted him so badly—

"Lucan and Rio are asleep," he whispered. "Mayhem and the medics, too. We have a little time."

"Kiss me, Kane. Oh, God, kiss—"

She didn't have to ask him twice. His lips found hers, and were not gentle. As the toolbox that hid the stairs slowly closed—because clearly he had willed it back into place—he picked her up and carried her over to a cot that was so small, she didn't think he would be able to fit on it with her.

Unless, of course, he mounted her.

Which he did.

Their clothes were a tangle of interference, but the desperation she had to get him inside of her made the desire to be fully naked something to be pushed aside. With his lips grinding on hers, and her breasts arching against his chest, she split her legs and welcomed him to her core. Everything was fast, fast, fast, for they didn't know when someone would rouse and there was little privacy here.

"Let me get . . ." She shoved her hands between them and started yanking at the surgical scrubs she had borrowed from the ambulance. "My bottoms are stuck."

"Here, maybe I can—"

Bang!

The sound and shock of the hard impact were enough to stop them both, and at first, Nadya thought they'd been shot at or maybe even bombed.

But then she realized they were both on the floor.

"We broke the wolf's cot," he said.

"Oops."

They both looked to the toolbox and stopped breathing. When no one came down, their laughter was shared, and then cut off by more kissing—and now that they had no distance to fall, he just rolled them over so he was on the bottom.

Splitting her legs over his hips, she rode his length, rolling her pelvis, stroking them both. And as he jerked his head back in response, she had never seen anything so beautiful. He was so different from her, thickened with muscle now, broader, bigger. Harder. In so many places.

But he was beautiful. Her eyes could have drunk in his appearance for hours.

Maybe longer.

It was hard to tell exactly when the urgency got out of hand, but suddenly she couldn't wait any longer. Easing back from him, she doubled-checked the stairs one last time—and then took her bottoms off.

The way he stared at the bare cleft of her sex told her exactly how he felt about her. No words were needed.

"Let me help you," she said hoarsely.

With hands that were surprisingly efficient, she pulled down his zipper and took out his—

"Oh . . ."

He stiffened. "Is that a good 'oh' or a bad one?"

"I didn't know they were this . . . big."

Kane barked a laugh. But then frowned. "Have you never . . ."

"No, I haven't. And I'm glad." She looked him right in the eye. "I want it to be you and only you."

With a surge, he sat up, took her face in his hands, and kissed her chastely. "Are you sure?"

"I've never been surer of anything in my life."

Shuddering, he kissed her again, gently now, brushing her lips with his own. And then he was laying her down with him, drawing her out flat so he could get on top of her.

After he mounted her, his hands traveled down her body, and when they paused, she was the one who guided his touch to where she wanted him to go, where he clearly wanted to be. And as she felt the slip of his fingers through her hot folds, she gasped.

He pleasured her, the caressing a circular stroke that made her body go languid, and then he was positioning himself between her thighs. Hypersensitive, hungry, in a hurry, she reached out for his erection—

"Oh, God," he hissed.

"Please. I need you."

She pulled him to her, or he went with a roll of the hips, or something happened, because she really wasn't following anything but the raw desire to get him inside—

The hot, blunt probing was even better than his hand. And she knew when he was in the right place.

"Nadya—"

"Please—"

The penetration was gentle and not very far in, some sort of a barrier reached. After that, there was a single surge from him, a punch from his hips, and a brief sting.

"You're inside me," she said with wonder.

As she looked up into his face, it felt like her male was the whole world. Everything else was a soft, unimportant blur.

"Are you okay," he asked tightly. "Did I hurt you?"

"No."

His jaw was grinding, his body shaking, sweat breaking out across his forehead.

"Make me yours, Kane."

◆   ◆   ◆

Kane hadn't been ready for any of it: The fact that he was her first, that she would want him as she did, that the feel of her tight core around his thick arousal was something akin to a lightning strike . . .

Then again, Nadya had been a revelation since he had first seen her. Why would that change, especially now?

With his mind jammed up, his sensations on overload, and his emotions vacillating between gratitude and high octane desire, he just let his body take over. And it knew what to do. Moving slowly at first, and then with increasing urgency, his hips pumped his arousal in and out of her, the friction cranking up his orgasm so fast, he knew he was going to—

"I'm coming," he groaned into her neck. "I can't stop—"

"Don't," came her guttural reply.

The pleasure peaked and exploded out of him, his ejaculations filling her up—and that seemed to carry her over her own ledge. A sudden stiffening of her body told him the release had come to her as well, and then he felt the powerful milking of her sex, the way his head and shaft were gripped in waves driving him wild.

He came again.

"More," she said. "Kane . . ."

She wanted him, he thought. She truly wanted him.

As he pushed his arms around her so he could hold on better, he dropped his head and just let go so he orgasmed again, and again, and another time.

He was a raw instrument of marking, his bonding creating a need to make sure that any male would know she was his, that she would carry his essence inside of her, that there would be a scent, a warning to others that she was taken, she was claimed.

And that a male would defend her. To the death, if necessary.

Beneath him, Nadya was riding the crests of her own pleasure, her eyes squeezed shut, her breath panting, a flush on her face. He wished she were naked, that they both were, but time was tight and privacy relative and fragile.

He had no idea how many times he came. It was like he had been pent up his entire adult life—then again, that was true. And he wanted to keep going forever.

But he also wanted to be careful not to hurt her.

When he finally slowed down, and then stopped, he had to recover, his head going down to the rail of the cot, his lungs burning, his body spent.

"Are you . . ."

Her laugh was magical. "Yes, I'm fine." Her hand made a slow circle on his back. "More than fine."

Rolling to the side, so he didn't crush her—he nearly cursed. She'd been on the hard floor.

Not that she seemed to mind or even notice. She was glowing, positively incandescent, as she lay on her side facing him.

"Hi," he said. Which was stupid.

"Hi."

They stayed together, touching softly, still joined, lips brushing from
time to time, for . . . he didn't know how long. But then he began to
worry someone would come down. Though they would not be judged,
he felt compelled to protect her modesty.

"My kingdom for a shower," she murmured.

"Your wish is my command."

Before she could tell him not to bother, he got up and stuffed his sex
back into his pants. A quick zip-up, and he was walking to the shower.
Cranking it on, he didn't see any soap or shampoo—no, wait. There
were some bottles on a little shelf.

"I'll watch out in case someone comes down."

He glanced behind himself. And forgot how to breathe.

Nadya had stood up and was pulling off the loose blue shirt that she
had borrowed from the ambulance. Revealed in glorious nakedness, her
body was all curves and planes that enticed, her breasts perfectly sized,
her bare sex something that made him lick his lips.

And his essence slicked the insides of her thighs.

"Come here, female," he said, holding out his hand.

Because she made his legs unreliable.

Nadya came to him like a summer breeze, gentle and warm, and as
she stepped under the warm spray, he eased back and watched her arch
to wet her newly grown hair.

Her nipples caught the water and the drips that fell were heavenly
rain . . .

That he just had to taste.

His clothes disappeared and then he was leaning down and capturing the water from her breasts, first one side and then the other. As her
hands went into his hair, she pulled him even closer, so he went down
on his knees to worship her properly.

And so he could go lower, down to her abdomen.

And lower still.

As she fell back against the tiled wall, he nuzzled between her thighs. His mouth sought out her sex, sucking at her, licking, tasting the combination of the two of them—and to get a better angle, he twisted around, leaned back, and braced his palms, his chin at the front of her.

Nadya lowered herself onto his face, and he licked into her.

When he came, his ejaculations went into thin air. But that was okay.

He had filled her up enough already.

CHAPTER THIRTY-NINE

When night finally fell, it was clear Lucan was going to pull through. Nadya was confident of it as she double-checked his vitals thanks to the ambulance's equipment.

"Well?" he asked.

She looked up at him. He'd angled the hospital bed up, and even with the verticality, his color was good. "You're doing so well."

He clapped his palms and pulled his mate in for a kiss. "Great, I'm healed—"

"But you're going to have to spend the night here at the garage. You need another twenty-four hours before you're ready to go."

"Oh, come on."

From up in front, the two medics who had done such wonderful work with his wound twisted around at the same time.

The blond woman looked at her patient as if he were insane. "We're taking you in to the medical center in Plattsburgh right now. Are you crazy? You almost died last night—"

The woman fell quiet as Kane appeared in the rear entry. "You guys were so great. We owe you."

There was a brief pause. Then Lucan twisted around to them. "Yes, thank you."

"Thank you so much," Rio echoed. "You saved his life. And mine."

Both of the medics started talking, but then went quiet. After which, they brought their hands up to their foreheads.

"Let me help you off the stretcher," Nadya said to Lucan.

As she stood up from the little bench seat, she was amazed at how easy it was to bend over and help the male off the examination bed. Though she found herself bracing for pain anytime she moved, it never materialized.

Not that she wasn't a little stiff.

In the most delicious of places.

Kane climbed in and helped get the patient out the back, steadying Lucan as the male got down off the high bumper of the rear.

They had a chair ready for the wolven, and as soon as he was settled in, with Rio by his side, Kane leaned into the ambulance.

"Thank you so much," Nadya murmured. It was just too emotional to say goodbye to those humans.

They had been through a trial together, and that created bonds that were hard to break.

On that note, Mayhem opened up the big door of the garage, and with a sweet diesel scent, and moments later, the ambulance trundled off . . . with the two heroic humans who would never know just how grateful a bunch of vampires were to them.

As a now familiar arm settled on her shoulders, Nadya glanced up at Kane. "Hi."

"Hi."

It was something they did, this greeting that was both silly and profound. Then again, when the world had been reborn all around you, you did kind of feel as if everything was new and fresh. Especially as you looked, once again, into the eyes of your lover.

After they got Lucan settled down underground on a pallet, Mayhem decided he needed a shower. While Kane worked with him to set up a rudimentary curtain for privacy, Nadya cooked up some freeze-dried chicken soup, using distilled water and the pan that had showed her her reflection.

A little butane stove did the trick for heat, and tired though she was, she loved making a meal for them all.

The five of them ate in a silence that was communal, the sense of having reached a plateau of survival making the simple meal a banquet.

"When are that wolven and Apex coming back?" Mayhem said between spoonfuls. "Are we just waiting for them here—"

As if on cue, a high-pitched whistle announced the return of—

Only Apex.

And the male was grim as he entered the garage without its owner.

Kane rose to his feet from his sitting position on the floor. "Where is the wolven?"

"I don't know. He never came back to the cabin. I have no idea where he is."

Kane cursed. "Okay, then we're going to look for him."

Mayhem got up, too. "Let's do it."

Apex glanced around. "I'd hoped he'd come back here. But I take it that's a no."

"We haven't seen any other wolven, though." Kane reached for a gun. "Maybe they're all together. Listen, we'll leave the others here and the three of us will go look up on the mountains."

"What if he was injured," Apex said numbly. "What if he's dead?"

As if that was all he'd thought of the whole day.

"Don't be like that. Not yet."

When Kane turned to her, the last thing Nadya wanted was for him to go out into the night, to where the guards were, where humans were.

"Go," she said hoarsely. "We'll be fine here."

"I won't be long." He kissed her. "I promise."

The males took a little time to get ready, and everyone shut down Lucan when the male said he wanted to go, too. Fortunately, Rio handled that bright idea, not that his loyalty to the group was unappreciated.

Kane was careful to kiss Nadya one more time, and as she watched him go out the garage's side door, she told herself that he had made good on that very vow the night before.

He had promised to not be gone long. And he hadn't been.

She just needed him to do the same thing again.

◆　◆　◆

The hut was back.

As Kane came into his corporeal form by the clearing's fire pit, that was his first thought: Over on the right, where it had been the first time he'd been at the site, the deep red draped shelter that was bifurcated by a river bed was exactly where it had been.

Even though finding Callum the wolven was his ultimate goal, he went over and pulled the flap back. The pallet of furs was where it had been, and he frowned. Ducking inside, he went over and knelt down. A tear of fabric, the corner of the towel he'd wrapped Nadya in when he had been determined to bring her to the old female, lay at the foot of the bedding.

Picking it up, he glanced around.

And then went back out.

Mayhem worked the periphery as Apex disappeared into the passageway that led to the hidden den with the spring. Kane went around back, to the trench behind the boulders.

And there, he found something, though not what they were looking for.

The burn marks of the guards they had killed in the trees marked the pine needles, the last resting places of the bodies unmarred by any disturbance made by boots. So no one from the prison camp had come to retrieve them or search for their weapons before the sun claimed them.

He wasn't sure what that meant. Maybe nothing. Maybe there were too few left to do the job.

But there was also no sign that any wolven had been back to the mountain, either. The fire pit was cold, there were no scents of food, and no one was moving around the territory.

It was deserted.

As Apex and Mayhem joined him, he said, "We head down the mountain searching for him. It'll be a needle in a haystack, but we can try to find clues—"

"He's at the prison camp." Apex looked back at the den's entrance. "Or he's dead. Those are the only two possibilities and I don't want to waste time fucking around out here if they've got him. I want to go to the source of the greatest harm."

Kane cursed. "But you don't know if he's in there."

"I can sure as hell find out—"

"Not on your own you can't—"

"Fuck you—"

Riding a surge of adrenaline that would have been impossible to comprehend, much less generate, just a couple of nights before, Kane grabbed a hold of the other prisoner's jacket and crammed his face directly into the other male's.

"You think you're going to help him if you get yourself killed? If you want to save him, you're going to be smart about it. You're going to search this fucking mountain with us, while Lucan gets back on his feet. And then the four of us can go together. But what is *not* going to happen is you going there alone."

Apex shoved him off and paced around. "They'll kill him if they've found him."

"Then what does it matter if you wait long enough to get proper backup. The four of us together can go." Damn, he wished the Jackal were still around. "We will go together first thing tomorrow night if we can't find him. But if you get ahead of yourself, you're not helping him— you're a liability I'm going to have to solve."

"I can't do this. I can't bear . . . this."

The admission was spoken roughly, in the kind of way that someone did when he was talking to himself.

"I'm not going to do this."

Kane shook the male. "No, we search the mountain in case he's injured and hiding. And then we go to the prison camp tomorrow night when we have more backup."

"Yeah, sure. Whatever."

When Apex broke off, Kane let him go, and he wasn't surprised when the male just walked down the trail.

"We're not finding the guy out here," Mayhem said. "It's worse than a waste of time. It's dangerous, because who the fuck else is on the mountain? And as for Apex, I don't think we'll see him again tonight and he'll either show up tomorrow or not. We can still go to the prison camp tomorrow at dark, though. You're right. We need Lucan—because maybe we'll end up rescuing them both."

Great. Something to look forward to.

Kane glanced around. The sense that time was running out struck him clear as a bell, not that he could pinpoint the why of the sudden feeling of dread.

But he couldn't ignore the premonition of doom.

CHAPTER FORTY

Well, he'd kept his promise. But Kane wasn't really back.

As Nadya glanced at him, again, he was staring off into space, his eyes full of shadows. They were upstairs in the garage, leaving the others down below. He had been silent since he'd returned from looking around the mountain for Callum. And likewise, Mayhem hadn't been his usual chatty self; especially after the pair of them had spoken to Lucan, who'd nodded and then gone really quiet as well.

"Are you okay?" As soon as the question left her, she wanted to take it back because she'd already asked him that. Twice. "I'm sorry, I don't mean to—"

"Do you ever feel like you're out of time?"

A chill went through her, and she blurted her biggest concern: "Are you all going back to the prison camp? Is that where you're going next."

"I don't know."

"Don't lie."

"That's not what's on my mind." He rubbed his face. "There's something I have to do after this. And you know what it is . . ."

"Cordelhia." When Kane looked up, she shrugged. "You don't need to explain. What's changed, really."

Except for everything, she tacked on to herself.

"I want to clean the slate," he said. "And find her killer."

"You sound apologetic. And that's totally unnecessary." When he started to shake his head, she interjected, "We had sex today. A couple of times. It's not surprising your *shellan* is on your mind."

When he didn't reply, she felt like she was losing him, even though he was right in front of her.

"I made a vow to myself," he said. "That I'd find her murderer. The only thing I know is that it wasn't me."

"So what are you going to do?"

"I've got to start somewhere. I think I need to go to her brother's. Assuming he's still alive."

As pain speared through her, Nadya stood up and wandered around, looking at the tools and oil cans, the gasoline jug, the spare tires and chains. Inside her chest, she was arctic cold, but she tried to stay grounded in what they'd found together. The closeness. The connection.

Plus his mate was dead.

So why did she feel like the two of them were suddenly going their separate ways? And wasn't that what she had wanted, what she had demanded of him before she had taken his vein?

"Do what you have to do." She turned back to him. "And listen, if you really want to go down to Caldwell and 'start somewhere,' there's no time like the present. We're safe here. Plus it's clear none of you are going anywhere tonight, and there's a good number of hours before dawn left."

He stared at her. "This is not about you."

Trust me, she thought. *I know that.*

"It's all right."

To his credit—or maybe his guilt—he didn't leave right away; he stayed where he was, on a folding chair that didn't look like it could support his full weight, his gaze still staring off into space.

"I just want the past to leave me," he said abruptly. "I want it gone, out of my head. And not only Cordelhia, but the prison camp, too. I don't want to ever think about that place again. I don't want to go back there and I sure as shit don't want to think about how I ended up in that pit of suffering."

She understood that, better than he knew.

"I need answers, Nadya. I feel like if I had them, I'd be able to let it all go."

When he looked over at her, she took a deep breath and nodded. "I get that. Like I said. Do what you need to do."

◆　◆　◆

Fools' paradises were good things.

Until the real world came back.

As Kane stared across the hood of an old, beat-up car, he knew he was fucking Nadya's head up. But when he'd been on the mountain, making the decision to go back to the prison camp, he'd realized in a stark way that as long as the past was not behind him, he was not fully free.

The prospect of returning to the place he'd been sent to for a murder he did not commit had brought everything to the forefront.

And in contrast to the way he'd been, now he had a future and a life he wanted to defend. Protect. Fucking enjoy.

He'd like being happy with the female he'd fallen in love with.

He wanted his life to be his own.

Getting to his feet, he knew where he was going to start—and he was frustrated that, on the night of the murder, he hadn't fought harder against the accusations. He should have been angrier at her brother. He should have hit back at the male and taken control of the situation.

"Nadya," came a voice from down below. "Lucan has a question about his drain?"

"Coming." His female gave him a tense smile. "You know where I'll be. Take care of yourself out there—"

"Nadya." He caught her hand. "I don't regret what happened today. Not at all. And I want to be with you again."

Her expression eased a little. "Really?"

"I swear. I'm doing this so I can lay the past to rest. So we can be together, if you'll have me."

His female took a deep breath as if she were trying to believe him. "Good. Because that's what I want, too."

Leaning in, he kissed her. "You take care of your patient."

"I will."

Kane watched her disappear down the stairs, and then he double-checked his gun, made sure the safety was off, and stepped out of the garage. Looking up at the sky, he saw that there was no moon tonight. Clouds had rolled in.

Funny, that he still knew where Caldwell was.

Closing his eyes, he sent himself off in a southerly direction, and he intended to go to Cordelhia's brother's estate. Instead, he went to where he had once lived for a year and some months, re-forming off to one side of the trail he'd taken his horses on, the one that came at the manor house from the rear.

The landscape had changed some, but the gardens had been largely kept as they'd been. And the mansion . . . was exactly as he remembered. Beautifully appointed, carefully tended, a place of elegance and standards.

He had expected that, in two hundred years, things would have been altered more; but in many ways, it was all so utterly preserved.

His boots started walking of their own volition, and as he approached from the rear, he thought of that last birthday party he had enjoyed. It had seemed so perfect.

Everything had seemed so perfect.

Off in the distance, a dog barked, and he could hear a rushing of cars. There was a road close by now, one on which the vehicles were permitted to travel at high velocity.

Lights were on behind the old-fashioned bubbled glass, and he had a thought that the draperies were not the same. Did vampires even live in it? Or had the estate found its way out of her brother's hands and into human ownership?

He stopped and glanced around.

The stables were gone, the whole of that structure removed and replaced with a body of water the color of an aquamarine and a matching little house that appeared to service the huge basin. He remembered his favorite horse and worried about what had happened to the stallion. As the thoroughbred had been of high quality, it was likely that he had been treated very well, but who knew?

There were no cars that he could see—

A figure passed by one of the windows on the first floor.

Even though his ultimate destination was elsewhere, he had to see who was living in his house. Not that it had been his for the right reason, not because he had purchased it with his money or his efforts, but rather because he had entered the mating rituals of the aristocracy.

And ended up with a female who had endured him.

Instead of one who wanted him.

He thought of what Apex had said, that he'd thought he knew what love and attraction were, until he'd met Callum.

Kane knew exactly what the male meant—

He stopped.

Then threw out a hand, even though there was no one and nothing around to steady himself on: The figure, walking through the first floor, was a narrow-shouldered female or woman, and she was dressed in a long pale gown, her blond hair piled up high on her head—

Kane tripped. Fell.

Got back up.

In a trance, he stumbled forward, feeling as though his feet weren't on the ground. And he only stopped when he was standing in the flower beds just outside the parlor's French doors.

The lovely room was kitted out with furniture he recognized: Though the arrangement had changed, and there was a different Persian rug on the floor, he knew the oil paintings of landscapes and the secretary and the lamps . . .

. . . and the female who drifted through the rooms like a ghost, beautiful as a statue.

And just as cold.

CHAPTER FORTY-ONE

Down at the Brotherhood mansion, in the great Blind King's French blue study, Vishous rolled a map out across Wrath's ornate desk. Even though the King couldn't see, the other brothers who had clustered around had peepers that worked just fine.

"So I performed a search on vacant facilities. Everything from schools to malls to churches and auditoriums." He glanced up. "You wouldn't believe how many things fucking fail. I found upward of a hundred that fit my loose criteria in the north country."

"Business is rough," someone said.

"Life is rough," somebody else muttered.

"But then I refined things."

Wrath cut in, glaring from behind his black wraparounds. "Fuck the back chatter. I don't care about your methodology, what's the conclusion."

"Three sites." He tapped his pen on the map. "A monastery just outside of Schenectady. A junior college up by Plattsburgh."

"And the third," the King said while he set George in his lap.

As the golden retriever looked at the map, too, V put his pen on a location just outside of a tiny town upstate. "This abandoned tuberculosis hospital, which happens to be not too far from the pharmacy break-in. All three properties have been recently purchased by someone, we're talking in the last year, and they have the infrastructure needed to maintain a professional drug processing business, as well as a population of workers and guards."

Tohr raised his hand, ever the rule abider. "But they could go underground, couldn't they?"

"You want to try digging a rabbit warren of spaces under someone's lawn in this environment where everything ends up on the Internet?"

"Maybe it was already extant."

"Well, I've been monitoring YouTube—"

"Are you a MrBeast fan?" Rhage said around his Tootsie Pop. "What. I like the guy. He has chocolate and gives away money."

V ignored the brother. "—and there are all these abandoned explorers. These three places have been visited before—and recently, a guy said that there was a new fence around the abandoned hospital. I'm suggesting we split into three groups and check these sites out. If they're empty, fine, I'll go back to the drawing board."

"And if they aren't," the King interjected.

"Then we circle the wagons, and get in there."

"To do what, though." Wrath sat forward. "Where do the prisoners go. How is an evac going to be managed?"

"Saxton told me today that you did revoke the aristocracy's charter."

"Yeah, and that's fucking great. But what do you do with the prisoners. You can't just get in there and bust shit up without having an after plan."

"Oh, so it's better to leave them as drug mules and processers?"

"Watch your fucking mouth, V."

"Sorry." Even though he didn't mean it. "Look, we only need to confirm that I'm right. Then we'll figure out the rest."

All kinds of chatter started up at that point, but he just stayed focused on the King. Opinions were great, but they were an asses-and-elbows situation. Everybody had one. Wrath was the decider.

"Okay," the King said. "Tomorrow at dusk so there's time to scope out and prepare. There's just one caveat."

V closed his eyes and gritted his teeth. "What's the catch."

◆   ◆   ◆

Nadya ascended the bolt-hole's steps and reemerged into the garage. She had stayed down with Lucan and Rio for a little bit, but the conversation with Kane had scrambled her mind.

Something he'd said really wouldn't leave her.

I feel like if I had the answer, I'd be able to let it all go.

It seemed like they both wanted the same thing for their futures, but it also was so fast, the whole of their relationship. She didn't doubt their emotions, but now that she was alone, she wasn't sure she could trust the good fortune. Plus he was heading back to his world, or what was left of it. Doubting his intentions with the aristocracy or his *shellan*'s family seemed disloyal, though—or maybe it was more her lack of self-esteem that made her question what they had together. Which was just too weak on her part.

Like him, she probably needed to find her own answers to make peace with her past.

After all, her father's decision to better her life had ended up ruining her for a very long time. And she had never been able to talk to him about it, not that any kind of conversation could have changed what had happened.

Full of nervous energy, she paced around a couple of times, then went over to the steps. "I'll be back in a little bit."

"You okay?" Rio called up.

"Yes. Just going to go clear my head."

What was good for the gander was good for the goose, right? Or whatever the quote was.

Stepping out of the side door, she hung on to what Kane had said as he left: That he had no regrets, and that this was a beginning, not an end for them. She had to trust him. What choice did she have?

And his *shellan* was dead. You didn't go back to a ghost out of a sense of duty, for godsakes.

Closing her eyes, she dematerialized in a direction she'd never thought she would head in again. And when she re-formed in front of a gracious mansion, she felt a piercing pain in her chest. As lovely as the house was . . . it was a grave. For her parents.

Looking at all the well-lit windows and the lovely grounds, she felt a stirring anger at how her parents had died.

She remembered what she'd heard about what had happened, the *lessers* breaking into the houses of the aristocracy, slaughtering everyone without regard to whether or not they were a target from the higher class or a lowly *doggen*. Or a worker.

She couldn't imagine the fear as her *mahmen* and her father were locked out of the safe room, left to be killed by the race's enemies along with all the other staff who had been denied shelter from the attack by the grand family they served.

As she stared up at the front of the formal house, she knew this was what her father had wanted for her, this materialistic upgrade. And instead, he'd ended up with a disfigured daughter who disappeared on him and then a terrible death at the altar of the very aspiration he had sought.

She had never blamed him, but nor could she forgive him—

Movement off to the left caught her attention—

Nadya gasped.

And then she simply couldn't believe what she was seeing. Surely that was someone else, another tall, broad figure, with dark hair . . . and a jacket . . . that was just like the one Kane had pulled off a hook down in the bolt-hole.

In a daze, Nadya walked forward.

As a set of glass doors was opened by someone inside.

The female who appeared on the threshold was beauty defined. Fair and lovely, with her hair up on her head, and the most perfect bone structure, she was ethereal in a pale yellow gown.

Clasping her hands to her mouth, the female seemed shocked.

Except then she launched herself forward and threw herself at Kane.

"Cordelhia," he said in a strangled tone.

Standing off to the side, Nadya thought, of all the outcomes she had considered for this night . . . the one that hadn't even been an option was that his *shellan* was alive.

CHAPTER FORTY-TWO

Kane knew things were actually happening because of Cordelhia's scent. It was the same one he remembered from many years ago, and as she held on to him, the fragrance of roses was all he could smell.

Dearest Virgin Scribe, she hung on so hard, he couldn't breathe. Then again, maybe that was shock on his part, not what she was doing to his neck.

Pulling himself together, he set her down, set her back.

"Cordelhia . . ."

"You're alive," she breathed through her tears.

He felt as though he were staring at her from a vast distance, even though they were merely a foot or two apart, his brain refusing to process anything. But he knew one thing for sure: He was suddenly angry, bitterly angry.

"Stop the crying," he snapped. Then he forced himself to calm down. "What the hell is going on here?"

"You got out of the prison. It's a miracle. We can—"

He moved her hands away as she reached for him again. "Don't touch me."

"You're free, though—"

"And you're alive. But you left me to rot in there. For two *hundred* years?"

Cordelhia's wide, hurt eyes did absolutely nothing for him. All he could think about was the decades upon decades of time he had spent suffering while she was prima facie proof he wasn't a murderer.

"Who the hell was upstairs in your bedroom that night?" he demanded. "Who died?"

With an elegant hand, Cordelhia motioned to the house. "May we please not do this here. I don't wish the gardeners to hear anything."

The last thing he wanted to do was go in that fucking house, but he stepped inside because information was the most important goal right now.

"Would you care for a libation," she said as she indicated the parlor's bar cart.

Which was the same one he'd taken the sherry off of.

Refusing to go any farther than the foyer, he laughed sharply. "That's what drugged me in the first place. So, no, I'm not drinking a damn thing—who was that body? Your scent was all over it!"

It was a while before Cordelhia answered, and when she did, her voice was so soft he could barely hear it.

"I had a twin." She put that long, lovely hand at the base of her throat. "She was an identical twin except for the fact that her eyes were mismatched."

Ah, but of course. That defect would have been considered irredeemable by *glymera* standards—and he could remember a time when, though he certainly wouldn't have condoned such a condemnation, he'd have understood it some. Now? After having been in the prison? Been deformed himself?

That way of thinking was an affront to everything that was moral.

"She wanted to get mated. The male was a commoner. My brother and *mahmen* were so upset—they knew it would ruin not only her, but our entire bloodline. My sister would not see reason, however, so they *sehcluded* her. It didn't matter. She snuck out of the house. It was pure insanity."

At this, Cordelhia went down to a display of stones that had been tumbled into the shapes of eggs. As she righted one that was off a mere degree or two, he saw her properly. She was painfully thin, twitchy as a bird, lost in a grand house with so many beautiful things.

"So you planned it all along," he said numbly. "You mated me, lived with me for a year, long enough so that things seemed on the up and up. Then when you both went into your needings at the same time, because you were twins, your brother killed her and drugged me, and the body swap was accomplished."

"Kane, you must understand." She floated over to him. "It was never anything personal."

When she reached for his hand, the expression on her face, the pleading, guileless beg to see their side of the situation, was scarier than anything he'd witnessed in prison.

"Don't touch me," he snarled.

Her brows lifted and she placed her hand back at the base of her throat.

"Your *mahmen*," he said, "she knew the plan, then."

"Yes."

"Hell of an acting job. And no doubt she repeated it in front of the servants of this household. So there were witnesses."

Now it was his turn to walk around, and as he peered in through the dining room, he remembered the way things had been.

He looked over his shoulder. "How did you end up living here, though. After it was all over? If you did this to preserve the bloodline, and you're alive and well, how does that work? I know the *glymera* is a cutthroat kind of place, but surely killing your own sister or daughter to survive socially is extreme even for them."

When she looked down at the carpet, he cursed under his breath as he figured it out. "You all told people it was your sister I was mating, the *exhile dhoble*. And that's why your *mahmen* chose me. I had no family and an elderly aunt who was dying. I was from the Old Country with no contacts here. That was why the mating ceremony was only your immediate family." He thought of that birthday party and laughed harshly. "That's why we never had anyone to this house, why there were never any gatherings, and of course the servants were too loyal to talk. You probably imprisoned your sister in the fucking basement for the year it took for both of you to go into your fertile period, and then when the time came, you executed the plan perfectly and swapped places."

Cordelhia stood before him, looking helpless. "You have no idea what it's like to be ostracized. No one to speak to you, nowhere to go—"

"I was in *prison*. For two hundred years. Spare me your version of suffering."

"We have suffered, too." She gestured about her. "This estate was attacked by the *lessers*. We hid for three nights after they slaughtered our servants and ransacked us—"

"Yes, this shit looks sooooo messy. Wow."

Her regal head lifted. "Your language. Please."

"By all means, do correct me on that. Because you've gotten so many other things dead right."

She cleared her throat. "However did you find release?"

Like this was a formal gathering and she was inquiring about plans for the festival season.

"I escaped." As she recoiled, Kane shook his head. How did she think prison worked? "You ruined my life."

"We did not intend to. And I am honestly sorry."

The strangest thing was, he believed that. He believed, down in her soul, she was sorry. She just had absolutely no frame of reference for the implications of what she and her bloodline had done.

"My *mahmen* is dead," she said. "My brother, too. He died in the raids. He was defending his property. I live here alone. I never mated."

No, you never did, he thought. Even when she'd been with him, she hadn't really been a *shellan*.

"I have to go," he heard himself say.

"Kane . . ."

"Shut up, Cordelhia. Just stop talking."

"But of course," she retorted in an icy tone. "Allow me to escort you—"

"No," he said roughly. "I'll see myself out."

He had a thought he would go to the front door, and do it properly. But that was a misfire of the old ways.

Kane went back to the French door she had opened upon seeing him standing outside her house. As he reached for the handle, he glanced back.

"They're all gone, then," he heard himself say. "Your family? What of your brother's young?"

"They were lost in the raids as well." Her voice choked up. "So, alas, it is only me. And I came back to this house after the difficulties with you and my sister because I have always favored it."

Thank the Virgin Scribe his aunt was gone unto the Fade, Kane thought. She would have been destroyed by all this.

"You will not see me again." He stepped out. "And lock this door behind me. You better keep protecting yourself from the real world."

"There is no reason to be rude."

"Goodbye, Cordelhia."

Outside, he looked down into the flower bed. He'd managed to plant his boots in the exact same position they'd been in when he'd peered through the glass.

There was a subtle click behind him and he glanced over his shoulder at the French door that had been closed on him. The female he had thought he loved was standing on the other side, staring out. He wasn't sure whether she saw him or not.

He didn't care.

Intending to dematerialize, he closed his eyes. But there was no way he could focus to scatter himself—

Abruptly, Kane's head cranked to the right as a scent was carried over to him on the breeze.

"Nadya . . . ?"

◆   ◆   ◆

Nadya had intended to leave the moment she saw the elegant female dressed in pale yellow race out and throw her arms around Kane. But emotions were the most powerful, invisible source of energy on the planet, and so she was felled by sensations that were not physical in the slightest.

No one had stabbed her in the heart.

Though she certainly felt that way.

Faced with the mated pair's embrace, she had blindly walked off, but she hadn't made it very far. When she'd passed a wrought iron bench that sat against the brick wall of what she assumed was a very formal garden, she'd fallen into its cold, hard palm.

The next thing she knew, Kane was standing in front of her.

As she looked at him, she discovered that the cloud cover overhead was breaking up some and the moon was making an appearance. Measuring its position, she was stunned to find that there was still some night left.

She felt as though it was time for dawn to arrive and burn her.

"What are you doing here?" he asked.

"How is your *shellan?*" She put her hand up. "I saw the reunion, actually. I'm so happy for you—"

"That was no reunion."

"Oh, so she ran into someone else's arms. My apologies." She touched her eye. "My vision is bad."

"You don't know what you're talking about."

His words were dead, his tone level to the point of being stony. And as she searched his face, it was that of a stranger.

"Why did you follow me," he said dully.

"I didn't."

Shaking his head, he looked back at the house. And remained silent.

"Allow me to spare you excuses." She got up. "I do have a question, though. Was anything you told me true? Or was it all a delusion—or something that didn't matter because I'm a commoner."

As she put the demand out there, she wasn't sure whether she was talking about what he'd told her in the last couple of nights . . . or what had come out of his mouth back when he'd been hovering on the brink of death. What she was certain about was that the female who had run into his arms had been his mate, and that she was alive and well.

"I can't do this right now," he said.

She nodded. "Then I'll spare you the effort."

"What are you talking about—"

"I want to thank you for . . ." She touched her face. "Whatever this gift was. I still don't know what happened to either one of us, but at least I've been set on a path where I don't have to hide anymore."

He'd also managed to destroy her, though.

The irony was that her insides were ruined now, even as her exterior had been set back to rights.

"Nadya. Stop, okay. This is not about you."

"Oh, I know. My life has rarely been about me. My father took control of it. My intended tried to destroy it. And here I am again, a male standing before me and reminding me that I don't matter."

He threw up his hands. "Oh, for chrissakes. I've just seen a female I thought was dead for two hundred years and learned that she sacrificed my life for a pair of mismatched eyes. Will you give me ten minutes to figure out how I feel?"

"And I just saw the male I thought I loved hold the female he talked about nonstop in his arms."

"It's not like that."

They stared at each other, and she relived what she'd witnessed.

"I can't be an aristocrat's little side secret. I won't be." Tears entered her eyes. "Pain has a way of getting through to our cores. Your love was real, and she's alive, and sooner or later, you're going to go back to her."

"You have no idea what you're talking about."

"Oh, I absolutely do." Nadya took a step back. "You're not going to be able to help it. I believe you have feelings for me, but I know the way the aristocracy works—"

"You don't know me. You have no *fucking* clue what you're saying."

"I know you're a male of honor and worth, and I know you come from the *glymera*." She shook her head. "I've already been burned once trying to get a leg up in this world. I can't do that again. You can say whatever you want right now, and I believe you feel terrible, and, yes, this timing is horrible. But I spent decades deformed because of a lie that was bigger and more important than me. I can't walk that path again."

"So you won't be with me because of my bloodline."

She thought of her father and his grasping social aggression. He hadn't thrown the acid at her, but his drive to distinguish their own bloodline had created a perfect storm—and she was the one who had borne the brunt of the hard lessons.

Sooner or later, Kane would have to go back to his mate. His sense of honor would demand his return, but more than that, his social position would dictate it.

She thought one last time of her father's scheming.

"No," she said roughly, "I won't be with you anymore because of mine."

CHAPTER FORTY-THREE

The fuck he was waiting for Lucan to get back on his feet.

As Apex scoped out the back of the prison camp from the parking lot, he knew only one thing for sure. If Callum was alive and on the premises, he would be held either at the wall or inside the head of the guards' private quarters. And wasn't it handy to narrow things down, given how big the place was.

God, he wished he'd saved that severed hand. And he didn't have enough ammo to blast a hole through the back door.

So under the theory you had to use what you had, he put two fingers to his mouth—

His whistle was so loud, it made his own ears ring, and the sound echoed off the five-story core of the winged building. When he needed a breath, he took one—and shoved his fingers back into his mouth, continuing the noise—

Well, what do you know.

He'd kicked a hornets' nest.

Guards came streaming out, and he ducked behind a vehicle and started picking them off, one by one. As he kept a count, he wondered whether that head of the guards had some kind of mold in the back room where she regenerated whole squadrons by pouring magic wax into a form and letting the shit dry.

His chance came as one of the guards poked his head out of the rear door. As bullets whizzed by, Apex surged forward in a crouch, running down the lineup of vehicles, pings and sparks following him from a shooter who was up in a third-story window.

Just as the guard lingered in his fish-or-cut-bait stage of exit, neither in nor out, Apex pile-drove him back into a staircase that funneled into the private quarters.

Curling up a fist, he beat the face of the male until there were no features to recognize, and then he looked up the steps to the interior locked door—

Sure as if he'd rung a bell, the last barrier swung open.

The head of the guards stood there in uniform, a bulletproof vest strapped on her chest. She was as she had always been, cold and calculating, a little smile on her face.

"I knew one of you would come for him. If I just remained patient, it was going to be so much more efficient than trying to hunt you all around that mountain."

"Let the wolf go," Apex said. "You can have me. Just let him go."

"I don't think so. He's proven to be quite a pet."

As she opened the door wider, what was on the far side was the last thing he wanted to see: Callum was alive, it was true. But that was only his body.

The male had been strapped naked to a bedding platform, and it was clear he had been used, his throat raw from bite marks, his sex lying across his thigh, bruised and deflated. But the worst of it was the way he stared up at the ceiling, his eyes unfocused and blinking slowly.

Like his soul was gone.

"You bitch!"

Apex attacked before he knew what he was doing, his lunge so violent that he nearly lost hold of his gun.

He didn't make it.

The head of the guards shot him in the thigh so that when his weight landed, his leg crumpled out from under him.

His head caught his fall.

Right on the last step.

The crack was like a lightning bolt. Just like the pain.

And then everything went black.

✦ ✦ ✦

Kane didn't go back to the garage. He knew that was where Nadya would go. Instead, he dematerialized to the clearing up on the mountain, to the hut. But there was no old female. No wolven, either.

Maybe that was for the best.

He sat down on one of the logs around the cold fire pit and stared at where the flames should have been. Behind him, the sounds of nature at night were a tiptoe into his ear, as if the whole world recognized he needed to be handled carefully.

He should have explained himself better to Nadya, but his head was fucked, and the anger that had entered him along with that resuscitation he'd been through, or whatever it was, made him volatile to the point where he didn't know if he could trust himself. He had once been so even-keeled.

Then again, back in the Old Country, the world had been his oyster. It was easy to keep a level head when there was no pressure.

As he thought about Cordelhia once again, he was shocked, and also not surprised. In his gut, he had known something was wrong about all of his good fortune in the New World.

Or maybe that was just hindsight talking.

As for Nadya, he wanted to be angry with her for doubting him, but how could he be. With the way her past had gone, he could see the why of it all for her, and though he wanted to talk her out of the way she felt, wasn't he just like her father?

Telling her what to do because of his own ambitions.

Which had been a future with her.

What the hell did it matter—

Fast approaching footfalls brought his head, and his gun, around to the sounds. But he didn't bother trying to take cover. Frankly, if someone shot him in the chest, it would probably hurt less, and then he could die.

If he *could* die, that was—

Mayhem shot out of the tree line. "Apex has gone to the prison camp."

"What?" Kane asked with exhaustion.

"I just came back after a food run to the bolt-hole, and Lucan said that he'd returned and taken a bunch of ammo and knives. Do not tell me he is just going to wander around the damn mountain looking for deer to hunt. He went to the camp. Alone. To try to find Callum."

As Kane slowly rose to his feet, he thought, well, he already felt like hitting something. Here was his chance.

"Lucan tried to come with me," Mayhem said. "I told him to not be a fucking liability."

"Wow. That's a totally reasonable thing to do."

"I'm turning over a new leaf. At least for tonight."

Kane took a deep breath. "Let's go. Frankly, I knew this was where we'd end up. I'd just been hoping if we gave it time, that white-haired wolven would magically reappear."

Closing his eyes, he meant to dematerialize back to the prison camp. But when he didn't move, he popped his lids.

Mayhem was still in front of him. "First things first," the male said softly. "We take care of Apex. Then you can deal with whatever blew up between you and Nadya. And don't tell me something didn't happen. She looks as bad as you do."

Kane glanced at the sky, at the way the moon was peeking out of the cloud cover. It was a beautiful sight, but cold and ultimately useless.

"There is nothing between me and Nadya."

On that note, he flew himself in a scatter back to Hell.

Which seemed the only proper destination for him.

CHAPTER FORTY-FOUR

As Kane re-formed off to the side of the abandoned hospital, he fell into a run. The gunshots in the back of the building were a snare drum of aggression, and his only thought was that he wished like hell he had more backup. More guns. More ammo.

Mayhem reappeared next to him, also in mid-stride. "That's where our party is."

I fucking know that, Kane wanted to holler as they bolted down the flank of the old brick building.

They didn't make it all the way around. Just as they were coming to the corner, as the smell of gunpowder, sweat, and blood wafted on a gust right into his central nervous system, a figure appeared from out of no-where.

A figure dressed in black and holstered with weapons.

But it wasn't Lucan. And it wasn't a guard. And . . . it wasn't the enemy.

As Kane skidded to a halt, Mayhem did the same. After which they just stood there panting.

"Jackal?" Kane shook his head to clear it. "Is it . . . you?"

Their old friend, who had escaped thanks to Kane's sacrifice, was staring across like he'd seen a ghost. "Kane? What happened to you— I thought you were dead."

"Oh, my God, do you have good timing," Mayhem cut in as he jumped forward and embraced the male they all had thought they'd never see again. "How the hell did you find us?"

The Jackal hugged the male absently, still staring over that shoulder at Kane, eyes bouncing around—and it was funny. Everybody who'd seen him since that old female had worked her magic, or whatever the hell it was, was used to the resurrection.

The Jackal's astonishment, to the contrary, was because Kane should never have survived the explosion of his restraint collar in the first place.

Kane stepped forward and put out his hand. "There's no time for explanations for anything."

"Yes," the Jackal whispered as they shook. "You're . . . right."

Kane pointed with his weapon to the parking lot. "We think the guards might have taken someone who isn't their problem to the prison, and we believe Apex has gone in there, alone. We've got to save the both of them."

The Jackal just kept staring at Kane. But then a bullet sizzled by the male's head and snapped the former prisoner out of his holy-shit.

"Let's go," Kane said. "If we survive, I promise I'll tell you everything."

When the Jackal nodded, the three of them moved into position at the corner of the building, peering around what cover they had. Guards were using the lineup of trucks and other vehicles as a shield, trading fire with a target that was not visible, but was clearly trying to get inside the prison itself. There was also a flank inside the ring of forest, their shadowy figures moving in and among the tree line.

"How do we get in?" the Jackal asked.

"I have an access code to the keypads." Mayhem glanced back. "But not everything is locked that way anymore, and I'm worried they changed the codes anyway after our escape. It's the first thing I'd do. I need to get to the back door that goes into the Executioner's private quarters to try what I have."

"That male is in charge now?" the Jackal muttered. "Great."

"No, we killed him. Now it's someone worse."

"Of course it is."

Kane was about to suggest a strategy when the wind changed direction, and the instant he felt the breeze on the back of his neck, he knew their presence was going to get announced. Sure enough, as their scents blew in to the guards, the gunfire that rained on them was well aimed and well timed.

Which was to say it was an absolute barrage.

As they returned fire at the guards, and bullets were traded in waves, they were forced back—and Kane experienced the strangest focus. Instead of being scattered and panicking, he became more and more calm as Mayhem and then the Jackal dematerialized up into the first aboveground floor for protection.

As opposed to taking their very prudent lead, he stayed where he was, even as the males stuck their heads out through some broken panes of glass and urged him to follow.

The inside of him was taking over. He could feel it.

And then . . . something happened.

His body floated off. That was the only way he could describe it. One moment he was up on his feet, shooting, ducking bullets. The next, he was flying.

No, he wasn't in the air . . .

He was on the ground. Moving smoothly through the grass. Staring out of a different set of eyes: The color of the world was suddenly in shades of red, all of the other hues gone.

With a strange sense of peace, he capitulated to the transformation, and the more he went with the altering of his form, the more leeway he was given in terms of awareness: He could feel the different sensations on his belly, the leaves of weeds, the coarse sand and small pebbles, the dirt. But the scents in his nose were not the same. Or perhaps, they were the same sources, but registered in a different way. Sounds were nothing as they usually were, either, the noises of the gunfight, the yelling, the footfalls, like the ocean rushing against a shore and retreating, undifferentiated.

Yet as he halted his forward progress, he heard what he recognized as the Jackal and Mayhem speaking. The codes weren't working . . . up on the first floor, where they were . . . the passcodes were not working in the stairwell.

How he could hear them from so far away, he had no idea. And though he was now in a form other than his vampire one, his mission had not changed. He still had to infiltrate the prison camp, and save the wolven, and find Apex.

But how—

The crack in the building's foundation was not large, just four inches or so wide, running at an angle from the seam of the brick siding to the concrete wall that was underground. It was not the kind of thing he could have fit his hand through, much less his body, yet he knew it was his way in.

The viper in him was not going to have a problem with the squeeze.

As he slithered through, somehow his serpent side knew the path to go, finding and following the routes that had been created in the concrete due to the exposure to the elements and neglect of the structure— and then abruptly, he was out of the compression and into the open, slithering along the floor at its intersection with a wall.

Halting his forward progress, his viewpoint swung back and forth, the viper moving its head around as if it knew he wanted to orientate, the red wash over everything not compromising his visual acuity.

He was inside the private quarters of the head of the guards.

And yes, there was Callum, over on a bed, tied down and unmoving— and past him, at the door that came in from the rear parking lot, the head of the guards was dragging an unconscious Apex inside, the male's dead weight something that with her physical strength was not a hard graft.

She was speaking, her mouth moving, but Kane didn't listen to any of it.

It didn't matter what the bitch said.

As Apex's boots cleared the door, the reinforced panel slammed shut and locked itself. And then she stood over the former prisoner with a smile that was vengeance personified.

She didn't see the attack coming. And Kane trusted his other side to do what it knew it could. With a sudden burst of speed, he was at her leg, and he shot up her calf and thigh faster than a blink.

The first strike went in right at the juncture of torso and leg, because Kane told his other side that that was the most effective circulatory access. The female screamed, or at least a loud noise emanated from her. And then she pointed the gun in her hand right at his head—

The popping sound of the discharge was loud as a lightning strike and Kane flinched inside his other skin, assuming he had been wounded and would be in immediate, debilitating pain.

Except, inexplicitly, the female was the one who was somehow hit by a bullet coming from a different direction, her arms throwing back as she arched and stumbled, her own gun firing into the room as it swung out to the side.

Kane's viper took it from there. In a split second, the snake sped up the female's torso and wound itself around its prey's throat, the constriction quick and deadly. But she didn't die from strangulation.

The bites were one after the other after the other, the fangs penetrating her face as she screamed and bled.

As the snake head went down repeatedly, the venom being injected again and again, Kane just let the attack happen.

And when her visage began to melt away, the flesh and bone going liquid, the eyes sinking back into the skull, before they, too, disintegrated . . . he was perfectly content with the outcome.

◆　◆　◆

From Apex's vantage point on the floor, he let go of the gun he'd taken out of where he'd hidden it inside his crotch and rolled onto his side so he could watch the hideous death happen. Though his head was throbbing and his vision iffy, he'd managed to retain enough awareness to get that one shot off into the chest of that evil fucking female—and now he had enough mental acuity left over to watch what appeared to be a massive black snake turning that female into a pincushion.

Kane. In his other form.

With the immediate threat neutralized—or soon to be denatured, as the case was—Apex focused on the bedding platform. Taking a deep breath, he meant to stand up, but he didn't have the strength to get on his feet. Fine. He'd crawl.

Dragging himself across the floor, he hoped that viper knew the difference between friend and foe because the damn thing was about to have nothing else to chew on. The female's head was totally disintegrating.

As Apex came up to the bed, he pulled himself up and—

"Callum. It's me."

There was no response from the male. Nothing but that blank stare at the ceiling and the autonomic blinking, which was somehow scarier than any moaning in pain could have been.

"I've got you," Apex said hoarsely. "I'm going to get you out."

From deep within him, a sense of purpose animated his body and strengthened him. Using the knife on his belt, he cut through the leather restraints, and when the wolven was free . . .

There was no response at all. Callum didn't look over, he didn't move, he didn't respond. He just laid exactly where he had been with his arms and legs splayed out from his naked torso, as if he were still tied down.

As those eyes just continued to stare up at the ceiling, it was as if he were nothing but a shell, his soul gone from the living husk that had seated it.

"Callum . . ."

With gentle hands, Apex reached out—

The flinching and pulling away was instinctual, the last reflexes of survival kicking in, nothing that seemed conscious.

"Here, I've got you," he whispered to the male.

Sitting himself on the edge of the bed, he shifted Callum into his lap, and as the wolven's head changed angle, he expected to finally see some recognition. There was none. The wolven just stared at the floor, as if his moonbeam-colored eyes were frozen in the forward position and whatever crossed their path was what he saw.

Apex brushed the sweat-matted white hair back. And as he stared down into the face he had seen in his memories with such clarity, blood from his own head wound fell on Callum's cold cheek.

"I've got you," he whispered. "You're safe now—"

An explosion loud enough to sting the ears, powerful enough to shake the foundations of the hospital, erupted from across the way— and the door leading out into the hallway fell forward into the private quarters with a tremendous bang.

As the smoke cleared, there were two males standing on the threshold.

Mayhem. And the Jackal.

As Apex looked across the debris field of weapons, ammo, and tactical supplies, he had a thought he should feel liberated or something. Especially as the pair raced in with guns—and was that a cell phone in the Jackal's hand?

They came over and gave him and Callum a look-see—but their eyes kept returning to what was happening over on the floor. The head of the guards was still disintegrating, the venom, or whatever the hell it was, moving down from what was left of her face and beginning to eat her body away as well.

"She's dead," Apex said unnecessarily, as the Jackal put the cell phone up to his ear.

To protect Callum's privacy, Apex reached out and pulled a blanket across the male's naked body . . . and that was when he noted the bruising where the restraints had been, and the scratches, and the other patterns consistent with a male having been used sexually and as a blood source.

"You're going to be okay, Callum," he whispered. "Reinforcements are coming."

People offered aid to him, made plans, and were reunited in the Jackal's case. But as if Callum's vegetative state was communicable, Apex found that he had nothing really to say in response and couldn't really train his eyes on anything other than whatever happened to pass through his line of sight.

Some rescues were too late.

Even if the person remained alive.

CHAPTER FORTY-FIVE

On the whole, V loved being right. And the good news was, ninety-nine percent of the time, he was correct about everything so it was a state of self-satisfaction he enjoyed a lot.

In the case of the prison camp's new location, he had been spot on with the logic about finding it—but the actual infiltration by the Brotherhood had been a total letdown. For one, he wished he could have used his daggers a little more. A lot more. The larger bummer, however, was that he had packed plenty of C-4 plastic explosives. It had been a while since he'd blown something up, and he'd been ready for all the false-sun, Fourth of July show.

And then there had been the satisfaction of just ripping the place apart.

'Cuz, yeah, fuck the *glymera*.

Instead, as he'd arrived at the abandoned tuberculosis hospital, and walked in a back entry thanks to the Jackal holding a secured door open, he had all of the satisfaction of being the brainiac in the room, but none of the workout or the pyrotechnics—

"What the *fuck* is that."

As he stepped into some kind of bedchamber/war room, there was a mess on the floor that had decomposing body written all over it. The slop appeared to be made up of bodily fluids and some bone, although the latter seemed to be turning to liquid before his eyes. There also appeared to be a trail of the goo across the bare floor, one that snaked around a bed that had a very naked male being cradled by a guy with one hell of a head wound on it. On the far side, the path of blood disappeared into a small hole in the corner down at the floor.

"Is there anyone else injured," he said as he took out his phone. "Never mind, I'll just take that as a yes."

"There are a lot of sick prisoners somewhere," the Jackal said. "By the way, this is Mayhem. Over there are Apex and Callum."

"I can take you to the prisoners," the guy named Mayhem murmured. "I'll show you where they are. I'd ask that you prioritize them over going after the guards."

Nodding, V texted his mate as well as Manny and the Brotherhood's own nurse, Ehlena. "You mean those males I saw running off?"

"Yeah. There have to be some of them left around somewhere."

"Not a problem. Prisoners first. I'm getting medical help right now and the Brotherhood is securing the perimeter. You're safe, all of you."

"I couldn't wait until tomorrow," the Jackal said. "Sorry."

V glanced up from his phone. "I'm glad you didn't. Can you guard these two while your boy takes me to the incarcerated?"

"Yes. I'll stay here."

V followed the other prisoner out of a door that appeared to have been—"Did you blow that in?"

"Yeah? I always like to keep some plastics handy. You know, for special occasions."

"Oh, my God, me too." He took out a hand-rolled. "Cigarette?"

"You know, I don't mind if I do."

As he turned to give the guy the coffin nail, he did a double take. The wall they had stepped out of was set with pairs of pegs, between which brown stains made their purpose self-defining.

"That's where they were punished," V said.

"Yes, at this location." The male—Mayhem? Yeah, that was the name—took what was offered and put it right between his front teeth. Talking around the hand-rolled, he said, "Back at the old camp, there was another setup where we were tortured."

"Fucking hell." V Bic'd up and extended the little flame. "Well, that shit's over now."

"We need to stay here," the male said as he lit the hand-rolled and exhaled. "This facility has beds and a kitchen, has a clinic. Don't move us, please. A lot of the prisoners didn't survive the trip here in the first place."

V glanced around. The long hallway had doors opening off of it, and he could smell the cocaine and the heroin.

"Show me everything." He started walking forward. "I want to see it all."

Unsurprisingly, the rest of the place was grim. The workrooms where the drugs were packaged were forced labor lockups, the very definition of a toxic environment, and the kitchen was a repurpose of a nineteen seventies facility that was filthy. But the worst was the sleeping quarters. As the male led him down a set of stairs, he could smell the corporeal decay and old sweat and infection already. Then he discovered that prisoners were relegated to sleeping pods that were barely big enough for dogs, the males and females slotted into the cramped spaces, most of them lacking the energy to care when V walked down a room as long as a soccer field.

At the far end, he turned around and couldn't believe what he was looking at. But what the fuck did he think it was going to be like?

"We're going to need even more medical help," he said to himself as he put his hand-rolled out on the bottom of his shitkicker.

"I know someone," Mayhem said, "who's going to be invaluable to us. She's the best of the best, and the prisoners already know and trust her."

◆　◆　◆

As Nadya re-formed in the back of the prison camp, she was escorted into the facility by the biggest, most beautiful blond male vampire she had ever seen—who introduced himself as the Black Dagger Brother Rhage. And when she entered the private quarters of the head of the guards, she stopped at a puddle that was . . .

"Yeeeeeeah," the Brother said, "whoever that was had a bad night."

Something in the scent of the remains drew her down to her haunches, and that was when she recognized the tool belt, the uniform, the boots.

"It's the head of the guards," she murmured as she stood back up. "The female who . . . well. I'm going to sleep better during the day, at any rate. She wasn't too fond of me."

"Something tells me that's a compliment."

Nadya looked across the room to a bedding platform—and her breath caught in her throat.

A female she didn't recognize, who was wearing the white coat of a human physician or nurse, was taking care of Callum, the wolven, while Apex sat aside, watching with an intensity that she'd seen before. It reminded her of the way he'd been with Kane . . .

And oh, no. Apex had a head wound that was still bleeding. From time to time, he wiped at it with a hand towel in annoyance. No doubt he had refused to be treated until Callum was.

Underneath his hard exterior, he was a male of worth, loyal and true. And, oh, God, what had happened to the wolven? He looked like he was in some kind of coma.

"Are you the nurse here?"

She glanced over her shoulder. Another member of the Black Dagger Brotherhood was striding into the chamber. With a goatee and tattoos at his temple, and those telltale black daggers strapped, handles down, under his leather jacket, he was intense, and that was before she met his icy eyes.

"Yes," she said to him. Then she cleared her throat, the sense that her life had been leading up to just this moment hitting her with a rush of purpose. "I am the nurse here. I've come because . . . well, it's a long story."

"You don't have to explain, but we got patients for you."

Okay, Nadya, she told herself as she took a deep breath. *It's time.*

"If we're dealing with the prison populace," she said with authority, "it'll be wiser to take the drugs and supplies from my clinic up to the sleeping quarters. We'll be looking at skin, bladder, and respiratory infections, but also tooth abscesses and malnutrition. I have a stock of antibiotics and painkillers, and there are enough opiates down the hall to treat half the continental United States. No, there are no records of identities that I've ever found, verbal accounts are going to have to suffice to establish a census and start to create files. It goes without saying that I am happy to take orders from anybody. I just want to finally be able to treat my patients the way they deserve."

The male with the goatee stared at her. Then he inclined his head with a sly smile. "I think you're going to be giving the orders, ma'am. Let me introduce you to our docs."

"Thank you," she murmured as she bowed. "I'm eager to meet them."

The rest of the night passed in a blur. She and the other medical professionals, who were great, worked together in the sleeping quarters, triaging the prisoners, providing food, starting to develop a list of names and conditions. Meanwhile, the Brotherhood continued to secure the premises, changing locks, confiscating keys to the vehicles out back, establishing a safe zone.

Mayhem and the Jackal were a great help, hauling supplies up from the clinic and helping to establish the triage and treatment area, and Lucan and Rio arrived to aid the effort just as dawn was arising.

When the sun came up, everything was locked tight and the work continued.

Except Kane was nowhere to be found.

CHAPTER FORTY-SIX

A week later, Nadya had things running smoothly in her new clinic location. The Black Dagger Brotherhood had proven to be invaluable, bringing food and more medical supplies, but never asking for anything in return, a regular rotation of fighters showing up and pulling shifts at the former prison. And the same was true for the medical staff that came with them.

They weren't the only ones who helped. The Jackal, as well as his son, his female, and his female's sister moved in, as did Rio and Lucan. There was just so much to do, like food to make, clothes to hand out—and oral histories to record.

If there were any prisoners who had committed petty crimes, their sentences were hundreds of years too long for the property infractions or social insults they'd committed. And the violent prisoners had already been weeded out, as the Executioner had killed any of the ones prone to physical attacks. And what was left after those two groups were those who had been thrown into the camp for nefarious reasons such as personal or familial slights, or other things that were unconscionable.

So they were making progress righting wrongs, for the most part.

But not in all areas. Apex was still just sitting beside his wolven, who remained mostly unresponsive. Because of the trauma Callum had endured, the two of them continued to stay in those private quarters, and Nadya was the one who brought them meals and kept assessing the comatose male's condition.

Apex only left the male for twenty minutes a night, allowing Nadya to sit with Callum as he disappeared to wherever he went. The only thing she knew was that every time he came back, it was with another white flower. The bed in the room was now surrounded by white blooms in various kinds of vases. She had a feeling the vampire was breaking into a florist's somewhere, the fragrance of his floral thieving the kind of perfume she looked forward to smelling and which he clearly hoped would rouse the male.

So far, he was still waiting.

And in her own way so was Nadya. For someone else.

Kane . . . remained nowhere to be found.

By the fourth night when he hadn't appeared or been discovered wounded, she had resigned herself to the conclusion she had been fighting.

He must have been killed during the infiltration.

The knowledge was horrifying enough, but when she thought about the way they'd left things, her heart ached to the point where she couldn't catch her breath. She'd had her reasons for what she'd done, though.

And she tried to remind herself that they hadn't spent all that much time together anyway—although that didn't hold water. They had had a lifetime in a matter of nights—and those memories of being with him were going to have to last her until she went unto the Fade.

Time to focus on her job, she thought sadly as she went to the first of the sleeping berths in the row on the right.

"You're looking much better," she said to an elderly female who'd had pneumonia. Then she made a note on her med chart. "The penicillin is doing its job, and I'll be back before dawn to give you another dose."

As she went to move away from the pod, a frail arm reached out and myopic eyes tried to focus on her. "Thank you."

Two words. Two syllables. And yet a wealth of meaning that even the *glymera* couldn't match with all their money and possessions.

What was left of the *glymera*, that was.

"You're welcome," Nadya murmured. "You just rest. I'll be back."

It took her a good hour to work her way around all the patients' check-ins. When she was finished, she returned to the desk Mayhem had set up for her at the far end, from which she logged doses and kept track of symptoms and vitals. As she sat down, Nadya frowned.

Another pebble was on her master ledger.

It was small and round, and of a pink tone this time. As she put it in her palm and rolled it around, she loved the smooth surface. The veining. The fact that it clearly had been chosen with care.

Then she looked to the little dish by her lineup of antibiotic bottles. There were five other little stones, of different sizes and colors, like flowers that had been picked from a riverbed.

She had no idea who had been leaving them, but when she was at her most pathetic, she fantasized that it was—

"Hi."

◆ ◆ ◆

As Kane spoke up, he wasn't sure what the reaction from Nadya was going to be. And as she looked up at him with a gasp, he told himself he should have given her more time. She had been working so hard, saving lives, easing pain, doing what she had been born to do, that she no doubt hadn't had a moment to reflect on the way they had left things.

Then again, how arrogant of him to assume he was even on her mind.

When this purpose of hers was so important.

Dearest Virgin Scribe, she was so beautiful, her brown hair pulled back to the base of her neck, her simple tunic and loose pants in green a ball gown to his eyes. She was glowing with health, her eyes sparkling—

and yet warily on him, although whether that was because she couldn't believe he was in the flesh or something else, he didn't know.

"You're alive," she whispered. "I thought you were . . ."

"I've been around."

"No one has seen you. I've asked . . . where you were." She cleared her throat. "But I guess you've had things to do—"

"I had some work I had to do on myself."

"Oh."

He wanted to explain to her that, after his viper side had come out as it had when they'd come to save Callum and Apex, he'd known he had to understand better, and make peace with, his other half. He had to learn how it worked, and who was in charge—so he was sure that people he cared about were safe.

Given the power of that bite, he had to protect those around him who mattered.

Especially . . . her.

"And how did the work go," she asked.

"Good. Very good." He thought back to Callum telling him he didn't need a weapon. The male had been so very right. "I'm really good."

"Well. I'm glad."

"You've been working hard, too." He glanced around at the prisoners' berths. "You're . . . doing what you're made to do."

"I think so."

There was a long silence, and then he rushed the story out, talking faster and faster, as if she wouldn't listen to him for longer than a minute or two: "Cordelhia was in on the plot to frame me. I just want you to know that. She knew what her brother planned and it was to get rid of her twin who was, in their eyes, a disgrace to their bloodline. They solved a problem that was no fault of that sister's by killing her and sending me to prison for two centuries. I'm telling you this not so you feel sorry for me, but so you know that there is no way I'm ever going back to Cordelhia. Ever. I was in love with an illusion set up and reinforced by the class I was in. I excused her behavior, which was about tolerating me, rather than wanting to be with me, at the altar of the modesty a female of worth was supposed to have. I do not love Cordelhia, I never truly did, and I never, ever will forgive her."

Nadya's eyes seemed to get wider and wider as he went along, and then as he paused for a breath, his name came out of her in a way that could have meant anything.

"Kane . . . ?" As if she couldn't believe it, and not because she didn't believe the story.

"You don't have to be with me," he said. "But what I can't bear is the idea you think I ever betrayed you or used you. What we had was precious and important, and it was every bit the resurrection I needed. You were never an illusion to me. You were always real. And it has nothing to do with how I started as your patient, and everything to do with who you are as a female, as a healer, as . . . the one that I love with all my heart."

Tears filled her eyes and she clasped the little pebble he'd left her tonight to her chest. "Kane."

He put his palms out to reassure her. "I'm not asking for anything. I just needed you to know how I f—"

Nadya burst up from her seat and all but jumped over the table she worked at. The next thing he knew, she was in his arms and kissing him.

"I'm sorry," she said against his mouth. "I didn't know—"

"Neither did I—"

"—about what had happened—"

"Don't apologize, I understand how you felt—"

"And I love you, too."

That stopped everything. But only for a moment. "You do . . . ?"

"Yes," she breathed. "I love you, I love you, I love you, do you want me to say it some more? And I'm sorry I doubted you. I had my own things to deal with from my past and—"

"Shh," he said as he dropped his mouth back down to hers. "All is forgiven. I understand completely."

They were kissing again now, holding each other, reconnecting. And it was a long time before they came up for air.

As he brushed her hair back, he saw her as she had been. Saw her as she was. Was looking forward to seeing her as she would become—

A spontaneous burst of applause exploded in the long, thin room, so unexpected and shocking that the two of them turned and faced the sleeping quarters. Every single one of the patients that Nadya had treated with such care had poked their heads out of their berths and were clapping their hands, supportive eyes and wide smiles a blessing that felt like destiny's approval that the pair of them had finally figured everything out.

And that all was as it should be.

Within the sound of so many hands being brought together, Kane tucked his female at his side, noting that she fit him perfectly. Then he stared down at her with love as she brushed shaking hands under her eyes to clear happy tears. When she was done with that, she looked up at him.

"Hi," his female breathed.

Kane smiled down at his one true love and gave her a kiss. "Hi."

EPILOGUE

I t was the scent that brought it all back. Wasn't that always true, though, the nose like an amplifier for long-term memories, sharpening the focus, the accuracy, the emotions, of them.

As Kane strode up the mountain trail, his footfalls cushioned by the layers of pine needles, a cool breeze against his face, he looked up through the entwined boughs above. The moon was full overhead and its radiant blue light pierced the canopy of pines, fracturing into cleaves of illumination that reminded him of the crystal chandeliers he had once lived with.

No more, though. He was no longer a member of the *glymera*.

And that was no loss at all.

He glanced over at Nadya. She was striding along with him, her hands in the pockets of a loose red jacket she borrowed from the Brotherhood's nurse, her hair streaming freely down her back, her lips lifted in a private smile that he knew meant she was thinking about what they had done together in their shared bunk during the day.

Kane smiled himself. "You're beautiful, you know that?"

Her eyes shifted to his. "Is it wrong that I never get tired of you saying those words?"

"Not at all, and hey, that works for both of us. I'm never going to be
tired of speaking them."

A quick tilt down and his lips found hers. Then he refocused on the
rising trail ahead. "Almost there."

When he'd told her he needed to come back to the mountain, she
hadn't hesitated. She'd clocked out of her shift at the clinic, with Ehlena,
owner of the red jacket, taking her place, and off they had gone. They'd
left the hospital through the front entrance, and walked out into the
underbrush, into the night. When they'd gotten to the chain-link fence,
he watched her dematerialize through it, but then he'd had to climb up
and over the old-fashioned way.

With every grip and and release of his strong hands, he had thought
about that night after the resurrection, when he'd returned to the camp
as a different version of himself, hell-bent on finding his female and getting her out of the prison. Back then, he'd had no appreciation for the
transformation he'd undergone. He'd only been along for the ride, with
no idea that he was a host to an entity, that freedom of thought and action was now and forevermore relative, a negotiation instead of something unilateral.

But he had absolutely no regrets.

The viper was a gift. For both him and Nadya.

Reaching out, he took her hand. "Thank you."

"For what?"

"Coming with me."

"You didn't even have to ask." Nadya squeezed his palm. "Plus this is
a wonderful walk. The way this air smells—I can't believe how delicious
and clean it is."

"That's what I was thinking, too." He frowned and remembered
Apex carrying him out of the back of the old hospital. "I don't remember
much from . . . that night I was brought up here. But the scent. The
scent brings me back—and speaking of scents . . ."

He glanced into the tree line as a shadow raced ahead, moving over the ground as fast and smooth as the wind.

"We've still got an escort," he said with a smile.

"I thought I saw something, too."

They'd started their climb at Callum's garage, heading around back to the trail that was hidden in the trees—and the moment they'd stepped onto the beaten path, a wolven in four-pawed form had appeared in their way. And then another. And a third.

For a split second, the viper had coiled into Kane's consciousness, narrowing his focus and assessment on a potential threat. Except then the wolven had lowered their heads as if they were bowing, and disappeared into the night—as if they had just come to welcome, to make sure he and Nadya had known they would be safe.

And as they continued to ascend, he had the sense that the wolven were keeping their distance out of respect because they knew why he was here and why he'd brought his mate.

Because they knew who he was. Or rather, what was inside of him.

As he and Nadya crested the final rise, and the turn in the trail took them around a tumble of rocks the size of cars . . .

There it was. The clearing with the fire pit in the center, and the hidden dens of the wolven, and the red hut.

As soon as they stepped free of the trees, a burst of flames lit the stack of logs that had been set in the circle of stones, and the *whoof!*-ing sound of spontaneous combustion was a greeting that was surprisingly cheery. And while the fire crackled and red sparks rode white smoke up to the clear, star-freckled sky, Kane turned to the hut.

He knew the old female who was not old would be emerging, and yes, there she was, holding the flap back so she could duck and step out. For a moment, he tensed up and moved in front of Nadya so that his body was protecting his female. But then the old female looked over at them and her smile was radiant.

"Greetings to you both. How wonderful to see you."

She was wearing the same kind of crimson dress she'd had on that first night, except the beading and smocking was different—no, wait . . . the embellishment was moving over the fabric, the swirls of stitches and red, yellow, and white beads shifting their positions slowly, the pattern like a living thing. Her gray-and-white hair was once again loose over her shoulders, and he realized that it was alive as well, the gossamer strands swirling around her body even though there was no breeze to animate them.

Kane opened his mouth. And when the words didn't come, he cleared his throat.

"It's all right, I know why you're here." The old female smiled again. "You're very welcome. And she is just lovely, inside and out. Aren't you, my dear."

The old female did not extend her arms, and neither of them walked forward, but the sense of warmth and comfort that came when one was embraced by somebody who loved unconditionally suddenly suffused Kane—and he sensed that it was the same for Nadya because she closed her eyes and took a deep breath.

"Now go," the Gray Wolf said, "and stand at the precipice and stare out over the valley. You will not find your future in the view, though, however beautiful it is. It is the one beside you who is your horizon. But you already know that, don't you."

Kane put his arm around his *shellan.* "You are too right, and yes, I do."

He looked down at Nadya, and as her eyes met his, he felt her arm go around his waist. The touch was so natural, so easy, her hand resting on the top of his hip a physical commentary on how much she just liked to touch him. And that still mattered to him, that she wanted to feel him and his body as much as he wanted to do the same to her.

"Will you join us to look at the—"

Kane glanced up. The old female was gone and so was the hut. And somehow, he wasn't surprised.

"Come on," he said to his mate. "I want to share this with you."

As they walked around the fire pit and out the other side, he thought briefly of Cordelhia and that empty beautiful house of hers, a relic of the past, a testimony to the female's lonely present and desolate future. There was no horizon for her, and maybe it made him vengeful, but that was okay with him. She deserved an even harsher punishment for what she had been a part of. Her blindness to the consequences of the actions of her family still astounded him. More than anything else, that was what had stuck with him.

It was a fresh definition for cruelty, such ignorance.

But as with learning to get along with the new side of him, finding a way to be at peace with something he couldn't understand and couldn't change was the internal challenge he was working on.

A little farther on, the trees gave way to a rock ledge and a cliff that dropped off to a sheer fall and a valley in the distance. The view was majestic, the rolling mountains descending to a gleaming lake, the thousands of acres of pines a fragrant blanket smoothing the contours of the undulating elevations of earth.

"This is the most beautiful thing I've ever seen," Nadya said with awe.

He looked at his mate. Her hair was getting longer, to the point where she always had to pull it back in a tie during work, and her face, though free of makeup, had a glow to it that was more about the soul than a good diet and being well fed from the vein of a loving mate.

"Yes," he whispered as he continued to stare. "I couldn't agree more."

Nadya turned to him, and stepped into his body. As he wrapped his arms around her, he thought about the things he had wanted for himself back in the Old Country, what he had hoped for, what he had dreamed of.

Funny, how all of that had come together in this female.

"I'm going to keep bringing you pebbles," he said as he stroked the flyaways from her hair tie back. "For the rest of our lives."

It wasn't like he had any kind of net worth, so it was never going to be diamonds. But diamonds were just rocks, weren't they, and to his female, his little stones were just as precious. She told him so every time he presented her with a new one.

"I'm going to cherish each and every one," she said with a smile.

Just as he leaned down to kiss her again, he saw, standing off to the side, a beautiful pale gray wolf. And the mystical, ghostly animal looked at him and seemed to wink.

Then she lifted her head to the heavens and let out a howl. And as the song of the wolven weaved through the dark night, Kane lowered his mouth to Nadya's.

And knew that community was a family that was chosen. Whether it was their friends and their mates, the prisoners, or the Black Dagger Brotherhood, they were surrounded by love.

Which made them richer than any amount of money ever could.

Family, after all, was priceless.

ACKNOWLEDGMENTS

With so many thanks to the readers of the Black Dagger Brotherhood books! This has been a long, marvelous, exciting journey, and I can't wait to see what happens next in this world we all love. I'd also like to thank Meg Ruley, Rebecca Scherer and everyone at JRA, as well as Hannah Braaten, Andrew Nguyễn, Jennifer Long, and Jennifer Bergstrom, and the entire family at Gallery Books and Simon & Schuster.

To Team Waud, I love you all. Truly. And as always, everything I do is with love to and adoration for both my family of origin and of adoption.

Oh, and thank you to Naamah, my Writer Dog II, and Obie, Writer Dog-in-Training, who work as hard as I do on my books!